Straight Lies

Books by Rob Byrnes

THE NIGHT WE MET

TRUST FUND BOYS

WHEN THE STARS COME OUT

STRAIGHT LIES

Published by Kensington Publishing Corporation

Straight Lies

ROB BYRNES

KENSINGTON BOOKS

KENSINGTON BOOKS are published by

Kensington Publishing Corp.
850 Third Avenue
New York, NY 10022

ISBN-13: 978-1-60751-879-2

Printed in the United States of America

Acknowledgments

Once again, I have probably been saved from myself by a crew that was more than generous with their edits and opinions. Special thanks go to Becky Cochrane, David Puterbaugh, and Jeffrey Ricker (who hates the word 'that'), who went above and beyond to help me whip the manuscript into shape; and to Wayne Chang, who asked some tough early questions that focused the narrative arc.

Not to mention my friends and (gentle) critics: Eve Ackerman, Timothy James Beck, Andrew W. M. Beierle, Julian Biddle, Margaret Campbell, Christopher Cornell, Greg Crane, James Daubs, Randy Ham, Scott Kaiser, Illyse Kaplan, Timothy J. Lambert, Darlene Marshall, Craig McKenzie, Denise Murphy McGraw, Steven Seegers, Elise Skidmore, Dan Weber, and Robert Widmaier. Yeah, I know. Sometimes it takes a village . . .

But wait! There's more!

Thanks to my partner, Brady Allen, who loves me enough to give me one-third of the bed, as long as I promise not to move in my sleep. Or snore. Or breathe.

Thanks to my agent, Katherine Fausset of Curtis Brown, who reminds me that "we do it for the love" when we can no longer convince ourselves that we do it for the Big Bucks.

And thanks to everyone at Kensington Publishing Corp., who have given me such great support and assistance over the years. Special thanks to Meryl Earl, Peter Senftleben, Frank Anthony Polito, and Craig Bentley. Oh, and the copyeditors! Mustn't forget the copyeditors!

Finally, it's only appropriate that I dedicate this book to

my one and only editor for the past eight years, John Scognamiglio, whose keen skills and eye for what works have served me well and taught me so much; and to Douglas A. Mendini, who discovered me in a seedy bar all those years ago and has been repaid with tantrums and martinis ever since.

Chapter One

"Miss?"

The passenger in 13C woke up to find the flight attendant lightly shaking her shoulder.

"I'm sorry to disturb you, miss," the flight attendant said, "but we're about to land at Kennedy. You're going to have to return your seat to its upright position."

"Oh . . . Yes, of course." She pushed the button to put her seat back in place. The flight attendant smiled, thanked her, and moved down the aisle.

When she was gone, Passenger 13C sifted through her purse for a compact, found it, and flipped it open, inspecting her face in the mirror. She sighed, not liking what she saw in the reflection. These early mornings didn't agree with her.

She slipped the compact back in the purse, then reached under the seat in front of her, where her backpack was stowed, and tucked the purse inside it.

Then she yawned again, gathering a blue jacket around her shoulders, and prepared for landing.

Henry Lemmon was late.

Keeping the speedometer at a steady seven miles per hour above the speed limit, his dark blue 2002 BMW 525i flew down the Van Wyck Expressway. His eyes darted left and right in the dawn sunlight as they searched for police cars.

Still, his foot never wavered on the gas pedal, not even when it officially entered the grounds of John F. Kennedy International Airport.

He loved driving this car, loved the way it handled as it zipped around banks of aggressive yellow taxis and the awkward movements of civilian automobiles jockeying for position in the crowded roadway. He loved the way he could ease it to the right, then left, then right again, and it never complained . . . The way it rode up one ramp and down another, shifted lanes, and did it all over again, threading through the congestion like it was the only car on the road. He loved it so much that he barely remembered he was ultimately in control of the machine, and not the other way around.

In a few years he'd have his twenty-five in, and then he could retire with a full pension. Maybe, thought Henry Lemmon, he could then sit behind the wheel of his 525i all day, and see where it took him.

It was only when he approached the traffic backing up outside Terminal 4—home of TriState Airlines—that he finally slowed, regretfully taking control back from the machine and patting the steering wheel, as if to assure the vehicle that it was nothing personal.

After pulling the car into an open space at the far end of the sidewalk adjacent to Arrivals, Henry Lemmon slapped a Suffolk County Sheriff's Department placard on the dashboard to make sure he wouldn't be hassled by airport security. Then he slid across to the passenger's side, let himself out at the curb, and cast an appreciative glance back at the car before briskly walking through the sliding glass doors.

Once inside, just past Baggage Claim, he reached into an inside pocket of his dark green windbreaker and pulled out a rolled sheet of paper, inspecting his careful lettering one last time as he opened it.

ARBOGAST.

The sheet of paper unfurled, he held it at chest level and

stood at the foot of the escalators, where—at any moment—
Amber Arbogast would be descending, fresh from her 6:43 AM
flight from Albany. She would see her name and rush into his
arms, free at last from the tyranny of her abusive parents,
and forever grateful that Henry Lemmon—Deputy Henry
Lemmon of the Suffolk County Sheriff's Department—had
been her savior.

And then they would be happy together. Happily ever after.

True, she was only sixteen years old, but she'd be seven-
teen in mere months. And after six weeks of on-line chats
and a few brief, furtive phone calls, Henry Lemmon already
knew they had a lot in common . . . Enough, certainly, to
compensate for the twenty-five-year gap between their ages.
She would get an education and be free of abuse and thrive;
in return, he would get unqualified love and affection. It was
a good deal for both of them.

Best of all, no one had to know the truth; the neighbors
had already been informed that Henry's wayward, runaway
niece was coming to stay with him. The cop as family disci-
plinarian . . . it was the perfect story to deflect suspicion.
Clever girl that she was, Amber had come up with that cover.
It just went to show how smart she was. He never ceased to
be amazed by how damn *smart* the girl was.

And, in an absolute worst-case scenario, sixteen was *almost* legal. Maybe it wasn't *normal* for a sixteen-year-old girl
to be with a forty-one-year-old man who was going to be
forty-two in a few weeks, but it was *almost* legal. And "normal" was in the eyes of the beholder. Or so he told himself.

Henry Lemmon smiled, sucked in his sagging belly, held
his ARBOGAST sign proudly, and thought how lucky they were
to have found each other. At any moment she would be
standing there in front of him, full of youthful gratitude. He
was sure of that—sure she'd be standing there, that was,
since he definitely knew she'd be grateful—because he had
checked and knew she had boarded the plane.

He hadn't wanted to do that—it seemed wrong to doubt his soul mate—but the cop in him made him cautious every now and then. He would have felt like a chump if Amber hadn't boarded the plane and had been playing him all along. But she hadn't; she was on that TriState plane.

Which, come to think of it, should have emptied its human cargo by now, if not their checked luggage.

His eyes misted a bit as he looked at the sign. ARBOGAST. Henry Lemmon and Amber Arbogast were going to start their new lives together in mere minutes. Henry, Amber, and the dark blue 2002 BMW 525i. Who could ask for anything more?

A trickle of people began to descend the escalator—the first arrivals from the 6:43 AM flight from Albany—and he started scanning their faces with excited anticipation. A woman in a blue jacket met his gaze, then glanced away, and his heart skipped a beat until he realized she was far too old to be his Amber.

At the bottom of the escalator, the woman brushed past him, and the cop in him sensed that something wasn't quite right. He looked over his shoulder at her as she bypassed Baggage Claim and walked toward the automatic doors.

It was the backpack . . . Yeah, that was all it was. It just seemed strange for a woman, probably in her late thirties, to be carrying such a big backpack.

He shrugged it off and held his sign—ARBOGAST—just a bit higher.

The woman in the blue jacket with the backpack walked out into the crisp morning and followed the sidewalk to the end of the terminal, where she proceeded to climb a flight of concrete stairs. Outside the Departures doorway—one level above the Arrivals gate, where Henry Lemmon waited expectantly, his sign held proudly—she scanned the row of cars dropping off passengers, looking for the one making an illegal pick-up. Finally she spotted a familiar, unsmiling man, staring and waving furiously while leaning across the passenger seat of a car parked at the curb.

Walking toward the car, she began dabbing cold cream on her face, not particularly caring who noticed—not that anyone would—until the real face of Chase LaMarca began to emerge through the heavy makeup.

Behind the wheel was his partner, Grant Lambert. Chase sighed when he saw he was unshaven, which was Grant's usual state on those days when he didn't feel the need to be presentable, which numbered approximately three hundred forty per year. As a religious moisturizer, Chase dreaded the effect of the scruffiness on his soft skin, made even more sensitive by this morning's application of makeup, but after fifteen years together he was resigned to it. Mostly.

Chase climbed in as Grant retreated to the driver's seat. Pulling off his wig and stuffing it in his backpack, Chase asked, without a word indicating affection, "Next time can I take the train?"

"If you take the train, maybe he takes the Long Island Rail Road into the city to meet you, and you're sort of trapped at Penn Station. If you fly, he drives, and has to go to a different door to wait for you. It's that simple."

Chase began pulling his male clothing out of the backpack. "But he doesn't even know what I look like. What's he gonna do, start interrogating every single person in Penn Station?"

"Maybe."

Chase rolled his eyes. "I *don't* think so."

"And *I* think," said Grant, as he turned the ignition, "that we wanted the car, too. Meaning, we go to the airport, where he has to drive; not Penn Station, where he doesn't."

Chase sighed again and tossed a makeup-smeared tissue over his shoulder. Out of the corner of his eye, he watched the early morning sun sparkle off Grant's graying hair and, regrettably, that three-day growth of beard sprinkled with even more silver among the brown. His partner had the look of George Clooney gone to seed, which—he had to admit—wasn't altogether a bad look, although deep down he thought a George Clooney tending to his appearance would have been preferable.

"Plus," Chase finally continued, as he took off the blue jacket and let the fake boobs that were under it fall to the floor, "I'm getting too old—not to mention too *male*—to keep getting on planes pretending to be a teenage girl. TSA isn't stupid. Mostly, at least. You know that, right, Lambert? They're developing this imaging technology now that can see right through your clothes."

"It's over, so don't worry about it." Grant turned off the parking blinkers and began slowly edging forward into a traffic lane.

"Right through your clothes. Next time, they could see my penis, and there goes *that* scam. Promise me: never again."

"Never again. Hopefully. And put your seat belt on."

"Let me put my shirt on."

Grant eyed the activity around them. "Make it quick."

Chase frowned and pulled a blue sweatshirt over his head. "By the way, that wasn't the most sincere apology I've ever received." The car entered the flow of traffic and he added, "Nice car."

"Yeah," Grant said. "Your boyfriend did right by us." He glanced at the dashboard and added, "That reminds me." With that, the Suffolk County Sheriff's Department parking placard joined the wadded-up tissue in the backseat.

Chase ran his hand along the leather seat. "Almost a shame to take it to a shop. But we've got to make a buck where we can make a buck, I guess."

"Mmmm-hmm."

Chase dropped the sun visor, opened the vanity mirror,

and continued removing the makeup. "So how long do you think we've got?"

"With the car?"

"No, with the credit card."

Grant thought about it. He had to recalculate after every one of these jobs. They were all so different, as he had learned when a bank president fell in love with Amber Arbogast, back when she was known as Becky Campanella. *That* particular scam had not gone well, but as long as they didn't end up in jail, he could chalk it up to experience.

"Well, on the minus side, he's a cop. My experience is, that's never a good thing. But on the plus side, we know he never checks his credit, so we've probably got a week, maybe two or three, before he knows for sure that something's going on." He thought a bit more. "And we also have six weeks' worth of chat-room transcripts. Just in case."

Chase flipped the visor up, but continued to wipe at his face with a tissue. "That's right. All those transcripts. What if he comes looking for me when he realizes that 'Amber' wasn't on that flight?"

"What's he gonna do?"

"Maybe I could string him along for a few more days. Keep him off guard. You know, tell him my monstrous parents caught me at the airport, dragged me off the plane, and TriState forgot to take me off the manifest . . . Something like that."

Grant shook his head as the dark blue BMW rounded a curve and exited the airport grounds. "Too risky. From this point on, we won't know when he catches on, or what he might do. If he brings in his fellow cops now and tells them that he's been investigating on-line identity theft, well . . . His story isn't all that convincing, but *he* gets to frame the story. It's better that Amber Arbogast disappears forever."

Chase leaned back in his bucket seat and thought about that. "I suppose so. It's just that . . ."

"What?"

"I dunno. I sort of got to like Amber Arbogast."

Grant Lambert took his eyes off the road for a split sec-ond—which he hated to do anywhere, but especially when leaving JFK and entering the Van Wyck—and stared at his partner before swiveling his eyes back to the road. "But you *are* Amber Arbogast."

"Was," Chase said with a sigh.

Grant patted Chase's knee and said, "Don't worry about it, baby. You can become a different teenage girl next week, okay? One that's even better than Amber Arbogast."

Chase didn't answer. Instead, he again dropped the visor and flipped open the mirror, giving himself a final once-over. The makeup was gone, but it left a slight rash on his face that blushed his cheeks, which annoyed him. And the wig had mussed the hair he was ordinarily so careful about, although maybe he had overdone the highlights the last time he was at the stylist. They were too memorable, which was good if you wanted to make an impression, but not so good if you were in his line of work.

Even though in age Chase and Grant were in the same ballpark, give or take a few years, in appearance, well . . . They were playing in different leagues. Everything about them—how they took care of themselves (Chase, obsessive; Grant, not at all); how they dressed (Chase, stylish; Grant, for comfort); how they saw the glass (Chase, half-full; Grant, completely empty and the water had been turned off)—was a polar opposite. Love held them together, but Chase knew—well, he *thought*, because the circumspect Grant would never confirm nor deny it—that the secret to their long relationship had been in the way they had managed to thrive off their dif-ferences.

Without him, Chase knew that Grant would have with-ered away into the depths of his despair long ago. He hadn't set out to be a criminal, but some early decisions had evolved into his only opportunities, and he had run with them as the easiest way to make something out of his life. Grant Lambert was a smart guy who hadn't been able to catch a break, but he was doing the best he could to keep above water.

As for Chase LaMarca, he had also found his opportunities limited by the twists and turns of life. But there was an undeniable thrill to this sort of sideline—which, for Chase, was a necessary supplemental income, not the whole paycheck—and he and Grant did everything possible to make sure that other bad guys—*worse* guys—were their targets, so he managed to justify it.

And if it hadn't been for a little larceny, they never would have met. That had to be put in the plus column, too.

In fact, the Pedophile Scam, as they came to call their current project, had even been Chase's idea. No one as initially computer-phobic as Grant would ever conceive of trolling Internet chat rooms for those logical victims.

At first, they found it astounding that otherwise solid citizens would fall in love with grainy pictures of teenage girls and stupid instant messaging . . . but, one after another, they did. Sometimes they even had to reject potential suitors because they were stringing along so many middle-age professional men that it was getting confusing. And so many of them—not that bank president; that had been a bad move on their part—were only too willing to give up their personal financial information in exchange for an opportunity to meet a teenager.

The world is full of twisted people, thought Chase, as he sat in the passenger seat of a stolen dark blue BMW 525i.

A few miles down the expressway, Grant slowed and merged right onto an exit ramp.

"It's time?" asked Chase.

"Yeah." Grant glanced at his watch. "Fifteen minutes for him to realize the girl didn't get off the plane, maybe another couple of minutes to figure out he didn't just forget where he left his car . . . I figure right about now he's screaming at an airport security officer. So it's time."

At the end of the ramp, he waited for the light to turn green before making a left turn and driving a few blocks until he spotted what he was looking for: a parked van with out-of-state plates. He pulled the BMW next to the van, then peeled Henry Lemmon's EZ Pass reader from the inside of the windshield behind the rearview mirror and handed it to his partner.

Then it was Chase's turn. He darted out of the door—the sun glinting off his blond highlights much the same way it had off Grant's gray—and skittered to the front of the van, where he affixed the EZ Pass to the most inconspicuous spot he could find on its grille before rushing back to the BMW. The stop had taken them less than thirty seconds.

"Seat belt," warned Grant as he took his foot off the brake and eased back onto the street. Chase rolled his eyes, but pulled the strap across his torso.

"Hopefully that guy's next stop will be Oregon."

Chase frowned. "I just hate it that the toll money comes out of *our* pockets now."

"You'd like it better if the cops followed our EZ Pass trail to the Bronx? The guy won't tell the cops that his teenage Amber never showed up, and he might not notice that we're bleeding his credit for a few weeks, and even when he does, I figure we've got a bit of time before he figures out how he's gonna explain why he gave all his personal information to a sixteen-year-old girl in an Internet chat room. But he's sure as hell gonna report that someone stole his car." Grant made a loopy right turn, knowing that continuing to take a major highway like the Van Wyck after boosting a cop's car would just be adding risk to the endeavor. "It's bad enough I don't have time to change the tags."

Again Chase stroked the leather seat. "How much you think this is worth?"

"I figure a grand. Maybe fifteen hundred."

"No, not from Charlie Chops. How much do you think this car would be worth if we owned it?"

Grant sighed and made a left turn, and a green sign told him that the borough president and mayor welcomed him to Brooklyn. "You get to ride in a different car—a different *nice* car—every couple of weeks or so, and you're gonna bother me about this?"

Chase settled back in his seat and tried to enjoy the ride. Grant had been doing this too long; he wasn't going to change anytime soon. And maybe Chase didn't want things to change too much, either.

The rest of the ride to Charlie Chops's garage in the Bronx went smoothly. While Grant drove the stolen car, Chase used a cell phone—purchased for $10 with no questions asked from a connection—to order several thousand dollars' worth of resellable merchandise with Henry Lemmon's stolen credit card number, which would all be delivered within two business days to a vacant apartment in an area that some people thought of as the upper Upper West Side and others as lower Morningside Heights, where they just happened to have an in.

It was small-time, but it was relatively risk-free, and after the bus trip to Albany, a few bucks to a friend for overnight accommodations and an early morning lift to the airport, and the plane ride back, it was all profit. They could consider it a good day. It would have been better if Amber could have coaxed Henry Lemmon into giving up his PIN—cash was always a better trade than fencing hot electronics—but Chase's subtle hints had either fallen on deaf ears, or the guy wasn't a total fool. Whatever . . . He was enough of a fool to make this worth their while.

And the car was gravy. After Amber Arbogast found out what kind of car Henry Lemmon drove—"That's hot!"

Chase typed in an IM conversation after he told her it was a seven-year-old BMW—Grant reached out to his dependable friend Charlie Chops, proprietor of an inconspicuous two-bay garage in Hunt's Point, at which very little legitimate garage work went on. Charlie said he'd be happy to take the car off his hands, and that was that. Gravy.

Yes, it had been a good day for the Lambert-LaMarca household.

Up in the Bronx, Charlie Chops was having a good day, too. After Grant talked the price up and he peeled sixteen well-worn hundred-dollar bills from the wad he always carried in his front pocket for situations like this, he calculated in his head that the BMW—in parts—would make him almost a three-thousand-dollar profit within the next twenty-four hours . . . Even after paying this guy he knew a few hundred to make the vehicle identification numbers disappear.

"Know why I like these older cars?" Charlie asked, then proceeded to tell them before they could answer. "Older parts are always in demand. That's the main thing. Also, those new cars have all that GPS crap built into them. That's trouble."

Grant shook his head. "They don't make 'em like they used to."

"Ain't that a fact. Someday I'm gonna have to close shop, if this antitheft paranoia keeps up. A small businessman just can't make it these days."

Charlie Chops liked Grant Lambert. The guy always made him pay top dollar, but every few weeks he brought him some profitable, high-quality pre-disassembled auto parts. And even without prompting, Grant was smart enough to stay away from the riskier newer luxury models.

He watched as the men trudged off, heading for a bus stop a few blocks away that would take them . . . Well, Charlie Chops didn't really know *where* that bus went. He owned a used auto parts company—one that was even mostly legitimate, if you squinted a lot at the books—so he never took the bus.

He knew that if you had asked him a year or so earlier what he thought of homosexuals, he'd fall back on traditional stereotypes: they were fey and neat and prissy and, well, *faggy*. Half black and half Puerto Rican, Charlie had dealt with just about every stereotype known to man in his fifty-six years, especially given the illicit nature of his business that didn't show up on the books, and generally had no use for those mental shortcuts. But with the gays, well . . . That used to be different.

Until Grant and Chase—especially Grant—came along.

That Chase guy, well . . . him, you could sort of see, if you didn't know he was helping to deliver, on average, a car every couple of weeks to Charlie's shop. He was just a bit too much out of the ordinary for this neighborhood, which would probably get him beat up at a Hunt's Point bus stop one of these days.

Grant, though, was prematurely grizzled, and looked and acted like most of the men Charlie Chops dealt with on a day-to-day basis. You could tell he had let himself cross over to the dark side. Grant Lambert had caught the crime bug, and it wasn't going to let go. No one in Hunt's Point was going to screw with him just for the sake of screwing with someone.

Charlie liked that about Grant. Liked it a lot, as a matter of fact. It was easier to deal with men who worked on his level and were up front about it, right down to their appearances.

He watched them turn the corner and disappear, then laughed to himself and said, "Gay car thieves. What a world."

With that, he wiped his oily hands on his shirttail and prepared to dismantle a dark blue BMW 525i.

Chapter Two

If he ever thought about how he ended up doing what he did for a living, in an entirely alternative—well, okay, *illegitimate*—field, Grant would have been hard-pressed for an answer. But he seldom thought about it, so it didn't really matter. What mattered to him as each day drew to a close was that he was working, putting bread on the table, and . . . that was about it.

The handful of times he *did* think about it, he thought it was a mostly wrong but inescapable career path, to the extent that being a professional thief was a career. Which it certainly was, to him.

Growing up in a fading industrial city in southern New Jersey, close but not too close to Philadelphia, Grant watched the rich get richer and the more numerous poor get poorer. Just like the song promised, except without a catchy tune. That's why he had to get out of there. Not only was it no place to live as a gay man, it was no place to make a decent living, unless you were fortunate enough—or lucky enough, which he figured was about the same thing—to be one of those rich getting richer.

But it wasn't a Marxian appraisal of economic inequality—not that he would know Karl from Zeppo from Richard—that led Grant Lambert to his alternative economic lifestyle.

It was New York City.

Newly arrived in New York, Grant thought he could aspire to a future that wasn't the floor of a struggling tool and die shop. He thought, like so many transplants to New York thought, that he could remake himself and rewrite the future that seemed bleak back home.

It turned out, he was wrong.

Things started out well enough. Within days he landed a job waiting tables in a restaurant on the Upper West Side that brought in more than he was earning in South Jersey, even when adjusted for the ridiculous prices in New York. And he made progress on the social scene, too, becoming acquainted with some of the regulars he met hanging around the bars.

But in New York, and especially among his new network of acquaintances, it didn't take him long to realize the economic tiers remained as rigid as ever. Not only that, but the New Yorkers were practicing the same unsavory behavior as he'd seen on a petty scale in South Jersey, where the Haves always seemed to have a scam going and the Have Nots always seemed to be getting scammed.

It didn't particularly shock Grant that successful gay Manhattan lawyers and nightclub owners and certified public accountants could be even more financially unscrupulous than in the small town he grew up in. If their self-satisfaction in how they maximized their bank accounts in ways that didn't quite pass the ethics test disappointed him, he could still live with it.

Not that Grant was necessarily pure of heart. In a pinch, he could shoplift with the best, and had not been averse to dipping into the petty cash drawer for some loans that he didn't intend to repay. But that was one thing; a down-on-his-luck guy just trying to get by.

These guys, though, they didn't have to worry about where the next meal was coming from. They were skimming and cheating and swindling for the hell of it. For pure avarice.

These guys were no better than the small-timers back home, except they tacked more zeroes onto their scams.

But even if they were crooks, they were still white-collar crooks, so Grant made a decision to keep his career in the table-waiting industry a secret. At least until he took a step or two up the ladder. Whenever someone asked, he'd just mumble something about being in restaurant management and change the subject. It almost worked.

On the day it *didn't* work, the lawyer stopped into the restaurant during Grant's shift and ended up seated in his section.

"This is 'restaurant management'?" asked the lawyer, recognizing Grant a split second before Grant recognized him and had an opportunity to hightail it back to the kitchen.

"I, uh . . ."

The lawyer smiled, but it wasn't a very nice smile. "There's nothing wrong with being a waiter, of course." And then he laughed, which told Grant that—to the lawyer—there *was* something wrong with being a waiter.

The subsequent marginalization by his status-conscious friends didn't take very long. Twenty-four hours after the lawyer had a chance to start spreading the news—that he had caught Grant in a lie, not to mention an apron and "Hello My Name is Grant" name tag—his social network started to box him out. They had pegged Grant as a loser—by their standards, that was, where waiters were potential victims, not members of their club—and began shedding his company accordingly. What had been conversation became vague nods, until vague nods became invisibility.

There was no room for someone like Grant Lambert in their lives, unless he was taking their order or bringing them a fresh drink. After a few months of friendship—and even a few instances of intimacy—he had ceased to exist to them.

So, like a lot of people who came face-to-face with an ugly truth, Grant acted out. He wanted them to pay.

His first inclination, when he realized that he had been exiled from the social network of gay professionals, had been to go after Tommy Wilkinson, the lawyer. He was, after all, the man who had set Grant's ostracism in motion.

Grant was neither surprised nor especially enraged to know that a lawyer was skimming from estates, billing clients for the hours he was drinking expensive scotch at the bar, or doing pretty much anything else lawyers were capable of doing and probably trained to do in law school. But he was afraid of lawyers, so he decided to let Tommy slide for a while.

The club owner, Devin Hannerty, was not only the biggest crook of the bunch—and that was before factoring in his larcenous drink prices—but had also, very briefly, been Grant's lover . . . or whatever you'd call a two-week paramour. The relationship had ended badly, and Grant found the thought that Devin had written him off particularly galling.

There was an important consideration, though: being the biggest crook, Devin also would be the most suspicious, and therefore hardest to steal from, so Grant figured he should wait for his revenge until he had some experience under his belt.

That left the CPA. Ted Langhorne was one of the last of the Big City Success Stories to excise him from his acquaintanceship, and for a while he still occasionally talked to him, so Grant wasn't quite as angry at Ted. And, like Devin, Ted had also once been a two-week paramour, which in that case Grant considered basically neutral, since—unlike with Devin—it had ended well enough.

But Ted, like the others, *did* eventually cut him out. And that was the one that really stung.

That was the one that set the rest of his life in motion.

Night after night, as he sat, ignored, at the end of the bar where they all tended to congregate, Grant's head was filled with revenge fantasies, which might have been worrisome if he thought he'd ever have the balls to implement them. Much as he wanted revenge—to relieve Tommy, Devin, and Ted of their ill-gotten funds and retaliate for their snubs—he didn't think he could really go through with it. That wasn't the way he had been raised, and a few minor incidents of shoplifting and minor theft did not a career criminal make. Plus, he was deathly afraid of failure, which would not only end up landing him in prison, but would make him an even bigger loser in their eyes.

Until one night, when he was at his lowest, wanting revenge but afraid to exact it. That was the night when Ted Langhorne, Certified Public Accountant, walked into the bar, saw him, and . . . looked right past him.

Tommy and Devin—the lawyer and the club owner—had been treating him like that, but somehow it didn't hurt quite as much, mostly because they were irredeemable assholes. Ted, though, well . . . His was the snub that pushed Grant over the edge.

Grant knew that Ted kept an outrageous amount of petty cash at the office . . . The things people talk about with a few dirty martinis in their bloodstream. The theft of petty cash was an act he knew something about, albeit on a much smaller scale, so Grant—feeling burned—started thinking.

A few hours later, almost without being aware of making a conscious decision, Grant found himself wearing coveralls and pushing a trash bucket in a Fifth Avenue office building where he was not technically on the maintenance staff. But the advantage of dating someone for a few weeks and seeing his office late at night was that it gave Grant a good idea of what time the cleaning crew came through.

Also, that English language skills were not required.

Grant walked into Ted's office wheeling his bucket, and the supervisor—some guy from Senegal who barely spoke English himself—asked why he was there.

"I clean," said Grant with a weary smile, affecting an accent of what he hoped sounded like it was of indeterminate Eastern European origin, and betting on easy odds that no one would try to communicate with him.

The supervisor said, "Where your badge?"

"Badge! Yes!" said Grant, smiling and, to the supervisor, clearly not understanding a damn thing.

"Badge," he said again, an index finger jabbing at his chest, pointing to his own.

Grant kept smiling. "Yes! Clean."

And, as he had anticipated—or at least hoped, which he figured amounted to the same thing, as long as he was right—the supervisor shook his head, muttered something about the quality of people they were letting into America, and walked off.

Grant wheeled his bucket down the hall to Ted's office, put on his latex gloves, and—taking care not to be seen—slowly rifled the desk until he found the metal lock box in the bottom right drawer. He felt *fairly* certain of success—he had been to the office, of course, but Ted hadn't actually waved the petty cash horde to show off for him—but he needed a key to unlock it. He was about to search the desk again when he heard footsteps, so he dropped the metal box into his bucket.

It was the Senegalese supervisor.

"You no clean here," he said.

Grant affixed the stupid smile to his face again, proudly swept a six-inch patch of floor with his broom, and said, "Yes! Clean."

It went on like that for a few minutes, until the frustrated supervisor again departed and Grant resumed his search for the key.

There was no key.

What happened next was what you would expect would happen. The Senegalese supervisor's supervisor showed up and physically marched Grant and his bucket out of the building. When they were at the loading dock, the supervisor's supervisor demanded his name one more time, and Grant, feigning sudden understanding despite having been asked the same question for fifteen minutes, said, "Tibor. Yes. Name Tibor."

"Well, T-Bone," said the supervisor's supervisor, himself not an obvious candidate for an ESL professorship, "you gots to report to the office tomorrow. Understand?"

"Yes. Clean office."

The supervisor's supervisor rolled his eyes. "No, just . . . no more work, okay, T-Bone? Understand?"

Even though Grant was beginning to enjoy the ruse, he also knew it was time to get out of there. So he said, "Tibor fire?"

"Yeah. Sorry, man."

And with that, the supervisor's supervisor departed, leaving Grant alone on the loading dock. After making sure he was gone—the door locking loudly behind him was pretty solid confirmation—Grant slipped out of the coveralls, tossed them to the side of the loading dock where he'd found them, grabbed the metal box from the bucket, and walked briskly to the subway.

It was a bitch to open that box without a key, but once it finally popped open, Grant Lambert was $2,684.35 richer.

At the time, he considered it a big step in settling scores. In reality, it was just a baby step for him on his long, slow slide down a very slippery slope.

A few weeks later, Grant heard through idle bar chatter that when Ted Langhorne noticed that his petty cash was missing, the theft was linked to a fired contracted employee named T-Bone. The office cleaning contractor reimbursed him the amount Ted claimed was in the box.

Four thousand six hundred dollars. And change.

Ted Langhorne had made almost a two-thousand-dollar profit off Grant's crime.

And, again, the rich got richer . . .

When Grant remembered his first foray into big-city crime, he occasionally felt nostalgic for the good old days. Back then, in the late 1980s, a guy could just wander into a building, don a pair of coveralls, grab a bucket, and access the world. If he knew then what he knew now, Grant was sure he could have cleaned out the Federal Reserve.

But times changed. These days you couldn't get within twenty feet of a loading dock without a photo ID and a fingerprint on file. Since Grant did not allow his photograph or fingerprint to be placed in anyone else's permanent record, he had to grow smarter. If he had just arrived in today's New York and been freshly dissed by Ted Langhorne, they both would have ended up with a lot less money.

So, in true Darwinian fashion, Grant evolved. The Langhorne not-so-petty cash gift was just a toe in the water, but it gave Grant an appreciation of what he could accomplish by applying his skills and utilizing the same ethics those Bright Young Gay Things used. Since there were a lot of white-collar crooks out there, they deserved what they had coming to them.

And he liked the fact that Ted Langhorne's petty cash box paid three months of rent. Oh, sure, Ted had made a profit, and he hated that unforeseen consequence, but still . . . three months of rent! Paid! In cash!

One day selfish Ted would get what was coming to him; that wasn't going to become Grant Lambert's obsession.

And one day, Devin Hannerty and Tommy Wilkinson, well . . . *maybe*. If the right opportunity came along, but only the *right* opportunity.

All in good time.

And as the years rolled by, Grant grew increasingly jaded, seeing that it wasn't just Devin and Tommy and Ted who were screwing everyone else. It was, well . . . Christ, it seemed as if *everyone* was doing it. Ivan Boesky begat Michael Milken begat Martha Stewart. People were always looking over their shoulders to make sure some common street thug wasn't approaching from the rear to swipe a twenty from their pockets, but then they'd fork over a few million to a crooked investment banker, who'd embezzle it and run off to Grand Cayman. And did they care? Maybe a little, but they'd just turn around and recoup the missing millions by siphoning it out of their Savings and Loans or jacking up the rent on their properties.

Everywhere Grant looked was another cesspool of corruption. There were no Mother Teresas in this city, and if even she had moved to New York she'd probably be day-trading on insider stock tips and running a brothel on the side.

Everyone's priorities were out of whack. And the people who ended up paying the tab were the ones at the bottom, the ones who had no one beneath them to screw over, although they'd probably do it if they could. People like Grant would have been, if he hadn't taken his alternative path.

And, he reasoned, if you can't beat 'em . . .

Chapter Three

Two days after the visit to Charlie Chops, Grant left the apartment he shared with Chase on a gritty, working-class block in Jackson Heights, Queens, and took the subway to Midtown Manhattan, where he transferred to another train that took him to Broadway and West 110th Street. He slowly climbed the stairs to street level until he finally emerged into the cool, sunny May morning.

Grant hated cool, sunny May mornings. On cool, sunny May mornings, the sun made promises that the temperature was not yet ready to keep. He wasn't wearing a scarf—he lost them too easily, and therefore considered them bad investments—so he bundled the collar of his threadbare coat to his neck with one hand and darted across the width of Broadway, racing against the flashing Don't Walk sign.

Several minutes later, he was standing in front of a battered brownstone just west of Broadway on West 108th Street. His free hand—the one that wasn't clutching the collar to his neck—found the front door key on a ring buried deep in his pocket. He let himself into the lobby, then proceeded to Apartment 2F, where he expected to find $8,957 worth of easily fence-able packages, courtesy of Henry Lemmon's MasterCard, which had had a $10,000 open credit limit just days earlier.

Grant knew better than to max out the credit, tempting as

it was. By leaving a thousand on it, Henry Lemmon would be able to afford some essentials—say, a rental car—for a while, until the card started to be declined, leading to the eventual discovery that his teenage Internet girlfriend might not have been quite as much in love with him as she'd professed. The theft would be discovered soon enough . . . no sense rushing things for the sake of another couple of iPods.

Except there were no packages.

No high-end electronics. No gaming systems. No computer equipment. No iPods. Not even the electric toothbrush he thought he'd keep for himself.

Grant leaned against the freshly painted but otherwise bare wall and slowly slumped, until he was sitting with his knees pressed together on the freshly mopped but otherwise bare hardwood floor. Then, with a sigh of hopelessness, he pulled out his cell phone—his *real* one, not one bought off the street—and punched in a number.

She answered on the first ring with a singsong lilt that was incongruous with her naturally husky, smoky voice, the result of a few decades of too much whiskey, too many cigarettes, and a hell of a lot of yelling.

"Lisa Cochrane."

"It's me," he said. A man of few words, he used even less of them on the telephone. He hated the telephone. "The place is empty."

"Vacant," she agreed.

"No, empty." And then she understood.

"Maybe the delivery hasn't—"

"No," he grumbled. "I tracked it on-line. The computer says that everything was delivered this morning."

Lisa Cochrane exhaled slowly and calmly, but still very audibly. "Let me put you on hold for a minute." With that, an announcer came on the line to inform Grant of all the wonderful living options he had in the five boroughs of New York City, courtesy of Lum Malverne Luxury Real Estate.

A few minutes later, Lisa was back on the line, and the announcer's voice disappeared just as he was describing The Quadrangle, a lovely new development on Roosevelt Island that the voice was trying to convince Grant and everyone else on hold was about to become the hottest luxury housing in New York. Grant knew Roosevelt Island and strongly doubted that.

Her voice was low; not a whisper, but obviously not meant to be overheard. And the lilt was gone. Now it was all smoke and whiskey. "The super says that the only outsiders he let in were the cleaning crew, and they only took their equipment when they left."

Grant shook his head. "He's sure?"

"He has a vested interest in being sure," she reminded him, not having to overtly mention the $300 the building superintendent was expecting for looking the other way while UPS delivered questionable goods to a vacant apartment.

"Right. Anyone else have a key?"

"No. Just the broker and the super. Oh, and the management company, of course. But when I'm trying to rent a unit, they usually stay away."

In the competitive and lucrative arena that is New York City residential real estate, the owner, manager, and broker of a single piece of property were often quite distinct and competitive, usually only working together in an effort to screw tenants out of every last possible quarter in their pockets. And the bigger the enterprise, the more complex the relationship between the players.

The owner, obviously, owned the building, almost always as a corporation, even if the actual owners were just Mom and Pop. Limited liability, and all that came with it. The corporation, in turn, often hired another company to manage the building. And when units became available, brokers like Lisa Cochrane stepped into the picture to get as much as they could out of either the owners, the prospective tenants, or both. Savvy apartment hunters understood that, with effort, they could skip a few layers—knowing the building superintendent when an apartment opened up was akin to winning the lottery—but most went along with the convoluted system, reasoning that their time was worth more than a broker fee of a few thousand dollars on top of the $2,500 monthly rent they'd be paying for 200 square feet of semi-habitable living space and a view of an airshaft.

This apartment, on either the upper Upper West Side or lower Morningside Heights, depending who you asked, went both ways: it was a small building, but in an increasingly desirable neighborhood. Meaning who knew how many hands were involved in the search for a tenant?

Grant knew when Lisa said "I," she was really referring to not only herself, but every other broker in the city hustling for the commission on that West 108th Street apartment, which made him wonder exactly how many people had been in and out of that vacancy between the hour when UPS delivered his packages and when *he* showed up. Sure, Lisa and the building super had stakes in it, too, and they had no reason to pad the truth, but the comings and goings were probably more frequent than either of them realized.

There were the contractors. And other realtors, hoping to beat Lisa to the commission. And the management company . . .

And Grant thought, if the contractors were working, wouldn't the management company want to check the work? They did have a vested interest in quality control, after all.

"What if management wanted to check on the work of the contractors?"

She didn't answer. She didn't have to. All she could finally bring herself to say, in her most professional voice, was, "I guess I can make some inquiries."

Grant managed to avoid the super and that $300 expected pay-off on his way out of the building. It was the only positive development of the morning.

* * *

An hour later, Grant was shuffling his feet awkwardly and filling in the morning's developments to the assistant manager at the Groc-O-Rama supermarket in Elmhurst. The fact that the assistant manager of the Groc-O-Rama—or "The Gross," as it was appropriately known throughout northern Queens—was Chase's day job didn't make things any easier.

As assistant manager, Chase's main duties were getting yelled at by the manager, getting attitude from the other employees, and, when he had an opportunity, keeping the shelves stocked and the customers moderately happy. He didn't like it; but he didn't hate it, either, which made him an exception among pretty much everyone else—employee and customer alike—who walked through the front doors.

Grant didn't like The Gross any better than everyone else, but—since he had news to deliver and hated the telephone, and because Elmhurst was more or less on the way home to Jackson Heights—he decided a visit was in order. The minute the automatic door opened with a pneumatic *whoosh*, though, he felt like he had made a mistake. The grungy floors and disorganized shelves—despite Chase's best efforts, and pretty much no one else's—gave the supermarket an air of desperation, as if the Groc-O-Rama Corporate Gods had decided to see just how far they could debase the public before they'd decide they would rather starve than shop there.

It didn't seem to Grant they had much further to go until they could end their experiment. The narrow aisles were close to empty, which made it easy to find Chase and deliver the bad news in relative privacy.

"So the people from the management office stole our stuff?" Chase asked, after listening to the story.

"We don't know that."

"But you think it."

Grant sighed in defeat. "Every last battery." He paused, then added, "Even my electric toothbrush."

Chase shook his head. Seeing a cashier eye him from the end of the aisle, he turned his attention to straightening a row of Pop-Tarts and hissed, "Well, we have to get it back."

Grant shrugged. "I've got no idea how to do that. We could break into the management office, I suppose, but the stuff could already be gone, so all we get are ... I don't know. Keys and apartment tear sheets, or something equally useless."

Without taking his eyes off the breakfast snack shelf, Chase said, "Grant, this is serious. That nine thousand dollars was just about everything we're gonna get off of Henry Lemmon's credit card, and by the time we fence it, even that will only get us ... What? Maybe a grand, fifteen hundred max? The fences in this city aren't exactly overly generous." He looked away from the Pop-Tarts for a brief second and added, "We're losing money on this job."

"I know." He shrugged again and looked at the floor. "Bad luck on this job."

"Real bad. It's good you grabbed the car. Otherwise, we'd be behind. And I don't even want to think about what our hourly wages have been, once you consider all the time I spent logged in on the computer. Probably less than I make here at Groc-O-Rama." Chase was a loyal company man— more loyal than the company would ever be to him—and he would never call his place of employment "The Gross."

Grant nodded. He knew his boyfriend was right. If Lisa couldn't find out the fate of the packages—and he doubted she could—this was going to be a minimum wage–level lesson in how *not* to be a criminal.

"Maybe next time," he said, in a feeble effort to save face, "we skip sending you to Albany. I mean, the guy doesn't absolutely have to know you got on the plane."

Chase blew a wisp of hair off his forehead and said, "Don't bullshit me, Grant. You wanted him at the airport because you wanted the car. You *always* want the car. God help us if someday a mark takes mass transit to JFK. We'll be screwed."

Grant was about to answer when Chase's cell phone rang. He pulled it from his pocket, looked at the caller ID, then put it away.

"Who was that?"

Chase was even more unhappy than he had been before the phone rang. "Jamie Brock. He keeps calling, but won't leave a message."

"Good." Grant wasn't a fan of Jamie Brock. The three of them—Grant and Chase on one side, Jamie on the other— had been distant acquaintances for most of the fifteen years Grant and Chase had been together, a fact he blamed on Chase. But Jamie was the type of person who only knew you when he needed something. In a sense, Grant felt he and Chase—both approaching career criminal status, despite his partner's low-paying Groc-O-Rama gig on the side—were *still* more sincere and productive than Jamie, who continued to play his "trust fund boy" game with the moneyed gay crowd a decade after the last time it had actually worked on a meaningful scale. Now that he was solidly joining Grant and Chase in what some would consider "middle age," the act was getting older than he was.

Chase allowed himself a smile as he returned to busywork. "Screw Jamie. I can hear about his latest Hamptons drama the next time we see him out in the bars. Anyway, at least we got that money from Chops for the BMW, because without it we'd *really* be screwed."

"Instead of just *mostly* screwed."

"Exactly."

This time, Grant allowed himself a smile, a rare emotion on what normally was a poker face even under the happiest of circumstances. Chase—who liked it when Grant smiled— smiled back.

"You know, I've been thinking," said Chase, taking advantage of Grant's rarely exhibited happiness. "We could probably make more money selling this stuff on eBay than from a fence."

"Ebay." Grant thought about that for a moment. "That's that Internet thingie, right?"

Chase laughed. " 'Internet thingie.' You get credit for trying, and I'm proud that you now know where the on-button is on the computer, but I am gonna have to bring you into this century one of these days."

"I'm learning." Chase realized that Grant was feeling defensive—he didn't like being considered a relic of the twentieth century, even though he generally was—so he didn't pursue it and let Grant continue speaking. "What's the advantage?"

"We can drop the stuff quick and anonymous, and probably make more money."

Grant thought about that. "I dunno. I'm used to dealing with who I deal with, not . . . strangers."

Chase neatened a box, turned to Grant, and said, "That's the beauty. It's all anonymous. They wouldn't know us, and we wouldn't know them." He paused for a moment while his cell phone trilled and frowned when Jamie's name again appeared in Caller ID before continuing. "The best thing is we can make money even when we don't have merchandise."

Grant squinted. "How do you sell something you don't have?"

"People look at the description, they bid on the item, they pay . . . and then nothing comes."

That confused Grant. "People buy things like that?" Chase nodded. "What happens when they don't get it?"

"They complain. And I'm sure eBay investigates, but by that time we've disappeared. Maybe pop up again later using a new name or something."

Grant sighed. This eBay thing was something he didn't want to talk about anymore, mostly because he didn't under-

stand it, let alone how people would let themselves get suck-
ered like that. He figured there had to be a fatal flaw to
Chase's idea, but now was not the time to discuss it.

And anyway, he thought of something else he wanted to
do, so when Chase started to pipe up again, he silenced his
partner with his palm and, surprisingly, smiled again.

"You're still smiling," mumbled Chase, from somewhere
behind the palm.

"Yeah. Because you know what I'm gonna do for you?"

"What?"

With a confidence belying a significant lack of faith in himself, Grant said, "I'm gonna find our packages. And maybe
then we can sell them on eBay or something."

Chase spun toward him, knocking a box of breakfast bars
off the shelf from the perch directly beneath the Pop-Tarts.
Grant hoped he wouldn't pick them up from the dingy
floor—just leave them for the rats—but he did.

For his part, Chase wanted to be supportive—that's how
boyfriends were supposed to be—but he couldn't help but express his cynicism as he collected the breakfast bars. "How are
you gonna do *that*?"

"It's a real estate office. How hard can it be?"

Chase laughed despite himself, adding, "You're an idiot.
So why is it again that I love you?"

"Because I'm an idiot."

"Oh, right. Anyway, are you sure you're not a bit rusty on
the breaking and entering stuff? It's been a while."

"It's like riding a bicycle." Grant showed a sliver of a
smile. "And like I said, it's a real estate office. Probably just a
storefront. It's not like I'm talking about breaking into the
Chrysler Building. I don't even figure this will require any
'breaking.' Just 'entering.' "

"But . . ."

"Stack your Pop-Tarts. I'll see you at home."

* * *

It was probably not surprising that someone like Grant Lambert would have a hard time finding love. People who don't trust, not to mention those who have adopted a criminal lifestyle, aren't usually the most requested men after a round of speed-dating, and those bar conversations that start with "so what do *you* do" tend to end unfortunately.

Which was why Grant and Chase met in probably the only way they could have met, when Chase caught Grant breaking into Groc-O-Rama in the middle of the night. That could have ended badly for Grant, had not Chase himself been in the dark store at 3:00 AM for the sole purpose of breaking into the manager's safe, which contained almost $5,000 waiting for an armored truck pick-up the next morning. So instead of getting arrested, Grant ended up sharing the loot with Chase, which led to sharing a bed with Chase. The rest was their own little piece of history. And so Grant Lambert and Chase LaMarca became partners in crime and love.

The Groc-O-Rama district manager thought Elmhurst was a bad location, but couldn't argue with its economic viability, even if the occasional thief emptied the safe and, on odd occasions when the cameras were actually working, stole the security tape, in those old, technologically prehistoric days. The net loss through theft to the major international firm that owned Groc-O-Rama was so insignificant that the corporation managed to convince itself it was performing a major public service by keeping the Elmhurst store open, even as they jacked up the prices to the consumer to make up for the shortfall and a little bit more.

Over the next few years, though, things began to change. They changed for the big Midtown office buildings, where security was stepped up and it was no longer possible to throw on a pair of coveralls and wander the halls, and they changed for Elmhurst supermarkets, too. A few years after that first night they'd emptied the safe, Chase broke the bad news to Grant. Groc-O-Rama was going to now be open twenty-four hours a day, and an armed guard would be on premises for each and every hour, as opposed to the Rent-A-Cops who used to make their hourly drive-bys.

With access to the locations where he did what he did quickly diminishing, so did Grant's economic status. After fifteen years living on the underside of the American economy, he had to grow more and more creative to make less and less.

But when they discovered the opportunities of the Internet, and realized that they could make technology work to their advantage, well . . . that's when things began to change for the relationship, as well as their wallets. With the Internet, they became more equal partners in their illegal enterprises: Grant, slower to adapt, often deferred to Chase, especially when it came to the electronic implementation of their schemes.

The best part of the Internet, Grant was beginning to understand, was quick and mobile anonymity. They were not foolish and without fear, but by exercising caution—a few keystrokes and a trip to a Starbucks to piggyback on a new wireless network—they could pretty well cover their tracks. Even a relative technophobe like Grant had to admit that was much preferable to breaking and entering.

Best of all, the victims were helpful enough to send their money and credit card numbers; Grant and Chase didn't even have to go get them.

And when they happened across the chat-room predators, like this Henry Lemmon guy, it was like striking gold.

Neither Grant nor Chase had any lingering trauma to address with the Henry Lemmons of the world; it just felt good to reverse the intended victimization, and they were willing to believe almost anything Chase typed to them. If a mark ended up feeling hurt and betrayed by his Internet teen lovers and stripped of his bank balances in the process, well, maybe he'd think things over a little bit more carefully in the future.

Not that they wanted that. They wanted their marks to stay careless.

It made their lives easier.

Chapter Four

The management company in this particular real estate food chain was called Kievers Properties. The company owned a string of mismatched, mismanaged properties throughout Manhattan, including the place on West 108th Street, and its offices were on York Avenue in the east 80s, on Manhattan's Upper East Side.

While hardly an embarrassment to the good citizens of New York, most of the neighborhood was still considered low-rent compared to those surrounding it; too far from the subway for an easy commute from a luxury high-rise, therefore meaning damn few luxury high-rises; yet not quite of the caliber of the elegant buildings with unobstructed East River views a block away on East End Avenue. Just a mélange of four- and five-story brick buildings with an occasional brownstone thrown in to class up the neighborhood, anchored by a bunch of small businesses on the ground floors.

As Grant had figured, Kievers Properties was housed in the first-floor storefront of a five-story walkup. Which made his life easier.

The Kievers Properties façade—a faded blue awning extending over the wide sidewalk that was almost certainly in violation of code, not that it was often enforced—fit right into the neighborhood. Its neighbors—a high-end florist and a low-end Chinese takeout joint—effected the same shabby look, less one of neglect than of "I don't care, I'm too busy doing important things *inside* the building to worry about the exterior."

Grant stood a block away, sizing up his surroundings. The traffic on York Avenue was on the heavy side, which he didn't like, but the side streets looked pretty clear. And there were double-parked cars everywhere; he considered that to be a good thing. He wished he could walk around the neighborhood a bit more to hone his bearings, but that would have been too conspicuous, given how he was dressed, so he just eyeballed the immediate couple of blocks and decided to trust the instincts that usually didn't fail him.

Ten minutes into his surveillance, when he saw a UPS truck double-park three blocks south on York, he decided it was time to move.

At 4:20 PM, a trim, if not especially toned, slightly graying man walked up to the front door of Kievers Properties and, finding it locked, pressed the buzzer off to the side. When the door was unlocked, Grant—in a brown UPS uniform—walked crisply into the office, flashed his clipboard, and said, "I'm here to pick up some packages that were delivered to the wrong address."

The receptionist furrowed her brow. "I'm sorry, but no one said anything about . . ."

"I'll just take a quick look around." He quickly assessed the interior, noting that the worn gray footpath on the otherwise green industrial carpet led to the middle of three doors in the room, meaning that the other two were closets and the path would lead to the interior offices. There was probably too much loot for a closet—not if they needed it for anything else—so he figured he'd find his stuff somewhere behind that third door.

Grant pointed to the door. "Back here?" Without waiting for an answer, he strode across the room, following the path to the door and exuding confidence in his UPS brown.

"Sir!" The receptionist began to rise, but was distracted by another buzz from the front door. She barcly looked at the monitor as she unlocked the door before standing and taking a few steps toward Grant.

"*Sir!*" she repeated, this time with much more assertiveness, and Grant stopped with his hand on the doorknob. He thought about trying to placate her for a split second, then thought better of that. The clock was ticking. He turned the knob and the door opened, revealing a hallway lit with harsh fluorescent tubes.

Ahead of him, office doors lined each side of the corridor, and Grant felt confident that his prize was behind one of them. Still, now that he had gotten this far, it was better to slow his roll and mollify the receptionist than risk her making a quick three-tone call to 911. Not to mention she'd need to tell him which room the packages were in.

"Sir?" Her voice had softened when he stopped, which he considered a good sign, and validation of his decision to slightly delay that march down the hall to liberate the stolen goods that had been stolen from him. "Sir, you really can't go back there without permission."

"UPS," he said with assurance and a half-smile, knowing from experience that almost everyone gave almost everything to the UPS man, no questions asked, which was why he had worn the uniform in the first place. "Which room are the packages in?"

"I told you I don't know anything about any packages."

"I really have to get back to my truck before I get a ticket." Grant took a gamble. "You new here?"

She shook her head. "Almost five years. *And* I know Vinnie." He was about to ask who Vinnie was, but she fortunately added, "If you were Vinnie, you could have the run of the place. But I don't know you."

He tried again. "I'm working Vinnie's route today, so if I could just grab the packages I'll be out of your hair."

"Ugh!" It wasn't disgust; it was clearly frustration.

He was about to respond with *something*—he wasn't quite sure what, but it would probably be a proud defense of his company's integrity and his own personal twenty-year career with The Brown—when the reception area door opened and a very familiar, very unwelcome face popped into view. And then one unwelcome hand belonging to the unwelcome body graced by the unwelcome face shot him an index finger, and the face grinned and said, "What's up, Grant?"

Jamie Brock. Jamie *Fucking* Brock.

He stared at one of the last people he wanted to see, not counting the police, as the tousled-headed, sun-weathered face of Jamie Brock grinned at him.

"Aren't you at least going to say hello?" asked Jamie, and his damn grin broadened. Catching the wary eyes of the receptionist in his peripheral vision, Grant tried to hold his poker face.

"I'm sorry, but I don't know who you are. I'm just the UPS man."

Jamie looked confused. "That explains the uniform. C'mon, Grant, it's *Jamie*! Jamie *Brock*!" When Grant again refused to break character, Jamie took a few steps forward, until he was just inches from Grant. Then he smiled and added, "What, are you pulling some kind of . . . ?"

Not a complete idiot—only about 98 percent—Jamie belatedly realized he was in mixed company—the mix being two people who didn't always abide by the law and one apparently law-abiding citizen—and shut up, but not before the receptionist picked up her phone, dialed furiously, and began whispering.

"You," Grant finally hissed into Jamie's ear, "are a fucking moron."

Jamie, wide-eyed, shrugged a "how was I to know?" apology and wisely took a few steps back, then tried for a save by trying to confide to the woman behind the desk, "I guess I was mistaken." He motioned to Grant, smiled, and added, "Just the UPS man."

Grant cleared his throat, hoping against hope that he could salvage the operation. "So if I could just get those packages . . ."

"I don't think so," said a tall, stooped, bald, and very angry man—not necessarily angry about the situation; he looked to Grant as if he were born angry—who was suddenly standing guard at the nexus of the front office and hallway.

Still, the faux UPS man pressed on. "And you are?"

"*I* am Stanley Kievers. And *you* are?"

"The UPS man."

Stanley Kievers was seventy if he was a day, but there was something about him—something born of owning and managing a network of overpriced tenements full of grousing, deadbeat tenants for four decades—that gave him a formidable, frightening presence. His stare—cold, glassy, hard—was targeted on Grant's poker face, and Grant felt beads of sweat begin to form. He pitied the tenant who fell two months behind in rent.

"You have identification, I suppose?" asked Stanley Kievers finally, although it was a demand, not a question.

Grant fumbled for the fairly professional laminated card he kept in an inside pocket for the possibility of something like this. It had never before happened—everyone just *trusted* the UPS delivery man—but now he was glad he had thought things out thoroughly a few years earlier when he bought the uniform from a disgruntled employee.

Kievers looked over the card, then put it in his own pocket. Before Grant had a chance to object beyond "What the . . . ?" the old man turned to the receptionist and said, "Go to my office and call 911."

"What the . . . ?" Grant started again, as the receptionist disappeared into the hallway behind her elderly protector.

"This expired three months ago, Mr. Talbott. *If* that's your real name." Grant suddenly realized that he hadn't quite thought things through as well as he should have. "You can sort it out with the police."

"But . . ."

Grant suddenly felt Jamie's hand on his shoulder and was grateful. He had almost forgotten that Jamie was there. "Let's go, Gr—uh, *Mr. Talbott.*"

"Uh . . . right." But Grant couldn't resist one last remark as he and Jamie fled, if "walking fast" could truly be described as fleeing. Jabbing a finger at Stanley Kievers from the safe distance of ten feet, he announced, "You're gonna hear from UPS about this."

As they escaped into the late-afternoon sun, the real UPS truck—driven by Vinnie, no doubt, a *real* UPS driver—pulled to a stop outside the blue awning. The driver did a double-take and hollered, but by then Grant and Jamie were lost in the protective labyrinth of double-parked cars and heavy York Avenue traffic.

Grant was reluctant to hail a cab—a uniformed UPS man hailing a cab on the Upper East Side of Manhattan, taking it to a subway entrance, then taking the subway home was probably not unheard of, but would certainly be memorable; and also Stanley Kievers, Vinnie the *real* UPS guy, and the cops would probably be looking for him—so he was happy to hear that Jamie Brock had a car parked around the block. Even though he was mad at Jamie.

It was a complicated set of emotions, but in a pinch, Grant went with the safest, least obvious one. Plus, that way he'd at least get to hear why the superficial son of a bitch had tracked him down on the Upper East Side and screwed up what should have been a simple retrieval job.

Jamie pulled his Lexus away from the curb, where it had been parked in a no-parking zone, and Grant stripped off his brown shirt so that any passing police car—and Jamie braked to let one pass, meaning it had been a quiet day in the 19th Precinct—would see just a guy in his T-shirt in the passenger seat. Strange for early May, maybe, but not excessively strange by New York City standards. In any event, it was good enough.

"So where am I going?" Jamie asked, following the patrol car down the block back to York Avenue.

"You mind taking me to Jackson Heights?"

"Not at all." Jamie drove a few more blocks before asking, "Uh . . . where exactly is Jackson Heights?"

"Queens." Confusion washed over Jamie's face, and Grant knew he'd have to fill in the blanks. "Near LaGuardia."

"That's . . . uh . . . on the way out to Long Island, isn't it?"

"Pull over."

When the car pulled to the curb at an open space next to a fire hydrant, Grant scanned the streetscape, then—clad in the telltale brown pants and a white T-shirt—darted out of the passenger side and around the front of the car. Following his lead, Jamie got out of the car and walked dejectedly around the back. Once they'd switched positions and Grant had them back in traffic, he turned to the new passenger and incredulously asked, "You really don't know how to get to Queens?"

"I've, uh . . . been to Astoria. Once. But if I go to Queens, it's just to the airport, and I get rides when I go to the airport."

"You don't pay attention to where they're taking you?"

Jamie felt slightly defensive. "They get *paid* to drive, Grant. I'm just a passenger. I'm not supposed to know how to get where I want to go."

Grant could barely bring himself to talk to Jamie, but—by the time they were on the FDR Drive headed north along Manhattan's East Side toward the Triborough Bridge—he managed to calm himself down.

"So, you must have something very important to tell me, if you had to interrupt my personal business."

A smile broke out across Jamie's face, crinkling his already crinkly features just a bit more. He ran a hand through his full head of brown hair. It had highlights, like Chase's. Grant thought that maybe he should start considering his own increasing silver content as highlights; maybe that would make him feel younger. It wouldn't make the back pain go away, but it'd be something.

Jamie stopped ruffling his annoyingly tousled-and-highlighted hair and clamped a hand on Grant's shoulder, which *also* annoyed Grant. "You are going to love this."

"I'd better." He began angling toward the cash lanes as he steered closer to the Triborough tollbooths, fighting the Friday afternoon traffic heading out to Long Island. "But first you're gonna tell me what you were doing at the Kievers office."

"Persistence," said Jamie, leaning back and obviously proud of himself. "I kept calling Chase—by the way, was he screening my calls?"

"No idea."

"Okay, whatever. Anyway, I kept calling Chase and eventually he picked up. I knew he would. No one can sit there and listen to the phone ring eight times in a single hour. After a while, you start to think someone is dead."

"I guess."

"Anyway, Chase told me where to find you—"

Grant felt a flash of anger. "Wait a minute! Chase told you I was at Kievers?"

"Don't be mad at him," Jamie said, reassuringly. "I was sort of insistent, and I might have indicated there was an urgent reason I needed to talk to you right away."

"So he just gave me up?" It would have been an understatement to say Grant was pissed off.

"Well, no. Wait." Jamie jiggled the window control and it

opened a few inches. He lit a cigarette—he usually hated the habit, which had been his off and on since he was a teenager, but it was different when he was "on" and *he* was the one smoking—then continued. "Okay, maybe he told me where to find you, but maybe that was because I told him one of our friends was dying, and I needed to see you right away. Because the friend might not last until you got home."

Grant's anger turned to immediate concern. "Who's dying?"

"Uh . . . well, no one, really." For a brief moment, Grant was about to make Jamie dramatically reconsider that statement. "But I have a huge emergency, and if we can't deal with this immediately, we're screwed."

"We?"

"Grant, you're the only one who can help me."

Keeping his eyes on the road, Grant made a half turn toward Jamie. He thought he saw his eyes welling up, but knew well enough not to be taken in. Jamie did emotional drama like most people did shoelace tying.

"Okay, you screwed up my little recovery mission, so this had better be good. Talk."

Jamie was immediately clear-eyed. "You know Romeo Romero?"

"Not personally."

"Yeah, but you know who he is, right?" Grant nodded noncommittally. He knew he was an actor, and he thought he was also some sort of gay political figure, but he couldn't quite picture his face, or anything he'd seen Romeo Romero do. On the rare occasions when Grant and Chase went to the movies, it was action or comedy. As far as he knew, Romeo Romero's entire filmography was comprised of the sort of boring, slow-moving crap that reviewers loved, and audiences didn't.

Jamie continued. "So the world thinks of Romeo Romero as this big, powerful, gay actor"—Grant allowed himself a smile at the knowledge that this was something he actually knew, sort of—"but it turns out, he's not all that gay."

Grant barely registered Jamie's last comment. He was closing in on the Triborough tollbooth and instinctively looked for—and saw—an EZ Pass box affixed to the windshield behind the rearview mirror.

"Get rid of the EZ Pass," he said, and Jamie looked confused, so Grant repeated his command.

"It's a five-dollar toll," Jamie whined. "And I don't want to mess up my windshield with all that glue and tape and stuff."

Grant looked at him for a second, then realized what he meant. "This is *your* car?"

"Sure."

"Oh." He wanted to ask how someone who had never had a real job in his entire worthless life was driving a 2008 Lexus GS 460, but decided to drop it. It would be bad—very bad—for Grant Lambert's self-image. Instead, he eased into an EZ Pass lane and cruised through the tollbooth, all the while wondering if Charlie Chops might be looking for spare parts for a late-model Lexus. Maybe he'd give him a call when he got home.

On the other side of the tollbooth, they headed east, and Grant told Jamie to continue. Which he did, excitedly.

"So Romeo Romero isn't gay! This guy has made a career out of being the brave gay actor who has stepped forward when all the closet cases were, uh, being closet cases, and it turns out the guy is faking it. He is one hundred percent heterosexual."

Jamie waited a moment for his earth-shattering announcement to sink in, but the response was somewhat less than enthusiastic.

"So you say."

"No, I know this." For a man pretty much used to being

considered full of shit by almost everyone, Jamie was strangely insistent. "Romeo Romero *isn't* gay!"

"So what does this mean for me?" Grant asked as he maneuvered around a slower car, and Jamie correctly thought he could not care less about the biggest news since, well, *ever!*

So it was time to up the ante.

"I want to blackmail him."

"Blackmail?" Grant barely raised an eyebrow. He had heard it all before, and from more imposing characters than the bullshitter sitting next to him in the passenger seat.

"Yeah, blackmail." Jamie leaned across the bucket seat, so close that Grant was afraid he was going to rest his head on his shoulder. "I was just out at his place in Water Mill—beautiful real estate, by the way—and the guy is dripping with money. I figure we could get a hundred thousand off of him."

"We?" Again.

Jamie returned his body to the upright position and shrugged, but never took his eyes off Grant. "Well, I really can't do it alone."

"You do everything alone, as I recall."

"Well . . . yeah, usually. But there's a slight complication."

Aha! Grant knew this scheme was dead in the water, and here was his confirmation. Still, he indulged him. "Which is?"

Jamie's hands began doing half the talking. "Okay, here's the deal. I'm out in the Hamptons and get invited to Romeo Romero's annual Tax Freedom Day party. Did you know there's a Tax Freedom Day?"

"I don't pay—"

"Right! You don't pay taxes . . . I forgot. Anyway, I'm with this mega-huge, super-rich openly gay celebrity, and it just so happens that I'm single right now—"

"And this car?"

"From when I *wasn't* single. Anyway, I figured it made

sense to get to know Romeo, because he seemed like a nice guy, and maybe things would work out between us. I mean, *yes*, he's, like, sixty years old, and *no*, he's not the hottest guy out there, but he's . . . he's . . . well, he's *Romeo Romero*! Openly gay actor and celebrity! A-list all the way. An 'A-Gay.' "

"Except for not so gay."

Jamie shook his head. "Not at all. I spent a week trying to get close to that guy and . . . nothing. But it wasn't totally wasted, because the more I hung around him, the more I started observing things."

"Things?" Grant slid into the left lane and passed a row of slow-moving cars.

"Things that the ordinary guy might not notice, but that I—as the man who couldn't get anywhere with him—sure did. Like the attention he paid to a certain female who seemed to be hanging out there a lot of the time."

Grant sighed as he moved back to the right lane. "You're seriously upset because he paid more attention to a woman than to you? Maybe *she* just had a personality."

"I was," Jamie acknowledged, ignoring the gratuitous insult. "But then I thought, maybe she's just his fag hag. And I tried to think that, but . . . it just didn't click for me. There was something more going on. So anyway, one night there's a party, and someone had a camcorder." He paused. "Can you believe they still make those things?"

Grant shrugged and kept his eyes on the road. He didn't know whether they still made them or not—most likely, it was just someone's dated toy—but he didn't want to get into it with Jamie. He was already feeling too old. Hopefully, the format was at least VHS; if it was an 8 millimeter model, like the one he once lifted from a city councilman's district office in Brooklyn and fenced for a few bucks, he was going to feel as ancient as the camcorder.

"Anyway," Jamie continued, when he realized he wasn't

going to get an answer, "I sort of started to follow him around, filming on the sly. You know, surreptly."

" 'Surreptly?' "

"You know, without being seen."

Grant sighed. "I think the word you want is 'surreptitiously.' "

Jamie scrunched up his face. "It is? Then what does 'surreptly' mean?"

"It means you're a fucking idiot."

"Listen, do you want me to tell the story or not?" Grant didn't answer, so Jamie took it upon himself to continue without permission. "So I'm sort of sneaking around in the dark and I see Romeo, and sure enough he's with that girl again. I follow them to the backyard . . . turns out he's got a hot tub back there. Fenced in, but he forgot to lock it, so I could get in. Anyway, they get in the hot tub and, well . . . *do it.*"

"Do it?" Grant thought about that. "You mean sex?"

"I mean sex." Jamie sat back in his seat and smiled contentedly. "And I got it all on tape."

For a split second, Grant lost control of the Lexus, and spit a few stray stones from the shoulder of the Grand Central Parkway. "You *taped* the fucking guy? You taped the fucking guy *fucking*? A *woman*?"

Jamie, briefly alarmed when they veered onto the shoulder, sat back again in his plush leather seat and said, "I taped him. And let me tell you, Grant Lambert, that woman was *no* fag hag."

"Okay, you'd better start at the beginning . . ."

Chapter Five

Jamie Brock repeated his story, ending at the point where he caught a twenty-minute hot-tub sexual encounter between Romeo Romero and his not so fag-haggish fag hag on tape, and the tape had been liberated from the camcorder and deposited in a pocket of his cargo shorts. Mission accomplished, as it were.

As Jamie finished recounting his tale, Grant exited the expressway and prepared to hit the surface roads.

"Well . . . it sounds like you did your homework," he said approvingly. "So you have the goods to make this 'A-Gay' a—what?—'D-Straight'?"

"More like a 'V-Straight,' I think," said Jamie. "Without his gay fabulousness, he's just another middle-aged-bordering-on-elderly actor whose career has gone bye-bye."

Something in Grant's gut hated the dismissive way Jamie used the phrase "his career has gone bye-bye." He wasn't sure if it was the childlike expression, or the fact that Jamie—who was only a few years younger than him, but *much* better at keeping himself up—seemed so dismissive of an aging man. Still, Grant swallowed his distaste and got back to the point.

"Okay, so where do I come in? Why did you have to interrupt me in the middle of a job? What is so friggin' urgent?

You've got the backup, and you've *certainly* got the balls, so just go and blackmail the guy. Simple!"

"Not so simple."

"Not so simple?" Grant didn't like the sound of that.

"Uh . . ." Jamie's face reddened. "There was a little problem."

Grant hiked an eyebrow. His sense of unease was about to be confirmed. "Yeah?"

"I don't have the tape anymore."

Grant whistled as he stopped for a red light. "That's more than a little problem." He thought for a moment, squinting as the sun glanced off a storefront window across the intersection. "So where is it?"

"That's where I thought you could help."

"So I figured. I'm psychic like that."

"You see, I left it in a cab."

The light turned green and Grant drove, glad to have the sun out of his eyes. He was also glad that Jamie, for once, was mercifully silent.

There were more than 12,000 licensed yellow cabs in New York City, and who knew how many livery cabs? Figured that Jamie Brock of all people would make him dig for a needle in a haystack.

"Okay," said Grant, trying to sort things out. "This cab: a yellow cab, or a black car?"

"What's a black car?"

"It's what they call the livery cabs."

"The . . . the *livery* cabs?"

Grant half turned toward Jamie and said, "Have you *ever* been out of Manhattan? And, if not, have you *ever* been north of Ninety-sixth Street?"

Jamie didn't answer, just muttered "livery cabs" a few times, rolling it around his tongue like it was a new taste. Then, still ignoring Grant's most recent question—which in any event was rhetorical—Jamie answered the important one. "It was a yellow cab. And I remember that the driver had some sort of foreign-sounding name."

Grant frowned while Jamie continued with some surprisingly helpful information. "I had him drop me at Ninetieth and Lex on Wednesday night when I got back from the Hamptons, but after he drove away I realized the tape wasn't in my bag. I tried to run after him, but after a block all the cabs sort of looked the same."

"They'll do that," said Grant, making an illegal right on red and heading down the home stretch.

"And that's when I started to call you. Leading us to . . . now!"

"Lucky me," grunted Grant, his brain reflexively thinking back to those electronics still hopefully stored securely in the offices of Kievers Properties, and wondering how soon he could get back there to liberate them. "Yeah, lucky me."

He rolled past a beaten, mixed-use red brick building at the next corner, housing a tailor and a vacant storefront on the ground floor and, three stories above, the small apartment he shared with Chase. He pulled the Lexus a bit too close to the 1977 Chevy Nova parked in front and said, "This is where I get out."

Jamie knit his brow. "You're gonna double-park?"

"No," said Grant, opening his door with only the briefest peek for oncoming traffic. "You're going home."

"But . . ."

"I know how to get you if I need you. First, though, I've got some thinking to do."

It took Jamie three hours to find his way back to Manhattan.

Four blocks after Abdul Mustafaa had deposited Jamie Brock at the southeast corner of East Ninetieth Street and Lexington Avenue two nights earlier, a short, roundish man hailed him, practically jumping from the curb to steal the cab from a trio of obnoxious frat boys—he didn't want to stereotype, but his frat boy fares were *always* obnoxious—who had converged at the same intersection. Abdul stopped the car short of the corner, giving the advantage to the short, roundish man, and the cab zipped through the yellow light as the frat boys screamed racial epithets in his wake.

It was all so . . . charming. Whereas earning money and bettering his life had once been the reason Abdul Mustafaa had immigrated from Ethiopia, after five years driving a yellow cab he was almost willing to admit that screwing over obnoxious frat boys as they waited for rides on the street corners of New York made even the harsh times and disappointments of his new American life worthwhile.

In the backseat, the short, roundish passenger—Will Whitcomb to his friends, who numbered approximately zero—gave the driver an address on the West Side of Manhattan, in Hell's Kitchen, then stretched back without bothering to buckle his seat belt. He looked out the window as the cab rolled fairly effortlessly south down Lex, patting one oversized breast pocket, then the other, of his cheap sport jacket and feeling reassured when his fingers felt the hard plastic of the half-dozen stolen DVDs he'd crammed in there. Once home—after he managed to stiff the driver of his fare, of course—he would replace the shrink-wrap (removal of which was needed to lift the merchandise in the first place) then sell them to that store on Ninth Avenue for half the suggested retail price, no questions asked. With no transportation costs and a net eighty dollars or so profit, Will Whitcomb could consider it a successful evening. He wasn't getting rich, but he was keeping his head above water, and—at fifty-six years of age—that's all he asked out of life. It was all in those little bits and pieces.

He slid a bit as the driver took a fast turn and felt something hard dig into his thigh. Not looking down, he blindly felt the seat next to him until he came in contact with a videotape, then quickly searched his memory. VHS was so last century . . . but had he grabbed one in his DVD-pilfering frenzy? No, he would have remembered that. *This* was not his.

When the cab stopped under a streetlight, he stole a look at the tape. In childish handwriting someone had labeled the plain cardboard casing "RR with Girl."

Ah . . . porn. Better yet, probably amateur porn. And if he was really lucky, RR was also a girl, which would make it amateur *lesbian* porn! Which was like the trifecta of videotape. Will Whitcomb was beginning to think it was a *very* successful evening after all, and he had no idea how right he was.

When the car reached Eighth Avenue, he told the driver that he just remembered that he only had a few dollars in his pocket, and asked him to pull to the corner so he could get money out of the ATM in the deli, and he'd be right back. Instead, he walked in through the side door and kept walking out through the door fronting Eighth, heading south so the driver wouldn't see him and he'd be able to flee against the flow of traffic, just in case the driver *did* see him.

Another free sixteen-dollar ride. It was all in those little bits and pieces.

An hour later, sitting in his crumbling studio apartment, the interior of which no human other than Will Whitcomb had seen in years, he put the hopefully-amateur-lesbian-porn tape into his VCR, popped open a beer, undid the flap of his blue-patterned boxer shorts, and prepared to enjoy himself. It had been close to a decade since he'd had the real thing, so a night enjoying someone else's pleasure by proxy would be the perfect nightcap.

He saw right away that the video was, indeed, amateur, which only heightened his excitement. He found the murky, grainy images highly arousing, and his hand slipped deep into his boxers. Even if the quality was bad—no, *horrible*—the fact that this had obviously been taped without the consent of one or both parties made it . . . irresistible. He wasn't even all that disappointed when he realized that one of those grainy, writhing bodies was a man.

For ten long minutes there was action both on the murky television screen and inside the blue-patterned boxer shorts . . .

Until something struck Will Whitcomb as uncomfortably familiar.

He *knew* that man.

That Man, that RR, who was at this very moment suckling on the breast of That Woman on his television screen . . . he *knew* him. Self-gratification forgotten, he edged his way off his chair, moving closer and staring intently at the screen as That Man began to receive oral sex from That Woman.

Who *was* he? Certainly no one Will Whitcomb knew in person. These people were clearly among the Beautiful People, as opposed to the literally Great Unwashed who were the sort of people he knew. *He* certainly didn't know anyone who had a hot tub.

No, these people were celebrities, or something like that. There was no other way he could have recognized That Man.

Now he was mere inches from the screen, still staring. Fifty years earlier and in an entirely more upright, comfortable setting, his mother would have warned him that he would go blind from being that close to the TV. Not to mention earlier, when his hand had been down his boxers, which would have caused him to go blind *and* grow hair on his palms.

"Oh, Romeo," moaned That Woman in a thick accent, as she broke away from That Man's impressive endowment, and Whitcomb wondered for a moment if they were engaged in a twisted Shakespearian reenactment . . .

Until it clicked.

He kept staring, and finally That Man turned toward the camera. He was well put together, but he was not young anymore. Handsome, in a "faded movie star" sort of way. And his name was Romeo. Which could possibly—*probably?*—make him . . .

Romeo Romero?

Whitcomb lifted an eyebrow, then looked at the videotape box. "RR with Girl."

RR.

Romeo Romero.

Bingo.

Except . . . something played at the corners of Will Whitcomb's memory. He was hardly an *Entertainment Tonight* addict or a *People* magazine connoisseur, but there was something about Romeo Romero that he thought he knew, but wasn't quite sure about.

He knew who would be, though.

"Ma," he barked into the phone, even though her apartment was in the same building just one floor below his. "I got a question. This actor, Romeo Romero, what do ya know? . . . Why? 'Cause I'm interested, is why . . . *Gay?*" He looked again at the screen, where Romero Romero was now preparing to mount That Woman. "You sure about that?" His mind raced, but the best he could add was, "Huh."

He kept his attention on the screen as his mother prattled on about the whole sordid, sinful business, only refocusing to reply to his mother, "No, Ma, I am *not* gay. That's not why I was askin'."

And with that, he hung up.

The next day found Will Whitcomb in the public library, a type of building he hadn't entered since the days when his mother worried about his impending blindness, mostly because everything in libraries was used, and therefore of no resale value whatsoever. Also because his reading, when he read, tended to be of the *Penthouse Forum* variety.

But it was, he vaguely recalled, a good place to do a little research for free.

The librarian—middle-aged, tall, thin, mustached, and wearing a powder blue sweater vest—had been thrilled when Whitcomb whispered to him that we was looking for references on Romeo Romero.

"The man is a hero," the librarian gushed.

"Yeah, well, I just want to get a read on him."

The librarian swatted at Whitcomb's shoulder and threw his head back, letting only a muted guffaw—it *was* the library, after all—escape. "Get a 'read.' And you're in the library. You are *too* funny, mister."

Whitcomb began to sweat a little. He wasn't enjoying the intimacy. Fortunately, the powder blue-vested librarian was suddenly walking him through the stacks. He would have been lost forever left on his own, but his new librarian friend was only too happy to cut through the orderliness and find everything he wanted. Minutes later, they were browsing a shelf in the library's biography section, hunting down the few short references.

Gathering the books in his arms, he found a table where he could be alone and began to read up on Romeo Romero, starting with a chapter in a book about openly gay celebrities that began, *"Before there was Ian McKellan, there was Romeo Romero..."*

Coincidentally, at the very same moment Will Whitcomb was reading about Romeo Romero, Romeo Romero was reading about Will Whitcomb. He just didn't know it yet... nor did anyone else.

It was an article in the *New York Post* titled, "Cabbies Say Drop 'n' Runs on the Rise." Ostensibly yet another story about the ongoing battle between the drivers and the Taxi and Limousine Commission over pretty much anything and everything, the article quoted one Abdul Mustafaa as claiming that the recently mandated global positioning units in the cars were encouraging fares to, well, not actually be *fares*, including one guy who bolted on him the previous night in Hell's Kitchen. Romeo Romero didn't buy Abdul Mustafaa's opinion that riders were rattled by the surveillance, but he found the story compelling.

It wasn't just because it was another example of the tax-sucking government run amok, although it was. It was also because, in the story of the cab driver and the skittish passenger, he found the germ of an idea.

What if I were to portray a rakish cab passenger—maybe a man paranoid about global positioning because the CIA could be watching me—who ran from the cab? And what if the driver . . . He thought about that. *Morgan Freeman? Samuel L. Jackson? No!* Jamie Foxx! *Jamie Foxx as the driver chases me down for the fare! And we end up paired as a buddy team, pooling our resources to elude the authorities.*

With delight, Romero imagined that his brilliant idea could very well even turn into a franchise! *Romero-Foxx II! Romero-Foxx III!* It was delicious to contemplate the loyal audiences and the hefty opening weekend box office receipts.

And maybe even . . . *action figures?* Dared he hope?

Well . . . if nothing else, it would be a lot more interesting than the Merchant-Ivory-esque yawn-inducers that had largely been his bread and butter since coming out as a gay man. That much was true. If Gielgud, Olivier, and O'Toole could do action and comedy, or sometimes both at the same time, why couldn't he? Hell, McKellan even got to be in those X-Men movies! If they could make popular films—and command the corresponding paychecks—why couldn't Romeo Romero?

He set the newspaper down and jotted a few notes on a

cocktail napkin, conveniently located under his first cocktail of the day. *Cab ... CIA? ... Some plot or something ... Foxx?* This he underlined twice. Then, work done, he drained his glass and prepared for the day's second cocktail. It was already 2:30 PM, and he was behind schedule.

He walked across his living room toward the small table tucked in the far corner. A table that had been in his family for generations and which now was used—in fitting homage to that family—to store a large and diverse selection of liquor bottles. He chose one of the clear bottles with a bright red label lettered in some westerner's idea of Cyrillic and began refilling his glass, briefly regretful that he had been reduced to acting as his own bartender.

Once, and not all that long ago, there would have been a person on staff to take care of these mundane tasks. Now, although he had enough money in the bank to keep a live-in assistant or two, he couldn't risk compromising his privacy, so he was usually the lone inhabitant of the six-bedroom house. Which meant he was reduced to the humiliation of acting as his own bartender.

But as he mixed his vodka and soda, he thought happier thoughts. Specifically, how an action role could allow him to break out of the "gay niche" he'd created for himself.

Maybe the man on the run could have a wife. Or, better yet, a younger, chic girlfriend.

He walked back to the cocktail napkin and scratched out: *chic girlfriend—Scarlett Johansson?*

Well, why not? Bill Murray had gotten away with something approximating a May-December romance with her in a film, and *he* wasn't even exotically European. Romeo Romero knew European exoticism made even the oddest coupling palatable to American audiences, as evidenced by pretty much everything ever done by Gerard Depardieu.

And did they come more exotic than Romeo Romero? Not often, they didn't. Italian and Spanish by birth—favoring the

Italian due to an upbringing just outside of Rome—for more than three decades he'd made a nice career out of his unique screen presence, enticing audiences—especially American audiences—with a smoldering charisma.

Well . . . when he was very young, at least. As age began creeping up on him, Romero began to understand that the raw charisma was starting to fade, that he'd need a new trick to stay on top. So he did what people had been doing for centuries, and moved to America to reinvent himself.

It was true that by declaring himself a homosexual, he had put new limits on his career. But that was all right; he still *had* a career, and he was still in the public eye, and he still made a lot of money. Not to mention that his fans—especially his gay fans—were rabidly loyal.

Still, even film stars who were also gay idols needed to pay the bills, especially given the heavy taxes levied on him as an upper-income earner. An action-adventure crowd pleaser could do that, and provide his career with a huge boost by exposing him to an entirely new audience.

Romeo Romero as the hero . . . Jamie Foxx as the buddy . . . Scarlett Johansson as the love interest . . . It was all coming together.

A thought occurred to him and, carefully balancing his drink, he walked briskly back to where he had left his pad, grabbed the pen, and wrote:

Christopher Walken as the villain!

Too obvious? No, he thought, and underlined it three times.

He felt brilliant.

Chapter Six

"The problem," said Grant Lambert, staring off into space, "is that there are more than twelve thousand taxi medallions in this city. And *that* is a problem I can't wrap my head around."

"Well, you're the problem solver, right?" asked Chase, who sat with Grant in the kitchen and grew increasingly concerned as every hour passed, which twenty of them had already. "So if you can't solve this, maybe it can't be solved."

Grant held up a hand to stop him. "No, I can solve this. I just need to focus."

And then he returned his gaze to the empty expanse of white wall over the corkboard they occasionally used to leave messages for each other.

Chase busied himself clearing the lunch plates, dumping Grant's uneaten sandwich in the trash and rinsing the dishes. When he was done, he announced, "Okay, Groc-O-Rama duty calls."

Grant didn't respond.

Chase leaned close to his ear and again said, "Groc-O-Rama duty calls." Again no response. "Which means . . . I'm going to work."

"Bye," was the half-aware response.

Chase shook his head. "Okay, then. Well . . . I'll see you later."

"Paul!"

"Uh . . . Chase."

But Grant was suddenly alive. "No, no . . . *Paul Farraday!* He'll be able to help us!" Grant leaped from his chair and kissed Chase full on the lips. "Paul knows the taxi system inside and out! If anyone can find this tape, it's him."

Chase tried not to roll his eyes. "Isn't Paul Farraday a big drunk?"

"Well, it's not as if I'm asking him to drive us anywhere."

"Didn't he get fired from driving a cab? Because he's a big drunk?"

Grant waved him away. "Water under the bridge. I believe in second chances. Anyway, he wasn't fired. He quit."

Another eye-roll. "Okay, Grant. Good luck with that." He gave his partner a kiss on the cheek and said, "I'm off at midnight. See you then?"

But Grant hadn't heard him. Much as he hated telephones, he was already dialing.

Chase, of course, was correct. Paul Farraday was a big drunk, which was the reason he was no longer driving a cab.

But in his prime—which he recalled as fondly and infrequently as Grant Lambert recalled the days before high-tech security and twenty-four-hour supermarkets—he was known as a driver's driver. There wasn't a block of New York City asphalt he didn't know intimately. Legend had it that he could make it from LaGuardia to Wall Street in fifteen minutes during the morning rush. He was just that good.

But Farraday loved his scotch on the rocks. Loved it more than that nagging shrew he married, before he realized she was a nagging shrew. Loved it more than his sainted mother. Loved it even more than his dream job driving a yellow cab through New York, dodging and weaving and detouring as if he'd sat on Robert Moses's lap while the legendary planner built, destroyed, and reconfigured the city's arterials decades earlier, all the while pointing at a map as he whispered in his ear, *"Bob, I could get back from Kennedy even faster if there was an exit here on the BQE."*

And he did it all without ever touching the horn. Now *that* was a driver's driver.

But Farraday refused to drive with even a drop of alcohol in his system. He prized his skill behind the wheel and his lightning-quick response to any backed-up intersection in the five boroughs too much to muddy his brain. Not to mention the whole "illegal'" and "not wanting to kill anyone" angles.

Which left Paul Farraday with a dilemma: a job he loved and an inviolable moral code versus a drink he loved even more.

The day a completely sober Farraday wheeled his cab back to the garage for the last time and handed in his keys, it is said the other cabbies wept. For those who witnessed the moment, it was like watching Lou Gehrig's retirement speech at Yankee Stadium.

Still, a guy had to make a living—especially now that the nagging shrew demanded alimony and the sainted mother needed a new hip—and it didn't take Farraday long to discover that his encyclopedic knowledge of the streets was in demand in the same underground economy where Grant Lambert and thousands of others made their living. He became the go-to guy for pretty much every job that required some transportation logistics work more complicated than stealing a car. Not that Farraday himself wasn't known to drop a delivery to Charlie Chops every now and then to supplement his income, which is where his path first crossed Grant's.

And now Grant was on the phone, asking Farraday about yellow cabs. Grant was dancing all over what he really wanted to say, but Farraday—well into his fourth scotch of the midafternoon—wasn't in the mood to dance.

"There are a lot of cabs," he said brusquely, after Grant

asked some pointless questions about garages and lost-and-founds and the like. "How's about you tell me what you're looking for, and I'll tell you what I know. And then I'll tell you how much it will cost for me to tell you what I know."

Grant knew Farraday, but not well enough to spill his guts. He tried to figure out if he had a choice.

"Someone came to me 'cause they lost a videotape in a cab," he finally said.

"So they pay a few bucks to replace it. You get that advice for free."

"Uh . . . this tape can't be replaced. It's, uh, from a wedding."

Farraday snorted bitterly. "Better off that the tape is lost. Fuckin' weddings should be illegal."

Grant had not known the former cabbie's marital status, but it was now easy enough to figure out. He steered away from that and said, "Okay, Farraday, truth is . . . it's a sex tape."

"Some guy getting it on with his lady?"

"Sorta."

"Tell him to rent some porn. And again, Lambert, that advice is on the house."

Grant sighed. This guy wasn't going to give him what he wanted without a lot more detail.

"Okay, Farraday, I'm shooting straight with you. I need to get the tape back, because . . . because I need it for a blackmail scam."

That got Farraday's attention. He even gently set his tumbler of scotch down. "Who?"

"I can't tell you."

"I need to know so I can set the price. Like, say, if you're blackmailing some nobody, my cut wouldn't be so big. But if you're blackmailing Trump . . ."

"It's not Trump."

"I wasn't saying you were. I was just saying *if* you were, my finder's fee would be higher. Understand?"

"I think so," said Grant. "You get more if we're black-mailing a big shot, and less if it's the assistant manager at Payless Shoes."

"Exactly."

Grant thought for a moment, and then said, "It's the assistant manager at Payless Shoes."

"Don't insult me, Lambert."

"It's—" Grant stopped himself. Word on the street was that Paul Farraday was loyal and trustworthy, and pretty damn brilliant when he put the bottle down. He also knew his way through the taxi system better than probably anyone else, including the Taxi and Limousine Commission. In their line of work, he was what people called "solid," which was just about the highest compliment one crook could pay another.

But . . . if he told him who was on the tape, one more person would be in on the scheme. And every person—he had pretty much decided that he had to include Jamie Brock, even though he didn't like him—diluted the pot of money and increased the chance of something going wrong. Someone could bungle . . . someone could talk . . . someone could, well, get drunk, at which point all bets were off.

Then again, no tape meant no blackmail scheme at all. Which is why Grant took a leap of faith with Paul Farraday and finally made up his mind.

"It's Romeo Romero."

There was a pause, followed by: "Who?"

"Romeo Romero? The actor?" No reaction. "The famous gay movie star?"

Farraday exhaled roughly. "You telling me you want me to ask around to find a gay sex tape? I ain't into that stuff, Lambert." He leaned into the phone, as if keeping an already private conversation even more private. "Listen, I am A-OK with you and Chase, and you know that. You guys do whatever makes you happy. But *I* can't be asking around for a gay sex tape . . . going to my buddies in the driving business and asking, 'You find a tape of two guys doing it?' Nope, sorry, but that ain't gonna happen."

Grant jumped in, knowing from the slight slur in his voice that the alcohol-fueled Farraday could very well go on in this vein for an hour if he wasn't stopped quickly.

"No, no, no!" he shouted, until he was sure the other man had stopped. "It's not like that. This is a sex tape, yeah, but it's him and a *woman*!"

This pause lasted a long time. Grant was starting to wonder if the connection had been broken when Farraday finally said, "A gay guy and . . . a *girl*? That doesn't sound right."

"It isn't. Which is why . . ."

"The blackmail."

"The blackmail," Grant confirmed.

Farraday picked up his tumbler, jiggled it until the ice swirled, and said, "This sounds like a five-thousand-dollar job."

Chapter Seven

Will Whitcomb, fresh off his weekend-long self-instructed 101-level course on Romeo Romero, courtesy of the Columbus Branch of the New York Public Library on Tenth Avenue, now definitely knew he had something in the videotape that had literally fallen into his lap five nights earlier. Something big.

He just didn't know what to do with it.

The way he saw it, there were two options. Option one was to sell it back to the actor. That was the best option . . . the cleanest. But how did a regular guy like Will Whitcomb even approach someone famous like Romeo Romero? Sure, the guy was no president of the United States, but he was bound to have people around specifically to keep other people—people like Will—away. Also, even if he *could* approach him, how was he going to find him? A couple of the magazines mentioned an apartment in Manhattan and an estate in the Hamptons, but the islands in question—Manhattan and Long—were big and full of people. It wasn't going to be easy.

Option two was to sell it to a third party . . . meaning, a gossip column. Pocket his finder's fee and let the professionals work out the logistics of either getting it back to Romero or—more likely, he thought—printing the story and humiliating him. The scandalmongers dealt with celebrities all the time, and they'd not only know how and where to find him, they'd probably have his private telephone number.

Which opened up yet another problem, quite similar to the first: how was a regular guy like Will Whitcomb supposed to get the ear of a gossip columnist? It was probably easier than getting the ear of a famous actor, but it still wouldn't be easy. It wasn't as if he could pick up the phone and get, say, Liz Smith on the line . . . and even if he could, she'd never believe him about the tape. Not until she'd seen it with her own eyes.

He knew he was a small-timer, and had never really had a problem with living a modest life based on the pettiest of petty theft and minor grifting. But now he had to step up and play in the big leagues, and the thought of it made his head swim. He had his golden ticket, but no idea what to do with it.

Or, for that matter, how much it was even worth. A thousand dollars? *Ten* thousand dollars? More? He decided he'd ask high, when he finally figured out whom to ask and how to ask them, and figure the rest out as the negotiations unfolded.

But how to find that middleman?

He sat in his apartment in a threadbare chair—the one in front of the TV—and tried to think things through. As he thought, he kept a wary eye on the tape cartridge, afraid it would somehow make a break for it. Not that a tape could walk away, but . . . well, wouldn't that be something if it did. As mysteriously as it had come to him, it would be gone.

Which is the thought that made him realize he was thinking too much. Thinking wasn't his strong suit. He knew it was time for action.

Grabbing the first newspaper he found strewn on his floor, of which there were several dating back over the past month, he opened the *New York Eye* to its gossip page. The column was called "Between the Streets"—reverentially self-acronymed to BtS—and the byline said the editor's name was Ian Hadley.

He flipped to the front of the paper, where *The Eye*'s phone numbers were listed, found the BtS number, and dialed.

"Mr. Ian Hadley, please," he said, when the phone was answered on something like the twenty-seventh ring. He was asked, so he replied, "My name's Whitcomb. Will Whitcomb. I have come into, uh, possession of something that I think Mr. Hadley will be interested in. A piece of, uh . . . uh . . . gossip, I guess." He was instructed to hold, and so he did.

And he held.

And he held.

And five minutes later the person was back on the line asking who he was again, then who he was representing, to which Whitcomb said, "Myself."

And he held.

And he held.

And finally the person at BtS took his number, thanked him for calling, and assured him that Mr. Hadley would call back, as soon as his schedule allowed.

Okay, Whitcomb thought, *I knew that wasn't going to be easy. But at least I left a message. When Hadley calls back, it will make this all worthwhile.*

And he waited.

And he waited . . .

Four hours later, his phone still silent, he called the "Between the Streets" line again. This time, the phone was answered on the fifteenth ring—he was making progress—but got no closer to Ian Hadley. He left another message and, feeling time slipping past, decided that it couldn't hurt to throw the fishing line back into the pond and see if he could get another bite.

He didn't, although he left messages for "Page Six" at the *Post,* the gossip columns at the *Daily News,* and even—because he was running out of options, and also because an issue was mixed in with the newspapers on the floor—the weekly supermarket tabloid *The Peeper*.

That was Monday.

It was Tuesday afternoon, and only after a battery of follow-up calls and a sleep-deprived night, before a woman at *The Peeper* finally returned Will Whitcomb's call. He had no way of knowing she was an intern, forced to return the call because no one else on staff would do it and they were getting sick of taking his messages, but at that point he might not have cared.

"So can you tell me the nature of your call, Mr. Whitcomb?"

"I have something," he said nervously, again eyeing the tape cartridge, which still hadn't walked away. "I have a videotape I think *The Peeper* would be interested in."

"Mmmkay," she said. "Does this involve a celebrity?"

"Yeah. Romeo Romero."

She put her hand to the mouthpiece, but he could still hear her when she asked some colleagues, "You know a guy named Romeo Romero?"

"Is that him on the phone?" asked one colleague.

"No, it's some guy named Whitcomb."

A second colleague said, "Old gay actor. Does a lot of those boring period pieces. Why? What's the caller have?"

"A videotape."

"Video?" It was the first colleague again. "Who uses video anymore?"

"Ask him what's on it," instructed Colleague Number Two.

She took her hand away. "And what is on this tape, Mr. Whitcomb?"

"Mr. Romero *in flangran . . . in flagrrrr . . .* uh, having sex."

"Ew," said the other three voices, and Whitcomb knew

they could hear him through the receiver. Or maybe he was on speakerphone.

"Grosser than the time that guy sent us pictures from Kitty Randolph's OB/GYN's office," said Colleague Number Two.

"Definitely," agreed Number One.

"Excuse me," snapped Whitcomb. "I can hear you, you know."

"Take him off speaker," whispered Number Two, and suddenly it was just him and the intern again.

"So," Whitcomb continued, "is *The Peeper* interested in making a deal with me?"

"Uh . . ." The woman was obviously confused. "Maybe?"

"This will be big. This will be a huge scandal! And the tape can be yours for"—he squeezed his eyes shut and hoped he was guessing on a number they could start working with—"twenty-five thousand dollars."

This time the intern didn't need assistance from her colleagues.

"Twenty-five thousand dollars? What, is he fucking a *goat*? While George Clooney holds it down?"

Self-destructively, and with very brief and misguided pride, Will Whitcomb slammed the phone down hard in its cradle. *Laugh at me, will you! Fine! Then you can't have the . . .*

He realized he had made a very bad mistake. One of them had actually called back, and he had hung up. Just because they laughed at his $25,000 asking price.

It was *negotiable*! He was a reasonable man! All they had to do was make a counteroffer. Twenty-five was too high? Fine, how about ten?

Five?

Something?

And more to the point: what the hell was he going to do with the videotape if he couldn't sell it? There were only going to be so many times he'd be able to watch Romeo

Romero and that girl in the hot tub. It wasn't exactly *Citizen Kane*. The only way it meant anything to him was if he could sell it.

He waited a half hour, hoping *The Peeper* would call back. When they didn't, he called them.

They wouldn't take his call. But in the background, he thought he heard laughter, and he was sure it was at the expense of both him and Romeo Romero.

Or maybe just at him.

Four days after Grant had handed him the assignment, Paul Farraday mixed himself a scotch and water and picked up the phone. He thought a stiff drink might help him break the news. The fact that it was 9:00 on Wednesday morning was of no great concern to him.

"Yeah," said Grant, on his end of the line in Jackson Heights.

"Bad news, Lambert. Your tape is gone."

Grant's expression, already dour that morning, and more so when he had to answer the ringing telephone, sagged a bit more. "Shit. You're sure?"

"Surer than sure. I managed to narrow it down to fifty-three cabs, and it wasn't in any of them. Searched 'em personally, too. Not in lost and found, either. I figure that whichever cab it was, another fare picked it up. People do that all the time, you know. Find a camera or a book or keys or something in the back of a cab, and keep it for themselves instead of turning it in."

"Bastards," said Grant, remembering that he found his very nice digital camera in the backseat of a cab he hailed in Midtown, but kept it because obviously only a rich thieving asshole would have a digital camera. "How can you be sure about the fifty-three cabs?"

"You know the new global positioning units? The ones all the drivers are griping about? Well, my buddy at the TLC got me the data for the cabs in the area give or take five minutes when your friend got dropped off at Ninetieth and Lex. Now, if your friend ain't remembering right, that's *his* fault."

"Fifty-three cabs around one intersection in a ten-minute span," said Grant, shaking his head.

"Must have been a slow night. Anyway, I even talked to a few drivers about any memorable customers. One asshole skipped out on the fare in Hell's Kitchen, but otherwise it was a quiet night."

"So what you're saying . . ."

"I'm saying that your tape is gone. And there is no way we're gonna find it. Not in a cab, at least. Especially now that an entire week's gone by since your friend lost it."

Grant let out a heavy sigh. This wasn't the most devastating news he had ever heard—it wasn't as if he had already spent the money—but it was still disappointing. "Okay, Farraday. Well . . . thanks. Guess I'll talk to you soon."

Was Grant Lambert hanging up the phone? Farraday thought not.

"Whoa. Wait a second."

"Yeah, what?"

"What are we going to do about my finder's fee?"

Oh, shit. Back in Jackson Heights, Grant rubbed his eyes, then let one hand drop to massage his aching lower back. This was going to be unpleasant. "No find, no fee. Isn't that how it works?"

"True," said Farraday. "I did not earn the five Gs we negotiated for. But I put in my time, and I did my job." He glanced at a bare shelf in the liquor cabinet. The one above the full shelf, which wouldn't last long. "And I'm running low on booze. So I think something is in order."

"What would make you happy?"

"Five Gs." When there was no response, Farraday laughed and said, "Just screwing with you. How about one."

"Hundred?" Grant hoped.

"Thousand."

"Uh . . ." Grant knew he didn't have that kind of money around. He also knew that if he didn't pay Paul Farraday—who *did* do his part of the job, after all—his reputation would suffer greatly in the small world they shared, where idle gossip was discouraged unless it told you who you could trust and who you couldn't trust and would therefore have to treat like a leper.

Grant didn't want to be the leper. It would be bad for business.

"Can you give me a few days?"

Paul looked at the liquor cabinet, which dictated his financial needs.

"Late tomorrow afternoon."

Grant agreed. Then he hung up the phone and let loose a string of expletives. For the next half hour.

Chapter Eight

Growing up, in an entire other lifetime, Ian Hadley had been groomed for success. Probably a financial career; perhaps eventually a seat in Parliament. Certainly riches and fame. He would dine with the queen ... maybe marry into royalty ... but no matter what, he would be an accomplished gentleman, carrying on the long family line of accomplished Hadley gentlemen.

Pretty much none of that happened.

Instead, he had become—in the words of his disapproving mother, most of his family, and a good share of the rest of the literate world—a scum-sucking, scandal-mongering yellow journalist.

One day after graduating from college he signed on with Sir Mortimer Morris, the king of London tabloid journalism, and never looked back. Coke-snorting princes, three-headed calves, spurned mistresses (and masters) of MPs, mass murderers, possible alien abductions, dramatic tragedies, illegitimate children of celebs, disapproving parents of celebs, angry exes of celebs—these were what became of Ian Hadley's promise. All the gentlemanly grooming had been for naught.

And he loved every minute of it.

An apt pupil, and even more apt sycophant, Hadley quickly rose through the ranks of Sir Mortimer's premier tabloid, *The London Air*. By the time he was twenty-seven, his name appeared on the masthead as the senior editor of *The Air*'s lively and widely read gossip column, "Air Pockets." And all the time he rose through the ranks, he followed Sir Mortimer's advice and partied harder than any celebrity the paper covered, because—in the publisher's words—"It's no fun if you're just sitting there in the newsroom reading about it, is it, mate?"

In the next few years, it was widely assumed by everyone who watched London's media, there would be an imminent promotion to managing editor of the entire newspaper. Ian Hadley was a young man who saw no limits to his future.

Until, on the day after his thirtieth birthday, Sir Mortimer called him into his office to discuss that future, and Hadley—for the first time in his otherwise charmed career—was concerned that he was about to be fired. The previous night's antics with George Michael and Fergie had no doubt already gotten back to the offices of *The Air*. How could they not? They *did* have a rather large audience.

But he need not have worried, even though his sinus cavity was so caked with cocaine that it numbed his entire head.

"I'm sending you to America, mate," said Sir Mortimer, his cheeks pink with either glee or drink or both. "You're going to lead us as we reclaim the colonies." No one used the word "colonies" anymore when referring to the U.S., but Sir Mortimer knew that Hadley's American maternal grandmother was a sore spot, so he needled him with it whenever he could. "Reclaim the queen's land from the rebels, right?"

"Uh . . . right?"

Sir Mortimer—not always the most perceptive man—sensed his obvious discomfort. "I've bought a paper in New York. *The Eye*. Heard of it?"

Hadley had actually stopped listening at "New York." So, no, he hadn't. He was being sent to New York? He wasn't sure how he felt about this news.

"You'll be editor of a new column I'm planning: 'Between the Streets.' "

Wait . . . he heard that. A *column*? He would be leaving London to edit another *column*? When he was in line to run *The Air*? He was trying to figure out if he was too hungover to spin on his heels and storm out when Sir Mortimer added:

"You don't realize what an opportunity I'm giving you, lad. The premier gossip column in the U.S . . . . or at least, it will be, when we get done with it. Celebrities will be eating out of your hand. You will be *of* them, but better. Do you understand?"

Hadley thought that, just maybe, he did.

"Best part is," said Sir Mortimer, laughing so hard they were both afraid he'd choke, "best part is our accents. With our accents, Americans think we can do no wrong . . . although they're also partial to the French and Italian accents, so you can see how low their standards are when it comes to discerning sophistication and class."

"Yes," said Hadley. "But still, there's the matter of the position. I assumed I was in line to become managing editor of *The Air*." Sir Mortimer nodded. "Well, to go from that to editor of a gossip column seems like, well, like a demotion."

"Rubbish. Let's face it, Ian, *The Air* is a joke. A bloody joke. I own it and you edit it, and we both know that for a fact. But this paper in New York City, *The Eye*, that's a different story. The president of the United States gets most of his news from *The Eye*! This is a big deal."

He was warming to the idea in concept, but had to ask: "My salary?"

"You'll do well. Very well, indeed." The older man looked at the younger, and put one hand on his cheek, the proud parent making a physical connection with his accomplished child. "A fifty-four percent increase, as a matter of fact, which is not a bad bump up."

Hadley seemed more responsive, but still conflicted, so Sir Mortimer continued to sell him on the concept. "This isn't a demotion, Ian. You are the only one I can trust to make this work. The *New York Post* pretty much rides on 'Page Six.' If you can take what is now a modest gossip page in *The Eye* and beat them at their own game, we will win the circulation wars." He winked. Unnecessarily. "Circulation means ad revenue. Ad revenue means staff salaries."

Which is why Sir Mortimer shouldn't have bothered to wink. After the initial shock—and the fear of being de-moted—Ian Hadley had worked out everything in his head. If he didn't screw this up, he was going to be richer and more powerful than he could ever hope to be as a mere managing editor of a major daily newspaper in London.

He was going to be a gossip kingpin. In New York City.

Cool.

"So," said Sir Mortimer, settling into his chair, "tell me about your night with George and the Duchess. And you might want to wipe under your nose . . ."

Twelve years later . . . not so cool.

Yes, Ian Hadley was rich. Yes, Ian Hadley was powerful. Yes, Ian Hadley was covered by the media almost as often as the celebrities his gossip column followed, although without quite the sarcastic, cynical edge.

But he was bored.

He knew the rest of the world—perhaps excluding his peers at the *News* and the *Post*—would be serenading him with the world's smallest violin, but he was bloody sick of the inunda-tion. Every day it was "Jennifer did not do that" and "Jennifer did do this" and "Jennifer is happy for Brad and Angie." It was "just saw Mary-Kate here" and "just saw Ashley there" and "Mary-Kate and Ashley are happy for Brad and Angie."

It was pimp my movie, pimp my art show. Pimp my gym,

my opening, my event. Or, "I'm seventy-two and coming out
of the closet and I'm writing a book about it!"

Snore.

Americans, he now believed, were crasser, if possible, than
the Londoners he had left behind. Too bad Sir Mortimer was
now doing hard time for—as the Americans and, to his great
regret, "Between the Streets" called it—stock manipulation.
Now he was never going back.

And it had nothing to do with that night with George
Michael and Fergie. Mostly. Although that *was* a memorable
night . . .

The offices of "Between the Streets" were housed on the
fifteenth floor of the Global Pan-Atlantic Mercantile West
Building, a glass tower rising high above the Avenue of the
Americas at West Fifty-fifth Street. *The Eye* rented floors ten
through sixteen of the forty-seven-story tower, meaning that
only the newspaper's top executives sat at a higher perch
than Ian Hadley and his crew. Which was just the way he
liked it.

For all the openness conveyed by the façade—floor-to-ceil-
ing windows, seemingly unbroken by actual steel or concrete—the interior of the building was considerably less
grand. The window glaze managed to keep most natural sunlight out of the building, and over the years more and more
HVAC equipment had been hidden by building management
above drop ceilings, until what looked like fourteen-foot ceilings from the outside were, in fact, generally about eight-feet
high.

And that was just what the owners had done to make the
building depressing. The owners of *The Eye* had made their
own alterations to the work space, ensuring that the news-
rooms—even in a prestigious address with an impressive
façade like the Global Pan-Atlantic Mercantile West Building—would look like every stereotypical overcrowded news-

room in the world. Even in Ian Hadley's realm on the fifteenth floor.

Many of the interior walls had long ago been demolished and replaced with padded five-foot-tall dividers, the better to reconfigure the workspace—then reconfigure it again on a whim—whenever someone in management had the inclination to actually change something, which admittedly was not often. The lack of personal space, of course, also had a secondary purpose: without privacy—no walls, no doors—the employees of *The Eye* would work while they were at work. There would be no computer solitaire or chatty calls to their boyfriends or staring into space and dreaming of a life that didn't include *The Eye*. Not on the company's dime, at least.

Because of his position—first as Sir Mortimer Morris's golden boy, and then as New York City's most feared gossipmonger—Ian Hadley was one of the few people to have a private office. It faced northwest across Fifty-fifth Street, offering him no sunshine at all; not even the light that occasionally broke through the window glaze for those fortunate enough to face east or south. But he didn't mind. His office was his own private domain, and over the years he had transformed it into a reflection of his personality.

The office jutted out into the newsroom, with open windows facing his underlings on two sides. While Hadley didn't really mind the fishbowl effect, he also valued his occasional privacy, as any man would who had to occasionally deal with celebrities in unpleasant situations. He had largely solved the problem by installing blinds on the internal windows; with the simple toggle of a switch he could raise or lower them without ever leaving the comfort of the leather chair behind his desk.

As for the rest of the office, it was remarkable what a man could do to transform his workspace with little more than flourishes of taste and money. Out went the industrial office furniture provided by *The Eye*; in came an imposing mahogany desk with matching bookshelves, and a few leather chairs to make the room cozy. Out went the battered file cabinets; in came a much more civilized credenza, along with a few other tasteful pieces to fill the office. The industrial carpet was pulled out and a parquet floor went in, along with area rugs to dull the noise.

In a short amount of time, his very plain office had become almost as cozy as his den at home. He even had an aquarium installed and stocked with colorful fish, the types of which he never bothered to learn because they were usually eaten by other fish before he could grow attached. Which he thought was appropriate, given their very temporary residence in the offices of "Between the Streets."

In recent years, Ian Hadley had even gotten high-tech. Now, in addition to the blinds on the window opposite his desk, he had a screen installed. A toggle from a second switch would lower it, which was helpful whenever he had to show an incriminating video to someone—or the someone's lawyer—who didn't believe he really had the goods on them. And hidden in the bookcase behind him was an array of electronic equipment—audio recorders, a VCR, a DVD player—all tied into his computer, which was angled to afford him the utmost privacy. An important consideration, he knew, given his predilection for viewing adult materials on his monitor during the slower moments of the workday.

There are worse ways to spend forty hours a week, he often thought, as he looked out through the fishbowl windows at dozens of "Between the Streets" staffers, plodding away in their workspaces surrounded by five-foot dividers with only an occasional *Dilbert* cartoon tacked to a wall to proclaim their individuality. Not that management ever let the *Dilbert* cartoons stay up for more than a few hours. They were too subversive to the corporate structure.

But the material comforts, of course, were not easing his

boredom. Yes, he was the undisputed Gossip King of New York City, but even *he* could feel as if work was nothing but a rut.

Which is why, when he walked into his office that Wednesday morning, impeccably dressed as always, he told his assistant, "I want to do something new."

She chomped on her gum for a second. "Well, I just read something about the Olsen twins . . ."

"You seem tense," said his second-in-command, J. P. Hunt, seconds after the young woman left in tears, which young women often did when Hadley fired them.

J. P., Ian knew, was inapt, without being inept. He didn't really belong on the gossip beat, but, as a former cop, he knew where a lot of bodies were buried. And he also knew a lot of private bodyguards and security, from his days "on the job." Writer material? No, not at all; at best he could forward an e-mail every now and then. But J. P. contributed in his own special way.

"We need to do something different," Ian said, taking off the jacket of his Brooks Brothers suit and draping it across the back of a chair. "Every day we follow the same rubbish. The same people." He paused for dramatic effect. "The same . . . *publicists.*"

"So what do you think we should do differently?"

"I don't know. Maybe nothing. I'm just bored." He pointed at his fired-as-of-ninety-seconds-ago assistant's desk and said, "Maybe we should just pick a random phone call from, uh . . . what was her name?"

J.P. shrugged. "Melanie? Melissa?"

"Eh, whatever. Maybe we should just grab a message from the pile and see where it takes us. Hopefully in a direction the publicists aren't taking us."

They chose a message slip at random. It was the one from when Will Whitcomb called back the most recent time.

Turned out the eighth time was the charm for Will Whitcomb.

* * *

"So, Mr. . . .Whitcomb, is it?" Hadley asked the odd, disheveled man sitting across from him, all the while regretting his spontaneous return phone call. He wanted to break a boring routine, not indulge a street person. But the man claimed to have something of interest, so the editor decided to see this through.

"Yes, Whitcomb. But you can call me Will."

"Very well, Will. I under—"

"Can I call you Ian?"

Hadley didn't bother to shield his eyes as he rolled them in the direction of the open doorway, where J. P. Hunt stood guard. "If you must, Mr. Whitcomb."

"Will."

Hadley gritted his teeth. "Yes, of course. *Will.* Now, I understand you have an item of interest. You were a bit mysterious on the phone . . ."

"Are you English?"

"Er, ah . . . yes. That was very perceptive, Will. Now, you were a bit mysterious on the phone . . ."

Whitcomb nodded. "I thought it was best that we talk in person."

"And here we are. So, this item. May I see it?"

Whitcomb nodded again, then shook his head.

"Is that a yes or a no, Mr. . . . *Will?*"

"I don't have it with me, Ian."

Hadley gave J. P. another roll of his eyes and confirmed what he had just heard by repeating it. "You don't have it with you." He dropped his eyes, examining a cuticle, and without looking up asked, "Do you have this item at all?"

"It's in safe-keeping." While Hadley closed his eyes, he continued. "I can describe it to you, and then when we agree on a price . . ."

Ian Hadley's eyes popped open. His voice was brusque.

"Mr. . . . *Will*, we are not in the habit of buying gossip at 'Between the Streets.' There's too much of the free stuff out there."

"You'll want this," said Whitcomb.

"I think not." He began to stand, a signal that the unfortunate conversation was over. "J. P., would you be kind enough to escort this gentleman out, please?"

J. P. took two steps forward and Whitcomb—seeing his opportunity vanish again—blurted out, "It's a videotape! With Romeo Romero!"

"How boring," said Hadley, waving him away.

"In a hot tub!"

"Boring."

"With a girl!"

"Bor—" Hadley stopped. Sensing that this Whitcomb fellow was not smart enough to play semantic games, but knowing a book should never be judged by its cover, he asked, "In a hot tub with a girl? Romeo Romero?" Hadley thought about that for a moment. "Were they . . . relaxing?"

"Screwing."

J. P. took another step forward, but this time Hadley raised a hand to stop him. The ex-cop backed up again into the doorway.

Relieved, Whitcomb slumped back down in his chair. He had rescued the opportunity! He was back in charge!

"So," said the editor, "Romeo Romero and a girl had sex in a hot tub, and you have a videotape of it?" Ian Hadley was not often surprised; this was one of those moments. "A recent one, I assume?"

"Yes," said Whitcomb, and hoped that was the truth.

"Hmm." Hadley stared deeply into the man's eyes and said, "You realize that Romero is gay, don't you?"

"Or maybe not so much. At least, that's what the tape tells me."

"You've seen the tape?" Whitcomb nodded. "You're sure?"

He nodded again. "And how did you come into possession of it?"

Whitcomb considered telling him the truth, but decided he had a better chance to maximize his earnings by fudging a bit. Or better yet, through outright, over-the-top lying.

"I'm tied in with some of those people."

Hadley regarded that skeptically. "You're tied in with actors? Or . . . the gays?"

"Not the gays!" said Whitcomb, who thought, *This guy is worse than my mother!*

"Of course not. Then . . . actors. You're tied in with actors." Hadley didn't have to add that he found that extremely implausible; he knew he could convey that with a subtle shift of tone in his crisp British accent.

Unfortunately, Will Whitcomb was not one for subtlety.

"Yeah, actors. Like Romeo Romero and, uh . . . other actors." He winked at Hadley. "In fact, if this works out between us, you might be hearing from me again."

"No doubt," said Hadley, with a sigh. The office was silent for a moment while he collected his thoughts, then: "So . . . please indulge me, Mr. . . . I mean, Will. I'm trying to follow this, but have to admit I'm confused. You are telling me that Romeo Romero is"—he grasped for the words—"a *closeted heterosexual*?"

"Nah. I just told you he likes *women*."

Another sigh. A deeper sigh. A sigh that Hadley meant to say, "This cannot be happening to me."

"Okay, so Romeo Romero likes women. I'm just trying to figure out why he'd *pretend* to be gay. It's usually done the other way around."

Whitcomb chuckled, and Ian Hadley hated him for that. "I dunno. Weird, huh? But I got it on tape."

Before he went any further, Hadley had a question guaranteed to trip up this round, unkempt, sweaty man dirtying up his office. "On the tape, can you see his, uh . . . his *member*?"

"Member of what?"

"His *penis*, you moron." Did that come out of his mouth? Yes, Ian knew; it did.

But Whitcomb was used to abuse and didn't even notice. "Yeah, you can see his dick." Unprompted he added, "Looks like he's got a big one." Remembering his mother's—and Hadley's—insinuations, he added, "Not that I'd really know what's big and what's not, but it *seemed* big."

And that sealed the deal for Ian Hadley. The idiot sitting in front of him was certainly not "tied into actors," and therefore would not know the rumor about Romero's member/penis/dick. Unless, that was, he was *really* in possession of a videotape showing Romeo Romero having sex with a woman in a hot tub, and featuring full frontal nudity.

True, it didn't absolutely mean that (a) there was a tape, or (b) if there was a tape, the hot tub action involved Romero. Maybe he had a well-endowed heterosexual doppelganger, a long-lost twin, or something of that sort. But Ian Hadley was now at least intrigued. Intrigued enough to take this to the next level.

Because why would a straight man pretend to be gay?

In a world racked by hate and discrimination—a world in which "Between the Streets" played its small, salacious part—it just didn't make sense. He could understand the Hollywood stars who hid behind their elegant and expensive beards. He could understand the Broadway actors and singers who avoided the question, then hid behind their less elegant and less expensive beards. And he understood the handful of celebrities who just got over it and lived their lives the way God made them, even though "Between the Streets" usually used the words "swishy" and "fabulous" a bit too often when writing up their usually not-so-scandalous (nor swishy; nor fabulous) items.

But he could not understand this. Not at all.

Which meant that he had to see that tape. And if it really

did involve Romeo Romero, a hot tub, and a woman, he had to have it.

"Mr. Whitcomb—"

"*Will.*"

"No," said Hadley, and he leaned forward, forcing a smile as his elbows came to rest on his desk. "I am in a formal business conversation." He noticed that Whitcomb smiled brightly. Idiot. "And, in business, I address people formally. So Mr. Whitcomb, I am interested in seeing this videotape. When can this be arranged?"

Whitcomb thought about that. But not too much. "I can get to my apartment and back in forty minutes."

"Give yourself an hour."

After Will Whitcomb scurried out of the office, J. P. asked, "Do you want me to get there before he does?"

"No," said Hadley, waving him away and undoing his cufflinks. "Let him do all the work, then we'll see what he's got. It's probably nothing . . . but I suppose it's worth a view." Cufflinks off and sleeves rolled up a bit, he added, "And tell Marilyn to cancel my lunch reservation at Michael's."

"Marilyn?"

"You know. That *girl* out there." He gestured at the empty desk directly outside his office door, and was puzzled for a moment to see it unattended. "Oh, that's right. I fired her, didn't I?"

"Uh . . . yeah."

"Then *you* do it."

After J. P. walked away to cancel lunch at Michael's, Hadley laughed . . . and for the first time in years, it was at his *own* naïveté and eagerness. A *straight* sex tape of Romeo Romero? Absurd. Impossible.

"J. P.?" Just outside the door to his office, at the desk where an assistant would be sitting had he not abruptly fired her, the ex-cop was just picking up the phone. "Don't cancel. Just move me to two-thirty. I have a feeling the viewing of this videotape won't take up too much of my time."

*   *   *

Ian Hadley never made it to Michael's.

An hour later, as promised, an even sweatier and slightly out of breath Will Whitcomb was escorted back into his office. In his hands he clutched a plastic bag from CVS, from which he delivered the tape into Ian Hadley's hands.

The blinds were closed, the door was locked, the screen descended against the wall opposite Hadley's desk, and a VCR on the bookshelf behind it was powered on. J. P. excused himself, and the remaining two mismatched men sat back to watch the videotape.

At first, there was no sound, so Hadley grabbed the remote and cranked it up a few notches. Finally, they heard the sound of water gurgling in a filter.

The tape—painfully grainy and about as close to black and white as color could be—darted about incomprehensibly for a few minutes, capturing only fleeting unblurred images, none of them human. Hadley, remote still in hand, was about to shut it down when the camera finally found the hot tub and steadied.

A young woman sat in it, looking away from the camera. Her large and obviously surgically enhanced breasts—bared, of course—bounced up and down, creating tiny splashes in the round tub of water. Hadley—a heterosexual of the standard definition, not the Will Whitcomb definition—watched in appreciation, more so after finally figuring out that all the jiggling and bouncing (and probably giggling; whoever was taping was standing too far away) was in anticipation of someone *joining* her in the tub.

And then, abruptly, he was there. Standing next to the hot tub, his sixtysomething body in a tiny Speedo inappropriate for a well-built man half his age, was Romeo Romero. Ninety-five percent in the flesh.

The remaining five percent followed, and even through the graininess Ian Hadley could tell that the rumors were true. It was also the final bit of confirmation he needed.

That was, inexplicably, Romeo Romero. *Naked* Romeo Romero. In a hot tub with a jiggling, mammary-enhanced woman.

And this creepy little man sitting across the desk had delivered the goods. Other than he and Will Whitcomb—and whoever had filmed the tryst in the first place—no one else knew about this tape.

As for confirmation, he thought he had enough. He recognized Romero, and the penis certainly met the rumored standards. There wasn't much more he could do to verify its authenticity. Not that he'd mind getting the name of the female hot tub paramour—that bouncing and jiggling and probably giggling had made him a bit stiff—but business was business.

Ian Hadley immediately knew he had to own this tape . . . and why.

When the copulation was over he powered off the VCR, plunging the room into near darkness, then turned on a faux Tiffany desk lamp. It would have been just as easy to turn the fluorescent overhead lights back on, but Hadley knew what he was doing. He was giving the immediate area around his desk lighting that was almost cinematic, making him look more intense and leaving the poor fool on the other side of the desk literally in the dark. He knew this because he employed his lighting strategy fairly often, usually with air-headed young socialites who had come to complain about one item or another and left not only cowed by him, but intimidated into sharing more society dirt with "Between the Streets."

It didn't work so well with the lawyers that celebrities occasionally sicced on him, but . . . whatever. Will Whitcomb was no lawyer.

Hadley cleared his throat. "So, Mr. Whitcomb. This is very interesting."

Whitcomb crumpled a tissue in his hand. All things considered, he thought everything was going well, although in the new lighting, the unsmiling Ian Hadley looked even scarier than he did ordinarily. "I thought you'd like it."

"But I don't think that was Romeo Romero on screen."

Whitcomb had done his research, and he was sure. But the brightly lit face of Ian Hadley, in stark contrast to the black background of the unlit bookshelves behind him, said otherwise. And he would *know*, wouldn't he?

Wouldn't he? Whitcomb felt doubt fall over him in the shadows.

Hadley blew on his nails, as if they had been freshly polished. The polish had actually been applied the day before.

"I know this is against company policy," he said, "but I can offer you two hundred dollars for this tape. Out of my personal funds."

"Two—" Whitcomb didn't have asthma, but he still felt his breath constrict. "That's . . . that's . . ."

"Fair, I think."

"No." Wheeze. "Not fair."

The Brit bore in on him, his intense blue eyes on Whitcomb's watery, washed-out gray. Not that Hadley could actually see the color of his eyes; in the dimness, everything about Will Whitcomb looked gray.

"It's fair, *Mr.* Whitcomb. You have brought me a poorly made videotape starring a man who is *not* Romeo Romero, although I admit he shares a resemblance. It would probably cause a sensation on YouTube. Other than that, I can't see what you'd do with it." He reached inside his suit jacket for his wallet. "But because you look like a man who's down on his luck, I'm willing to help you out."

"How do you"—wheeze—"know it's not him?"

Hadley didn't even bother shaking his head, or rolling his eyes, or anything else he could do to belittle the small-timer. He simply kept staring at him and, in his crispest accent, said, "Because Romeo Romero is a homosexual. A gay man. A poofter. Whatever you want to call it, that's what he is. Ergo, this videotape—"

"It's him!"

"It's *not* him." Hadley inflected an edge into his voice that—combined with the lighting—showed him at his most intimidating. Whitcomb actually recoiled, and Hadley took a tiny bit of pity as the poor guy he was blatantly ripping off slid back in his chair. "So . . . two hundred dollars?"

Hadley might have been willing to go to three, maybe four, but the poor guy abruptly got an attitude.

"*The Peeper* offered me twenty-five thousand dollars."

And Ian Hadley thought, *What? This sniveling imbecile is fighting back?* He didn't show it, but it ruffled him. That almost never happened.

Instead, the gossip column editor reached behind him and pushed a button, discharging a tape from the VCR. He stood and walked around the desk until he towered over the stout, sweating man, then handed the tape to Whitcomb with his left hand while, with his right, he took Whitcomb's clammy hand and shook.

"In that case, Mr. Whitcomb, I wish you good luck with *The Peeper.*"

All color drained from Will Whitcomb's face. He had fucked up the deal once again. "But . . . but . . ." was all he could get out when he finally remembered to speak. But by then it was too late.

Hadley turned on the fluorescent lights, opened the office door, and said to his number two man, "J. P., please escort Mr. Whitcomb out."

Seven minutes later, J. P. was back, lapel ripped, saying, "He didn't want to go."

"They never do. Make sure when you get your jacket sewn up to charge it to BtS."

J. P. smiled. "Yes, boss." His smile faded. "So the tape was a fake?"

Hadley shrugged. "Why not?"

Chapter Nine

Most of the day and a half he had promised Paul Farraday had passed, and Grant was getting nervous. The guy wanted a thousand dollars, and probably deserved it, because it wasn't *his* fault that Jamie's tape had vanished. But in the bank, Grant and Chase—well, technically just Chase, since Grant didn't believe in banks, because he knew people who robbed them—had maybe a grand total of forty. Dollars, not thousands of.

So Grant needed to make some cash quickly. But although desperate times called for desperate measures, he was nervous about even *thinking* of doing what he was about to do.

He was *thinking* he was about to rob a bank.

And though he had been committed to a life of crime for many years, this was one crime he had never committed. He didn't like the odds.

Sure, every dime he lifted would be covered by insurance, and that made it all right, in theory. But in reality, banks had armed guards, and cameras, and little old ladies waiting in line who could have a heart attack or stroke when some middle-aged guy pulled a gun and yelled, "Freeze! This is a hold-up!"

Or worse, the little old lady could cold-cock him, which would result not only in imprisonment, but eternal humiliation.

Willie Sutton once famously *didn't* say—but thanks to history, got credit for it anyway—that he robbed banks because that's where the money was. Grant Lambert knew the money was there, but would rather find it somewhere else.

But there was nowhere else. Charlie Chops didn't need a car. Groc-O-Rama didn't need another theft if it was going to stay in Elmhurst. And while preying on the Internet predators would continue to pay off in the long run, it wouldn't be paying off before Farraday came to collect his grand.

And even Grant had to agree that Farraday probably deserved his money. Especially if Grant wanted to hold his head up and get a fair deal the next time he had a Lexus to deliver to Chops. Hell, the next time he had to do *anything* that skirted the legal system, which—to Grant—was pretty much everything.

It was all so depressing. Like some damn "crime doesn't pay" government public service announcement, although he was pretty sure if the government ever made a "crime doesn't pay" PSA, they'd manage to screw it up and triple the crime rate.

He wondered if he could find a way to make money off a campaign like that. Damn "honor among thieves"; it was putting him in a very bad position right now. It never occurred to him that he didn't understand the expression.

He stood at East Fifty-second Street and Third Avenue in Manhattan, which gave him easy access to the major bank branches anchoring three of the four corners, making it a pretty typical Manhattan intersection except there was no Starbucks. He told himself his delay in deciding which branch to rob was procrastination, but deep down he knew it was because he was hoping he wouldn't have to do it.

Unfortunately, the lottery scratch-cards had not been in his favor an hour earlier.

Finally, he picked a bank and walked in, flipping up his collar to partially block the cameras. Grant had a ski mask in his pocket, but even *he* knew that would be far too obvious, so he was just going to duck down behind his collar and . . .

"Good afternoon, sir! Welcome to M-M-M!" said a perky girl in a business suit and, strangely, pigtails, when he walked through the door.

He had to ask: "M-M-M?"

"Milwaukee-Massachusetts Mutual! Your three-M bank for three-M care!"

"Three-M care?"

She beamed. "Money, mortgages, and *more!*"

" 'More'? Couldn't think of a third M, huh?"

She stood there, confused, and Grant suddenly wondered why he wasn't a communist. Well . . . robbing the Three-Ms would be a good place to start. He was about to draw his fake gun when his cell phone twittered.

Perky Miss Pigtails said, "You're ringing."

He scowled. This was another reason he hated the telephone; it never rang at convenient times. Someone was always trying to reach you when you were in the shower, or having dinner, or about to rob a bank.

"Sir?" she asked, when he took a bit too long trying to decide if he should answer it or not.

On the fourth ring he finally pulled the phone from his pocket and looked at the Caller ID. It was Chase. He was going to ignore it again when he saw that Perky Miss Pigtails had lost her smile, which wasn't a positive development, so he decided to answer.

He waved one "just a second" finger at the woman, clicked open the phone, and said, "Yeah."

"Whatcha doing?"

He let his grip on the fake gun loose. "Just, uh . . . hanging out." Perky Miss Pigtails gave him a strange look, so he added, "At a bank." And added further, sotto voce, "With some people I don't know, and who don't know me . . ."

Chase knew instinctively where he was going with this. "You're not going to rob—"

"No!"

With that yell, Perky Miss Pigtails walked away. And even though he needed a quick grand, the way that she walked directly toward the uniformed security guard he hadn't noticed before—being a novice to the bank robbery line of work—made Grant think it might be a good idea to walk a few blocks away and scout out another three-banks-on-one-corner intersection. He clutched the phone to his ear and faked a quiet but animated conversation to cover what he hoped looked like a distracted exit from the Three-M bank.

Once outside, still on his cell, connection still open, Grant asked, "So why did you call me?"

"I just heard from Jamie."

"Jamie? Jamie . . . ?" Oh. "Jamie *Brock*?"

"Yeah. Three calls in two minutes. A new record. Anyway, there's this Web site that's uploaded a teaser and—"

"What do you mean?"

"A teaser!" Chase fought for the words. "A . . . a . . . a sort of preview of upcoming news items. Except at this site, news equals gossip."

"And this affects me *how*?"

"To quote—well, *paraphrase*—the Web site: 'Which gay blade isn't too gay to romance a buxom female beauty in his Hamptons hot tub? Pick up *The Eye* next week and read 'Between the Streets' to learn more about the shocking, *naked* truth!'" And even though Chase was paraphrasing, he emphasized the "naked," because that's the way he had heard it when the Groc-O-Rama produce department supervisor had read it to him, ostensibly while on her break.

Grant was silent for a moment, then said, "So someone got their hands on our tape."

"*The Eye*. The friggin' *New York Eye*. Now we're never gonna get it."

"Well," said Grant, "the good news is that we know who's got it. And we know it isn't lost." He stopped and began scoping out the banks on a new corner.

"For all the good that does. If *The Eye* has the tape, how are we going to get our hands on it?"

"You let me worry about that."

Grant broke off the connection, took another look around, and abruptly decided that bank robbery was something he really didn't want to get involved with. He had to save his energy for something infinitely riskier and less likely: getting the tape out of the hands of the *New York Eye*.

But first, there was something important that needed his immediate attention. Frowning because he would have to use the phone for the second time in minutes, he punched out a number.

"Hello."

"Farraday? Grant Lambert here."

"Hey, Lambert." Not surprisingly, Farraday's voice was slightly slurred. "Got good news for me?"

"Better than good, I think. But I'm going to need a little bit more time."

Back at his basement apartment in East Williamsburg, Brooklyn—not the fashionable hipster section of East Williamsburg; the part that remained gritty and ungentrified—Farraday stole a glance at the quickly diminishing row of liquor bottles. A little bit more time didn't sound good to him.

"We had a deal, Lambert."

"And I'm gonna make good on it," Grant said, walking away from the intersection, where a blocked box was resulting in all kinds of blaring car horns. "But I think I found the tape, so we're gonna get back on track."

Farraday thought about that. True, those scotch bottles weren't going to fill themselves, but maybe he could find a silver lining.

"I'll wait," he finally said. "For a few more days, at least. But it's gonna cost you."

Grant sighed. "How much?"

"The original five thousand."

"*Five*—! But we agreed on a grand."

"And I'll still take a grand. If you can get it to me by the end of the day. If you can't, well . . . It's back up to the original five. Hey, I don't abet crimes as a hobby, you know. I have to pay rent, too."

Grant's frown deepened, and he wondered how much was required of him to keep his good name in the criminal economy. Paul Farraday had him in a bind, that was for sure.

"All right," he finally spat out, unhappily. "Five thousand."

"In that case," said Paul Farraday, allowing himself a smile, "I wish you Godspeed on your mission, Lambert."

Out on Long Island, at his Water Mill estate, Romeo Romero took a break from drafting his dream cast for the spy/cabbie/CIA adventure he could not stop thinking about to take a call. It was his agent, *finally* returning his call! He could afford her his time. In fact, he couldn't wait to tell her how they were going to reinvent his career, and not a moment too soon.

"Darling," he said, purring in a vaguely Italian accent that had notably faded over his years as an American, but which he could still lay on thick for roles, or for added charm. "I am in the midst of a project that you will die for. Think of this: Romeo Romero and Jamie Foxx starring in . . ." He realized that she was talking, not listening, so decided to give her the floor. "What's that?"

He listened to her talk for a minute and a half, then hung up the phone with the briefest of assurances that there was nothing to worry about. Hands free again, he went upstairs to his office, powered up the computer, and clicked over to the *New York Eye*'s Web site.

And there it was, just as she had told him: "Between the

Streets" was hinting that an unnamed "gay blade" wasn't really very gay.

He thought immediately to that recent Saturday night, with the luscious Scandinavian beauty whose name he could not quite remember anymore. That had been indiscreet, and he chided himself. Even though there had been no witnesses, *and* the girl was leaving for Europe the following day, *and* she spoke maybe three words of English, *and* she had no idea who he was, it had been very indiscreet.

But could she really have turned him in to "Between the Streets"? That seemed unlikely. She was the guest of his closest friend, the director Sven Nordstrom, who also happened to be one of the few people who knew of Romeo Romero's little secret. It was preposterous to think that the two of them—or even just the girl—had turned on him. Preposterous.

Which meant that *The Eye* had nabbed some other gay blade with a hot tub.

Good, he thought. *I hope it's McKellan. Bastard.*

Ian Hadley clicked on the BtS webpage to make sure the teaser had been uploaded; then, satisfied, he clicked back to the column he had been editing. He stared at the screen for a few minutes but couldn't concentrate. His thoughts were on the videotape.

Those thoughts made him smile.

Will Whitcomb no longer had the tape. The videotape that he now held was worthless, a blank cartridge handed to the squat, sweaty man while the Romeo Romero sex tape still sat secure in the VCR. Hadley had gambled that the small-timer wouldn't notice a difference and he was correct.

But no matter what the BtS Web site claimed, he had no intention of running the story in *The Eye*. That was Hadley's ruse, a shot fired across Romeo Romero's bow.

A way to draw his attention.

There was no value to Hadley in having the hot tub session made public, whether through the newspaper or by uploading it to the Internet, where it could theoretically be viewed and downloaded as often as the Paris Hilton sex tape. Theoretically, that was, because he seriously doubted there were significant numbers of people interested in seeing a naked senior citizen have carnal knowledge with a silicone-laden bimbo.

No, the tape's value was in its extremely limited distribution.

Oh, he'd *threaten* to run a story and put the tape on the Internet, of course. That was his leverage. But he couldn't imagine actually doing it.

And speaking of those threats, it was now time to place a call to actor and gay icon Romeo Romero.

"Monica!" he called out, then remembered he had fired her.

Ian Hadley was pissed. He hated placing his own calls. He was going to have to hire someone new, and soon.

He dialed the phone and listened to it ring on the other end, briefly disappointed when his call went to voice mail. Still, he pressed on.

"Romeo, this is Ian Hadley of 'Between the Streets.' Please return my call at your earliest opportunity. We have something rather important to discuss . . ."

Chapter Ten

With every passing day, Grant Lambert was learning to appreciate the modern age a little bit more. Sure, a lot of bad things came with it: you could no longer casually walk into an office building and blend in with the cleaning staff; and the increasing frequency of those GPS units meant stolen cars had to be gotten rid of immediately, if you really had to grab a late model instead of an older one; and alarms were trickier and more pervasive.

Still, with all those inconveniences, the modern age could be a good thing.

Take the Internet. It was great for scams, and it was also pretty damn good when used to glean detailed information about people. The editor of "Between the Streets," for example. A certain Ian Hadley.

Once they figured out that *The Eye* had the videotape, Grant began making inquiries among his acquaintances. But no one had an in at the paper. Social-climbing Jamie Brock had yet to mount anyone at the tabloid . . . Paul Farraday didn't know any of their drivers . . . No real estate connections through Lisa Cochrane . . . No one had anything positive to contribute. So he decided to go right to the top, reasoning that something like a sex tape featuring gay actor Romeo Romero and a woman could only be in the possession of Hadley, the column's editor.

Him or the lawyers, that was. And he hoped it wasn't the lawyers. Hadley would bc tough enough.

And so he booted up his rickety computer and went to work researching Ian Hadley. Forget about his work, and forget about the society stuff. What Grant wanted the Internet to tell him was where he could find Hadley and what his weaknesses were.

The Internet delivered. It usually did when people got themselves written about on a regular basis.

Finding him would be easy. Every day, without fail, he walked into the *New York Eye* building at West Fifty-fifth Street and Avenue of the Americas—or, as Grant and every other New Yorker called it, Sixth Avenue—at 9:15 AM. You could set your watch by him.

Lunch was more problematic; half the time he was at Michael's, the publishing industry's place to see and be seen by everyone else in the publishing industry. The rest of the time he mixed it up a bit, although lunch seldom involved eating at his desk.

And every evening, between 6:00 PM and 6:30 PM, depending on loose ends that had to be addressed at the office, he held court at a back table at Galan's Irish Pub, just a few doors down from *The Eye*'s building on West Fifty-fifth Street.

It didn't matter what soirées were on his schedule; Galan's was his after-work habit. No, more than a habit; it was an addiction. Weekday nights at Galan's were as much a part of the Ian Hadley persona as the perfect haircut, the perfect tailoring, and the occasional drunk-driving arrest pleaded to a misdemeanor in front of one judge or another who would therefore not see their names attached to anything unsavory in "Between the Streets" as long as Ian Hadley was its editor. New York City judges were used to making bigger compromises with their integrity.

So the guy didn't live in his office; which was good. If Grant could figure out a way to get in and out at any time between 7:00 PM and 9:00 AM, or while Hadley was out to lunch, they stood a decent chance of recovering the tape.

As for his weaknesses, they included adult beverages— hence his regular presence at Galan's—and women. Specifically, he seemed to have an appetite for dry martinis and women in their forties, which was a strangely age-appropriate personality tic for a wealthy man in Manhattan.

That was pretty much it, as far as the public would ever know, but it was enough for Grant. It offered him two paths into Ian Hadley's office: an off-hours break-and-enter, or—if he could figure out how to pull it off—an escort courtesy of Hadley straight into the offices of *The Eye*. But only if he could find a person whom Hadley would want to escort in, meaning a woman in her forties. Preferably one with a shared taste for dry martinis.

He could handle the martinis, but he was no fortyish woman, and that presented a problem.

Grant thought about it, and realized he did know one woman who might fit the bill. Maybe a bit on the older edge of Hadley's tastes—if asked, she'd have to lie about her age— but still presentable.

And the thought made him so excited that he even broke down and used the phone, instead of paying a personal call.

"Are you out of your mind?" asked Lisa Cochrane, when he reached her at her office at Lum Malverne Luxury Real Estate. "Lambert, I can't believe you want to pimp me out."

"Nah, not like that. I just want you to make nice with this Hadley guy, and maybe get invited back to his office or something. Or swipe his key. I dunno . . . You've got a lot of latitude here to be creative. The thing is, he's got something I need."

"A couple things are wrong here," she said, her smoky voice firm. "But let's start with the big one: I'm a lesbian."

"I didn't say you had to sleep with him."

"You make me crazy, you know that?" She paused, thought, and asked, "So what's this mysterious 'thing' you

need so desperately? If I'm going to even consider this—
which, I should warn you, is iffy—you're going to have to let
me know what I'm in for."

Grant was afraid she was going to say that, and he didn't
know how much he wanted to tell. Five grand was already
going to Paul Farraday, one-third of the take was pledged to
Jamie Brock—well, eventually . . . *hopefully*—and he was reluctant to further dilute his cut.

But if he didn't tell her, he would be minus a fortysome-
thing woman, even though this particular one was more like
fiftysomething. Which would make for a significant problem,
especially because he wanted to avoid a B-and-E if at all possible.

"If I tell you," he said finally, "you have to promise a few
things. First, keep it to yourself. No talking about it to your
girlfriend." He thought her girlfriend didn't like him.

"Okay." She knew her girlfriend didn't like him.

"And then . . . we have to discuss your fee."

"That's easy," she said. "Half."

"*Half?*" Oh no. "Ten percent."

"You want *me* to do all the work," she said. "So I get half."

"Planning the thing is a lot of work, you know."

"Not the way you do it. Okay, if you aren't doing even
shares, I guess you're going to have to find yourself another
girl."

Oh hell no! Among other things, Grant didn't really know
any other girls. Or at least not ones he could trust to have a
minor taste for larceny. In other words, he didn't know any
other girls like Lisa Cochrane.

So he told her.

And when he was finished, she was on board.

"You are a lucky man," she said. "That was a nice present
to fall into your lap."

"Yeah, but there's still work to do, because the tape isn't
exactly *in* my lap."

"Now that I know what's up, I'm much more motivated. This is going to be big, Lambert." She paused, and added, "I get a quarter."

He held firm. "Ten percent."

They went on like that for a while, until he finally got her to agree to twenty-five percent—or at least that's how he'd tell Chase it went down—and she got off the phone with one more burst of enthusiasm. For a woman who only had a toe in this business—unlike Grant, who was totally immersed— she was certainly confident. More so, of course, now that she was in it for one-quarter of the take.

He knew she was right, though. This was the big score he had been waiting for years to come his way.

If, that was, he could pull it off. With Lisa Cochrane on board, he allowed himself to feel just a tiny bit more confident.

Lisa kept her criminal interactions restricted to Grant and Chase, but on the handful of occasions that she was needed for a job and other people were brought in, inevitably someone would ask her how she had gotten mixed up in "the life." After all, she was a fairly successful real estate broker, with more than a few million-dollar deals in her portfolio. Why would she risk that career on random small-time larceny?

She'd explain how she became friendly with Grant years earlier through their mutual patronage of a decidedly seedy gay bar in Brooklyn. How in time she came to understand what he did to earn a living, and eventually gave him a helping hand here and there before discovering she sort of had an aptitude for the criminal life.

All of which was true. And no one ever questioned the pursuit of more cash in New York City. Everyone—from the wizards of Wall Street to the chronic homeless—knew that whatever money you had was never enough. Everyone was picking up a few bucks on the side; her way of doing it was just a bit less orthodox, and only more illegal than the way a lot of people made it on the side by a small matter of degree . . . although she was aware that *this* matter of degree was defined in the New York State criminal statutes.

She was just a working woman picking up a few extra bucks, and with a girlfriend like Mary Beth Reuss—who wanted the best of everything but didn't quite comprehend that she could work for at least some of it—there was always a need for more income. Especially *untaxed* income.

Still, the "everybody's doing it" line was mostly just for show.

The truth was that she got a thrill from crime she'd never get selling a condominium. Lisa didn't really want Grant to know that money wasn't her only motivation, though, because if he knew he'd probably try to reduce her cut of the take.

Maybe if the dark-haired, dark-eyed Mary Beth had not walked into Lisa's life five very expensive years earlier, she never would have fallen into a sideline as Grant's accomplice. But that was what happened, and she was happy with the way things turned out. She got to pick and choose her jobs; not scramble for every crumb, like Grant and Chase.

She thought it was great that Grant had found Chase, but wasn't especially impressed watching two men work hard to cobble together one income. Hers was the opposite sort of problem—with, she was sure, even better sex—but it worked for them, and she didn't need anyone's approval.

If she had one wish, it was that working-class Grant and upper-class Mary Beth would someday end their not-so-Cold War. She appreciated both of them for entirely different reasons, but their mutual resentment drove her to distraction.

But that could wait. In the meantime, this lesbian in her mid-fifties—albeit a well-put-together lesbian in her mid-fifties—had to prepare herself to seduce a man.

Chapter Eleven

Unlike Grant, Will Whitcomb had never seen anything all that great about the modern age. Then again, he had never used the Internet, although even if he had, he would have still been a small-timer.

No, Whitcomb longed for the old days, when even a half-wit could make a subsistence living off petty crime. He could have never seen the potential in electronic crime that Grant Lambert and Chase LaMarca did.

Fortunately, there was still a lot of old-fashioned crime to be committed, and even if a guy wasn't the smartest in the city, he could still get by with a small scam here and there and dream that the big one was just around the corner.

What annoyed him was that he had *hit* his big one—won the Lucky Crook Lottery—when he came into possession of that videotape. And *still* his ship hadn't come in.

That cheap bastard Ian Hadley had insulted him with a lowball number, and those people at *The Peeper* had laughed—*laughed*—at him! How was a poor guy supposed to make a dime—not to mention keep his dignity, which had never been one of his particular strong points—in the business these days?

The $200 offer from Hadley still burned him two days later. He had even *seen* the tape! And no matter what the editor said, Whitcomb was still sure—well, *pretty* sure—that was really Romeo Romero on the screen. He even had a big dick, which Hadley had mentioned was the actor's well-known trait and which Whitcomb had confirmed with the helpful librarian, although that question had earned him a very disquieting wink and an invitation for coffee someday.

He paced the apartment anxiously, willing the phone to ring . . . willing a return call from "Between the Streets" or *The Peeper*. They owed him that much.

But the phone remained silent.

He decided to watch the tape again for the first time since that disastrous meeting with Ian Hadley. Maybe he'd see something to disavow him of his certainty that it was Romeo Romero. Or maybe he would find reinforcement. At this point, anything was preferable to just sitting around, waiting.

He popped the tape into the VCR. Watched for twenty seconds. Smacked the VCR a few times with the flat palm of his hand and cursed secondhand, probably stolen electronics. Tried to watch again. Suddenly realized that the problem was *not* with the VCR.

And then he screamed.

When Will Whitcomb called, Ian Hadley was on the other line speaking to Romeo Romero, who—the editor sourly noted—had taken his time returning the phone message. Without an assistant to pick up the incoming call, Whitcomb went straight to voice mail after a half dozen rings. Ian Hadley never bothered to check his voice mail. He was too important for that. People who wanted to talk to him should just keep calling.

"Romeo, something came into my possession and, well . . . I can't believe it's really you."

"And why is that, Ian?" the actor asked guardedly. They had never met, but—coming from the realm of people whom other people were supposed to know—immediately and casually began using first names, as if they had a long acquaintance.

"Because you're gay."

Romero paused only briefly, although beads of sweat began forming on his brow. "I hope this call isn't to tell me you're outing me, Ian. Because, if so, you're almost thirty years too late."

"That's the thing, Romeo. You see, this videotape I've seen, well . . . it looks as if you're . . . well . . ."

"Yes?"

"Fucking a girl in a hot tub."

As a classically trained actor, Romeo Romero was averse to the cheap laugh that comes from a spit-take. That didn't stop him from spitting a mouthful of Pinot Grigio into his lap and across the coffee table.

"Romeo? Oh, Romeo?" No sound from the Water Mill side of the line. "Wherefore art thou, Romeo?"

"Sorry," said Romero, clearing his throat and letting things come back into focus, and very happy that he hadn't indulged in his craving for Merlot, given the current state of the off-white couch. "Went down the wrong way." He cleared his throat again. "You were saying, *Ian?*"

"Yes, *Rrrrrromeo.*" Hadley trilled his R, all the better to aggravate him. "I was saying that someone brought me a videotape, and it looks to me as if you're having sex with a woman. In a hot tub."

"Having sex with a woman?"

"In a hot tub." Hadley cleared his throat. "Which I assume a gay man does not ordinarily do. Unless the rules have changed."

Romero decided to turn on the charm. That, and lie a lot. He turned up his accent a notch.

"Ian, if you have a videotape of me having sex with a woman, it is either a fraud or from the nineteen seventies."

"You may very well be correct, Romeo," said Hadley, no

stranger to charm himself. "I suppose that's possible. Then again, that's why we at *The Eye* have technicians on staff to ferret these things out. I doubt it's thirty-some-odd years old because of the technology, but the techies can tell us if it's a forgery, or if that's not really you . . ."

"Yes."

". . . *walking around naked with a huge hard-on before he fucks a hot girl with big tits in his hot tub.*"

Ah, thought Hadley, *the old change-up*. There was nothing like an abrupt shift from erudition into vulgarity to rattle even the most composed subject. And now he had had the delectable opportunity to employ two change-ups in one conversation. It didn't get much better than that.

And, of course, it worked. The beads of sweat—there were more of them now; a lot more; a gusher, in fact—began dripping into Romero's lap, commingling with the spit-take Pinot Grigio. Still, he tried to save himself, which was more than most people did when Ian Hadley went on the offensive.

"I don't know what to say, my friend. It is hard enough in this world to be openly gay without being the victim of fraud or mistaken identity."

"You know what's harder?" asked Hadley, his voice soft and kind and suddenly—it sounded to Romero—much more reasonable. Until, that is, he continued: "Being a heterosexual Caucasian actor of no great renown whose career is tanking and who will end up touring Eastern Europe in a Slavic version of *Hello, Dolly!* if he doesn't find a way to separate himself from the pack."

Romero froze. It wasn't that Hadley was harsh, although he was. It was that his analysis was so incredibly dead-on that it was as if his mind had been read thirty years ago and regurgitated today for his embarrassment and mortification. And if he had stopped sweating, it was only because all moisture had been drained from his body.

The phone line was quiet for an uncomfortably long time.

Uncomfortable for Romero, that was; Hadley was rather enjoying himself.

"Any feedback?" the editor finally asked to break the silence.

"Ian, you . . . you . . ." *Think, dammit!* "Ian, you have quite an imagination. Before we discuss this further, I would like to see this tape."

"I would insist on it, Romeo."

"Privately."

"I would insist on that, too," Hadley agreed, because the fewer people who saw the tape, the better. Especially if Romero was planning to involve, oh, his *lawyers*. "Why don't you come to my office on"—he flipped through his calendar—"Monday."

Romero tried to regain control of the situation. "Monday is no good. Why don't *you* come to *my home* on Wednesday?"

Hadley didn't bother checking his calendar. "Booked all day. And really, it would be a lot easier to do it at my office. We're completely wired up here. We can review the tape in my office and no one will be the wiser."

"But here," said Romero, "there is no one around. Not a soul in the entire house. And I have a screening room."

No, thought Hadley. *Going out to Water Mill is not an option.*

"Romeo, much as I would love to accommodate you, please understand I'm a very busy man, with a lot of commitments here in New York. I regret to say that it would be very inconvenient for me to travel all the way out to the Hamptons just to spend twenty minutes reviewing a videotape. I don't have the same, uh, *flexibility* and free time you have with your schedule."

Flexibility? Free time? Romeo Romero knew when he was being insulted, and he didn't like it. But he managed to hold his tongue, which was at least civilized on his part.

"Oh, Ian, I only wish you had caught me at a time when I'm less busy. But I've got so many things that need my attention right now. Next weekend, I'm hosting a gay rights fundraiser out here." That much was true. "And I have a half dozen scripts I have to read." That much wasn't. "So I just don't see . . ."

"That's all right, Romeo. I quite understand your schedule. I was hoping that I could discuss this with you before we go to press, but if you're too busy . . ."

"How about next Tuesday at your office," the actor said quickly, and Ian Hadley smiled. "Will twelve o'clock work?"

"Next Tuesday it is. Twelve noon." The men began to say their good-byes, one with considerably more satisfaction than the other.

"One more thing before we sign off," said Romero, hopeful that this unpleasant situation could be resolved peacefully, subtly, and cheaply.

"I'm all ears."

"Do you happen to have Jamie Foxx's phone number?"

"Jamie? Sure." He looked at his watch; he was twelve minutes late for his Friday night appearance at Galan's, so this would have to be fast.

Chapter Twelve

Grant, Chase, and Lisa got to Galan's Irish Pub twenty minutes before the earliest they expected Ian Hadley to arrive. Still, they entered separately, several minutes apart, each taking time to scan the bar after their eyes adjusted to the dark interior. Customers 1 through 31—they knew, because they counted—did not yet include their target.

Galan's had been a fixture at its mid-block location on West Fifty-fifth Street for longer than even its owners knew. Certainly it predated the office towers now surrounding it. The regulars—drinkers from *The Eye*, plus more than a few people who enjoyed practicing their alcoholism in an old-fashioned and flat-out-cheap pub, lining the long wooden bar in the same stools night after night—appreciated it as an oasis from the hyperkinetic energy outside its battered door.

Grant eyed the joint appreciatively. If his ragtag gang ever needed to adopt a bar as a meeting place, Galan's would be the right place. Quiet . . . not too crowded . . . He wondered how many crimes had been planned here over the years, not including the crimes against journalistic standards and common decency perpetrated by the staff of *The Eye*.

They walked to the end of the bar, near the bathrooms, until they were standing in a loose knot as far as possible from any prying ears. Then they again reviewed the plan, worked through a few kinks and potential hitches, prayed for success, and finally ordered a round of drinks to unwind, because thinking this up had been the easy part; the tough part would be in the implementation.

Even Grant, now surprisingly the most optimistic of the group, since he was seldom optimistic about much of anything, knew that luck and perfect timing were going to be the keys to their success. His plan had seemed much more doable twenty-four hours earlier; tonight he wasn't so sure. But at least they had nothing up their sleeves that could lead to arrest, so even if everything fell apart, the worst that would happen was they'd walk away empty-handed.

The first thing they agreed on was to use their real names. It would lessen the potential for a slip-up, especially in the unlikely occurrence they happened across someone they knew. It wasn't likely, here in this dingy bar, but Grant's unfortunate encounter with Jamie Brock while he was trying to pass himself off as a UPS deliveryman had recently driven the lesson home. Good plans were always getting derailed because of stupid slip-ups. Using real names would eliminate at least one potential stupid slip-up.

Real names were also safe because they weren't likely to cross paths with Ian Hadley again. Theirs were not the sort of names likely to show up on invitations to a gala at the Waldorf. Although they decided that prudence dictated that Chase use his unbeloved *real* first name, Charles, which didn't make him happy.

Grant had planned out two possible courses of action, either one of which he hoped would get them close to that videotape. Improvisation would be key: much as he hated to admit it—especially since the stars didn't always line up for him—success was going to fall back on a little luck and a little skill. He was confident about their skill; less so about the things that were out of their hands.

The plans could be simply summarized: Plan A was to get Chase in; Plan B was to get Lisa in. And Plan C . . . well, there was no Plan C, except Grant's certainty that if plans A and B failed, he'd end up breaking into Hadley's office in the dead of night. He didn't want to, of course, but he'd do it before he gave up on retrieving that vidcotape.

For their parts, Chase and Lisa were ready to play their roles.

Chase—"Charles," that was—was going to pretend to be new to the city and looking for some sort of job that could utilize the skills he had developed working for a small weekly paper in upstate New York. In the dim bar lighting—which the rear dining room of Galan's Irish Pub, where Ian Hadley held court, had in abundance—he could easily pass for someone not yet hardened by decades on the streets of New York. Or so they hoped.

He would be the first to approach Hadley. He'd express his admiration, flatter him, and finally drop a few hints that he'd like to work for him at "Between the Streets." Chase's overture would almost certainly be rejected, which was when it would be Lisa's turn to step up to the plate.

Providing that Hadley had not yet had Chase thrown out of the joint—a possibility they considered, but knew there wasn't much that could be done of a preventative nature— she would approach the men, and Chase would introduce her as his aunt. His *single* aunt. His single, *man-hungry* aunt, if it had to come to that.

At which point their only hope was that sexual attraction would propel things forward in a way that careful criminal planning had not.

Not that it had been easy to convince Lisa of the merits of her role.

"*Aunt?*" she had asked. "Listen, I can swallow my big old lesbian pride and do the 'man-hungry'; take one for the team, or whatever, as long as I don't have to sleep with him. But how come I have to be Chase's *aunt?*"

"You'd prefer?" Grant had asked.

"What's wrong with cousin?"

Grant thought about that, but not for more than a few seconds. "Aunt," he said definitively.

"But we're the same age!"

He cast the sort of glance at her that said "I know better than that," and that had more or less ended the discussion.

Should the first part of the plan unfold without a hitch, and Chase and his aunt Lisa made the personal connection, they were prepared to take one of two different paths straight into Ian Hadley's office.

The first, and easiest for all concerned, was for Lisa to convince Hadley that it would be a good idea for him to hire her "nephew." If Chase had access to the office, it was only a short matter of time until he'd be able to put his hands on the videotape and get it back into their hands, where it belonged.

But if Hadley held firm, Lisa would have to take over. Ideally, by seducing Hadley into taking her back to his office for a rendezvous. It would be a lot trickier—especially because it would almost certainly mean that Lisa would end up knocking him cold, tying him up and gagging him, rifling his office, finding the tape, and somehow getting back out of the building—but it was better than nothing.

Yeah, Grant thought, there were a lot of things that could go wrong. He looked at Lisa and wondered if maybe she should open another button on her shirt. Show a little more cleavage.

Grant's role was to play Bar Customer Number 32. He was going to stand there and pretend not to see a thing as he nursed a Molson and kept watch. If he saw a problem develop—with them, Hadley, the joint—he would set his beer on the bar, which was their signal to meet him in the bathroom. If he didn't, they wouldn't. Well . . . unless they had to use the bathroom.

And so the three of them, well versed on what needed to happen, waited for Ian Hadley and hoped they'd recognize him without too much trouble from pictures on the Internet.

And as each minute passed they got just a little bit more nervous. Until . . .

"There he is," whispered Grant, who was pretending to not really be with the other two, except when there was a need to whisper.

Sure enough, Ian Hadley was finally walking through the front door and into the gloom of Galan's. Even if he hadn't been recognizable, which he was, they would have known him by the way he swaggered down the bar, treating it almost as an extension of his office, clapping the backs and shoulders of *Eye* employees and Irish alcoholics alike as he made his way to the empty dining room in the back.

He brushed past Grant and Chase without notice, but gave Lisa a second glance. That made Grant smile ever so slightly, despite the stone face he was trying to hold. It was a good sign.

When Hadley reached a booth in the back of the bar—where people ate lunch, but was empty at night—he sat. The way he slid into the bench and began adjusting the condiment bottles on the table made it obvious it was his regular spot to hold court in the bar. He gave off the aura of territorial possession. The lone waitress didn't bother approaching him; she just nodded and smiled to acknowledge him and went to fetch his martini.

"Ready?" asked Grant, out of the side of his mouth. He scanned the room, watching for sycophants who might be making their way to Hadley and consequently screwing up their plans. No one yet. "You'd better get going, before someone grabs him and starts gabbing his ear off."

"Ready," said Lisa and Chase.

"One more thing." Grant looked Lisa in the eye. "Pop another button."

She looked down at her cleavage. "Grant, three are already open! Who am I supposed to be? Madonna?"

"Make it four. Remember that this is a British horndog who has an obsession with breasts." He knew that from the Internet, of course.

She griped and grumbled and otherwise ignored him.

"Okay," muttered Chase, speaking without looking at them. "I'm going in."

"Good luck," they whispered in unison, apparently to no one in particular, causing a patron near them at the bar to lift his pint and say, "Thanks."

Grant moved away from Lisa, who in turn backed up a few steps until she could see Hadley's booth, but not Hadley. They watched Chase as he approached the booth . . . watched him in animated and apparently one-sided conversation . . . watched him extend his hand to Hadley, only to withdraw it, unshaken, seconds later.

"Oh shit," Lisa said to herself. "Looks like it's my turn already." She waited until the waitress maneuvered around Chase and deposited the martini in front of Hadley before making her move.

Standing in front of the Gossip King, who was pointedly ignoring him, Chase was doubting the wisdom of the plan. Trying to befriend someone who didn't want to be friendly was definitely a major flaw in their plan.

Lisa approached, grabbed him around the waist, and said, "Hey, kiddo. I was wondering where you ran off to."

"Hi, uh, Aunt Lisa," he said, grateful that he wouldn't have to suffer alone, and not noticing when she recoiled at his use of the word "aunt." "I just spotted Mr. Hadley here and wanted to say hello."

She looked down at the editor, who was sitting in his booth, glancing over a few typewritten pages and not looking back at them.

So . . .

"*Ian* Hadley?!" she gushed.

He sighed, but kept his eyes on the pages.

So she tried again. "The editor of 'Between the Streets'? Is this really him?"

"Uh . . . yes," said Chase. "Yes, it is."

Again, Hadley sighed, and this time he shook his head slightly. But his eyes didn't move.

Okay, Lisa thought, *if you're going to be like that . . .*

She thrust her chest out, and the fourth shirt button, already straining from the weight of her breasts, popped free of the fabric. It arced through the air until it bounced off Ian Hadley's nose.

He looked up angrily, wondering what the hell had just hit him. There was the insipid young man, the wannabe reporter, still not having gone away, still staring at him nervously. And next to him was . . .

"Well, hello," said Ian Hadley, suddenly forgetting he had been angry as he stared at the woman's almost-exposed breasts. He looked down at the table. Saw the shiny piece of gold.

"Did you happen to lose a button, my dear?"

Lisa smiled. "You're such a gentleman."

At a couple of points during the next two hours, Lisa and Chase were afraid they were going to lose him. He'd appear bored with them . . . or distracted by something or someone . . . and once he even indicated it was time for him to go home.

But they had hung in there, through those difficult moments and interruptions from a parade of well-wishers trooping to the table to pay respect to Ian Hadley. Through all of that, Lisa and Chase hung in there.

And they learned an important lesson as the minutes ticked by.

When dealing with Ian Hadley, there was apparently no

obstacle that couldn't be overcome by ordering him another dry martini.

Chase's first day at *The Eye* would be the following Monday, when he would begin a probationary try-out as Ian Hadley's new executive assistant at a ridiculously low rate of pay.

Not that it mattered. He didn't intend to be there long enough to collect a paycheck.

Chapter Thirteen

The new guy, Charlie LaMarca, seemed to be working out, thought Hadley, watching him through the fishbowl window of his office. Sure, it had only been an hour or so, but it was nice to have someone around to answer the phones in a professional manner, which hadn't happened since he'd fired . . . whatsername. Millicent? Maggie? Something like that.

He considered the appearance of Charlie—not to mention his delightful and bosomy aunt—to be nothing short of serendipity. All of them were at the right place at the right time. Then again, when was Galan's ever the *wrong* place?

Obviously, all those very dry martinis played a role in his spontaneous decision to offer Charlie employment, but, well . . . he *had* wanted to break his routine, hadn't he? And it wasn't as if he would ever regret it. No, he'd fire Charlie's ass long before it ever came to the point of regret.

But hopefully that wouldn't happen, as it seemed to happen to almost everyone else who had ever worked for him.

That morning, J. P. Hunt had begun the vetting process, and in another day or two Hadley had already decided he'd go outside corporate policy and move Charlie's status from probationary to permanent. Just as he had already thumbed his nose at the process by hiring him without going through the annoying Human Resources routine. It was a good way to foster staff loyalty.

And in any event, he was Ian Hadley; he did *not* answer to HR.

Not to mention, it would probably help earn him another introduction to Charlie's aunt. That evening at Galan's, he had been intrigued by the way the woman ran hot and cold, seducing him with her exposed cleavage while at the same time not really seeming to like being touched by him. In any other circumstance, Ian Hadley—a connoisseur of the gentler sex—might have thought Charlie's Aunt Lisa wasn't really into men . . . but how then to explain her playfully popped button, and the subsequent display of cleavage. Not to mention the risqué conversation . . . well, what he could remember of it. Those memories were certainly risqué, and that's all that mattered.

No, she must like men. Most likely she was one of those flirtatious yet cautious women found in abundance in New York City these days, burned a few times too often in the past and now insistent on calling the shots.

Very well then, he thought. I can wait if you can, Aunt Lisa. You can call the shots all you want.

Best of all, that morning Charlie had instinctively understood when he had explained his creeping sense of Gossip Item Ennui.

" 'Between the Streets' needs new sources," Charlie had said, which sounded fresh to Hadley but was really just a regurgitation of his own words, changed only slightly to mimic original thought. "When the column follows the same people and publicists every day, each one starts to sound alike. They're interchangeable."

Hearing his words come back to him, Hadley smiled. "So what do you suggest we do, Charlie?"

Chase, now a passable expert on "Between the Streets" by virtue of a weekend spent on-line immersed with several years of back columns, said, "First, maybe it would help to get out of Michael's and listen to some new voices."

Hadley gasped. *Get out of Michael's? Sacrilege!*

"You're a smart man, but you've still got a lot to learn about this business." He patted Chase on the shoulder and walked back into his office, all the while thinking about what a thoroughly ridiculous idea it was to not go where everyone else went.

For his part, Chase—who hated being called Charlie even more than he hated being called Charles, but what could he do?—was feeling more ambivalent about the situation.

First, when he recommended that Ian Hadley get out of Michael's, he really, truly meant it. Not because he had anything against Michael's per se (he had never been, and doubted he ever would), but because it took less than an hour at *The Eye* before he grew sick of hearing pretty much everyone talk about the place. And it never was about the food; it was always about the other people who were there, or going to be there, or had been there. The fifteenth floor of the Global Pan-Atlantic Mercantile West Building sometimes sounded like a beehive with "Michael's" substituted for "bzzz." And that was only in the first hour. He couldn't imagine what the rest of the day was going to be like.

Second, there was the background check. The minute he walked into the office, he got a bad vibe from J. P. Hunt, whom nobody needed to tell him was an ex-cop. Even though he and Grant had spent the weekend building a respectable background, complete with fake references who would vouch for him—meaning lie—for small amounts of cash, he got the sense that J. P. Hunt wasn't going to be content skimming the surface. That was the reason Chase spontaneously decided to use his own social security number, instead of one they found on-line courtesy of a dead person.

Real name, real social security number, fake references that would never be found out, and therefore could be considered real . . . It was almost as if he actually had a job in this place. Of course, Groc-O-Rama would be expecting him back when he returned from what they believed was his great-uncle's funeral in Odessa, Texas, in the very near future, but it was nice to know he could always get another job.

Third, there was the telephone. Chase didn't share Grant's aversion to the phone, but the line to Hadley's office rang constantly. If there were eight million stories in the Naked City, people were trying to plant seven million of them in "Between the Streets." That, or the callers were angry about something that had already appeared in print . . . or, in the case of one strange caller named Will Whitcomb, they were just generically angry, sputtering and spitting and demanding to speak privately to Hadley, but unwilling to offer up any details. This Whitcomb's rudeness to Chase got his hourly messages put on the bottom of the pile.

Finally, there was Ian Hadley himself. His new boss had been a little too friendly, in sharp contrast to his dismissiveness a few nights earlier, which Chase knew was mostly because he wanted to get into Lisa Cochrane's pants. Knowing it wasn't going to happen—but that Chase would continue to be the point man as long as he sat just outside Hadley's office door—made him uncomfortable.

Still, he kept in mind that he was there for a purpose, and once his mission was complete he'd be gone. Hopefully before the background check was complete or Hadley's obsession with Lisa drove him to distraction or the buzzing about Michael's made him snap.

The phone rang and, in his head, he added, *Or before I throw the damn phone out the window.*

Hopefully as early as today.

To Chase's deep regret, that particular rainy Monday in May was one of those days when Ian Hadley pretty much planted himself behind his desk and didn't move. Until, of course, it was time for him to walk the few blocks to Michael's for lunch, a black umbrella emblazoned with *The Eye* logo in his hands.

"You know where to reach me," he said, as he finished buttoning his Burberry raincoat, and Chase did. And he silently thanked him for not actually saying the name of the restaurant this time.

He waited for ten minutes to pass after his new boss disappeared through the elevator door to minimize the likelihood he'd pop back in, having realized he'd forgotten something. Then, comfortable that Hadley would be gone for a while, he grabbed a pile of papers, none of which pertained to the others, and walked into the private office.

He was going to have to make this fast and discreet. He didn't have a lot of time, and prying eyes could figure out what he was up to if anyone decided to be suspicious. Or even if they just happened to innocently look through the large windows.

Chase ducked down beneath the fishbowl window, that handful of papers wedged against his hip, and pulled open a drawer on the credenza. Nothing but stacks of old editions of *The Eye* . . . probably a collection of Ian Hadley's greatest hits.

He opened another drawer. Blank travel vouchers. Requisition forms. Nothing of use.

He opened a third drawer.

A half dozen videotape cartridges, and another eight or nine DVDs.

Ian Hadley's stash.

Bingo!

Bing-*fuckin'*—

"What are you doing?"

Startled, Chase fell backward on his ass. The papers—his props—spilled across the parquet floor, sliding in every direction. He looked up and J. P. Hunt towered above him.

"I'm, uh . . . I'm, uh . . . Jeez, you scared me!"

The ex-cop just stood there, one hand on the corresponding hip, and stared at him. Gray eyes, gray hair, gray face . . . just staring.

"I was, was, was . . . filing," Chase said finally. He cast a glance at the papers strewn across the floor, as if to say, "See?"

J. P. let the tension hang in the air for a few beats, then said, "Ian doesn't like people in his office when he's not here."

"I–I–I . . . I was just trying to do my job."

"Yeah, well . . . Do it later. When he's here."

After Chase collected the papers and returned to his desk, J. P. shut and locked the door to Ian Hadley's elegant outpost on the fifteenth floor. As he walked away, he kept tossing suspicious glances back over his shoulder at Chase, as if he was going to try something.

Which, of course, Chase was going to do. The very next time he again had access to that credenza.

Opportunity finally knocked again in the late afternoon.

Ian Hadley was only human, or at least as human as any other gossip editor. Meaning, eventually he had to use the facilities. Chase was going to have to work fast, but knowing the exact drawer he wanted to raid would work in his favor.

When Hadley walked out of his office, Chase scanned the room. Several cubicles away, he saw J. P. Hunt's gray head hovering above the five-foot-tall dividers, and while he wasn't looking in Chase's direction, it seemed to make sense to wait him out.

Which only took two minutes, although to Chase, it felt like hours. Plus, it had cost him precious time, and he'd have to move even faster than he'd already planned to move.

With J. P. finally out of sight, Chase again grabbed some random pieces of paper as a prop, and this time added a plastic bag to spirit away his haul. Ten seconds later he was huddled close to the floor, hunched over the credenza drawer and filling the plastic bag with the tapes and DVDs.

He was taking the last DVD from the drawer when he heard Hadley's voice.

"Charlie?"

The DVD dropped from his fingers and bounced silently off the edge of an area rug before rolling to a stop, making only the slightest sound as it flattened on the parquet floor.

Chase didn't dare look up. He had no idea how he could plausibly explain why he was emptying the drawer. He was going to have to run for it . . . try to evade security and get out of the building. Maybe he and Grant could figure out another way to get the tape.

"Charlie?" Another pause, then he heard Hadley ask, "J. P., do you know where Charlie is?"

Wait a second, he thought. *Hadley isn't standing over me, after all. He's outside the office, out by my desk.* Chase dared himself to look up, and, sure enough, he couldn't see him, although he could now hear Hadley and J. P. in conversation just outside the open door.

"Maybe he's in the can," said J. P.

"No, I was just there. Ah well . . . he could be in the break room. It can wait."

Chase carefully, silently, closed the drawer. Now it would look *awkward* when he was discovered crouching in the boss's office, but it would not necessarily look criminal. He hoped.

"I don't know about that guy, Ian. There's something about him that I don't trust."

"Too many years of police work, J. P. It's made you suspicious of everyone."

Chase was about to rise from his crouch when he realized that he was holding a plastic bag full of VHS tapes and DVDs, which *would* look criminal. He dropped to his knees and slid it underneath the credenza, pushing it until it wouldn't go any farther. Another potential disaster averted.

"Charlie!"

Chase spun around, and this time was not surprised to see Ian Hadley was now in his office.

"Oh, hi, Ian!"

The editor regarded him warily, although not quite as warily as J. P. regarded him from the doorway where he literally had Ian Hadley's back. "Didn't you hear me?"

"Oh. Uh . . . I'm partially deaf in my left ear. So, uh, I guess not." Hadley crossed his arms and stood, with an expression that told Chase he still might need some convincing. "Uh . . . too much loud music in my youth."

Hadley scowled. "Well . . . hopefully this disability won't negatively impact your performance here. I cannot be expected to chase after you. I need an assistant who hears me and responds to me."

Chase nodded earnestly. "I'll make sure this never happens again, Ian."

The scowl didn't exactly disappear, but at least it diminished. "Very good." A quizzical expression crossed his face; the look of a man who knew there was another question he wanted to ask, but couldn't quite remember what it was. When he did, the scowl returned. "And what the devil are you doing in my office?"

"Uh . . ." Chase waved the random papers. "I thought I'd file a few things. But then I realized that I don't know where anything goes, and . . . uh . . ."

"I caught him in here when you were at lunch, too," said J. P., who eyed Chase up and down and added, "I told him *then* that he wasn't supposed to be in here."

That was when Ian Hadley surprised Chase LaMarca . . . by smiling.

"J. P.," he said, clapping a hand on his Number Two's shoulder, "you are indeed our pit bull." He turned to Chase and said, "But, Charlie, J. P. is correct. Nothing personal, but I really don't like people in my office when I'm not here." He winked. "Here at BtS, we deal in the business of secrets, and I like to think I'm entitled to have a few of my own."

"I apol—" Chase stopped when he saw something out of the corner of his eye. It was a DVD, just lying there on the floor in plain sight, which was when he remembered the disc that had fallen from his hand when he first heard Hadley's voice. He swallowed hard and said, "I apologize, Ian. I was just trying to be a good assistant."

It didn't seem as if Hadley or J. P. had seen the disc yet, so he took a step back until he felt it under the sole of his shoe.

"I appreciate your industriousness, but there will be time to deal with all the mundane chores around here. In the meantime, it might be helpful if you were out there"—he pointed at Chase's desk—"instead of in here, because that telephone isn't going to answer itself."

"Of course, Ian. Absolutely, Ian." With that, he flicked his foot slightly, and the DVD slid under the credenza. "And again, I'm sorry."

J. P. Hunt glowered as he passed by on the way back to his desk, then he closed the door, leaving Chase on the outside and Hadley, J. P., and the tapes on the inside. Which wasn't where those tapes were supposed to be.

He called Grant, and, after he explained the latest twist, Grant simply said:

"Bagels."

"What do bagels have to do with anything?"

So Grant explained.

At 4:00 that afternoon, Chase popped his head into Hadley's office and said, "Would you like a bagel, Ian?"

Hadley looked up from his computer monitor and said, "A bagel?"

Chase lifted up an oversized plastic bag. "I've got plain,

sesame, onion . . . pretty much whatever you want. I was going to take them to the break room, but figured I'd give you the first choice, since you're the boss."

Hadley flashed him a tight, dismissive smile. "No, thank you."

Chase pulled a bagel from the bag and held it up. "Are you sure? They're fresh."

"No, I'm fine."

Chase was about to answer when the bagel fell out of his hand, then bounced once and began a slow roll across the floor toward the credenza.

"Sorry, Ian," he said, as he followed the errant piece of dough. "Guess I'm a little clumsy today."

Hadley offered him an unhappy grunt and returned his gaze to the monitor.

Chase reached the bagel and knelt down to collect it. In the process, he managed to reach under the credenza and collect the plastic bag with the tapes, as well as the unbagged DVD, and stuffed them in the bagel bag.

"Got it," he said seconds later when his recovery mission was complete.

"That's nice," said Hadley, who did not seem to be paying attention, until he looked over just as Chase was putting the bagel back into the bag and preparing to leave.

"I'm very disappointed in you, Charlie. I expected better."

What did he see?

"Uh . . . what did I do?"

"That bagel has been rolling around a dirty floor. Don't put it back. Throw it out!"

"Yes sir."

As soon as he got back to Jackson Heights that evening, Chase and Grant began viewing those tapes and DVDs that had been smuggled out of the Global Pan-Atlantic Mercantile West Building in a bagel bag.

There was not a trace of Romeo Romero in any of them.

But there was a lot of hardcore pornography. Six VHS tapes and eight DVDs worth, to be precise.

"Nun porn?" asked Grant, watching one scene unfold on the TV.

"To be fair," said Chase, "I kind of doubt she's really a nun."

"This guy is sick."

Chase nodded, and wondered what the gang at Michael's would think if they knew of Ian Hadley's secret stash of "whips-and-wimples" pornography.

When Grant finally turned off the DVD player after forty-seven minutes of fruitless fast-forwarding, Chase asked, "Now what?"

"Now you go back to *The Eye* and figure out what else Hadley has stashed in his office."

Chase shook his head. "I don't know, Grant. I think they're on to me. I've already been caught twice snooping around the office, and it's only my first day."

"Maybe," said Grant, "I could get a job on the cleaning crew. I've done that before."

They thought for a minute or two before simultaneously sighing.

"I'd better get to bed," Chase said finally. "Looks like I'll be reporting for work tomorrow at *The Eye*, and Charlie LaMarca needs his shuteye."

The worst part, he thought, was now he was going to have to smuggle the porn back *into* Hadley's office, which seemed to be the opposite direction of how they should be doing things. He consoled himself with the knowledge that at least there was one less drawer he'd have to search. Which wasn't much, but it was something.

Chapter Fourteen

In the first few hours after Will Whitcomb discovered he had a blank videotape instead of the Romeo Romero sex tape he once possessed, he was immersed in a boiling rage without any idea of how to rectify the situation. He had tried to play in the big leagues, and had been soundly defeated.

Defeated by that snake, Ian Hadley.

He had called *The Eye*, of course. He had called several times, but each call went straight to voice mail. Will Whitcomb might not have known much, but by now he knew the messages he left in voice mail were never going to be returned.

Finally he had decided to personally confront Hadley, and marched the eleven blocks from his apartment to the glass office tower on West Fifty-fifth Street. Marched past a hole-in-the-wall Irish bar called Galan's, as a matter of fact, where—if he had bothered to look inside—he would have found the object of his ire sipping his first dry martini of the night as a button popped off a tall woman's shirt and hit him in the nose.

But he didn't. He marched straight up to the front door of the Global Pan-Atlantic Mercantile West Building, marched inside, and marched to the security desk.

Three minutes later he was marched back out to the sidewalk by building security.

So that strategy hadn't worked. But then the weekend came, and there was nothing he could do about the situation until the following Monday, so Will Whitcomb did whatever he could to put his mind at ease. Mostly boosting CDs from music stores and stiffing cab drivers.

The passage of a few days did serve to calm him down, though, and by Monday morning—no longer irrationally hotheaded, mostly, although still angry—he decided to try a new approach. He would reach out to Ian Hadley in a mature, businesslike manner. He would make a deal. He would even take a small sum—maybe even a *very* small sum—to give up his claim to the tape, walk away, and disappear from Ian Hadley's life forever. It wouldn't be the big pay-off he had once anticipated, but it would be a net profit. And any acknowledgment from Hadley, no matter how slight, would go a long way toward giving him back some of his normally inadequate self-esteem. Hell, a *ten-spot* would put him back to where he had been, in terms of dignity.

And so he called, and left an insistent message with the pleasant young man who seemed to have replaced voice mail over the weekend. And a while later, not getting a returned call and thinking that maybe his first call had been a bit *too* insistent, he called again, although this time the young man was a bit less pleasant.

Still no returned call, so he called again . . .

By 5:30, after eight messages during which Will Whitcomb's tone grew increasingly less mature and businesslike and the young man's tone grew increasingly annoyed, it was clear that reasoning with Ian Hadley was not going to be a productive approach. The guy had screwed him and was never going to give him the time of day.

And the saddest part of that, to Whitcomb, was that there wasn't a damn thing he could do about it.

Which was why he was surprised very early on Tuesday morning when the young man—pleasant, again—called and told him that Mr. Hadley would like him to come to the office at 3:00 that afternoon.

*   *   *

When Chase hung up the telephone, he felt unclean. There was something about that Whitcomb fellow that seemed to ooze through the line. And why Hadley, of all people, wanted to see him was incomprehensible. But his was not to reason why . . . his was to sneak the tapes back into the credenza before Hadley noticed they were missing, then start all over again with a new search of the office.

In fact . . .

Chase glanced in through the fishbowl windows. Hadley had left a few minutes earlier for an editorial meeting, and Chase thought this might be his best opportunity. He stood at his desk . . . looked for J. P. Hunt . . . looked to see if *anyone* was paying any attention to him . . .

Nothing. Everything was clear. He might only have a few minutes, but maybe he could make that work.

He opened the desk drawer and slid out the plastic bagel bag containing the Nun Porn and other pieces from the Ian Hadley collection . . .

He started to walk toward Hadley's office . . .

"Ah, Charlie!"

Chase dropped the bag, which landed with a thump at his feet. Hadley looked at it as he approached from the general direction of the elevators, then back at Chase. "Not bagels again."

"Uh . . . no." As he collected the bag, hoping that what was inside it wouldn't be too obvious, he said, "I thought you were in an editorial meeting."

"Forgot something."

Chase walked back to his desk, trying to make it look like he was just stretching his legs. As he pretend-stretched, Hadley entered his office, grabbed a file folder from his desk, and exited again.

"You spoke to Whitcomb?" he asked, on his way back out.

"Yeah. He'll be here at three."

Hadley smiled. "Excellent. In that case, I'll need you to get something for me."

"Sir?"

"A metal wastepaper basket."

Chase scrunched up his face. "A metal . . . ?"

"Exactly. And I shall need it before my three o'clock."

Well, at least Chase wasn't the only one who thought of trash when they thought of Will Whitcomb. A metal trash can was an odd request, but not in context.

After Hadley was gone, he got in and out of the office quickly, taking only the time necessary to return the tapes and DVDs. Ian Hadley had been surprising him a bit too often lately; he would wait for a wider window of opportunity to launch his next search.

He knew Hadley had booked out his calendar from noon to two. Two hours. That would give him plenty of time.

In the meantime, he had to order a metal wastepaper basket.

An hour later, Hadley was back in his office. Which is when bad things started happening.

They started, like bad things usually do, with a ringing telephone.

"Ian Hadley, please," said the accented voice on the other end of the phone.

"I'll see if he's in. Who's calling, please?"

"Romeo Romero." Which is when the accent made a lot of sense to Chase.

He gagged. "Ro—Ro—"

"Romero," said Romero, with obvious impatience. "Romeo Romero."

Sweat broke along Chase's brow. This wasn't good. He was too close. He'd have to lose this call.

"He's stepped out of the office, sir." And of course that was the moment when Chase looked up and saw Hadley still in his office, but striding toward the doorway. Toward him. Toward him on the phone with Romeo Romero. He was going to have to make this a quick abort. "Can I take a message?"

"We are supposed to meet today. At noon. I am in the city now and want to confirm that I am scheduled."

"Uh . . . can I call you back?" Chase whispered.

"I don't want to talk to you. I want to confirm that with *him*."

"Charlie," said Hadley, advancing only as far as the threshold of his office door, as if restrained by some invisible fence separating him from the lesser mortals on the fifteenth floor. "Could you come here for a moment?" Chase was confused for a moment, until he remembered he was Charlie.

"I, uh . . ."

"Isn't that Hadley's voice?" asked Romero brusquely. "Please transfer me in. I need to speak to him."

Chase turned away from Hadley, buried the phone close to his neck, and mumbled, "No, it's someone else. Uh . . . could you repeat that message?"

"Charlie," said Hadley sternly.

"One moment," said Chase, waving a finger, and into the phone he said, "I don't think he's free at noon."

"I hear his voice. I *must* speak to him."

"Charlie, *come on! Off the phone! Now!*"

"And there it is again!"

"It's not him." Chase, usually so cool under pressure, felt himself cracking under the dual hectoring from Ian Hadley and Romeo Romero.

"Charlie, what the hell . . . ?"

And with that, Chase hung up. One problem was gone, at least.

"Sorry, Ian." He stood and followed the gossip mogul into his office. " 'Between the Streets' seems to bring out the crazies, doesn't it?"

Hadley sighed and smiled, and Chase knew that all was forgiven. He played with a cufflink and said, "Son, if you only *knew* how this column brings out the crazies." He led the way to his desk and, after sitting down, asked, "So which one was this? I don't think you've yet to be properly introduced to some of our regulars. The Sarah Jessica Parker stalker? The fellow who claims he's Jann Wenner? . . . Come to think of it, I'm not sure it's not really Wenner, but still . . ."

"Uh . . . more of a routine crazy. This guy said he saw Tina Brown at Michael's. Drunk and canoodling with, uh . . . the waiter."

Hadley cocked an eyebrow. "Did you get a phone number? We could call back and confirm . . ."

"No, sorry. He . . . he said he works for her. Paranoid about staying anonymous."

"But that doesn't sound crazy."

"You should have heard him yelling." Chase looped one finger around his ear. "Crazy. Trust me."

Ian Hadley looked out his window at the roof of the crappy little low-rise across West Fifty-fifth Street. "That's a shame," he said wistfully. When he turned back to Chase he added, "But I have my own sources at Michael's, so if it happened—or if there was a *possibility* it happened—I'll get to the bottom of it." He smiled, showing two rows of straight white teeth that didn't *look* sharp, although they were. "Too bad you couldn't get your caller to confirm, Charlie. You could have earned your first BtS byline."

And that, of all things, made Chase regretful. It would have been so cool to earn a byline in a major newspaper. Albeit in a tabloid gossip column. And albeit based on an item he had just made up in a mad effort to cover up the phone call from Romeo Romero. Still . . . in a way, it was cool to come that close to a byline. He'd have to remember that if he ever decided to leave Groc-O-Rama.

"One more thing." Hadley wagged a long, manicured finger at him. "Nobody ever actually *says* the word 'canoodling.' It's fine for print; not for conversation. Got it?"

"Got it."

"I hate that word," he continued, almost to himself. "Sorry I ever invented it."

"Got it," Chase said again, and, as he did, he heard his phone start ringing.

So did Hadley.

"Maybe that's your source again. You'd better answer that."

"No, I'm sure he wouldn't call back. Too paranoid."

"Then *I'll* get it," he said, with a playful wink. "Remember, Charlie, we're going to try to do some new things to break up the monotony." And, with that, Ian was hurrying off to Chase's desk. Chase made an effort to beat him to the phone, but Hadley's head start was too much for him to overcome without tackling him, or doing something else that would be a bit too obvious.

"Hello," he said, grabbing the receiver. Then: "Speaking." His brow furrowed and he looked at Chase, who now— slightly out of breath—joined him at the desk. "Good morning, Romeo. Please hold for one moment, and I'll have my assistant transfer you into my office." He pushed the hold button and said, "Charlie, please transfer this in to me." He began to walk away, then half turned and asked, "Did you take a message from Romeo Romero a few minutes ago?"

Chase tried to keep his cool. "Who?"

"Romeo Romero? Come on, Charlie, he's a huge star." He waved his thoughts away. "Never mind. Actors are *so* self-important. He must have misdialed. Anyway, transfer him into me when I get to my desk."

When Hadley was out of earshot, Chase took the call off hold and, in the deepest, most Brooklyn-ish accent he could muster, said, "I'll transfer you to Mr. Hadley, sir."

When he began talking to Ian Hadley, Romeo Romero first noted that the man who had transferred the call was not the same one who had given him such a hard time just minutes earlier, which put both of them at ease. For his part, Chase would never know this, because the moment after he sent Romeo Romero's voice to Ian's desk phone, he called Grant and announced, "We've got a problem."

As he filled Grant in on the new development, he kept one eye on Ian Hadley chatting away with the compromised actor, until his partner finally said, "So we have to move the timeline up. Can you go through his office again when he goes to lunch?"

"That's my plan." Chase looked around the newsroom, again noting just how open it was. But at least he didn't see J. P. lurking around . . . which didn't mean he wasn't out there somewhere, watching him from between the rows of cubicles. "But it'll be tough, Grant. Pretty much everyone can see everything if they're looking."

"Well . . . you can narrow things down. Go through part of the office now . . . maybe another part later. I figure the tape is in there somewhere, so eventually we'll get our hands on it."

Chase took another long look at Ian, who was still in animated conversation. "The other problem is, what if he doesn't go out for lunch today?"

"Doesn't he always?"

"Mostly. But he's cleared two hours from his schedule, and now we know at least part of that time he's meeting Romero. What if they're meeting here? Or . . ."

Grant waited for Chase to continue. Which seemed to take forever, so he finally asked: "Or *what*?"

"What if this is it? What if he's gonna sell him the tape this afternoon?"

Grant thought about that. "Think you can get Hadley to tell you where he's going when he meets Romero? You know, tell him you need to know in case something important comes up."

"I can try."

They hung up.

Seconds after Chase ended his conversation with Grant, Hadley ended his with Romeo Romero. And then, as Chase watched from his desk, the editor pulled a black plastic cartridge from the bookshelf behind him.

For the first few beats, Chase's eyes didn't quite register what he was seeing. But then he realized it had to be the tape.

The *Tape!*

The Motherfucking Goddamn Tape! Ian Hadley was holding it in his hands.

And smiling.

Chase glanced at the clock on the wall. It was 11:30. No time to call Grant back right now. He was going to have to think and act fast on his own.

And then Ian Hadley was walking out of his office, buttoning his coat as he approached Chase's desk. The tape stayed with him, disappearing into an outer pocket.

Meaning Chase was going to have to think and act even faster than he was anticipating.

"Early lunch, Ian?"

Fortunately, Hadley gave him the information he desperately wanted without a round of questions, which only would have raised suspicion. "Yes, I'm meeting Romeo Romero for lunch at the Four Seasons."

"You are?" Chase's voice was tiny. All he could focus on was the pocket with the videotape. He wondered if he could pick the pocket, although that had never been one of his more successful criminal skills.

"I am. And then we have a meeting scheduled here after lunch. We'll probably be back around two or two-thirty."

Chase tried to rally and not think too much about knocking Hadley down, ripping off the coat, and running like hell, because that wouldn't really be very practical. "Remember you have a three o'clock with Mr. Whitcomb."

Hadley's smile broadened. "I wouldn't miss that meeting for the world. But my meeting here with Romero won't last long." And then he added breezily, almost to himself, "I'm sure we can fast-forward through a lot of it."

He rapped his knuckles against Chase's desk, then strode toward the bank of elevators.

Chase picked up the phone and dialed.

The decision to meet for lunch at the Four Seasons had been Hadley's and Hadley's alone. It was a way to draw out Romeo Romero's pain . . . to make him understand what Ian Hadley was capable of doing if the actor chose not to play along. And he also sort of enjoyed it, in the way a cat enjoys playing with its prey up until the point where it gets bored and kills it.

Plus, he liked the food.

Left to his own devices, of course, Romeo Romero would have opted to skip lunch, skip their meeting, skip everything. He just wanted this problem to go away.

Hadley waited until they had ordered and the waiter was out of earshot.

"So tell me, Romeo . . . Is it difficult to pretend to be gay, when you're really straight?"

Romero dabbed at the corner of his mouth with a napkin, taking his time before answering. As a general rule, he didn't like to improvise. With words that had been written for him, he could perform like a master. With his own words, it was better to exercise caution.

"There is a sexual continuum," he said, finally, slightly exaggerating his accent in case he was forced to play the "no speak English good" card. "How do you define what is 'gay' and what is 'straight'?"

"It's quite simple, actually. If a person is caught on tape having sex with a woman, I'd say that person is straight." He paused. "Or are you trying to wiggle out of this using the Kinsey scale?" He nodded to Cindy Adams as she passed, chuckled to himself that *she* didn't know what *he* knew, and continued. "Because let's face it, Romeo, a revelation like this would ruin you."

"What do you mean?" He knew exactly what Hadley meant, of course; he just needed time before saying anything else with a passing resemblance to meaningfulness.

"Your gay fans will abandon you. Your straight fans, well . . . do you even *have* any of them? The fact is that your base of support will disappear overnight. Poof! And there goes your career . . . your money . . . your home . . ." He sat back and looked thoughtfully at Romero. "You know, Romeo, having this tape fall into my hands might be the best thing that could have happened to you."

Romero's eyes crossed. Was this guy crazy?

Seeing he was not going to get a reply, Hadley leaned forward and said, "Others wouldn't protect you, Romeo. But I will. If someone unscrupulous had come across this tape— those bottom-feeders at 'Page Six,' for instance—you wouldn't be having this discussion. They would have plastered stills from the tape over the front page for weeks without even having the decency to give you advance warning." He sat back again. "I can see the headlines now: GAY-FOR-PAY ROMEO IN STRAIGHT SEX SHOCKER! And, yes, they *would* use an exclamation point."

Romero sat quietly, not really looking at anything, wanting nothing more than to get the tape and get back to the Hamptons. So Hadley continued to do the talking for both of them.

"Yes, thank God for me."

And he gently stroked the black tape cartridge that lay on the tablecloth, just out of Romeo Romero's reach.

Chapter Fifteen

Had they dawdled over dessert, or even made one last stop at the men's room, on their way out of the restaurant, Ian Hadley and Romeo Romero would have encountered an unshaved, graying man with a realistic-looking fake gun who would have forcibly stolen the tape, along with their wallets and watches to add a touch of verisimilitude. But after getting Chase's desperate call, Grant had a commuting nightmare coming into Manhattan from Jackson Heights, and missed their exit from the Four Seasons by mere minutes.

Chase figured that would happen, which was why he wasn't especially shocked when the editor and actor walked into the office a few minutes before two. Spontaneous criminal acts like that seldom worked out for him and Grant. They would have been abysmal failures as run-of-the-mill street criminals eking out a living on random muggings.

Both men were wearing coats, but Chase didn't bother wondering which of them had the tape. He knew Ian Hadley wouldn't let it out of his hands until the transaction was complete. If even then.

With barely a word to him they walked into Hadley's office. Chase heard the door lock behind them, and then watched sadly as the blinds descended over the windows, sealing off the fishbowl.

Okay, he thought, *there are still options. If Romero has the tape, Grant could catch up to him on the street outside. Or if Hadley keeps it in his office, I've still got another chance. All hope is not lost.*

But then J. P. Hunt walked up to Hadley's office door—without so much as a sidelong glance at Chase—and, folding his arms, took up sentry duty. And Chase knew whatever his options were, they wouldn't be exercised this afternoon.

Inside that office, Ian Hadley was tiring of toying with his prey. Romeo Romero had fallen into a sullen silence almost the moment they met at the Four Seasons, and Hadley was getting bored with him. The whole point of meeting for lunch was to draw out his pain, but without anger, or tears, or prayers, it wasn't any fun for Hadley. Now he just wanted to get past the main event and move on.

Not as much as Romero wanted to move on, but close enough.

Hadley toggled the switch on his desk and the screen descended. Then he popped the videotape into his VCR and dimmed the lights.

Twenty minutes later, the lights were turned back up. Hadley glanced over at Romero and, sure enough, the actor was ashen. This was going to be easier than he had hoped.

"So you see the problem here," he said, and Romero nodded, not making eye contact with anything but the aquarium. "If this tape were to get out, well . . . like I said earlier, it would mean the destruction of your career. Romeo, everything you've worked forty years to build would be destroyed within days."

"What do you want, Ian?" His voice was weak.

Hadley laughed. "I assumed that was obvious."

Romero nodded his understanding of the unspoken blackmail demand. "And the tape? I will get possession of it, of course."

"Of course." The smile disappeared. "As soon as I'm adequately compensated for my silence and discretion, you will get the tape." He paused, then: "Can I ask you a question, Romeo? Why did you do it?"

Romero finally looked at him. His eyes were tired. "Because I am a human being, and I'm weak."

"Hmm." Hadley tented his fingers on the desk and stared at them. "That's interesting. You see, I've always been fascinated by the things people do to self-destruct. And you, well . . . you especially fascinate me. Thirty years out of a forty-year acting career spent pretending to be gay, just to keep your calling alive. And then to almost have it undone by an indiscreet romp in a hot tub, well . . . that's fascinating."

"That's one way to look at it."

"And you know what made it worse, Romeo? You know what made the thing so sordid?"

"What?"

"That Speedo you were wearing. I mean, *what* were you thinking, man?"

Romeo Romero had no response to that question. When he saw himself on the grainy tape, he was more embarrassed by his Fashion Don't than the fact that he was taped having sex with a woman.

To change the subject away from the Speedo, as much as anything else, Romero asked, "Shall we discuss the financial terms?"

"If you'd like." He jotted a number on a piece of paper and slid it across his desk to the actor, who barely lifted an eyebrow at the amount.

"And for this number, I get the tape back and this incident goes away."

"You have my word."

Romero thought about that. The number was a big one, but it didn't really matter. He would have happily agreed to a number ten times that amount without losing his cool. Still, he felt he had to bargain a bit.

"Okay, but I assume you want cash?" Hadley nodded. "It

will take me a few days to get that much cash together. Maybe a week or so, maybe a little bit longer. I trust that won't derail our arrangement?"

"No," said Hadley. "I completely understand."

"Sunday. My house in Water Mill. I will have your first installment."

Hadley thought about that. He wasn't inclined to deal on enemy turf—and make no mistake about it, Romeo Romero was the enemy in this instance—but a quick drive out to the Hamptons might be pleasant, so he smiled and said, "Very good."

"I want one more thing thrown in."

Hadley's smile flickered. "Try me."

"I know that *The Eye* and 'Between the Streets' are not particularly known as gay-friendly, but I'm hosting a huge Memorial Day fund-raiser for the Eastern Seaboard LGBTQI Pride organization this coming Saturday—"

"Hold on," Hadley interrupted. "I get the LGBT, but what are the Q and I?"

"Q is for 'queer' and 'questioning' . . ."

"Ah, so you get sort of a twofer on the Q."

"Uh . . . yes. And the I is for 'intersex.' "

"Intersex?"

"It usually means sexually ambiguous. Sometimes applied to the transgendered community, too."

"So . . ." Hadley scratched his head. "So it's like the transgendereds get both a T and an I."

"No, not really. You see, in some cases—" Romero abruptly stopped, realizing that it was a pointless discussion to have with this man.

"I'll give you credit," said Hadley. "You're quite educated on your sexual abnormalities. Especially for a straight man. No wonder you're their celebrity spokesmodel."

Romero bit his lip until he regained his composure, but finally managed to continue. "Anyway, about this fund-raiser.

A lot of famous people will be there, and I'd like some publicity. Especially since I seem to have had a shot fired across my bow on my commitment to homosexuality, and I'd like to reinforce my position as the world's most famous gay actor."

That would be easy enough, thought Hadley. Plus it would give BtS a lot of fresh fodder for mockery over upcoming months. The same old wire-service articles and photos were getting stale. And anyway, wasn't Ian Hadley a man who wanted to break his routine?

"I'll send a photographer," he said. "And I'll even run something in the column tomorrow. A little advance publicity for your efforts."

Forty-five minutes after the men entered the office, the meeting was over. First Chase saw the blinds ascend, then J. P. stepped aside as the door was unlocked and Romero and Hadley walked out of the fishbowl.

Chase tried to figure out who had the tape while they shook hands just yards away from him. Nothing was obvious.

Finally, Hadley said, "J. P., would you escort Mr. Romero back to his car?" And Chase thought, *Great, that's another thing we can't do now* as he started text-messaging Grant to make sure he didn't try to mug Romero outside the building, which they had considered to be an option up until that point.

He hit Send and looked up just in time to see the elevator doors close, sending Romeo Romero and J. P. Hunt down to street level. Seconds later, a ding announced the arrival of a different elevator . . . and a roundish, disheveled man in a coffee-stained trench coat that had seen better decades stepped off. Chase glanced at his watch to confirm the time, because that man could only be Will Whitcomb. He looked like his voice.

Hadley, who had been whistling, stopped when he laid eyes on the man.

"Ian, thanks for meeting me," said Whitcomb, managing a smile and extending his hand.

Hadley looked at him, ignoring the outstretched hand, and a sneer crept across his face.

Which wasn't the look Whitcomb had anticipated.

"Oh, yes," he said. "Whitcomb. I had almost managed to forget about you."

The short, sweaty man's face turned red. "But *you* called *me*." He thought about that, then decided to make it sound more professional. "*Your* people called *my* people."

Hadley nodded reluctantly. "So I did. Or rather . . . so *they* did." With one more nod, he said, "Very well. Come into my office and we'll talk."

Whitcomb charged into the office, a smirk of victory on his face and the tail of the trench coat flapping behind him. Hadley followed him without enthusiasm.

Since he didn't see how any of this concerned him, and since the thought of even being in the same zip code with Will Whitcomb made his skin crawl, Chase asked Hadley, "Want me to close your door?"

He turned, and Chase was surprised to see him smile. It was a half-smile, but still it was a smile.

"Actually, I'd prefer that the door be left open. The office will need to be ventilated."

Chase laughed. He knew exactly what Hadley meant.

Except, he didn't.

Hadley began the long walk to his desk, where he would deal with this pest, but turned around once more after a few steps. "My metal wastepaper basket?"

"Oh yeah," said Chase. He collected it from beside his desk and handed it over, although he was surprised moments later when the fastidious, orderly Ian Hadley placed the basket directly in the center of his office, which was not where people usually put their trash.

He hadn't planned on listening in on the session between

Hadley and Whitcomb, but there was something about the wastepaper basket that piqued his interest, so he hovered near the doorway.

"Mr. Whitcomb," intoned Hadley, now seated in his comfortable leather desk chair, and Whitcomb leaned forward expectantly. This time, Hadley was not bothering with the dramatic lighting or other intimidation factors. He just wanted this man out of his life . . . but first he wanted to enjoy the destruction.

He continued. "As I suspected, the videotape you gave me was a fraud."

Wait a minute, thought Chase. Videotape? Whitcomb was the guy who found the tape?

"I don't know how you had the balls to try to pass it off to me as authentic, but you did. Kudos; some day perhaps you'll become a publicist. But *I* am personally offended. *Insulted*, even."

Whitcomb, up until that point still trapped in his dreams of getting something—a hundred? Fifty? A dollar?—out of "Between the Streets," began sputtering. "But . . . but . . . but . . ."

Hadley stood and leaned forward, seeming to stretch across the desk toward Will Whitcomb. In reality, he made sure to keep an appropriate amount of distance, because he really didn't want to be flecked with any of Whitcomb's spittle.

"Mr. Whitcomb, I invited you here today to put this matter to rest once and for all."

"But . . . but . . ."

"Mr. Whitcomb, your attempt to defame Romeo Romero and defraud the *New York Eye* ends right now." With that, Hadley seemed to produce a tape cartridge out of thin air, although it had been sitting unnoticed, half hidden by memos on top of his desk, for the entire time he had been talking. If he had to waste a dramatic flourish on this loser, that was as good as he was willing to give.

The tape! It's right there! Chase was so close to rushing Hadley and snatching the tape that he could almost feel his legs moving. Except they weren't, of course.

"*Here* is what I think of your tape." Ian Hadley walked around his desk, past Will Whitcomb, and up to the metal trash can. And then . . . he began pulling the grayish brown tape from the cartridge, letting it loop in ribbons as it unspooled into the receptacle.

"No!" gasped Whitcomb, but he was helpless, paralyzed in his chair.

Chase thought the same thing.

And then . . .

Oh no, thought Chase. *Oh God, no!*

Hadley took a disposable lighter from his pocket and flicked once. The flame touched the tape and fizzled for a half second before bursting to life, at which point he dropped it into the can along with the cartridge.

Whitcomb could finally move. He tried to throw his chubby body on the fire, but only got as far as almost—but not quite—tipping over the trash can before Hadley restrained him.

"It's over, Mr. Whitcomb," he said, very crisply. "Now all of us—you, me, and especially poor Romeo Romero—can go back and live our lives."

The fire was getting smoky, and Chase finally understood why Hadley wanted the ventilation. For his part, realizing he was getting flames that were a bit more intense than he had anticipated, Hadley put out the fire with the water from a nearby vase before the sprinklers went off.

There was silence in the room for a moment, until the stunned Whitcomb began fuming.

"You know what was on that tape, Hadley! You're cutting me out of the deal!"

"Deal?"

Whitcomb briefly considered taking what was left of the

tape and shopping it around. Maybe he'd have better luck with *The Peeper* through sheer persistence. But when he looked in the metal can, all he saw were blackened tendrils that used to be tape. Not a useful frame in the entire basket. Even *he* could see that.

But that wouldn't stop him from putting on a show, and he did, stumbling around the office and shouting mostly unintelligibly, except for the expletives, which came through loud and clear. Finally, he steadied himself against the back of a chair, took a few deep breaths in a partially successful attempt to regain his composure, and pointed a finger across the room at Ian Hadley.

"I'll be back, Hadley. You'll regret this one day."

And with that, he was finally gone.

"It's quite all right, Charlie," Hadley said a short time later, after Whitcomb's departure, noting the glum expression on his assistant's face. "Just some old video I no longer need."

Chase felt like crying. "But . . ."

"And . . ." He winked conspiratorially, because he felt like he was buddies with his new hire at BtS. "Nothing anyone else needs to know about. Do you understand me, Charlie?"

Chase nodded dully. "Yes, I understand."

"Good, then." Hadley smiled broadly. "Charlie, I just made a quarter million dollars today, and I think a celebration is in order. If anyone needs me—*really* needs me, not just wants to annoy me—I'll be at Galan's." He paused. "I don't suppose your aunt Lisa will be there."

"Doubt it," Chase said, still stunned. "Probably at softball practice."

Hadley gave him a strange look, but simply said, "Pity."

Chase didn't quite know how he was going to break the news to Grant, but he knew it was not going to be a pleasant conversation.

Chapter Sixteen

"You want the good news first? Or the bad news?"

"Start me with the good news," said Grant, "and we'll take it from there."

"Okay, but don't get too excited when I tell you I found the tape."

The line was silent for a few long beats, while Grant tried to prepare himself for the bad news. Prepared, he said, "And?"

"And I just watched Ian Hadley burn it to a crisp."

"Yeah," said Grant, in a voice just above a whisper. "Yeah, that qualifies as bad news. You'd better start from the beginning."

After Chase filled him in on the very eventful day at the office, Grant said, "So Hadley ends up being the only one who makes out on this thing, right?"

"Right," said Chase. "To the tune of two hundred fifty thousand dollars. Which is a nice way to make out."

Grant was silent for a moment. "All right. I think I've figured out what we've been doing wrong."

"You have?"

"I have. See, we're used to dealing with people like us, but these people are on a higher level of criminal. I mean, compared to them, we're on a par with that Combover guy . . ."

"Combover?" Chase thought. "No, *Whitcomb*."

"Whitcomb. Whatever. Anyway, see what happened to a

small-time crook who tried to mess with Ian Hadley? Not pretty, was it?"

"No. But we're not—"

"No, we're not as pathetic as Comb—*Whit*comb. And we can even outsmart the normal rich guys. But these people—Hadley, Romero—they've spent decades playing sort of a variation of the thing we do. Ian Hadley lies before he brushes his teeth in the morning. Romeo Romero has spent thirty years getting rich and famous by faking his homosexuality. This is the type of thing we're not used to. We're used to dupes like your Internet dates, not people who all they do is lie and cheat."

Chase had to agree with that assessment. But . . . "Okay, so what do we do?"

"We accept the fact that this job is bigger than the two of us, plus Lisa every now and then to pop her buttons. We've got to get a gang together and do this right."

"A gang?" Chase almost laughed. "Every now and then we bring in an extra hand like Lisa, but where are we going to get a gang?"

Grant thought about that. "Well . . . Lisa is already in. Jamie Brock is expecting a cut, and so is Paul Farraday. Let's make them all work for it."

"I dunno, Grant . . ."

"It's that, or we take our losses and get out. Deeper in debt, I might add, especially since you took the week off from The Gross."

"I wish you wouldn't call it that."

"Sorry. Force of habit. So let's get everyone together tonight to talk this over. Maybe if we toss some ideas around, we can come up with something. We won't have the tape, but we're some of the only people in the world who know Romeo Romero's secret. There's got to be some way to make this pay off for us."

"Okay. We can talk, at least."

"One more thing," said Grant, before he hung up. "If I give you the phone numbers, would you mind calling?"

Yeah, Chase said, he already knew one of his jobs was to work the phones.

Their small kitchen felt unimaginably smaller that evening with not only Grant and Chase crammed into it, which was usually more than enough people, but also the rest of their newly formed gang: Paul Farraday, Jamie Brock, and Lisa Cochrane. And Lisa had brought her girlfriend, Mary Beth Reuss, which—given her oil-and-water relationship with Grant—was especially troublesome in such tight quarters.

Chase had brewed a pot of coffee, but it sat untouched. Instead, they decided as soon as Farraday arrived to break open the hard stuff. Which was Farraday's idea, of course.

Farraday had been the hardest one to lure into the gang, until Grant finally explained that he wasn't going to see anything—not $5,000; not even $1,000—unless he bought in. In exchange, Grant offered to up his share to twenty grand if the gang figured out a way to pull off a job on Romero, figuring that he definitely would need an extra pair of hands and probably would need a driver, so it was a small price to pay.

As for Jamie, Grant reassured him the one-third finder's fee was still on the table, since he did film the original video, even though he subsequently lost it. Lisa's share they could work out later.

"We should've had a Plan B," Grant said, gripping a Corona and staring at the battered kitchen table, the exact wood of which was no longer discernible after years of spills, nicks, and scalding. "Rule Number One: never put all your eggs in one basket."

"We *had* a Plan B," said Lisa, who was standing in the corner of the kitchen by the open window, doing what she could with a Marlboro Light to smoke up her already smoky voice. "If he wouldn't hire Chase, I was going to seduce him. Remember?"

"You were *not!*" shrieked Mary Beth.

"Not really. Just enough to get into his office, get the tape, and get out."

"But you're a *lesbian!*"

Jamie, who had been mercifully silent to that point, decided to pipe up. "It was sort of like an acting job, Mary Beth. You know, like Jodie Foster acts like she's into Richard Gere in a movie, but that doesn't mean she really is. Or like how that Will guy, from the book *Will and Grace*, was played by a straight man—"

"*Will and Grace* wasn't a book," said Grant. "It was a TV show."

"But it was a book first." Jamie looked around the kitchen. "Wasn't it?"

The closest there came to an answer was when Chase whispered into Grant's ear, "Let's bring a top-notch gang together! Good idea, baby!"

"Shut up." To the rest of them, Grant said, "Okay, we had a shortage of women, so we asked Lisa to take one for the team, and she did. Now let's—"

"Why couldn't Chase have been the girl?" asked Mary Beth, who obviously didn't want to let it go. Probably, thought Grant, just to annoy him. "We know he does your airport scams in drag."

Grant looked at Chase. "You told them?"

"Uh . . ." Chase was embarrassed. "One night, we were out having a few drinks, and maybe it slipped . . ."

Grant again addressed the others. "If this Hadley guy grabbed a balloon or a penis, the plan wasn't gonna work, which is why we needed a *real* woman. Now can we get back on topic? The fact is that the tape is gone."

"Burned to a crisp," said Chase.

"Burned to a crisp. So we have to figure out how to use what we know about Romeo Romero *without* the tape. This is a big secret he's got, so he'll probably do almost anything to keep it under wraps."

"Oh, why bother?" Lisa exhaled the smoke from her Marlboro Light into the airshaft, where it was no doubt annoying Mrs. Palmiere from 4C, not that anyone cared, then flicked the still-lit butt into the darkness. "We gave it a shot, Lambert. And now at least you know you can always get Chase into 'Between the Streets.' Good to know for future reference."

"Yeah," he grunted. "Good to know. If I ever want to meet Lindsay Lohan. But it would be really helpful if someone in this room could figure out how we can get this scheme back on track."

They sat in silence for a few minutes, each lost in regret for what could have been. It was not surprising that Mary Beth broke the silence, but it *was* surprising that her contribution was actually meaningful.

"Can I ask a question?" she said, and continued without waiting for an answer. "Why did you need that tape?"

Grant scoffed. "Because without the tape, we've got nothing."

"No, I get that. But why *that* tape?"

"You know of another?"

Mary Beth shook her head. "It just seems to me that if Jamie could make one tape, maybe . . . well, maybe he can make another."

That caught Grant's attention. "We make another?"

"Sure." Mary Beth, to that point mostly uninterested in the blackmail scheme, except when it came to Lisa's possible seduction of a *man*, began to come alive. "We already know that Romeo Romero is straight, right? At least according to what Jamie tells us."

"It's a fact," said Jamie.

"Yeah, okay. *Hopefully* it is. Anyway, all we have to do is get a girl to seduce him while we get it on tape, and we've got our own personal blackmail material. No dealing with 'Between the Streets' or anyone else. *We* own it; no one else."

They sat looking at each other across the small kitchen for a few seconds, until Grant took a swig of his beer and said, "Pretty much impossible."

"Well, it happened before."

"Jamie was lucky. We can't count on that kind of luck again."

"Hey!" shouted Jamie, in weak self-defense that dematerialized as soon as it was clear he had nothing more to say.

Mary Beth sat back and crossed her arms. There was sarcasm in her voice. "I thought you were the big problem solver, Lambert."

"Yeah, well you've certainly thrown out a big problem, honey. Bigger than I'm used to. First, we were lucky getting to Hadley. It's going to be next to impossible to get to Romero. He's a big celebrity and we're just a bunch of nothings sitting around a kitchen table in Queens. Even with Jamie, it was a fluke he got into Romero's house." He turned and eyed Jamie. "The people who got you into his house. You've probably already burned those bridges, right?"

"Uh . . ." was all Jamie had to say in response, so Grant turned back to Mary Beth.

"Second, the guy has already had a heads-up. He's gonna be on guard, so the Ian Hadleys of the world—or us, for that matter—don't get the chance to blackmail him again."

She rolled her eyes. "Some problem solver you are."

"Some problems," he said, "aren't meant to be solved."

And so he thought—so all of them thought—for the rest of that evening and into the morning. They had their gang, and even a halfway decent idea, but no way to make it all come together. The easy thing would have been to snatch the tape, but—since the tape no longer existed—that idea was no longer on the table. And although Mary Beth's idea had merit, it would be next to impossible to get close enough to Romeo Romero to pull it off.

It was an unsolvable problem, all right.

Until the next day's edition of *The Eye* hit the newsstands.

Chapter Seventeen

Grant didn't usually drop by Lisa Cochrane's office for two reasons. First, because as occasional business partners—with that business, when it occurred, being of an illicit nature—it wasn't a smart thing to do. Second, because he tended to avoid Midtown Manhattan unless there was a job to do. Too many people. Too many eyes.

And third, because she told him she'd crack his skull with a baseball bat if he made a routine out of it, and Grant knew she had a powerful swing.

But after he saw the item in *The Eye*, he figured it was appropriate to make an exception to his rule, which is how he found himself walking into a nondescript office building at Madison Avenue and East Fifty-seventh Street and riding an elevator to the offices of Lum Malverne Luxury Real Estate on the twenty-eighth floor.

He was about to tell the receptionist his name when Lisa walked out of an office carrying a thick folder, glared at him, and said: "I thought I heard your voice. This had better be good."

"It is," he said, motioning with one hand to the copy of *The Eye* tucked under his other arm.

She sighed. "Okay, Mr. Riley, let's go into my office and discuss the place on Lexington Avenue again. But I already told you the sellers aren't budging."

Grant frowned. "Riley? Sellers?" But then he saw Lisa motioning urgently at the fortunately oblivious receptionist and he got it. "Well then, Ms. Cochrane, I hope I won't take up too much of your time."

"That makes two of us."

He followed her down the hall to her private office, and she closed the door behind them. It was roomy but stark in there, all glass desktops and glass tabletops and glass windows and white walls.

"Are you sure you're a professional criminal?" she asked, when the private office was truly private.

"You didn't tell me I had to use an alias. If I was supposed to do a bit, you should have warned me in advance."

"I would have. *If*, that is, I knew you were coming here."

"You know how I feel about phones."

She shook her head. "I have a busy day, Lambert, so get down to business." She sat in a very streamlined black chair on one side of the glass desk; he sat in an identical chair on the other. "Why are you here?"

He took *The Eye* out from under his arm, opened it to the right page, and set it in front of her on the desk.

"What am I looking for?" she asked.

He pointed. She read. And when she was done, she said, "Oh, Christ, Lambert. Not Romeo Romero again! Can we please drop this topic? Forever?"

"But—"

She pushed the paper back toward his side of the desk. "Look, we can't touch the guy, so let's stop obsessing about it. I love my girlfriend, but if you think it's going to be that easy to find a woman to waltz into Romeo Romero's house and seduce him, you're as crazy as she is. And I've already been down that road; I can't do it again." She pushed the paper another few inches toward him. "Take this away."

"Now, Lisa . . ."

"Get it out of my office, Lambert. And follow it."

But Grant didn't move. If Lisa didn't see the opportunity that presented itself in the pages of *The Eye*—in the form of an announcement that Romeo Romero was hosting a Memorial Day Pool Party fund-raiser for the Eastern Seaboard LGBTQI Pride at his very exclusive Water Mill estate—then he'd have to convince her of the merits. And he'd have to do it fast, because the party was on Saturday night, just three days away.

"You see, the thing about an"—and here he had to read from the invitation—"an LGBT . . . uh . . . Q . . . I event, especially a major one like this—"

"By the way," she said. "I get the LGBT stuff, but what are Q and I?"

"Queer, I think. And, uh . . ." He shrugged. "Intelligent?"

She shook her head. "Seldom do non-answers answer my questions so thoroughly."

"Here's my idea," he said, hoping that by speaking quickly, he could get the words out before the baseball bat appeared. "We send two good-looking people to this fund-raiser. A hot boy and a hot girl. And both of them are geared up with digital cameras, maybe tape recorders . . . you know, make it like a police sting. Except the opposite, obviously. You follow?"

"I follow," she said, with only the most barely perceptible interest, which—since there was at least *that* much interest there—Grant found encouraging.

"So when the hot girl gets Romero, and the hot boy gets rejected, and we get it on film, we've got all the evidence we need to prove he's not gay. Then we blackmail him, and walk away with his money." He slapped a hand on his knee. "See? It will work."

"It *could* work."

He shrugged. "Okay, 'could.' But probably will."

She shook her head and frowned, and in her smoky voice said, "You're like one of those people who are always surprised they didn't win the lottery, aren't you." The frown and smokiness both deepened as she continued. "Lambert, I don't know where to start. There are so many holes in your plan it sounds like Jamie Brock thought it up. But let's start with the big one: what if Romeo Romero isn't interested in either your hot boy *or* your hot girl? What if he's got something else going on there? Like, he already has a girlfriend or something."

"The beauty of this plan," he said, "is that both of our colleagues will be ready to capture anything that happens. And if nothing happens during the party, they could just hide themselves in the house—"

"I am *not* hearing this."

"—and sneak around later that night. If Romero's got a girlfriend, then they take a picture of *that*. Get whatever we need and get out of there."

"With Romero's home security system? With maybe even armed guards? Are you nuts?"

"I figured we'd take a ride out there before the party and check out the system. It'll have to be off—or at least partly disabled—during the party, with all those people coming and going. It shouldn't be that hard to keep it off for the rest of the night if we can figure what kind of system he's got."

"Another job entrusted to your boy and girl seductress/ spies, I assume."

"Probably."

She moaned.

"Now, I'll admit there are some details we have to work out. Who we'll get to go in there, for example. At first I thought Chase could do it, but we used him at *The Eye*, and Romero has seen him, so that wouldn't be smart. And we probably shouldn't use you." She nodded. "And getting around security is another problem. But this just came to me a little over an hour ago, so I haven't had a lot of time to think through all the steps."

"It sounds like a nightmare."

"Lisa," he said, as he stood up and collected his newspaper from the desk, "after twenty-five years of this business, I know nightmares. And this is not a nightmare. It's a challenge." With that, he walked to the door, put his hand on the knob, and—as he twisted—winked at her and said, "And, Ms. Cochrane, tell the owners from Lexington Avenue that I *always* get what I want. And I want this very badly."

When he was gone, she realized she had a pounding headache.

Lisa would hear from Grant again that day. Not that seeing him would make her measurably happier, but it would happen.

First, though, Grant called Chase, who was a few hours into his third day at the office. Even though the tape was gone, they still held hope that Ian Hadley might be a source of information; also, Chase wasn't getting paid for his leave from Groc-O-Rama, so they needed the income.

"You see that thing in the column this morning?" Grant asked.

"In 'Between the Streets'? No, I haven't read it yet."

So Grant read it to him, and when he finished, he said, "I figure if we can get some people into that party, maybe we can use Mary Beth's idea to entrap Romero. What do you think?"

Chase agreed, and—since Grant was standing outside Lisa's building, talking against the wind into the cell phone, which only made the "talking on the phone" experience more miserable to him—clicked on his web browser. Seconds later the Eastern Seaboard LGBTQI Pride Web site opened up.

"Good news or bad news, Grant?" asked Chase, after he

clicked on the Events button and a new page opened, advertising their Tenth Annual Pool Party fund-raiser at Romero's place.

Grant didn't like this "good/bad" game much, but again opted for good.

"Tickets are still available."

"Yeah," said Grant, "that is good. Okay, so what's the bad news."

Chase told him the ticket price.

"Shit." And then there was silence.

"Uh . . . Grant? Baby?"

"I'm here. Okay, here's what I need you to do. Call Lisa at her office and tell her that Mr. Riley's on his way back up . . ."

She nodded solemnly when she found him in the reception area and said, "Please come back to my office, Mr. Riley." And she kept it entirely professional until the door was closed and her face turned red.

"What is it, Lambert? *Why* do you feel the need to bother me today?"

"There's another problem," said Grant.

Lisa sighed. "With you, it seems there always is. So what now?"

"The tickets. I can't afford them."

"How much?"

"Twenty-five hundred."

She whistled. "That's over a thousand dollars per ticket. Pretty pricey."

"No," he said. "Twenty-five each. Meaning this thing is gonna run five grand for two tickets."

There was a long pause before she replied.

"Yeah, Lambert, I can do math. But Christ . . . five thousand dollars? That's a lot of money."

"I know. Money that I don't have."

And Lisa understood. "But money that I *do* have, right?"

"Right."

She shook her head. "You greatly overestimate how much money I can throw around."

"But you have investments, right? Think of *this* as an investment."

She closed her eyes. "Grant Lambert, I can't believe I am letting you talk me into this, when I'm smart enough to know better. But . . . okay, I'll do it."

"You'll do it?" He was surprised to hear the surprise in his voice.

"On one condition. I want a fair cut of the blackmail money."

"What's fair?"

"Same as before. Twenty-five percent."

"*Twenty*—" He had to catch his breath. "Come on, Lisa, this is the score I need to meet the cost of living. This is the big one! If I shortchange myself on this, I'll have to go back to the riskier stuff. Uh . . . I'll have to go back to it *sooner*. You want to feel responsible if I end up in jail because I had to take a risk that I wouldn't have had to take if I could have lived longer on the Romeo Romero money?"

"Twenty-five percent."

"Most bankers get double, so if you put up five, you get back ten. Tell you what . . . we've been friends for a long time, so I'll bump it up to twenty thou. Four-to-one. That's a great return."

"No," she said flatly. "Listen, Grant, when all is said and done, I *do* have a real job. I don't need to break the law to make ends meet."

He sat down, grabbed a pad and a pen, and started doing the math. "So if we blackmail Romero for a quarter million like Hadley did, and you get twenty-five percent, and I promised a one-third finder's fee to Jamie Brock and money to Paul Farraday . . ." Grant worked the numbers for a minute, then said, "Shit, that means Chase and I make less than eighty thousand dollars for taking almost all of the risk and doing most of the work." He set the pen down. "Does that seem fair to you?"

She flashed him a tight smile, then picked up the pad and pen, jotted something down, and handed it to him.

"What's with the zero?" he asked.

"The amount of money you'll get from Romero if I don't lay out money for your tickets."

"I think I understand. You drive a hard bargain."

"I'm a Realtor, Lambert. That's what I'm paid to do."

He stole another glance at Lisa's scrawled zero. That was definitely not a good number. "But not even eighty thousand . . ."

"That's your problem, Grant. And I mean that in the nicest way. First, I don't know why you promised Jamie one-third. The idiot didn't even have the tape when he came to you."

"A moment of weakness, back when I thought this was going to be easier. You know, the simpler times a few days ago, before we knew *The Eye* had the tape."

"Live and learn," she said. "I'm also not quite sure why Farraday is getting that much money. It's not like he brought you the tape."

"But he tried. And I think we'll need him, and the twenty will be enough to keep him drunk and happy."

"Well, the way I see it, the second I lay out five thousand dollars for your tickets, I've already done more for this enterprise than either of them, so I think I should be rewarded appropriately. And twenty-five percent is, in my mind, appropriate."

He was defeated, and he knew it. He would have to agree to Lisa Cochrane's demand if his plan was going to work. Still . . . *his share would be less than $80,000.* That grated on him.

Until the thought occurred to him that he was playing by

the wrong rules. He was playing by Ian Hadley's rules. It was Hadley who had set an arbitrary blackmail level of $250,000, not Grant.

Again with the pad and pen, he reworked the numbers, and this time he was happier with the result.

"Why are you smiling?" she asked.

"Everyone is going to be smiling," he said. "Because you're about to double your take from this scheme. Jamie, too. And Farraday will still be happy."

"I'm not sure I follow."

"We're going to blackmail Romeo Romero for a half million dollars."

"Ah. *Now* I understand."

Chapter Eighteen

With the money issue resolved—at least temporarily—Grant could move to the next stage of planning. Namely, who could he pay off with two expensive tickets to a high-cost party, and maybe a couple of hundred on the side, who could also be trusted to do what needed to be done *and* keep their mouths shut.

It was at times like this he regretted wasting Chase on the infiltration of Ian Hadley's offices. Chase would have been the perfect man to send to the party to try to seduce Romeo Romero, but now it was too risky he'd be recognized. No, they needed a new man to send in . . . and Grant was drawing a blank.

And he hadn't even started thinking about the girl. And they only had three days. And if Grant Lambert was the type of man to panic, he'd be a puddling mess right now.

But he wasn't. He kept his cool and thought things over, and finally knew where he had to turn.

When Chase arrived home from Groc-O-Rama that evening, Grant was waiting for him, and he barely had a chance to close the door before Grant asked, "Remember that kid you used to hang out with? Jared or something like that?"

Chase knew damned well that Grant knew the kid's name was Jared, which made him wary. When he wanted to, Grant could be a convincing actor, but the two of them had been together for a long time and he immediately saw through the act.

"Jared . . . Jared . . ." Chase scratched his chin thoughtfully, then shrugged. "I'm drawing a blank."

"If you think I'm going to start accusing you of having a crush again, well . . . you're wrong." Grant figured that was what Chase was up to, because a few years earlier when Jared had briefly entered their lives, that's exactly what he accused Chase of having. And he wasn't convinced he had been wrong, although it was now ancient history.

"Oh, *Jared!*" Chase was enjoying his moment. "Now I remember him. Yeah, he was a real cutie. Really adorable . . . those green eyes . . . and that hot little *body*!"

Grant knew he was paying for the past and held his tongue. He wasn't an excitable man in the worst of situations, but—in this particular case—he had a goal that kept him focused.

"That's the kid. Think he might be available for a job?"

Now it was Chase's turn to see the light. And he was delighted, as always, by his boyfriend's flash of brilliance.

"You want Jared to seduce Romeo Romero!"

"No, I want him to *try* to seduce Romeo Romero, but fail."

"That's what I meant."

"So do you think you can track him down?"

Chase didn't think twice. "That shouldn't be too hard."

"And," Grant added, "do you think he can keep his mouth shut?"

Chase *did* think twice. "That could be a problem. Cash would probably help make it happen."

"It always does. I was thinking we give him five, along with the ticket."

Chase shook his head. "Better make it ten."

It took a moment for Chase's words to sink in. "Wait, I was talking hundreds. You're talking *thousands*?"

Chase was surprised. "You weren't?" He paused, then chuckled at Grant's expression, which was that of a man re-calculating the lower amount of his share of a blackmail scheme, although Chase didn't know that. He just thought it was a comically perplexed expression, so he continued. "Five hundred—hell, five *thousand*—means nothing to a lot of these young guys. If they need it that badly, some sugar daddy will be there for them, and they'll never even bother to call him back. Ten thou, well . . . now you're starting to talk the language of silence and discretion."

Grant raised an eyebrow. "How do you know this? You're only a few years younger than me."

"Yeah, but they were crucial years, baby. That's why you were late to the Internet, home computers, blond highlights, and all that other fun stuff."

"Sometimes you make me feel old."

"Would a blow job help?"

Grant laughed, despite himself. "Yeah. But *only* after you call the kid. We've got work to do before we play."

After a meeting with "the kid" was secured, and after that other business was taken care of, and after a few hours of sleep, Grant had to start thinking again. It was one thing—and a difficult enough thing, at that—to come up with gay male temptation to fling at Romeo Romero. It would be quite another to find the girl who would prove once and for all that the actor was a closet heterosexual.

Because the sad fact was that, of their few female acquaintances, all were middle-aged and almost all—Lisa being a rare exception—were very butch lesbians. Which he didn't see as a successful component in the seduction of Romeo Romero.

Grant was sitting in bed, dark circles under his eyes and deep in thought, when Chase awoke the next morning. He didn't even have to ask; Grant just offered.

"A girl. I can't think of a girl. And we're down to two days." He sighed. "You might have to cover this gig in drag after all."

"Uh . . . no." But Chase couldn't think of a woman, either, although he helpfully offered. "Maybe Jared knows someone."

"By the time this is over, Jared is already gonna know more than I want him to know. The last thing we need is for him *and* a girlfriend to get into this too deep."

"Agreed." Chase laid his head back into the pillow for a few minutes and tried to think through the problem, although mostly what he thought was that coffee would help. Finally he crawled out of bed and headed for the kitchen.

Ten minutes later, when he returned with two hot mugs of coffee, Grant still hadn't found a solution. But Chase thought he might have an idea.

"What about Mary Beth?"

"Mary Beth?"

Chase laughed. "Lisa's girlfriend."

Grant frowned. "Lisa *Cochrane's* girlfriend? The twit?"

"Think about it," said Chase, as he sat on the edge of the bed and tried not to spill his coffee. "They're already in this, aren't they? And Mary Beth is definitely what you'd call a lipstick lesbian . . ."

"She's a twit. *And* a bitch!"

"Well, yeah. But she's *our* twit and bitch, Grant! She is totally part of Team Lisa, and since Lisa is already in this thing, why not use Mary Beth to further the cause? Look, she's a really hot girl . . . probably the type a straight guy like Romeo Romero would fall all over. Lisa sure does. And we'd be keeping it in the family, so to speak."

Grant thought about that. For maybe seven seconds.

"I don't like the idea."

"You don't like the idea? Or you don't like Mary Beth?"

"Exactly." Grant climbed out of bed and headed to the

bathroom, hopeful that a warm shower would stir his creative juices. He always did his best thinking in the shower.

And it was in the shower the thought occurred to him that,
well . . . maybe Mary Beth was a good idea. Or at least not a
horrible one, which—considering the options—elevated her
status considerably.

Fifteen minutes later, when he emerged from the bathroom
with a towel around his waist and headed for more coffee in
the kitchen, he held up one finger to Chase and said, "If this
Mary Beth thing doesn't work out, I'm blaming you."

Chase smiled. And then he got ready for another day playing the role of Charlie LaMarca at "Between the Streets."

At 5:30 that evening they were sitting with Jared Parsells
in his living room. Jared Parsells was smiling. Jared Parsells
always smiled. This was one of the problems Grant Lambert
had with him.

Another was the fact that he was named Jared Parsells. Or
rather, *not* named Jared Parsells.

Jared Parsells, he knew, was really Jerry Stanley. The kid
had actually changed his name—well, maybe not legally;
Grant didn't know that—to make it sound prettier, more attractive to gay men. That bothered him.

Okay, sure, Chase was really a Charles, but it was still in
the same family. Also, he loved Chase; he didn't particularly
even like Jerry Stanley, although he was trying not to show it
as they sat on a futon in this living room on West Fiftieth
Street in Manhattan's Hell's Kitchen neighborhood.

"Can I get anyone some herbal tea?" asked Jared/Jerry,
and Grant had another reason to hate him.

Chase and Grant passed. Politely.

"Nice place," said Chase, although it was only so-so, fur-
nished in a style about what you'd expect a twenty-five-year-
old with no discernible source of regular income to cobble
together.

"Don't you *love* it?" asked Jared, taking Chase's mild compliment to another dimension. "And only nineteen fifty-six a month!"

That was almost twice as much as Grant and Chase paid in Jackson Heights, just to live in a hotter neighborhood, and that made Grant smile. It meant that one night at Romeo Romero's mansion would pay five months of the kid's rent, which was going to look sweet to him when the offer was made.

Plus, he'd have enough left over to buy more herbal tea. Or maybe a *real* drink.

Jared sat on an ottoman pulled close to Chase and touched his hand, which Grant willed himself not to notice. "It has been so long since I've seen you," he gushed, then glanced at Grant as if to assure him, *hey, you're sort of included, too.*

Grant coughed into his hand and got down to business. "It's good to see you, too, Jerry"—wait, had he really said that? "*Jared!* So, how are you paying for this . . . *beautiful* apartment?"

Jared smiled. Perfect straight white teeth. "Odd jobs, here and there. A little of this, a little of that."

"Oh, the Penthouse?" Grant regretted insinuating that Jared was hanging out at Manhattan's premier young-men-on-the-make/old-men-wanting-to-make-them watering hole the minute the words escaped his lips, but, well . . . now it was out there. Like the "Jerry" remark. There was something about this kid that left him unable to keep his darker thoughts to himself.

He need not have worried. "I *love* the Penthouse. Hey, we should all go some night!"

"We should," said Chase quickly, before Grant had another opportunity to inflict damage. "In the meantime . . ." He glanced at his partner. "In the meantime, we have a proposition for you."

"A proposition?"

Jared was confused. He wasn't necessarily averse to three-somes, but the approach was usually a bit more subtle. Also, he was more than a little scared of Grant Lambert. That's why he was especially relieved when Chase continued.

"A *business* proposition."

"Ah." Jared thought about that. Then he thought again. A *business* proposition? He wasn't sure he knew what that meant. Fortunately, Chase was ready to clarify.

"We need you to seduce someone."

Jared thought a bit more. All this thinking was making him slightly dizzy. Finally he asked, "A man?"

"Yes."

Phew! *Finally* Jared was getting his equilibrium back.

"Because I'm better at seducing men. I just don't under-stand women. They're just so . . ."

"Yes," said Grant, jumping in not only to expedite the conversation, but to prevent Jared from saying something that he would regret hearing.

Jared fixed Grant with his surprisingly clear green eyes. "So, this seduction . . . does it involve anything illegal?"

"Uh . . . no, not at all." Feeling that further explanation might be required he added, "We've been asked to help a pri-vate detective friend, and you seemed like the right man for the job. That's all."

"Will I actually have to have sex with him?"

Grant and Chase looked at each other.

"If you want," said Grant, with a shrug, knowing—well, *hoping* at least—that it wouldn't happen. Because if it hap-pened, that meant there was a serious, fundamental flaw in their scheme.

"Yeah, it's not like a requirement," Chase added. He was thinking the same thing as Grant. "Mostly, we just need to try to get the guy in a compromising position and get a few photos. Anything else is up to you."

Jared reached for Chase's hand again, and again Grant

tried to pay it no attention. Even when it became clear that, this time, Grant really wasn't even in the room to the kid.

"I can do it," Jared told Chase. "If you want me to."

"Uh . . ."

He finally let go of Chase's hand, but it was only to lift his shirt up, exposing a stomach that had apparently been sandwich-free for the past decade.

"Think he'll like this?"

"Uh . . ."

"We don't need to see the goods," snarled Grant, conflicted between resentment at being cut out of the conversation and wanting to be cut out of the conversation. "That's between you and this guy."

But it was too late to stop Jared, who now was pulling the shirt over his head, showing off an upper body that could have been depicted in the dictionary next to the definition of "twink." Free of the shirt, he cocked one hip, put an insouciant half-pout on his lips, and said, "This is my 'seductive' look. Think it will work?"

"You've got 'looks'?" asked Grant.

"Oh sure," he said, answering Grant without taking his eyes off Chase. "I can do 'boyish.' I can do 'attitude.' "

"I'd like to see 'masculine.' "

Jared curled his lip, and Grant thought he looked about as masculine as Dakota Fanning, but let that go unsaid.

Chase tried to bring the conversation back. "Very nice, Jared. But . . ."

"You think so?" In fact, Chase did sort of think so, especially when Jared cocked that hip again and exposed some skin, and he suddenly realized that the kid probably wasn't wearing underwear. But wasn't going to say that. Especially in front of Grant, who he noticed seemed to be getting edgier. "I've been going to the gym."

Grant was pretty sure "going to the gym" meant going to the steam room, because it was clear only two of Jared's body parts were getting any workout, and neither of them were currently on display. Still, he again managed to keep his thoughts to himself. Although it was getting more and more difficult.

"Good for you." Chase forced himself to look away from Jared's hip. "Now, let's talk terms."

"Terms?"

"Money."

"Oh."

"Grant and I were figuring ten thousand."

Jared did some quick math in his head. Ten thousand dollars would pay for this apartment for . . . three? Four? Well, a few months, anyway. And all he had to do to earn the money was seduce a man, which would be easy. Plus, he had the bonus option of sleeping with him, if he thought he was hot, which he probably would since he had yet to meet a man with money who *wasn't* hot.

"I'm in," he said. "Just tell me what I have to do."

So they did. At least, they told him all they thought he should know for now, leaving out a few details, like the fact that their target was almost certainly a heterosexual.

When the name "Romeo Romero" finally came up, and Jared processed the information and realized he was the man he was to seduce, he beamed.

"Now *that*," he said, "is *hot*. You mean, if this works out for me I could be *Mr.* Romeo Romero?"

"Uh . . . I guess so," said Chase.

"Why not?" Grant shrugged.

And then Chase and Grant went back to talking, which Jared sort of listened to while he was daydreaming about how fabulous it would be to be internationally known as Romeo Romero's boy toy. Galas . . . yachts . . . mansions . . . expensive cars . . . *People* . . . *Us* . . . "Between the Streets" . . . red carpets . . . the Hamptons . . . St. Barts . . . Cannes . . . the Oscars . . .

His head only came out of the clouds when he heard Grant mention something about a girl.

"A girl?" he repeated, confused. "As in, a *real* girl?"

"Technically," said Grant, "as in, a real *woman*. But, yes, we're talking about the same thing."

"I don't understand."

Grant snarled. Just a little bit, but it was still a snarl. "Have you been listening?"

"Yes," Jared lied.

But Grant knew the kid had gone into a very private, probably very vacant space, so he again summarized the scheme for Jared's benefit. When he finished, Jared said:

"Okay, a few things have me confused."

"No doubt," said Grant, earning an elbow to the ribs from Chase.

"First of all, how am I supposed to look my best while I'm carrying a camera?"

Chase smiled broadly, as much to reassure Jared as to quiet Grant. "It's easy. These things are very small."

"Yeah, but if I'm going to seduce Romeo Romero, I want to show some flesh."

Grant and Chase looked at each other, then back at Jared's shirtless torso. He had to show *more* flesh?

"I have this outfit that's sure to get him into bed," Jared continued. "But there wouldn't be any room to hide the equipment."

Chase tried flashing his smile again, although this time there was a strain to it. "Then you'll have to wear something, uh . . . a little *looser.*"

Jared sulked. These old men obviously had no idea how to seduce a rich and powerful man. No wonder they lived in Jackson Heights.

"You'll be fine," said Grant. "And anyway, maybe Romero will be more interested in the girl than you."

"That's the other thing. I still don't understand why there has to be a girl there."

"Because," Chase said, and this time he didn't even try to smile, "like we said, we want to catch him with a woman, if possible."

"I get *that*. But I don't get why a gay dude would want to be with a woman. Except, you know, as friends."

Grant and Chase were walking a thin line between keeping Jared in the dark, where he'd be useless, and telling him too much, where he'd be dangerous. Chase kept them balancing on that line when he said:

"We think Romero's bisexual."

Jared looked confused. "Bisexual? You mean, he's into guys *and* girls?"

"That would be how you'd define bisexual," muttered Grant.

A confident look came to Jared's face. He smiled and said, "Bisexual men are just gay guys who are afraid to come out. Meaning, he's mine."

"Uh . . . yeah, okay," said Chase. "Just remember we want to catch him with a woman. As soon as we lock that in, you get your ten thousand and you're free to do whatever you'd like with Romeo Romero."

Jared's smile grew wider. A whole new world was about to open up for him. He was sure of it. By the time this little scheme dreamed up by Chase and Grant was over, that $10,000 would be pocket change.

Not that he'd give it back, of course. He wasn't stupid.

As far as *he* knew, at least.

Chapter Nineteen

Fifteen minutes later, when they were back on Fiftieth Street, walking west toward the subways at Eighth Avenue, Grant said to Chase, "I don't know what you see in that kid."

"I see nothing in him. This is all about the blackmail plan, that's all."

Grant continued, as if he hadn't heard. "I'm, like, twice his age, and pretty much different in every way. Plus, he's about as sharp as an unplugged toaster oven. I just can't figure out how you could find both of us attractive."

Chase shook his head. "I don't find him attractive. I'm all about you."

Grant might have believed him if there wasn't still a slight tenting in Chase's pants. But he let the matter drop.

"Anyway," said Chase, "while we were in his apartment, I had a new idea." Grant didn't reply. "Maybe we've been too limited in our Internet scams."

Now he had Grant's interest. "Meaning?"

"Meaning, we keep scamming horny heterosexual men. How come we aren't scamming the guys who are trolling around looking for teenage boys?"

Grant saw where he was going. "Using photos of Jared's body."

"Exactly. Crop out the head and you've got a picture of a sixteen-year-old. Gay jailbait. Plus, a lot of the guys are closet cases and wouldn't dream of going to the cops."

"How come we didn't think of this earlier?" asked Grant.

"Because when was the last time you even *thought* of a naked teenage boy, until a half hour ago?"

"Good point."

They stopped at Eighth Avenue, waiting for the walk sign to come on.

"One question," said Grant. "Think we'd have to cut Jared in on the deal?"

"To use his pictures? *Hell*, no! You saw how eager he was to strip for us—"

"You."

"Whatever. It'll be a snap to get him to pose for a few photos. He'll never know what we're going to use them for."

"Okay," said Grant, as they started across the intersection. "We have a new plan."

"Yeah, but first let's finish putting together the plan we're in the middle of. We've got to secure our girl now."

"Maybe we should just put Jared in a dress. That would work."

"Grant."

"Okay, okay . . . Cheap shot."

"So are you ready to pay a visit on Lisa and Mary Beth?"

Grant sighed. "No. But let's do it."

On the west side of Eighth Avenue, as they descended the staircase to the subway, Grant said, "I'm a little worried about Jared, you know. I don't think he was quite getting the plan, which means you'd better go over it a few more times with him, before he gets too caught up with his fantasies about being the next *Mr.* Romeo Romero. Otherwise, he could blow this for us."

"Gotcha," said Chase, swiping his MetroCard.

"Oh, and baby?"

"Yeah?"

"Do it over the phone, please."

Lisa Cochrane and Mary Beth Reuss lived on an upper floor of a new luxury high-rise in Long Island City in Queens, somewhere behind the iconic Pepsi sign that rose above the East River. The views went both ways in that area of the city. From Manhattan, you got to look out on the Pepsi sign and the developing Queens skyline; from Queens, you got the United Nations Building and the Manhattan skyline. Lisa knew her real estate, and preferred *her* view, even though the Pepsi sign looked a lot less charming when you were situated behind it.

Plus, in Queens, rents were a lot cheaper. The $2,900 a month she was paying in Long Island City would have been $4,000 or more on the other side of the East River, and since she was only one stop on the 7 train from Grand Central Terminal, she considered that a good deal.

Not to mention the terrace . . . the square footage . . . the amenities . . . Yeah, Manhattan snobs—and there were a lot in her industry, although less every year—could look down on her, but she knew a real estate deal when she saw one. And this was a deal.

The fact that Mary Beth was a Manhattan snob, well, that had resulted in some awkward moments. But at some point Lisa had to put her foot down, and Mary Beth had to live with it. Lisa was sure she'd grow to love Long Island City eventually. It hadn't happened in the fifteen months they'd lived there, but . . . eventually. She was sure of it. Almost.

One thing they didn't like doing was entertaining. They had a great apartment with a breathtaking view—everything from the Queensboro Bridge to the Empire State Building—but they could count the number of visitors they had in any given year on both hands and maybe a stray toe or two.

And that was when they wanted the visitors.

Which was why, even though Chase had called ahead, the women didn't seem particularly happy to see them, and made that obvious. Which in turn was why Grant, picking up on their discomfort, got right down to business.

"We think Mary Beth should be the girl," he said, and they looked at him as though he had suggested Mary Beth should leap off the balcony. Which he probably would have under other circumstances, but not tonight.

"No way," said Lisa.

"But this was her idea," said Grant. "And it was a good one. If we're gonna put it to the test, though, we need a woman."

"A *hot* woman," Chase added.

"Exactly."

"No," said Mary Beth and Lisa in unison.

Lisa expanded on that. "Lambert, this is *your* life. Yours and Chase's. And, okay, a little bit of my life. But it's not Mary Beth's." She stroked her girlfriend's hair. "I'm not going to get Mary Beth involved in this scheme. That is off the table."

"But where are we going to get another girl?" asked Chase, and Grant again thought of Jared in a dress. "After all we've been through. It'd be a shame to end everything now, just because we don't have a woman to seduce Romeo Romero."

Grant pointed at Lisa. "Plus you're out five grand for the tickets if we can't pull this together."

Mary Beth stared at Lisa; in turn, Lisa scowled at Grant.

"Is that true?" Mary Beth asked. "You gave this idiot five thousand dollars?"

"Hey," said Grant. "It was *your* scheme."

"This wasn't," she said. "My scheme involved having a woman seduce Romero and getting it on tape. *You're* the one who overcomplicated everything. As usual. Christ, Lambert, you could have paid a hooker a couple hundred bucks and had everything you wanted."

He was annoyed. "I don't know any hookers."

She picked up on his annoyance and raised. "Jamie Brock is pretty damn close."

"Okay, then. I don't know any hookers *I can trust*." Grant realized, too late, that his voice was showing anger, which was definitely not what he wanted to show. He was there to persuade, not fight. No matter how much they didn't like each other.

Chase did, too, which is why he jumped in between them, waving his hands to try to calm everyone down.

"Listen," he said, "whether we like it or not, we're a team. This plan—now, wait a minute, Mary Beth—this plan has a lot going for it. First, it gets us close to Romeo Romero, and, with all due respect, I don't know if a random hooker would work out that well for us on that end. Next, if we send in the right people, with the right cameras, we're *way* ahead of the game. On one hand there's us—with a plan—and on the other hand there's our mark, who's got no idea what we're up to. This could work."

Mary Beth frowned. "Five thousand dollars."

"If it works," said Grant, "your return will be over a hundred thousand. Which will more than cover the tickets. Think about *that*."

Lisa and Mary Beth asked for some time alone, and when the men thought that meant they'd talk things over in the bedroom, they were advised that it meant that the men should go to the lobby and make themselves comfortable, because the talk might take some time.

It took an hour. Which seemed a lot longer to Grant and Chase, because the lobby didn't have things like magazines, and there were only so many times they could stare at the glass box near the elevator and read up on the building's new recycling policies. The lobby was nice—all marble and expensive-looking uncomfortable furniture that probably wasn't expensive, although it delivered on the discomfort—but it was still just a lobby. Underheated, too, because—besides the doorman, who was called a "concierge" at this particular building—which person in this building wanted to pay more money for *real* expensive furniture and heat in the lobby? It's not like they lived here.

Speaking of living there, though, Grant had a question for Chase.

"You know, if we can get our act together, we're looking at some real money. What would you think of moving into a building like this?"

Chase thought about that. "I assume you mean *like* this, and not this exact building."

"Right." Not that there was anything wrong with the building, if you didn't have to spend too much time in the lobby, but this particular building would be a little too close to Lisa and Mary Beth—especially Mary Beth—for comfort. "A place like this."

Chase thought some more. "I don't know. I sort of like Jackson Heights."

That answer made Grant happy. Not that he showed it. Instead he went, "Huh." But deep down, he knew they'd always belong to Jackson Heights, and he was glad Chase shared his sentiment. Lisa's place was nice, with the view and the nice furniture and the doorman and the lobby and the *newness*, but some people belonged here, and others didn't.

Eventually, after that hour passed, Chase's cell phone rang—the women knew better than to call Grant—and Lisa told them to come back upstairs.

She got right to business. "Okay, here's the deal. Mary Beth is in."

"Great!" said Chase.

"Not so fast. Mary Beth is in, but our cut has to go up to a third."

Grant thought about that. That would add another $40,000 or so to their share, and it would come directly from the Lambert-LaMarca side of the ledger.

"I can't do that," he said finally.

Mary Beth crossed her arms. "Then neither can I."

Chase tugged at Grant's sleeve. "Can I talk to you for a sec?"

"Sure."

"In private?"

No way the lesbians were budging, so they headed back down to the lobby.

"I know what you're gonna say," said Grant, when they entered the elevator. "And the answer is no."

Chased pushed the button for 1. "But Grant, if this works out, we're still walking away with over a hundred thousand dollars."

"Over a hundred thirty, actually, after we give ten grand to Jared. But I don't like the idea that Jamie and Lisa and the bitch all end up with more money than us. It isn't right. We've done all the work."

"I know, I know." He touched Grant's shoulder gently. "But if this is our only way to get Mary Beth on board, it's worth it."

The elevator stopped on the sixteenth floor and a small Asian woman boarded. She got off on the fourth floor and their conversation continued.

"As I was saying," Chase said, "we need her . . . and let's face it, we'd be nowhere without Lisa financing us. They deserve a bit more for that."

"I dunno."

The reached the ground floor, and Chase pushed the button for Lisa's floor. "Let's take it up again."

Grant shrugged. "Okay."

The door was half closed when someone called out "Hold that," and an arm stopped it. As Grant and Chase backed into a corner, a small army entered the elevator, most likely meaning a 7 train had passed through Long Island City a few minutes earlier.

The buttons lit up: 2 - 4 - 8 - 9 - 12 - 18 . . .

Two? Two couldn't *walk* a flight? He looked healthy.

After 18 got off, they had a few seconds alone. So Chase said, "I'd just hate to see us lose a shot at a hundred thirty thousand because we got stubborn. Let's face it: this is the big one. The big score. If this doesn't pan out, we'll have to steal something like one hundred cars to make that kind of money. That's a lot of Internet predators, Grant."

His shoulders slumped. He hated it when Chase made so much sense.

The elevator *ding*ed. They were back at Lisa's floor.

"Want to ride it back down?" asked Chase.

"No." They stepped off the elevator and Grant said, "Okay. They get a third."

And so they delivered the news. No one really felt like breaking out champagne—there were too many strained and ambivalent feelings in the room to feel *too* good about it— but at least there were smiles and some vague sense that, for the first time, they were truly in this together.

"So," said Mary Beth, "do you have your boy yet?"

Grant rolled his eyes. "Yeah. And you're gonna love *this* one."

Chapter Twenty

Early the next afternoon they drove to Water Mill, far out on the south fork of the east end of Long Island, to look over Romeo Romero's house. Since they were using Jamie's car—even though they made him ride in the back—they didn't even have to steal one, although they still sort of wanted to. Somehow, it felt wrong to take a day trip to case a job in a car that was legit.

In the car were Grant, because he was the one who primarily needed to size up the place; Jamie, because he was the one who had been there before and actually wandered around; and Farraday, because he was the one who needed to know the roads in case they had to make a quick getaway, which they considered a possibility worth planning for.

Meaning Farraday got to drive, not that he would have had it any other way, as long as he was sober.

Left behind were Chase, who called in sick to *The Eye* so he could continue to tutor Mary Beth and Jared—*especially* Jared—on what was expected of them; and Lisa, who was looking through the listings for an empty house near Romero's they could borrow, since Grant figured the rest of them might need to stay overnight while Jared and Mary Beth were working their respective wiles on the actor.

"There it is," said Jamie, after Farraday had driven a few

hours and the second story of a two-story Victorian came into view above a hedgerow.

Farraday slowed the car slightly. "Want me to park?"

"No." Grant eyed the neighboring houses for signs of life. There weren't any, but he thought it likely that someone was standing behind a curtain in one of the half dozen houses in range of Jamie's Lexus. "This isn't a walking neighborhood. Three guys who look like us walking around, we're gonna attract attention."

"I could pass for a local," said Jamie's voice from the backseat.

"Fine. Two guys who look like us and one guy who looks like you. It's still not a neighborhood where strangers just wander around without someone who actually belongs here calling the cops."

The car rolled past the house, then past a break in the hedgerow where a half-open metal gate led up the driveway, then past more shrubbery until there was another break and a closed gate where the circular driveway exited.

On the other side of the property line, Farraday guided the car around a bend in the road and said, "So?"

Grant shook his head. "All I could see were bushes."

"Technically, *hedges*," said Jamie, and Grant answered him with a stare.

Farraday said, "I could take it again, more slowly. You know, pretend like we're lost or something . . . looking for a house number."

And they did. This time Grant could make out a few more details—most importantly the small metal sign planted in the sliver of lawn at the driveway entrance informing them that the property was protected by Wilbourne Security, just below a keypad attached to the gate that probably opened and closed it—but not much else besides a corner of a big white truck parked up near the house.

"Want me to make another pass?" Farraday asked when they reached the other end of the lot.

"No good," said Grant. "Too obvious. Just pull over to the side of the road."

"Here?"

"Here."

Farraday pulled the two right tires onto the grassy edge of somebody's lawn and stopped. "Now what?"

"Open the hood." The latch was pulled and there was a metallic pop. Grant opened the passenger door and, as he stepped out onto the grass, said, "We'd better try to find out what's wrong with the engine."

Behind him, Jamie scrambled out of the car. "What's wrong? It sounded fine!"

Grant's voice was a growled whisper. "We need an excuse to park here for a minute and try to get a better look at the house. Engine trouble makes a hell of a better excuse than having a picnic."

"Uh," said Jamie, and Grant could tell his eyes were squinting in confusion behind his knock-off Oakleys. "Got it."

Grant lifted the hood and propped it open, then pretended to look at a lot of parts that would have delighted Charlie Chops . . . and maybe still could, if Jamie kept annoying him. The three men feigned a consultation—complete with a lot of pointing at perfectly good auto parts—until Grant said to Jamie:

"Give this to me quick, and keep your voice down. What do I have to know about what's on the other side of those bushes?"

"Hedges."

"Just answer my question."

"Okay, okay. Uh . . . the house has two stories and a basement. There's a big lawn on the south side . . ."

"Which is south?"

"To the right when you go up the driveway. There's a big

in-ground pool on that side, too. At the back of the house, past the pool, is the infamous hot tub. It's fenced in."

"So if—*when*—Mary Beth gets lucky with Romero, no one else will be able to see?"

"Exactly. Uh . . . unless he leaves the gate unlocked again, like that night I was out here."

"I'll make sure she knows to leave it unlocked so Jared can get in. There are places to hide, right?"

"How do you think I took that video? It's a pretty big space, and he's had it landscaped. There's a shed, too. Lots of places to hide."

"Good. What about the house?"

"Pretty standard. Downstairs there's a living room, with a glass door out to the pool. There's a formal dining room, a kitchen in the back . . ." He tried to remember. "There's a guest room back there, too, near the kitchen. I think you can get to the hot tub through it. And another big room set up like a movie theater. He calls it the 'media room.' " Jamie punctuated that with air quotes; Grant really hated people who used air quotes. "There are a bunch of bedrooms and an office upstairs."

"That's where Romero sleeps?"

"Yeah."

"Nothing else?"

Jamie shrugged. "There's an attached garage on the other side of the house from the pool, if you're thinking of taking his car."

"Maybe. Okay, I think I'm ready to eyeball it." For the benefit of any nosy neighbors, Grant raised his voice slightly and said, "Let me go see if one of these houses has a phone we can use."

"Just use my cell," said Jamie.

Grant shook his head sadly and began walking toward Romeo Romero's house, leaving the other two men standing at the side of the road.

He reached the driveway and walked through the open gate with a casual stride, just another harmless disabled motorist. Albeit one who was taking everything in out of the periphery of his vision as he walked up the blacktop toward the house.

He now saw that the white truck was from a party rental company, which made sense. Romero's big bash for Eastern Seaboard LGBTQI Pride was one day away. Over the next twenty-four hours there would be a lot of trucks in and out of the driveway, which Grant figured was both good and bad. Good, because it eased access; bad, because it increased the number of people he might encounter. He decided not to overstay his inspection of Romero's estate.

As a couple of workers unloaded folding tables from the back of the truck, ignoring him, Grant casually ran his eyes over the grounds.

The bushes—okay, *hedges*—formed a natural fence around the property, an unbroken eight-foot-high fence. That would present a problem. Not an unsolvable problem, but a problem. If someone had to get in or out in a hurry, they'd have to find a way over or through them. Given their thickness, "through" didn't seem like a very workable option.

The landscaping inside the compound was another one. He had no idea what the rear of the property looked like, but the part he could see was mostly open lawn and flower beds. Not much opportunity to hide, if the need were to arise.

And then he finally located the big problem he had been expecting. Attached high up on one of the few trees, very close to the hedgerow, was a black box. A motion detector, which was obvious to the criminally inclined trained eye. He glanced past the truck to the other edge of the property, near the garage, and sure enough there was another. Not a good thing.

Grant nodded to the workmen without making eye contact as he passed them on his way to make an inspection of the interior. They nodded back, as if it were perfectly natural for him to be wandering around.

He had counted on that.

Out at the car, Jamie snipped, "Nice of Grant to invite us along."

"It's a one-man job," said Farraday gruffly.

"Maybe." Jamie paused to light a cigarette, then continued. "But I'm the one who's actually been there before. I already know my way around."

"Did you ever think that maybe that's why Lambert wants you out here with me? If Romero's already met you, it doesn't make sense for you to be inside that gate. He might recognize you."

Jamie thought about that. "I suppose . . ." He was thinking about saying something else—what, he wasn't quite sure—when he looked over Farraday's shoulder and said, "Oh shit."

"What is it?"

"Don't look behind you."

"What is it?"

And then Farraday didn't have to worry about looking behind him, because a Suffolk County Sheriff's Department patrol car was braking next to them and the pretend-disabled Lexus.

"Let me do the talking," said Farraday out of the corner of his mouth as the cop stepped out into the roadway and looked at them over the roof of the patrol car from behind mirrored sunglasses.

"Broke down," said Jamie, ignoring Farraday and without being asked by the cop.

"I figured. This your car?"

Shit, Jamie thought, until he remembered that it actually *was* his car and he relaxed. "Yeah. Do you need my license and registration?"

The deputy adjusted himself and said, "If you'd be so kind."

Jamie dropped his cigarette in the grass and ground it out with his heel, then went to retrieve what he needed from the glove compartment. As he did, the deputy walked around the front of his patrol car and kept walking until he was standing just a few feet from Farraday.

"You men from around here?"

"No, just looking for a summer rental," said Farraday implausibly, given that he looked exactly like an alcoholic ex-cab driver, which was not the type of man who generally summered in the Hamptons. Those would be the alcoholic ex-hedge fund managers.

"Uh . . . yeah," said Jamie, once again part of the conversation and eyeing his colleague every bit as critically as the lawman. To take attention away from Farraday he handed over his license and registration with a "Here you go."

"James J. Brock III," the cop read off the license, then looked at Jamie, sunglasses to sunglasses. "So where were you looking at rentals, Mr. Brock?"

For once, a subject arose which Jamie could actually speak to somewhat intelligently, and so he prattled on about East Hampton and Southampton and Westhampton and what sounded to Farraday like Hamptonhampton for several minutes until the cop finally had to force the conversation to a close. Still holding the license and registration, he said he'd be right back and returned to the patrol car.

"He's gonna run your license and registration," hissed Farraday, stating the obvious. "Anything I should know before he slaps the cuffs on?"

"Nothing," said Jamie. "Nothing that's going to be in a police computer, at least."

"You'd better be right about that. Or after I'm released from prison, I *will* hunt you down and kill you."

But Jamie was right. If there was anything out there on him, it had not yet made it into a police database. A few minutes later he was returning his registration to the glove compartment and the license to his wallet.

The cop asked, "Want me to call for a tow truck?"

Farraday smiled politely, trying his best to look amiable and almost succeeding. "That won't be necessary, deputy." He pointed at Romero's house. "Our friend is over there, using the phone."

The cop followed Farraday's finger, and let out a low whistle. "You know whose house that is?"

"No-why-would-we-know-that?" replied Jamie, more than a bit too quickly.

The cop didn't seem to notice. "Romeo Romero, the movie star. That's *his* place."

"Huh," said Farraday, feigning cool. "Go figure."

Minutes later, driving away in his patrol car, Suffolk County Deputy Sheriff Henry Lemmon felt an almost crippling wave of sadness wash over him. This was what had become of his life: interrogating people at the scene of routine motor vehicle breakdowns instead of building a life with his beloved Amber.

Just two weeks earlier, he had lost the two great loves of his life within minutes of each other. Amber Arbogast had never gotten off the plane at Kennedy, and someone had stolen his beloved 2002 BMW 525i. And now all he had to look forward to was . . . *this*. It was too disappointing—too *depressing*—to contemplate.

Henry Lemmon thought about his future as he drove past the manicured estates of Water Mill. Maybe he could call his uncle Howard, the judge, and see if strings could be pulled to get him into the court security system. It wouldn't solve all his problems—that beloved BMW was probably gone forever—but young girls often found themselves in legal trouble, and Henry Lemmon knew he could provide them with a strong, supportive shoulder to cry on.

Well, it would sure as hell beat running license checks. Plus, the young girls he met on patrol in the Hamptons always looked down on him. *Rich bitches.* The girls in *need* would understand him.

Grant wasn't happy knowing that a Suffolk cop had had his hands on Jamie's ID, but agreed there was nothing they could do about it. And just because an outsider now knew that Jamie had been in Water Mill on a Friday afternoon didn't mean much. If everything went according to plan, when this was over no one but the seven of them and Romero would even know anything illegal had happened.

It would only be a concern if everything *didn't* go as planned.

He told Farraday to circle the block so he could get a look at the back of the estate, and as they drove he filled them in.

"I didn't see Romero. Just a bunch of delivery people. No one seemed to know anyone except their coworkers, so they left me to myself. Romero must have been out . . . or hiding from the little people."

"Little people?" asked Jamie. "Like . . . *little* people?"

Farraday said, "Midgets give me the creeps."

"You *both* give me the creeps," said Grant. "But that's not what I'm talking about. I'm talking about 'the little people.' Like 'common' people. Like us."

"Okay," growled Farraday. "You coulda just said that."

"I'm saying that now, God help me. Anyway . . . I got a pretty good look at the house and yard."

"And?" asked Jamie.

"The big thing is he's got motion detectors around the perimeter of the yard. As far as I can tell, when those things are on, they trip about a yard or so from the hedges. That's going to make it tough for Mary Beth and Jared to let themselves out if they have to wait out Romero tomorrow night."

"Or anyone to get in, if we have to rescue them," added Jamie.

"Exactly. Forget a ladder to go over the hedges. Even if those things could support the weight, the angle would be tough to work with. We'll have to figure out a way to disable them." He thought about that. "I'd better give *that* job to Mary Beth. Anyway, from what I could tell, it doesn't look like the house itself is overly wired. I couldn't check out every inch of the place, but it looks like he's got basic alarms on the doors, and nothing on the windows. So I have two thoughts . . ."

"Which way?" asked Farraday, who was suddenly idling at an intersection where neither of the two winding routes seemed to logically go in the direction Grant wanted them to go.

"Uh . . . go the straightish way. And when you see a left, take it."

"Nothing really goes left or right around here," said Farraday, as the car eased through the intersection.

"Left*ish*, then."

"Straightish . . . leftish . . . I miss the Manhattan grid."

Grant ignored him. "So as I was saying, I have two thoughts. One is that we check out the rear of the property. All I could see from the kitchen windows was that the yard goes deep in back, and there are woods out there. Maybe the hedges don't surround the entire property."

Jamie asked, "So you want Jared and Mary Beth to escape through the woods in the middle of the night?"

"That's my Plan C, if they can't disable the alarm," said Grant, although now that he was thinking about it, it didn't seem like a bad idea to send Jerry Stanley and that bitch Mary Beth Reuss flailing around in the woods in the dark. Maybe he'd be especially lucky and there'd be wolves out there. The smile flickered from his face when he remembered that they would also have the blackmail material, so maybe that wasn't such a good idea after all. A nice daydream; not necessarily a good idea.

"My Plan A," he continued, "is to turn off the alarm. Plan B is to leave them in the house overnight, let them get the goods, then sneak them out with the workers the next morning."

"What workers?" asked Jamie as Farraday finally made a leftish turn.

"Have you been listening to me?" Jamie sort of nodded, which told Grant he was only half tuned in. "You saw that truck back there? Workers dropping off tables, chairs, and all that other crap for the big party tomorrow night. They drop it off and set it up today, tomorrow the caterers probably come, and then on Sunday—after the party—the rental people and the caterers come back to pick up their stuff. And when they take everything out, they take Jared and Mary Beth with them."

The car slowed and Farraday said, "I think that's the back."

Yes, Grant sadly realized, *that is indeed the back of Romeo Romero's house.* He recognized the reddish gray towers rising above the structure, visible above the trees that hid everything above the top few feet of the second floor.

But between them and the trees was . . .

"It's a pond," said Jamie. "A big pond."

"Yeah, I can see that." Grant sat back and signed. "Okay, then, I guess we're gonna have to hope that my Plan A works." He looked hopefully to Farraday.

"Sorry, Lambert. I don't know how to drive a boat."

"Actually," said Jamie, "you *pilot* a boat."

"Shut up, Jamie. Okay, Farraday, take us back past the house one more time."

"What for?"

"The delivery people. I want to remember exactly how they're dressed."

When the three men returned to the Jackson Heights apartment early that evening, the others were already waiting. Grant barely took time to say hello before reeling off his mental to-do list.

"Lisa, you find a place for us to stay tomorrow night?"

"I did," she said, flicking an ash from her cigarette into the air shaft. "And only a quarter mile away. The only hitch is that the owners have taken out most of the furniture. *Against* the advice of their Realtor, I might add."

"We'll survive." He looked at Chase. "And you've got Mary Beth and Jared up to speed."

Chase smiled tightly. "To the best of my ability."

"You could be more reassuring . . ."

Mary Beth rolled her eyes and said, "I'll make it work, Lambert. Don't worry about me."

Grant's eyes darted to Jared, who was deep in concentration over a freckle on his right forearm. "And you?"

No answer.

"Jared?"

Jared's eyes blinked twice. "What?"

Grant suppressed his sigh for the good of the team. "I want to make sure you understand what has to happen tomorrow."

He rolled his eyes, too, but in a manner much more exaggerated than Mary Beth. It made him look like a gay bobblehead. "We get out to Romero's around four, have a cocktail, take a swim . . ."

Grant cocked an eyebrow at Chase. "A swim?"

Chase shrugged. "Eastern Seaboard Pride's Tenth Annual Memorial Day Weekend Pool Party. Remember? *Pool*?" This time, Grant let the sigh come out. "Hey, I didn't plan the theme."

"Here's the problem," said Grant, looking at Chase, Mary Beth, and Jared, but he focused mainly on Jared. "You're gonna be carrying cameras, which I'm pretty sure you'll ruin frolicking in chlorinated water."

It was Mary Beth who spoke. "Believe it or not, Lambert, we're *way* ahead of you, not that that's an especially high hurdle to clear. First, I'm not going in the pool. Not with all those other people . . . who *knows* where they've been? Second, before Twinkenstein strips down to God knows what and reenacts his favorite gay porn pool orgy scenes, he's gonna give me his equipment."

Jared giggled; Mary Beth glowered.

"Don't for a minute think I want the equipment you're thinking of, or you'll be singing like Minnie Ripperton before you leave." She shook it off and finished. "Anyway, he only gets it back when he's dry. That way, we look realistic and we also get the goods on Romero."

Grant thought about that, and was unhappy that he couldn't find anything wrong in a plan Mary Beth had obviously devised.

"Okay, then. Good thinking. So, Jared, after your *short* dip in the pool . . ."

"Then I try to seduce Romeo Romero!" He practically squealed.

"But fail."

Jared's smile vanished. "Okay . . ."

"We added a few things," said Chase.

Jared brightened. "Oh, right! Mary Beth and I are going to be brother and sister."

"Which one's which?" asked Grant, to scowls from everyone except Farraday, who actually thought it was funny but was unsure of the appropriate level of political correctness he should display as the lone heterosexual in the room, so he played it safe and focused instead on his scotch.

Chase explained. "We want Romero to think Mary Beth is

straight and available, right? So we figured it would be easier
to pass her off as Jared's straight sister than his straight girlfriend, because, well . . . you know how straight men sometimes feel about fag hags."

"I do?"

"You would if you thought about it. Romero would probably think their relationship was too intimate . . . that she'd
run back and tell Jared *everything* the minute their rendezvous was over. I figured—"

"*I* figured!"

"*Mary Beth* figured if she was the supportive sister who
was maybe just a little too cool for this Eastern Seaboard
party foolishness, Romero would find her more appealing."

"And," Mary Beth added, "besides the fag hags and a few
suck-up celebrities and politicians, the only women who will
be there will probably be lesbians." She smiled. "I'll stand
out."

"But you *are* a lesbian."

She brushed away Grant's comment. "Details."

Grant had a new, grudging respect for Mary Beth. He was
going to have to work his brain overtime to quash it. In the
meantime, he filled them in on what they had learned in
Water Mill. When he was done, Jared finally had a question
of his own.

"You want us to dress in orange T-shirts and cut-offs?"

"Just to get out of there," Grant said. "It's what all the delivery people were wearing."

"I'd rather die."

Maybe tonight, thought Grant, but he said: "If you have to
leave with the workers, you'll only have to be dressed like
that for an hour, maybe less. Just long enough to blend in and
get out before anyone realizes you don't belong. Piece of
cake."

"Chase . . ."

Chase shook his head. "This isn't a fashion shoot, Jared.

Just follow Grant's lead. You'll be back in your . . . uh, whatever you want to wear before you know it."

Jared leered, and even though he was seven feet away from Chase, it made everyone uncomfortable. Even Farraday shuddered as he studied an ice cube.

"Maybe what I *want* to wear is nothing . . ."

The kitchen become uncomfortable squared. Or cubed, in the case of Farraday.

"Okay, then," said Jamie, who had been leaning quietly near the airshaft window where Lisa still flicked nonexistent ashes from a now-dead cigarette. "I, uh . . . I guess you have a plan, Grant. I can't wait until we get together on Sunday to hear how it went."

"What do you mean 'you'? *We* have a plan, not just me. And what's this about Sunday? Aren't you part of the team anymore?"

"Well, I meant . . ."

"Because if you want out, I'm sure everyone else would be happy to divvy up your share."

"That's not what I meant," said Jamie. "I just figured, you know . . . you have your team to work the party, and your driver, and your, uh, Chase and Lisa . . . And I *did* bring the whole thing to your attention. So I figured my part was over."

"That's what you figured, huh?"

"It's just that . . . You know me, Grant. I'm not a criminal, technically. Not like you. Uh . . . no offense. I just sort of take advantage of opportunities."

"No offense taken." Grant cleared his throat. "So what you're telling us is, you're out of this job? Because we need to know how we're gonna divide up the take."

"Well . . ." He slumped against the wall in resignation. "I guess I'm going to Water Mill, right?"

"You are if you want a cut. We have no idea what's going

to happen tomorrow night, and I want everyone there in case we need to improvise."

"Sounds fair," said Jamie, clearly not meaning it.

"Okay," Grant said, looking around the room as if daring anyone else to challenge him. "*We* have a plan. So let's get some sleep because tomorrow we're rolling it out."

Grant slept for maybe forty-five minutes that night. Chase, Jamie, Farraday, Lisa, and Mary Beth maybe three hours, give or take.

Jared slept for ten hours. Right through his alarm.

Chapter Twenty-One

They were outside the Jamaica subway station—a little nervous, because the minivan they were standing next to had been taken by Paul Farraday from LaGuardia long-term parking a half hour earlier—when Mary Beth pointed at her watch and said, "He's late."

Chase looked at his own watch. "Just a few minutes."

She fumed. "I knew Lambert would find a way to screw this up."

To which Grant said, "Wait a second. *I* was here on time."

"No, you screwed this up by bringing Twinkenstein to the party."

Grant slipped his cell phone out of a pocket. Not that he had any intention of actually using it. "You got a better twink? We'll call him."

She waved him away. "If I weren't already a lesbian, you would have turned me into one over the past few days."

"The men of the world would thank me . . ."

Jamie waved his hands. "Uh, could everyone calm down."

They probably wouldn't have paid any attention to him. He was, after all, Jamie Brock. But it didn't matter because that's when they heard Jared call to them from the top of the stairs at the subway entrance, having just emerged from an E train.

"Yoo-hoo! I'm ready to go!"

They turned in unison. And then they gaped in unison. Even Farraday, who had been trying so hard to be neutral about everything, gaped.

It was finally Lisa who broke the silence when she rasped, "What the fuck?"

It wasn't what Jared was wearing, although that was certainly noteworthy: his jeans and shirt had been sliced by razor blades so thoroughly that they were literally held together by threads. And this time, while Chase still found the lack of underwear distracting, it wasn't in a good way.

And it wasn't because his hair had gone blonder by several shades overnight, although both Chase and Jamie subconsciously brushed their hair with their fingers and hoped that they weren't doing the same damage to their follicles.

And it wasn't even because Jared's spray-on tan would only pass for realistic in a dark place. Late at night. During an eclipse. And a blackout. It certainly wasn't working on a sunny late-spring morning in Queens.

No, those were the things about Jared that *didn't* surprise them.

What *did* was that he was carrying two suitcases for what, at most, would be an overnight trip.

No one else—with the exception of the women, who had handbags, Mary Beth's obviously and necessarily much larger than Lisa's, since she had a couple of cameras, orange tees, and denim cut-offs in there—had brought more than the clothes on their backs.

"Little help?" Jared asked, but they continued to gape. So he had to drag his costume changes to the minivan by himself, all the while muttering, "Whatever . . ."

Farraday, who was driving, decided that their best bet was to take the Van Wyck Expressway to the Southern Parkway until they got to Nassau County, at which point they'd take county roads. The highways were riskier if the cops were looking for the minivan, but it was the fastest way out of

New York City. Plus, he figured the cops would assume that a van lifted from LaGuardia would be headed farther into New York, not due east, deeper into suburban Long Island.

"What, no DVD player?" asked Jared, who had not yet realized that it would be in his best interest to shut the hell up.

"Newer models have DVD players," said Chase, next to him in the second row of seats, vaguely behind his partner, who was riding shotgun. "Newer models *also* have more antitheft devices. They could track us."

"But I wanted to watch *The Little Mermaid*."

Chase unbelted himself, leaned forward, and wrapped his arms around Grant's shoulders. "Please tell me we didn't make a mistake," he whispered not especially quietly into Grant's left ear.

"I can't do that."

A little more muted he said, "Okay, then, hope for the best?"

"That I can do. That I *have* been doing."

Chase settled back and buckled himself in just as Mary Beth leaned over from the back seat and asked Jared, "So what's in the bags?"

Jared became animated, smacking Chase in the chest with his elbow as he turned to talk to her. "Well, DVDs, although I guess *that* was a waste of space, and I wish someone had told me. Also clothes for the party and—"

She looked up and down the razor-slashed jeans and shirt. "This isn't your party outfit?"

"Oh, *hell* no! These are my traveling clothes. Anyway, I have my party clothes, and my first bathing suit—"

"Your *first* bathing suit?"

"Yeah, the Etro board shorts for the late afternoon. Very cute. Then the Prada square cut for the early evening. Very cute, too."

"Isn't that exces—"

"And then, for the late night dip—you know, after everyone's been drinking and things start getting crazy—there's the Speedo." He winked at Chase. "You know . . . for when it's time to show a little more skin."

Mary Beth stole another glance at Jared's already-too-revealing ensemble. She and Lisa had a joke whenever they considered the possibility of seeing a penis: "Lesbian Blindness." Jared was not quite at the "blindness" stage, but probably "cataracts."

"*More* skin?"

"Oh, Christ," Grant said to himself, and to Jared he said, "You realize that the goal here is for you to not actually sleep with Romeo Romero, right?"

"Well, duh. Jeez, you make it sound like I overpacked or something." He paused. "And if the dude is straight, he wouldn't be interested in me and my cute little swim-wear anyway. But there will be other hot guys with money there . . ."

"Guys with money, maybe," said Grant. "I can't vouch for the 'hot.' "

"Guys with money *are* hot. End of story." He seemed lost for a moment, then recovered. "And then I have an outfit change for later, in case it gets cold. Then one for brunch . . ."

"Brunch?" asked Chase. "By the time brunch rolls around, you're gonna be in an orange T-shirt and cut-offs."

Jared sulked the rest of the way to the Hamptons.

After a few wrong turns down unfamiliar roads, Lisa finally directed them to the house she had borrowed to use as their hideout. It was a Victorian very similar to Romeo Romero's, Grant noted, except without the damn hedges. And it came with an attached garage, which was a requirement when Lisa was house-hunting, since they needed to keep the minivan out of sight as much as possible.

"Okay," said Chase, when they were all out of the vehicle

and he could once again take on the role of tutor. "Let's review one more time."

"We go to the party and try to get Romeo Romero to sleep with us," said Jared, boredom in his voice as he hauled the second suitcase from the minivan. It was the bag that held his brunch outfit; that made him frown.

"*I* try to get him to sleep with *me*," Mary Beth corrected him, before adding, "But he won't."

"No one's actually asking you to have sex with him," said Grant. "Just . . . you know, make it *look* like he's having sex with you so Jared can get a picture."

"It's still disgusting."

"Yeah, a half million dollars worth of disgusting. Think of that as your motivation."

"And don't worry," added Lisa. "We'll only be a few minutes away. If he tries anything . . ."

"He won't try anything." Mary Beth's smile didn't quite hide her steeliness, and her hand dropped into her oversized bag. "If he gets too close, I've got protection."

"Condoms?" asked Jared.

Her hand reappeared. She was holding a small metallic canister.

"What's that?" asked Grant.

"Pepper spray."

Grant mumbled, "Pepper spray. Great. What could possibly go wrong?"

"If that letch tries to put a hand on me . . . *zap!*" She sprayed very briefly, but it was still enough to send Jamie—standing a few yards downwind—into a coughing spasm. She looked at him, then nodded triumphantly. "See?"

"Okay," said Chase. "Back to business. So you get into the party and what?"

"Find Romero and introduce ourselves. 'Hi, I'm Mary Beth, and this is my retarded gay brother! Nice to meet you.' "

"Jared, what's your last name supposed to be?" Not that

they expected a last name to play any sort of significant role, but Grant felt that the name should match the check that had paid for the tickets. Not to mention muddy the waters and make Mary Beth and Jared slightly less traceable, in case something went horribly wrong. Lisa would be the benevolent aunt—again, she hated being the aunt—but they figured she was old enough and resourceful enough to take care of herself if something went wrong.

Speaking of things going wrong . . .

"Jared?" Grant not-quite yelled.

"Huh?"

"What's your last name supposed to be?"

He was, as usual, quick with the wrong answer. "Parsells."

"Try again."

Jared thought for a second. *What did Chase . . . ? Oh, I know!* "Cockring!"

Chase turned warily, and—as he expected—Lisa's face was turning crimson. "Try again."

Again, Jared thought. "I thought it was . . . Oh! Right! *Cochrane!*" The triumph on his face was almost heartbreaking.

"Thank you," said Lisa icily.

Grant sighed and said to Mary Beth, "What next?"

She ticked off the steps in her assignment on the fingers of her right hand. "*I* get into the house and look for a place to hide, in case we have to sneak out with the delivery people. *I* look for the alarm and get the code, in case we have to turn it off. And *he*"—she jabbed her thumb toward Jared—"gets lost, so I can start putting the moves on Romero."

"Subtly."

"Well, *duh*. Don't worry, Lambert. If Romeo Romero is really straight, I'll get what you want."

"And I get to take the picture!" said Jared.

She shook her head. "Un-freakin'-believable. Yes, you get

to take the picture. Just try to do it fast, before I have to spray him."

Grant had a bad feeling in the pit of his stomach. If possible, Mary Beth had more contempt for Jared than he did.

He sighed. "So you're pretty confident about this?"

"Like I said, if the guy is heterosexual—even a little bit—I won't be coming back without the blackmail material." She smiled. It was all teeth. "Trust me, Lambert."

"Trust me, too!" said Jared, who was now dancing to the music playing in his head in the middle of the driveway.

A few hours later, after Jared had made several wardrobe changes before settling on something that met his taste as well as the acceptance of the adults in the house, the brother-and-sister act left with Farraday, their chauffeur, for Romeo Romero's estate. The others stood silent in the cavernous foyer of the large, empty house until long after the sound of the minivan's engine had faded away.

"So," said Chase finally, more to break the uncomfortable silence than any other reason. "This is it. Two weeks after Jamie lost the videotape . . . two weeks of sneaking around and conniving and plotting . . . and our half million dollars is now riding on Mary Beth and Jared."

Lisa turned to Grant. "How are you feeling about this?"

"I'm feeling," Grant said, "like we don't have much choice about how this is going to play out now, so we'd better hope for the best."

"Yeah." She stared at nothing for a while before continuing in the tone of voice flight attendants use to tell the passengers the engines have stopped working. "I'm sure it will turn out just fine. Hey, we wouldn't still be in this if we thought it would be a disaster, right?"

The others muttered cautious agreement.

"But do you mind a little constructive criticism, Lambert? For the future?" He shrugged. "If you ever have to do something like this again, maybe you should find male bait that doesn't want to sleep with the straight guy, and female bait who's not a lesbian. The way we did this today is sort of backward."

"In so many ways," he said, and he joined her in staring at nothing. "But we had to work with what we had. Minimal budget; minimal time . . . minimal talent."

"All in all," said Jamie, "I think it's working out pretty well."

No one bothered to respond. It just wasn't worth it. Their fate was now in the hands of a higher power.

Romeo Romero's closeted heterosexual horniness.

Chapter Twenty-Two

Romeo Romero did not exactly revel in the role of host to a few hundred homosexuals for the late afternoon-into-evening fund-raiser known as the Eastern Seaboard LGBTQI Pride Annual Memorial Day Weekend Pool Party. In fact, he hated every moment of the four parties he had hosted over the previous ten years.

First, there were the organizers, who never seem to conceive of an idea they wouldn't impose upon him. One year, they even had him take out the red rose bushes in the back and replace them with yellow, to better mesh with the evening's color scheme. The garden had never recovered. It seemed to him they acted the opposite of how people borrowing his house, yard, and pool should act, but whenever he balked they gave him the "look at all your worldly goods, thanks to the support of the LGBTQI community" speech, and he backed off.

Then there were the workers tromping in and out of his house. Caterers, deliverymen, people who seemed to have no other purpose but contribute to the tromping . . . and everyone, *always*, in his way. Besides the complete rearrangement of most of his house and grounds, it wasn't unbearable when they were setting up; but the breakdown on the day after the party was pure hell. Dirt, dust and mud everywhere . . . broken glass and uncollected trash . . . *Pure hell.*

Worst of all, though, were the guests. The first time he hosted a pool party, Romero had assumed the ticket price would deter all but the cultivated, sophisticated, and mature gay elite. He had underestimated the number of loud, overly boisterous, young gay men who had a spare couple thousand dollars of disposable income they didn't mind spending for the opportunity to run around a Hamptons estate in their bathing suits snapping towels at other loud, overly boisterous, young gay men. And over the years, it had only gotten worse, to the point where that cultivated, sophisticated, mature gay elite now tended to avoid the Pool Party altogether.

But, alas, it was still a very profitable undertaking for Eastern Seaboard Pride, so, well . . . here he was again.

And the things he always found around the house the next day? The things the workers left behind with the broken glass and trash? His stomach churned just thinking about it.

If there wasn't a healthy tax deduction involved . . .

Ah well, at least there *was* that. That, and the fact that this year he had been able to use the delivery trucks to cart a lot of his most valuable possessions out of the house and into very secure storage. The wrong people would not be putting their hands on his artwork and antiques and other treasures. That was now certain. Except for a few last items stashed in the basement for later removal, the house was clean.

The setup for the Tenth Annual Pool Party was following the usual routine, meaning that crew after crew of men and a few women in matching orange T-shirts and denim cut-offs— none of whom seemed to recognize him, to his chagrin— stormed through the house on Thursday and Friday putting everything—from tables and lawn chairs to a volleyball net— together. They were followed early on Saturday by a flock of fussy caterers bearing chafing dishes and boxes and grocery bags, taking over not only the kitchen but most of the entire first floor and forcing him to seek refuge in his bedroom.

It was only when midafternoon arrived and the fleet of delivery trucks swept back out the driveway that he dared to come downstairs. A dozen workers still slaved away in the kitchen, but the house was finally approaching a tolerable noise level. He wanted to enjoy it for—he glanced at his watch—the fifteen minutes he had before the guests would start arriving.

"Mr. Romero?"

Startled, the actor spun around and was face-to-face with a man in a suit, which would have seemed out of place any-where on a warm Saturday at the end of May, but especially at a pool party.

The man introduced himself as an employee of Eastern Seaboard Pride, but his name immediately escaped Romero's memory. No matter. He'd know to look for the thirtyish man in a suit—certain to be the *only* man in a suit, if history was a guide—if he needed anything Eastern Seaboard Pride–re-lated. Which he seriously doubted.

He realized the Man in the Suit was talking and he hadn't been listening, so he tuned in as the man said, ". . . and there might be some press, so if you can make yourself available, that would be great."

"The media." Romero thought about that for a moment. "Yes, I suppose I can do some brief interviews. Which re-minds me, *The Eye* is sending a photographer."

"*The Eye?*" The Man in the Suit frowned. "The *New York Eye?*" Romero nodded. "Gee, sir, I don't know. It's not a very gay-friendly paper."

Romero offered him half a smile. "All the more reason for us to be polite. And hopefully keep our guests on their best behavior." Because, honestly, if he found one more empty lube packet in the rose bushes, *The Eye* would be the least of their problems . . .

Unlike some of the pushier Eastern Seaboard Pride repre-sentatives from Pool Parties past, at least the Man in the Suit had the decency to swallow hard and say, "I see your point, Mr. Romero."

"Good." Maybe this wouldn't be another hellish experience after all. "In that case, let me quickly show you around before our guests arrive. I want to let you know where guests do *not* belong . . ."

The tour was brief. Romero declared as off-limits the entire second floor of the house, the basement and kitchen, the fenced enclosure in the backyard behind which the hot tub—his private refuge—was secluded, and the wooded area at the rear of the property, which he claimed was for safety reasons—mossy tree stumps over which someone could trip, a pond beyond the trees where someone could drown—but was really because he knew the woods were a natural magnet for the horny young gay men, and he wanted none of that. Not this year. His yard was *not* the Fire Island Pines.

The Man in the Suit nodded politely and jotted a few notes, and they were at the front of the house before he could finish his jotting. Romero unhappily noted that a trickle of guests was already walking up the driveway.

"Okay, then," said the Man in the Suit. "Time for me to get to work. Thanks for everything, Mr. Romero."

"Call me . . ." He stopped himself. Oh, hell, let him say *Mister* Romero. It would remind him who was in charge.

Within a half hour, the yard was full of people, and a few of the more adventurous pretty gay men were already in the water, splashing each other and, in the process, managing to wet down everyone in the vicinity of the pool. He scanned the crowd and, as expected, the only women in attendance were either obviously with each other or clinging a little too desperately to their gay male friends.

Great . . . He was heating the hot tub for nothing. The gay card he was playing had been key to his career, but there was a definite downside.

He brightened for a moment, noticing a somewhat attractive woman who didn't seem to fit into either of the usual demographics, only to dim seconds later when he got a closer look and realized she was wearing a press badge on a red lanyard around her neck. She looked about as happy as he did to be there, and when he drew closer he saw why: she was the photographer from *The Eye.*

He flashed his most sincere smile. "Ian Hadley sent you?"

"Sent me? Oh, he didn't have to send me. I had a choice of either covering this or spending my Saturday with my boyfriend out on the boat, and I chose this."

Okay, then, thought Romero. Nothing like a bitter, sarcastic photographer to lighten things up.

He sort of wished he'd said that, but instead he smiled again, put on his accent, and said, "Enjoy the party."

He wandered through the party, largely ignored by the overwhelming majority of the crowd young enough to be his children . . . although if they *were,* he would have raised them better. Ah well . . . the recognition factor would change when the action-adventure movie with Jamie Foxx and Scarlett Johansson was in the theaters. *Then* they'd appreciate him.

From across the yard, the actor Quinn Scott—the gay flavor of the moment since coming out of the closet in his dotage—waved to him, and Romero waved back, smiling even as he thought, *That's right, old man. Enjoy the recognition while you can. Just remember who was openly gay a generation before you screwed your courage up. My fans will remember . . .*

He was distracted by a flash of purple.

Oh, wait. What do we have here? Romero's eyes zeroed in on an attractive woman in a purple bikini, following her as she navigated the crowd until she stopped and kissed . . . *Damn, she's kissing another woman! Why do some lesbians have to be so attractive? It isn't fair.*

The Man in the Suit, cell phone pressed to his ear, walked up to him nervously, weaving his way through the lawn chairs dotting the yard. When he reached Romero, he closed his phone and solemnly announced, "Tori Spelling will be here in five minutes. Can you do a photo op with her?"

"I will do," he said wearily, without bothering to force a smile, "whatever I have to do . . ."

It was while he was waiting at the top of the driveway for Tori Spelling that yet another attractive woman caught his eye. Mid-to-late twenties . . . dark hair and eyes . . . big breasts . . . Romeo Romero approved, but told himself not to get his hopes up. Not after that photographer from *The Eye* and the hot lesbian in the purple bikini. She was almost certainly the best girlfriend to the ninety-five-pound twink— hell, maybe eighty-five pounds—bouncing along next to her.

Still, he wanted to be a polite host. It was the least he could do.

"Hello," he purred as the woman approached. "Welcome. I am Romeo Romero."

The twink—whom he had not even been looking at— grabbed his hand and began pumping.

"Hi! I'm Jared Cockring!"

"What?!"

"Jared *Cochrane*," said the woman, nudging—well, a bit more than nudging, really—the twink in the ribs. She pulled their hands apart and took over, shaking politely. "And I'm his sister, Mary Beth Cochrane."

"That hurt."

"You'll be fine, Jared."

"His *sister*!" said Romero, because that was one pool party dynamic he had not encountered over the past decade. PFLAG-style mothers would occasionally appear to show their support, but *never* an attractive sister. "Interesting."

Her voice was sunny. "Yes, well, nice meeting you! I'm a

big fan!" With that, she yanked her brother's arm and walked away toward the large side yard and pool.

That was disappointing, he thought, until he remembered that *of course* she would just walk away. To her, he was Romeo Romero, the gay icon. Again, the gay card was his blessing and his curse. Tonight, it was nothing but a curse.

Then again, she was the only possibility at the moment. Maybe . . .

"Romeo! Darling!" He turned to see Tori Spelling storming up the driveway, a small entourage—more gay men—in tow.

He sighed, and pasted on that damn smile again.

Mary Beth found a rum and Coke and a lawn chair, then took her cell phone out of the handbag, careful not to pull out an orange T-shirt or a camera with it. She texted Lisa.

ALL OK. GOT HIS ATTN

She hit Send, then thought of something else she wanted to add.

JARED = MORON

Messages delivered, she put the phone back in the bag and tried to figure out what her next move should be. And also, where the hell Jared had twitted off to, because he sure wasn't getting the concept of teamwork.

"Hi!" said a woman, who was suddenly towering over her, blocking Mary Beth's sun. "I'm Tori Spelling! Thanks for coming to my party!"

"Uh . . . okay."

With the hosting duties he was performing for all these horrible people—and they seemed more horrible with every passing minute, parading around in almost nothing and giving him that "I know the name, but not the face" attitude—it took Romeo Romero an hour before he again found the fascinating sister of that annoying gay child. But he did finally spot her as she texted on her cell phone, seemingly apart from the crowd surrounding her and her lawn chair. He walked up behind her, and the sight of the fullness of her bosom made him stir slightly, which he would have been self-conscious about had semiturgidity not been the state of things for about half the male guests.

"My darling," he said, in a low register, barely noticing when she slapped her cell phone closed at the sound of his voice. "Mary Beth, is it not?" She nodded. "Are you having a good time?"

He was rewarded when she arched her back—*God, those tits were big!*—and looked at him with an appreciative smile. "Not my usual crowd, Mr. Romero. But, yes, I *am* having a good time. Thanks for asking."

And then she turned her head away.

Maybe a more direct approach would work better. "Do you not want to talk to me?"

"Oh!" She arched her back again, thrusting out those breasts, and Romero squatted next to her because suddenly she had taken the "semi" out of semiturgidity. "I just assumed that with all these attractive men, you had your hands full." She giggled. "I didn't mean your actual hands, although . . . well, you know . . ."

He duckwalked a half-step back, the better to adjust himself without being too obvious. If she only knew where he wanted to place his hands . . . his lips . . . his . . . uh . . . "There is more than enough of me to go around. I find you fascinating. Please tell me you'll stay until the end of the party?"

"Well, that will depend on Jared, of course."

"Jared?"

"My brother."

"Oh, of course. Jared Cockring. Yes . . ."

"Stage name," she said, without further explanation. And she would never mention that to either Jared, who might actually use it, or Lisa, who would probably kill someone. Hopefully Jared.

Romero flashed his eyes toward the pool, pretending to look for Jared but not caring enough to focus. "Yes, your brother. Well, encourage him to stay." He nudged her, but was careful to stay in his squat, because the "puppies in a blender" and "grandparents having sex" mantras weren't doing much to deflate his erection. "I think we will have an after-party, and I would like you to be there."

The woman giggled again. And Romeo Romero thought, *Score!*

Two minutes later Mary Beth texted Lisa again:

SCORE

The message was sent seconds before Jared materialized at her side.

"What?" she moaned, because he was in her sunlight, which was growing sketchy enough at this hour of the evening. She looked up and was unhappy to see almost all of Jared's body naked and looming over her, her only protection from Lesbian Blindness a swimsuit approximately the size of a bandage.

"Well, while you were laying out here in the sun giving Romero a hard-on . . ."

"I was?" Mary Beth was genuinely surprised. She knew she was making progress, but she didn't know she was making *that* much progress.

"You were. I saw him adjusting his junk from the window."

"What window?"

Jared squatted like Romero had, but for a different reason. "The kitchen window." He jerked a bony shoulder toward the house.

She didn't want to, but had to ask. "So why were you in the kitchen? It was supposed to be my job to check out the house."

"Well . . . beat you to it." He shrugged. "See that hot guy over there?" Mary Beth looked where the bony shoulder again directed her, but the men all looked *eh* to her, so she passed on answering. Not that Jared noticed. "He's president of the company that rented out all the tables and chairs and shit."

"Okay, very nice. Have fun."

"No, you don't understand." Jared was a bit too proud of himself, but maybe he should have been. "I got the code."

"The code?"

"For the alarm!"

Mary Beth looked at Jared with a combination of astonishment and annoyance. "You got the code?"

"Four-three-six-three."

"But . . . how?"

"Romero gave it up because the delivery people would have to be in and out while he wasn't home. But we're into the party weekend, so I figure there's no way he's going to change it until late tomorrow, at the earliest, because everything they brought in, they have to take out. Follow?"

"Uh-huh . . . Okay . . . Four-three-six-three. You're sure about that?" Jared nodded. "And how did you get this guy to tell you that?"

Leaning forward, Jared said, "I told him I was gonna sleep with Romero tonight, and he said there was no way, so we made a bet. The only thing is that I said I needed the code so I could sneak out if I had to."

She arched an eyebrow. "He believed that?"

Jared stood and cocked his hip in the way Chase found interesting but Mary Beth found annoying. "We have a bet. If I lose, I have to sleep with him."

"Well, you're going to lose."

"I *know*! See? It's win-win!"

Mary Beth again pulled out her cell phone, this time to send herself a message: the code—well, she *hoped* it was the code, otherwise Jared was going to learn there was a big, bloody "lose" in his "win-win" scenario—to disable Romeo Romero's motion detectors.

She was starting to type when a woman's voice said, "Hi! Can we take a picture together?"

4 . . . 3 . . .

"Oh my God!" Jared squealed.

6 . . .

"*Tori Spelling*! I *loved* you on *90210*!"

1 . . . 0 . . .

No, wait . . .

Shit!

The picture of Tori Spelling and Jared Parsells was lovely. But the expression on Mary Beth's face looked a lot like the one worn by the photographer from *The Eye,* the woman who could have been sailing with her boyfriend. They were women who were there to do a job, not have fun.

When the photographer and Tori Spelling left, Mary Beth asked, "So that number was four-three-six . . . what?"

"You didn't get it?"

"I had it until—" She stopped herself. She had a temper; she knew that. And no good would come out of disemboweling Jared in the middle of the Eastern Seaboard Pride Pool Party, no matter how good it would feel.

She tried to smile sweetly and said, "I couldn't catch that last number."

He shrugged, and both bony shoulders went in different directions. "I think it started with a four."

"The *last* number!"

He shrugged again. Two more directions. "Seven?"

"Now you're just guessing."

"I thought that's what you wanted."

She took a deep breath to calm herself. It was against her nature, and she was sure that she'd take out the accumulating rage on someone as soon as she was out of the party, but for now . . .

Then he smiled. "It was a three. Four-three-six-three. That's the code. What, you thought I'd go through all the trouble of getting it just to forget it?"

Still struggling for serenity, she punched in the last digit and didn't answer him.

"I'm not an idiot, you know."

She muttered "I know" and tried not to look at him.

"The other thing you should probably know is that the control panel is behind the kitchen door."

This time she *did* look up. "You managed to get a lot of information."

Jared ran his tongue over his lips. "I know how to make people talk."

Mary Beth was surprised by the realization that she really *was* calm. And she was happy. This stunt was going to work!

"I think I've underestimated you, Jared. You're pretty clever."

"Thanks." He looked thoughtful for a moment, then added, "So you think I should get a tattoo?"

No, she thought, she had not underestimated him at all.

Chapter Twenty-Three

After sunset, and after many of the guests had decamped, Romeo Romero surveyed the yard. It was a mess, but to his reluctant satisfaction he had to admit that it was not as bad a mess as it had been the previous year, which meant that the Man in the Suit had done his job. Not that there would be a *next* year at the Romero Estate, but it was good to know that someone could keep it together.

A dozen young men—including Jared Cockring, the twink brother of the beautiful Mary Beth—were still splashing in the pool, and he frowned when he saw a few tiny bathing suits on the deck instead of where they belonged: covering the gay boys. Ah well, nothing a tractor-trailer of chlorine wouldn't kill. And although the lawn was littered with unarranged chairs, plastic cups, and plates and napkins, at least his guests hadn't torn it up this year. Resodding was ridiculously expensive.

He spotted the skinny kid's sister, still sitting aloofly by herself in the dark. She wasn't like the others. It was as if she and Romeo Romero had a kinship. The thought made his manhood stir. He would have to tread delicately, but . . . *maybe*.

"Mary Beth," he said, approaching. "I am so glad you decided to stay."

She looked up. "Mr. Romero, you threw a very nice party

today." In a lower, *sexier* register she added, "And I can't wait to see what kind of after-party you throw."

Again, Romero was forced to crouch slightly. "Please call me Romeo. *All* my friends call me Romeo."

He righted a toppled lawn chair and pulled it next to her. "Have you had an opportunity to see the house?"

"No, not yet."

"Then can I give you a tour?"

"Me?" She seemed genuinely surprised. Then again, Romero knew that most mortals could never imagine being given a private tour by an internationally acclaimed film icon. He smiled, knowing that she must be thrilled, and knowing that he had been the one to thrill her.

Looking deep into her eyes he said, "You and only you."

"I'd—I'd be honored!"

He took her hand, steadying her as she stood, and then an annoyed look came to her face, as if she remembered something particularly unpleasant.

"Would you excuse me for one moment? I just want to let my brother know I haven't abandoned him."

Mary Beth texted Lisa two short words: I'M IN. Then she found Jared splashing in the pool and waved him to the side.

"What's up, sis?"

"It's time," she whispered, taking a camera from her oversized handbag and setting it near the edge of the pool. "He's going to show me the house."

"Okay. I'm on it."

"Don't screw this up." She looked down, and was immediately struck by Lesbian Blindness. "And put your bathing suit back on, you little whore."

Romero, ever the gentleman, took her arm to escort her when she returned, and they began a slow stroll toward the front of the house.

"I hope you won't be too disappointed," he said, as they

walked. "It's a bit bare in there tonight. I had most of the valuables removed because of the party. The art, the antiques . . ."

"Would people really steal things?" she asked, with a hint
of irony that only she could hear.

He laughed. "Oh, no, nothing like that. But, well, things
happen when you have a lot of young people partying."

The Man in the Suit, phone pressed to his ear, was standing near the driveway when they approached, shaking his
head. From the phone they could hear the tinny sound of
someone yelling.

"Is something wrong?" asked Romero.

He put his hand over the mouthpiece. "Just the usual
Kathy Griffin problems. When she got here one of the volun-
teers called her 'Kathy Lee Gifford,' so now she's . . ." The
voice on the other end flared. "Sorry, I've got to put out this
fire."

"Good luck," said Romero, sure he'd need it.

He walked Mary Beth up the front steps, through the half-
open front door, and into the foyer. He waved his arms as he
explained where valuable things would be if they were still
there, but Mary Beth wasn't really listening. She pretty much
wanted to first find the kitchen, and then get this over with.

"Romeo!" A tall, overweight, older man with a pinkish
face approached. Mary Beth sized him up, mostly because he
didn't look like most of the other guests, who had an average
age, waist, and IQ well below 30.

Romero turned to greet him. "David. I didn't even know
you were here."

"Yes, well . . ." He sighed, gesturing toward the living
room. "I arrived very late, and brought along a houseguest.
She has a touch of hay fever, so we've planted ourselves in the
house."

At the word "she," Romero looked hopefully through the
door off the foyer into the living room. And, yes, there was a
"she" there . . . but a short "she" in her mid-forties, not a she

that interested him. He returned his exclusive attention back
to Mary Beth.

"Pardon my rudeness. Mary Beth Cockring—*Cochrane!*—
this is my friend, David Carlyle. David, Mary Beth." They
nodded and exchanged hellos. "So your houseguest," said
Romero. "Is she a relative?"

"Oh, God, that's perhaps the only thing that could make it
worse. No, Romeo, that's Margaret Campbell, one of my au-
thors."

"I've read her books," said Mary Beth, and she remembered the title *People* magazine had given her. "The grande
dame of the American mystery, right? And you're her . . . ?"

"Editor." David sighed. "Editor, and punching bag."

Romero wasn't happy. "I've heard about her. Isn't she the
one who had the entire concierge staff at the St. Regis fired
last year?"

"Not the *entire* staff. Just one concierge. Maybe two. That
story was *greatly* exaggerated by the time it hit the papers. In
any event, we're only making a brief stop, and she's being very
well-behaved tonight. Just three bourbons and she hasn't had
a single cigarette. It's like she's a new wom—"

"*Carlyle!*" Margaret Campbell yelled from the living
room. "Get over here!"

David groaned. "Duty calls. Well, good to see you,
Romeo. And nice to meet you, Miss—"

"*Now!*"

After David Carlyle returned to the living room, Romero
said, "So that is obviously the living room, but for now I
think we'll skip that part of the tour."

Mary Beth agreed, so they strolled down the hallway that
ran through the center of the house, pausing briefly at door-
ways where she looked inside and he continued to explain
what wasn't there. Finally, at the end of the hall only two
doors remained.

"What's in here?" she asked, pointing to the left.

"Nothing. Just the kitchen."

"Can I see it?"

"It's just a kitchen. I would really like to show you the other . . ."

Mary Beth pushed the door open and walked in. The six remaining employees from the catering company, their work all but done for the night, glanced at her and went back to whatever they had been doing, which Mary Beth—who used the kitchen only as storage for the refrigerator—couldn't have begun to describe.

Not that it mattered. She wasn't in the kitchen to see the caterers. She was here to see if the alarm panel was where Jared said it was. Before Romero could catch up to her, she looked behind the door and, sure enough, saw it mounted on the wall. A green light on the panel flashed.

"Mary Beth? Darling?" He was following her through the door, so she spun around.

"I was just admiring your, uh, kitchen things."

"Hmm. Okay, yes, it is a very nice room, for a kitchen." He nodded cordially at the catering crew. "Would you like some champagne? The refrigerator is fully stocked."

"No, thank you." Her job was done, and she didn't want to spend a moment more than necessary in a room with appliances.

"Very well. Maybe later." He took her arm. "If you will come with me, I'll show you my favorite room in the house."

They left the kitchen and walked across the hall.

"And this," he said, opening the door opposite the kitchen with a flourish, "is the guest room."

"Very nice," said Mary Beth by rote, until she took a few steps into the room, sized it up, and realized it was perfect. A guest bedroom with ground-floor windows was just what she needed: easy viewing access for Jared and, if necessary, an escape route that wouldn't require her to jump from a second-story window. Not that she had any intention of doing that, of course; that's what the pepper spray was for.

She didn't even mind when she heard Romero close the door behind them . . . although she waited apprehensively for the click of a lock, because if he was going to lock it, she was going to have to unlock it. When that didn't happen, she turned to him and said, "What a cute room."

He took a step toward her. "It used to be for the maid. Before I trimmed back my staff."

"Why'd you do that?" Casually, she put just a little more space between them, walking to the other side of the bed and pretending to be interested in the décor, which mostly consisted of framed film stills from the career of Romeo Romero.

"A man like me, well, I like my privacy. These days, you can't be too careful. One disloyal employee could sell secrets to a tabloid like *The Peeper* and do untold damage." He paused, and added, "You seem like the type of woman who can keep a secret."

"Oh yes, Romeo. I *never* tell . . ."

Romero smiled. "Of course you don't. I can see that in your eyes." He sat on the edge of the bed, patting the mattress next to him. "Please . . ."

She looked hopefully out the window but saw nothing. *If Jared blows this . . .*

"Where's that go?" she asked, pointing to a door in the corner of the room.

"Outside." He smiled. "To the hot tub. But please . . . Sit with me for a moment."

"Uh . . . okay." And she sat.

"I have to tell you something," said Romero, arching an eyebrow. "When I invited you to the after-party . . ."

"That was very sweet," she said abruptly, knowing what was coming next and trying to steady herself. The words would be good for the blackmail scheme, but bad for her

Sapphic sensibilities. Although if Jared didn't make an appearance soon, the words were just going to be uniformly bad.

Romero cleared his throat. "Yes, well . . . yes, it *was* sweet. But I was thinking about something more than sweetness. I was thinking about an after-party . . . *for two*."

Mary Beth hoped she seemed appropriately receptive to his charm. "An after-party for two? As in just the two of us? Just you and me? Or as in . . ."

He stopped her. "We should talk less, my dear, and leave some thoughts unexplored. Now, your brother—will he be looking for you? If you were to leave him alone for, oh, an hour, will the boys in the pool be sufficient entertainment for him?"

She willed herself to lean closer to the actor, but the movement was awkward. It was one thing to be seduced by Romeo Romero in theory; quite another in practice. "I think Jared's got a crush on you, Romeo. Don't you like him?"

His voice was low, almost a purr, and his accent thickened. "There are a lot of crushes in the air tonight, Mary Beth."

She forced a giggle, figuring that a man in full seductive mode would appreciate a giggly woman. "You Europeans are *so* mysterious."

"Aren't we?" Romero's lips grazed her neck, and Mary Beth closed her eyes, hoping to conjure up a more welcome mental image. She had just about managed to pretend his lips were Kate Hudson's when he abruptly pulled back.

"What's wrong?" asked Mary Beth, suddenly afraid the catch of the day had rejected the bait of the moment.

"I should lock the door."

She couldn't let him do that. She didn't know which direction Jared would be coming from.

"No, don't lock it."

"Don't lock it?"

"I ... uh ... I have a phobia about locked doors. I ... I get nauseous."

"You have a ... ?" That didn't make sense to him, but ... okay. He was close to sexual intimacy with this attractive woman, and there was no need to upset her. When they were outside, under the open night sky in the hot tub ... then he would make sure they could not be disturbed.

And it was time to take it to that next level. He furrowed his brow, offering her the same expression of heightened concern that had won him a Golden Globe supporting actor nomination as the selfless and compassionate doctor treating Jane Fonda for cancer.

"Let me ask you something, my darling. What do you know about the Kinsey Scale?"

She actually knew quite a lot about Dr. Kinsey and his scale. As a committed "Kinsey 6" for almost ten years, she knew pretty much everything there was to know about human sexuality. But she also knew that this was not the time or place to show off her brain.

"A little bit," she said, because she *also* didn't want to come off as thick as her supposed brother.

"If you know even a little bit, you know that human beings are capable of a complex variety of sexual expression. For example, I am gay ... but I am not without attraction to some females."

"Uh-huh. So you consider yourself to be bisexual?"

"I do not like labels. But there are some rare women—you, for example ..." He put his hand on her back and began gently stroking, which was a signal even Jared would have been able to figure out.

"That's, uh ... sweet," she said, and willed herself not to zap him with pepper spray or break his fingers because $500,000 was riding on this—this *ickiness*.

His mouth was next to her ear. "Again, just sweet? My

darling, I don't think you truly appreciate the *passion* that is Romeo Romero."

Had he really just said that? Had she really just felt his hot breath in her ear? *Where the hell is Jared with his camera?*

"Oh, Romeo," she said. Reluctantly. "That's so . . . *hot.*"

She heard a faint noise from outside, near the window. Jared? Maybe this entire unpalatable episode would be over soon.

"I would like to make you a proposition."

"You would?"

"I would like you to open yourself to me."

"Open myself?"

"Sexually. To explore a little of my 'Kinsey five' side."

"Uh . . ."

"Only for an hour or so." His large hands clamped over her wrists, preventing her from acting out on her impulse to grab the pepper spray and empty the entire canister in his face.

"My dear . . . my darling . . ." He moaned, and his eyes closed. "I *want* you. I *need* you."

"But there ain't no way you're ever gonna love me?"

"What?" he asked, eyes popping open.

"Sorry. Old song lyrics."

His eyes closed again. "Old songs, like old wine—and even older people—have a sophistication the young can never understand. Don't you agree?"

She knew it was coming, and wanted it to come, but that didn't make it any less annoying. So she kept thinking "*$500,000*"to keep her focused.

There was a slight movement from beyond the window treatment, out there in the darkness. Yes, he was definitely out there. She was saved, and this sordid episode—digitally captured forever—would be over in mere moments.

"Romeo," she moaned, squirming her wrists out of his grip, then placing one hand on each side of his face and turning it toward hers, more to keep him from seeing Jared in the window than to gaze into his eyes.

"Oh, yes, my darling," he cooed. His eyes lowered, and she thought, *Is he staring at my breasts? My God, he's staring at my breasts!* "We have shed our pretenses tonight, and now it is time to shed everything else. Our clothing, along with our pretenses."

She swallowed hard and yanked his head up a few inches to take his eyes off her breasts. "Romeo, I am very attracted to you." He tried to pull away, but she firmly held his face in place. "Very!"

"And I . . ."

"*Very!*" She shook his head until she thought she heard something crack that maybe shouldn't have been cracking.

"Yes, my dear. Thank you." He was less concerned about the cracking noise, being roughly thirty-five years older than her and used to hearing similar sounds. "Now—"

There was a tap at the window, and she spread her fingers to cover his ears. *That idiot Jared! Can't he be quiet about this?* She glanced over the actor's shoulder and, sure enough, she could now see the bedroom light bouncing off something metallic, which had to be the camera. No sooner had she seen it then the lens again made contact with the pane of glass, emitting a tiny *tap*.

Idiot!

But it was time for action. A picture of a clothed woman holding Romeo Romero's ears wasn't worth a half million dollars. She was going to have to make this look real . . .

"Romeo," she whispered breathlessly, moving her lips perilously close to his mouth. "I would love to explore your Kinsey Five-ness."

"What?"

Oh. Right. She took her hands off his ears and again said, "I would love to explore your Kinsey Five-ness."

He smiled. "The hot tub, then? It is just outside the door."

She smiled. On the outside, if not the inside. "Please, darling. Please take me to your hot tub."

Click-clunk. Click-clunk.

They both turned as the doorknob to the enclosure where the hot tub awaited them jiggled slightly.

"Did you hear something?" She hoped he hadn't, but realized ignorance was pointless in the wake of stupid Jared's noisiness.

"This is an old house. Even a slight breeze makes it creak and groan." Again, his lips brushed her neck, and he quietly added, "Or maybe it's a ghost. Shall we investigate? Shall we see if there are ghosts . . . in the hot tub?"

Kate Hudson . . . Kate Hudson . . . Kate Hudson . . .

Romeo Romero's lips were on hers. There was no mistaking them for Kate's, which would be soft . . . and welcome.

He pulled away, but only millimeters, and his voice was a whisper. "There is nothing like a warm tub in the cool breeze."

She looked out the window. Jared was still there—she could see the silhouette of his head in the moonlight—and she hoped he'd have the sense to duck out of sight before they walked outside.

But he wouldn't have to do any ducking.

Because that was the exact moment Jared, wearing nothing but his damp Speedo and a towel wrapped around his shoulders, walked into the guest room, leaving the door ajar.

Romero snapped to an upright position on the edge of the bed and adjusted himself.

"So *here* you are!" Jared said, flouncing down between them on Romero's bed. He patted Mary Beth on the thigh. "Hi, sis! I've been looking all over for you."

Stunned, Mary Beth spent a few seconds wondering how the idiot managed to walk into the room moments after she had seen him in the window . . .

She looked back at the window. The silhouette had vanished.

"How . . . ?" She looked at Jared. Then at Romero. Then back at the window.

Romero, annoyed that Jared had interrupted them—let alone planted himself between them—leaned across the boy and asked her, "How *what*?"

"Nothing," she said, trying to suppress the alarm going off in her head. Turning to Jared, she said, "Brother, dear, would you be a sweetheart and leave us alone?"

"In a second. Uh, sis." He patted Mary Beth's thigh again, and she was afraid she might have to pepper spray both of them. "I just needed to get away from Tori Spelling for a minute. Every time I try to talk to someone, she's in my face. I never should have told her I was such a big fan."

Mary Beth's smile was frozen. "And don't you have something you're supposed to be doing?"

"Uh . . . Oh. Right."

"Then do it!"

"Is everything all right?" asked Romero.

She attempted a smile that was a little less frightening. "We're fine. You know how brothers and sisters are."

And Jared said, "Okay, maybe I can avoid her . . ."

Which was, coincidentally, when they heard Tori Spelling's voice from the other side of the door, somewhere back in the party.

And she was screaming.

"He pushed me! That son of a bitch pushed me!"

The decibel level of everyone who *wasn't* Tori Spelling seemed to grow, too. There was the sound of shouting . . . something being upturned . . . breaking stemware . . .

And the chaos seemed to be getting closer.

Romero cocked his ear toward the door, confusion etched on his face.

"What the hell is going on out there?" His accent had almost disappeared.

The decibels continued to climb. Now there were male voices that almost drowned out Tori Spelling, and all of them were yelling words that had to do with "cops" and "police" and "don't shove Tori Spelling."

And then the guest room door flew open and a short, roundish man, gripping a camera, was framed in the center of the doorway. He was middle-aged, rumpled, and clearly didn't belong at the party, whether or not he had shoved Tori Spelling. Behind him, they could see others approaching.

"Aha!" yelled Will Whitcomb, pointing an accusing finger at Romeo Romero. "You're with a *woman*! I saw it through the window! I *knew* it!"

In one swift motion, Romero reached over and knocked Mary Beth off the edge of the bed—her ass hit the hard floor with an audible thud—and had his arm around Jared before Whitcomb could aim his camera. By the time it clicked, and before anyone but Whitcomb had the chance to focus on anything except the angry, foaming, Tori Spelling–pushing man who had just crashed the party, Jared was on Romero's lap . . . a move that delighted Jared, who squirmed suggestively, much to Romero's intense discomfort. The actor was beginning to wonder if he would ever be able to have an erection again, with or without supplements.

"Sorry, Mr. Romero," said the Man in the Suit, who was suddenly tugging at Whitcomb's stained windbreaker. "He got past us."

"He shoved me!" yelled a woman from somewhere in the crowd, and everyone knew who it was.

"Who is this man? Why is he in my house?" *And why in hell's name won't this kid stop squirming on my lap?*

Whitcomb was sputtering agitatedly and trying to pull away from the Man in the Suit. "You—you—you were just with a girl! I saw it! You're not gay!"

Romeo Romero wasn't a famous and well-respected actor for nothing. "Clearly he's deranged."

"Clearly," said the Man in the Suit, still trying to get a grip on Whitcomb, though not too much of a grip, because the guy looked a bit stained and oily to him. Maybe even contagious.

"But he—he—"

"Want me to call the police, Mr. Romero?"

Romeo Romero looked at the struggling men in the doorway, and then at the crowd that had gathered behind them, straining to see what the fuss was about. And he quickly figured out that the only way to make the crazy little man's story go away was to make the crazy little man go away. Promptly. Especially with the media in his home. No police . . . no publicity . . . nothing.

"No," he said. "No police. Just escort the gentleman out of here."

"But—but—"

The Man in the suit finally got a grip on Whitcomb—he would thoroughly wash later, to the verge of scalding—and yanked him out of the doorway. Much of the crowd dispersed, following the sideshow as it played out on its way back to the driveway, although a handful of people lingered to take in the sight of Jared Parsells smiling and grinding his ass into Romeo Romero's lap.

Including the sour-faced photographer from *The Eye*.

"One quick picture for 'Between the Streets'?" she asked, and, before Romero had a chance to consider the request, Jared's tongue was in his ear. A flash went off, and, with a glance at her watch, she said, "Okay, that's the money shot. I can get this in before deadline, so I'm out of here."

On the floor next to the bed, Mary Beth moaned, rubbed her bruised posterior, and said to herself, "Lambert and his dumbass plans . . ."

Chapter Twenty-Four

A few minutes before 10:00 that night, Lisa Cochrane got a brief text message from Mary Beth Reuss: PICK ME UP NOW

"That's not the way it was supposed to work," said Jamie.

"No shit," said Grant.

No way was Farraday going to drive, and, surprisingly, that wasn't because he was drunk. There was something about a night of abstinence, along with the keyed-up tension of the job, that put him to sleep like a baby. Grant, who hadn't had a decent night of sleep in weeks, thought that he'd have to look into that.

Since he *was* wide awake, Grant grabbed the keys to the minivan out of the sleeping Farraday's fist, collected Lisa, and drove the quarter mile to Romero's house. Mary Beth was waiting at the end of the driveway, and she didn't look happy.

"He made me leave," she said, as she got into the minivan. "It was a freakin' disaster."

"Where's Jared?" asked Grant, putting the vehicle in gear.

"You don't want to know."

"What happened?" asked Lisa.

She shook her head. "I was *so* close! I mean, we were on a bed and he was about to take me to the hot tub. I had it *made*. But then this crazy guy bursts into the room and makes a scene . . . He even tried to take a picture of us!"

"Who?" asked Grant, trying to imagine who else might be trying to blackmail Romero—besides himself and Ian Hadley, of course—but drawing a blank. That Combover guy, or whatever his name was? Unlikely; Ian Hadley had taken him out of the picture. Although if two or three people were already doing it, who knew how many others were out there?

"I dunno. Some fat, sweaty, crazy guy. He knocked down Tori Spelling. Anyway, after that happened, Romero couldn't get away from me fast enough. Next thing I know, I'm on the floor with a bruised ass and Jared is grinding *his* ass into Romero's crotch. About which, let me add: gross."

Grant and Lisa silently agreed.

"So they kicked the crazy guy out, but by then it was too late. Romero was spooked. I was pretty much the only biological woman left at the party—except for Tori Spelling—so he made me leave, and said that maybe we'd get together some other time. Now, I haven't seen a penis in a *long* time, but I know a man's brush-off when I hear it. 'Some other time' means 'never.' "

Lisa shook her head. "Uh . . . you sound disappointed about that."

Mary Beth folded her arms across her chest and said, "I have my pride."

For his part, Grant just wanted to bring the conversation back to the more important item at hand. "And Jared . . . ?"

"*That* idiot! Get this: *he* got invited to spend the night. I get sent home, and Twinkenstein gets to spend the night. Is that fair?"

Grant was confused. "But . . . wait. If Romeo Romero is heterosexual, why would he want Jared to spend the night? He *is* straight, right?"

"I told you he was spooked. Right before I left, he was asking all the cute boys to stay for an after-hours pool party." She imagined the X-rated antics that were probably going on at Romero's house even as she spoke. It wasn't pretty. *Major Lesbian Blindness.* "Oh, I'm sure he's double-locked himself in his bedroom and will let the rest of them run around all night without him, like the rutting pigs they are. But this is all about his *image* now. After that guy accused him of being straight, Romero couldn't gay it up fast enough."

They pulled into the driveway of the vacant house. Grant got out, opened the garage door, and pulled the minivan inside.

"So what do you think?" asked Lisa, as they stood on the cold concrete floor of the garage after Grant finally managed to wrestle the door back down, thinking all the time how it was probably a lot easier with the automatic opener. "Do we go over the hedge?"

Grant wasn't happy. "For what? Pictures of Romeo Romero and a bunch of gay boys splashing around in the pool? I don't see how that helps us blackmail him."

"But our Plan B—"

"Our Plan B was based on having a woman in the house. I didn't figure that Romero was going to turn the place into a big gay stag party tonight."

"So what do we do?"

Grant sighed. He was getting a headache.

"Hope that Jared can think of something spontaneous," he said, following them from the garage into the darkened house. And if Lisa and Mary Beth thought they heard tears in his voice, they were right.

When Lisa first told him she had secured an unfurnished house, Grant figured it was no big deal. They weren't going to live it in, after all . . . just borrow it for a few hours.

He hadn't thought it through about how sleeping on a

hard floor was going to feel to his back the next morning. If he had, they would have stayed at the Holiday Inn.

Not that Grant was the only one ailing; they were all suffering from soreness and stiff muscles. But since Grant started out with the worst back, he was the one who suffered the most.

"I've got bad news," said Farraday, as he lurched into the foyer. "I don't think I can drive."

"What do you mean you can't drive? You're the *driver*! Driving is what you're here to do!"

"My neck." He turned it maybe one inch to the right, and a little less to the left. "It's stiff from sleeping on the floor. Sorry, Lambert, but if I can't turn my neck, I won't be a safe driver."

"Hold on a second," Grant said, and then he frisked him for a flask. Not finding one, he said, "Okay, I guess I believe you."

Farraday laughed, which somehow still seemed threatening. "Figures. First night without booze in six months, and look what happens to me. The scotch keeps you loose. That's my theory."

"If you say so."

"I can drive," said Jamie, who was also walking stiffly, although not as bad as Farraday.

"The hell you can. You'll hit the Queens border and somehow send us to Connecticut. *I'll* do the driving."

And so it was settled. But first they had to pick someone up.

"You left Jared with his cell phone?" Grant asked Mary Beth.

"Yeah, he's got it. Unless he managed to drop it in the pool, which I wouldn't put past him."

"Call him. Tell him we're on our way."

There was no answer, so she left a message. And then they painfully climbed into the minivan, drove it out of the garage without bothering to close the door, and headed toward Romero's house.

As they drove, Chase asked, "So what do you think the odds are that Jared got what we need?"

"On a scale of one to ten," Grant said, "I'd say minus thirty."

A few minutes later, Grant braked by the side of the road, just down the street from the actor's home. And then they waited.

They waited for a long time.

"Hit the horn," Jamie finally said, after almost twenty minutes had ticked past in silence. "Let him know we're here."

Grant considered that, because, really, what did they have to hide anymore? Well . . . except it was generally bad form for the occupants to draw attention to the stolen minivan in which they were sitting.

Besides, Farraday would never go for that. "The single worst thing most drivers do today," he said, "is lay on the horn. It's rude."

"There you go," said Grant."It's your morning quality-of-life lecture from Paul Farraday."

A few minutes later, Jared wandered out to the street and spotted the van.

"Oh my God," muttered Mary Beth. "He hasn't gotten dressed *yet*?"

Spotting Grant in the driver's seat and Chase in the passenger's, he opted for Chase's side of the car, and, through the open window, said, "Heeeey! You missed a great party. Wasn't it a good time, Mary Beth?"

"Mmph, sort of," said Mary Beth.

"Where are your clothes?" asked Chase. "We've got to get going."

Jared placed a naked forearm on the ledge of the open

window. "That's what I wanted to tell you. I need to get my brunch outfit out of my bags."

"What?" It was Grant, although the rest of them were thinking the same thing.

"I'm staying for brunch!"

Chase shook his head. "You can't stay for brunch, Jared. It's over. Time to get back to the city."

"Wait a second," said Jamie, and he leaned forward from his seat in the back. "I think I'm following what Jared is saying. They're having brunch, so Mary Beth goes back inside . . ."

"Right!" said Chase, getting it, too. "She goes to collect Jared, and *then* she gets another shot with Romero!"

"That would work!" said Jamie. "And this time we get the pictures and—"

"Yeah, except that's not what Jared was saying," said Jared, who would know. "That place is totally no girls allowed." He looked at their faces, and they still didn't seem to quite grasp what he was saying, so he made it simpler. "I just want to stay for brunch."

"Okay, then," said Grant, and he turned the key in the ignition. "See you around some day."

They left him, dressed only in a Speedo and flip-flops, at the side of the road.

They needed coffee, so after they drove ten miles or so Farraday directed them to a convenience store. They stocked up on caffeine, snacks, and newspapers to make the next several hours of their trip back to the city slightly more bearable. Then Farraday guided Grant to a fairly isolated road running through Long Island's vanishing south shore farmland, where the odds were better no cops would be looking for a stolen minivan, and they were on their way.

It was Lisa who, because she was holding the newspaper,

won the privilege of opening to "Between the Streets." And then she simply said:

"Oh, crap."

"Oh, crap?" asked Lambert. Taking his eyes off the road, he glanced at the tabloid in Lisa's hands. He saw the headline first. It was hard to miss.

CAUGHT IN THE CLINCH: ACTOR AND HIS BOY TOY SIZZLE THE HAMPTONS!

And below it was a photograph of Romeo Romero and Jared Parsells that was, indeed, sizzling.

"Oh, crap," said Lambert, and he didn't return his eyes to the road until he heard gravel from the shoulder kicking up under the undercarriage. Which was too late for a helpful reaction.

Chapter Twenty-Five

The minivan wasn't drivable. No doubt about that. It had gone off the right shoulder and knocked down a potato farmer's mailbox on its way into the drainage ditch, before coming to a jarring stop where the potato farmer's very sturdy driveway crossed the ditch at grade; grade being road-grade, not ditch-grade. It caught the minivan in the center of the grill at a rate of speed that was slow for the road but pretty damn fast for a drainage ditch.

It took Grant a few seconds to shake off the shock of the accident, time he spent staring at a mailbox reading SUFFOLK SPUDS POTATO FARM that now rested tentatively against one windshield wiper. By the time he finally unbuckled himself from the driver's seat and stepped out into the ankle-deep ditch water, the others were already outside the van.

He slammed the door, and the mailbox slid off the wiper blade and tumbled into the water.

"Everyone all right?" he asked, above the hissing steam from the radiator escaping from under the hood. They nodded unhappily as they rubbed various sore spots on their bodies and glared at him.

Grant's back ached more than usual as he slogged through the water to higher ground, where he turned and looked back at the crumpled front end of the van. "Well, this sort of sucks," he mumbled.

"First rule of driving," said Farraday, annoyed he hadn't been behind the wheel, because none of this would have happened, and also a bit surlier than usual because of the absence of alcohol in his blood system."Never take your eyes off the road."

"Yeah, I knew that. Now I know that *better*."

"I'm just sayin' . . ."

"I heard you the first time."

"That was just carelessness . . ."

"Guys," said Chase, trying to head off Grant's comeback and be the voice of reason. Or at least prevent a fistfight. "Before this gets any worse, I want to remind you that we just crashed a stolen motor vehicle." He looked up and down the road, then back to the potato farmer's house, mercifully set back a distance from the road. "And even though it's quiet out here right now, it isn't going to be long before someone comes along and calls the police. Understand?"

Mary Beth wasn't quite as inclined toward reason. "But the van's busted. What are we supposed to do?"

"Walk," said Chase.

"Walk?" It was as if she had never heard the word before.

"Yeah, walk," said Grant, with a surliness inappropriate for the guy who crashed the van. "Unless you can fly."

Mary Beth didn't like the idea of walking very much. She did *not* believe in walking, which was something prehistoric man did before God created motor vehicles. "We don't even know where we are! We don't know where we're going!"

"Then you can think of this as an adventure," said Grant.

She folded her arms and said to Lisa, "I'm not going."

"Honey, be reasonable . . ."

"I'm wearing heels. And it's dirty out here."

Grant decided it was time to put an end to her nonsense. "Fine. You stay here with the van, and we'll find a way to get home. If the cops come before we have a chance to get back, maybe they won't think *you* stole the van. They *probably* will, but *maybe* they won't."

With that, he turned and began walking back the direction they had come from, hoping that his vague recollection of seeing a sign directing traffic to the Long Island Rail Road a mile or two back was accurate. And, if it was, hoping that the station was located somewhat close to the sign.

One by one, the others shrugged a "what can you do" and began to follow him down the dusty shoulder of the road, with Lisa and the still-complaining Mary Beth bringing up the rear.

"One thing," said Jamie, when he caught up with Grant. "What about Jared's stuff? He's got two suitcases in the van."

"You want to carry them?"

"No."

"Go back and make sure the idiot didn't leave any ID inside. If he did, grab the ID and leave the bags."

"Leave them?"

"Your choice, Jamie. Carry them or leave them."

Jamie shrugged and went to do what he was told, which was not going to include carrying Jared's suitcases.

"You know what annoys me?" Grant asked Chase when his partner finally reached him. "That idiot Jared is the only one of us who's gonna make out on this deal, and we're the ones who brought him in. He made the papers, and you can bet that Romero is gonna slip him some cash. *That* annoys me."

"You can't blame him. We put him up to it."

"I don't blame him. I just don't appreciate the irony. Everybody else here—" The sound of Mary Beth's shrill whining somewhere behind him made him reconsider. "Everyone here contributed something practical, although mostly at a tolerable noise level. Even Jamie was useful for once in his life, by bringing us the idea. But all Jared contributed was prettiness."

"You sound jealous."

Grant frowned. "Maybe I am. Twenty years ago, maybe I could have planned this scheme *and* been the pretty boy."

Chase patted his back. "Aw, baby, I still think you're pretty."

"For an old guy."

"Wouldn't want it any other way." He paused, momentarily forgetting the fix they were in as he admired the way the sun glinted off the silver in Grant's hair, then thoughtfully added, "And maybe you shouldn't dismiss Mary Beth like that. Yeah, she's loud, but she did a lot for us. Hey, she even got close to getting Romeo Romero in a compromising position. I know she gets on your nerves, but you've got to give her credit for delivering."

"Eh . . . maybe," Grant said, as Mary Beth's voice welled up in the background, which only annoyed him all over again. "And anyway, why was that picture in the paper this morning? Christ, it's Sunday. The party was only last night. What, this is breaking news? Every day do they make a judgment call between whether they should cover Jerry Stanley or the Middle East?"

As they stepped over roadkill—small roadkill, but Grant saw even in that a bad omen—Chase put his hand on his partner's back and said, "You have got to calm down, baby. All of us—all seven of us, *including* Jared—are in this thing together. You already know that Ian Hadley has his fangs in Romero. That's probably why the picture ran today. Does it matter? It would have run eventually, you know."

"Maybe."

"What's eating at you? Seriously!"

Grant walked another dozen paces before answering. When he did, his voice was heavy. "I just botched the biggest score of our lives. That's what's eating me. We were looking at a half million bucks—well, a half million split between everyone—and we blew it. The nickel-and-dime stuff we've been doing for all these years . . . Eh, I guess that's what we're gonna keep having to do."

He looked away for a second before adding, "I failed."

Grant began walking faster. Chase kept pace with him for a while before gently grabbing Grant's arm, slowing him slightly.

"So how do we un-fail?"

"Un-fail? What do you mean?"

"Wait, are you telling me you're giving up?"

"I already quit. I quit last night when Mary Beth got tossed out of the party." Grant glanced over his shoulder before continuing. "Look who we've got. A drunk cabbie, a Realtor who does this for the cash but mostly for the adrenaline rush, her psychotic girlfriend, *Jamie Brock*, who defies categorization, *Jared!*, and the two of us, who maybe aren't up to a big score like this. And we thought we could pull one over on Romeo Romero and Ian Hadley? We were insane."

"No, we weren't." From behind him, Chase heard Mary Beth screech, which probably meant she had finally come across the roadkill. "We weren't insane. We were *ambitious*. There's a difference."

"How do you figure?"

This time when Chase grabbed Grant's elbow, he stopped him altogether.

"Maybe we went too big too soon, Grant, but that's not a crime." He laughed. "Okay, in this case it *is* a crime, but you know what I'm saying. Look, we got so close to scoring a big one here . . . minor leaguers playing in the major leagues who scrambled and improvised and almost won the World Series. It'd be a shame if we were to quit just because we're behind in the eighth inning."

Grant looked at him. "When did you get so basebally?"

Chase looked down. "I would have used football metaphors, but I don't understand the game."

"Chase Rockne, All-American."

"Now you're getting footbally on me."

Grant laughed, despite himself. "Yeah, we're both too butch for words."

"It's good for you," said Chase, dancing around the shoulder like a prize fighter. "Gets those competitive juices flowing."

Grant looked out at the wide countryside. "Well, here's the thing, Rockne. You made a nice, impassioned speech—very inspirational—but it sounds like it could also have been from a World War II movie about a team of lovable misfits, just before everyone dies. At a certain point you have to realize that we've put together a bunch of lovable misfits—also with Mary Beth and Jared, who aren't so lovable—but it doesn't matter."

"What's going on?" asked Farraday, who was suddenly behind them. "Are we gonna find this train station? Or chat?"

"I'm trying to get Grant to go back," said Chase. "He doesn't want to."

Farraday asked Chase, "*You* think we should go back?"

"Absolutely."

Farraday smiled, a rare sight. "I thought I was the only one."

"*You* want to go back?" asked Grant.

"Hell yeah. I want my thirty grand."

Grant thought about that. "You were in for twenty."

"That was then," said Farraday. "And this is now."

"Two to one," said Chase, smiling.

"Not to overuse your baseball metaphor, but that sounds like the score from a low-hitting game." Grant looked down the road and saw Jamie trudging closer. He hated the idea that Jamie might be the only voice of reason besides his, but already knowing that Jamie wanted to keep his distance from the actual commission of felonies made it an easier call . . . to abuse the baseball metaphor one last time.

Except before Jamie got close enough to bring into the conversation, Farraday lifted up his head at a distant sound.

Then he shouted, "Sirens! Everybody down!"

They scrambled for cover off the road and, sure enough, less than a minute later a wailing patrol car zipped past.

"I guess that means they found the van," said Chase over the receding noise, as he emerged from behind a tree a few yards from the roadbed.

"Guess so." Grant, who had hidden behind the tree next to his, looked back down the road, and was satisfied the stragglers had avoided being seen, although the nearest—Jamie—seemed a bit worse for the experience.

"I had to take the ditch," he said, trying to wipe the mud off but only smearing it as he approached.

"Jamie!" Grant wrapped his arm around Jamie's shoulder, taking care to avoid the mud. It was a gesture that let Jamie know something was wrong, because Grant never did things like that. Not to him, at least. "Sorry this thing fell apart, but maybe we can work together again someday." He left unsaid the "when hell freezes over" part.

"Uh . . . actually, I was just thinking." To emphasize that he was, in fact, thinking, he even took off the knock-off Oakleys. "If Jared is still *inside* the house, should we be giving up so soon?"

"Told you," said Chase.

"Shuddup." Grant trained his eyes on Jamie's, boring into them. "You'd trust your freedom to Jared? Because if we do something and *don't* succeed, at this point we're looking at breaking and entering, at a minimum."

Jamie thought about that. His scams tended to be of the unconscionable type, not the illegal, and he knew he wouldn't look good in an orange jumpsuit with his coloring. Not unless they had tanning beds in prison, which he sort of doubted. Grant was making a good point.

Still . . . *$500,000*. And a third of it would be his. He had taken foolish risks for a lot less.

"I say we do it," he said, with a finality that made Chase sort of worried that he had missed a major flaw in his advocacy of returning to Romeo Romero's house.

But there were two more people who still had to be convinced.

"No way," said Mary Beth, after she and Lisa limped up the shoulder and met up with the men. "I am done with this, and so is Lisa."

"A half million dollars," said Chase.

A half-million dollars, thought Lisa.

"I don't care. Lisa and I are out of this. She can sell more apartments if we need more money."

"I can?"

"You can." Mary Beth had made their decision, and that was that. "We're going back to New York."

To which Lisa said, "But—but—yes, baby. Of course."

They took the lead, and the men watched them walk away.

"This doesn't happen without Mary Beth," said Grant to the others. "Jared may be inside that house, but Mary Beth is the only one who can get Romero naked. Without that, this scheme doesn't happen."

"Never thought Grant Lambert would be a quitter," snarled Farraday, and he started to follow the women. Followed by Jamie. And finally followed by Chase, after a mournful glance at his partner.

"Don't give me that look," said Grant, almost to himself. And then he brought up the rear.

Chapter Twenty-Six

The question that confronted them when they reached the Long Island Rail Road station twenty minutes later was, should they buy a train ticket? Or steal a car from the parking lot?

So Grant asked.

Farraday shrugged. "You wanna steal a car, be my guest. Not that I believe you're really gonna do it. You don't seem to have the fire anymore."

"I've got the fire. Just not for *this* job."

"Yeah, well, this job is—*was*—the only game in town. But maybe you're right. Maybe you should stick to the small-time stuff . . . the stuff you've got the balls for."

"I know what you're doing, Farraday. Reverse psychology. You're saying I can't do something just so I'll prove I can do it."

Farraday shrugged again. "Nah. I just figure you don't have the balls. But if you think I'm psychologizing you, go right ahead."

Mary Beth, standing defiantly behind Farraday, said, "The problem is he didn't have the balls to do it *right* this time. Cutting and running now is the smartest thing he's done in the past two weeks."

And that's when Grant finally snapped, because Mary Beth was the last person he was going to take it from.

"Okay, that's it! I've *had* it with you!"

She was ready to boil over anyway, so when Grant snapped, Mary Beth did, too. "You haven't heard *anything* yet, Grant Lambert. I am tired, and hot, and dirty, and I just walked two miles in heels to get to this goddamn train station. Oh, and did I mention that, because of *you*, I had a man's lips on me last night?"

"Ehhh . . ."

Mary Beth's face glowed a fiery red. "Let me tell you something, Lambert. I am *not* shutting up and you're gonna listen to it. *All* the way back to New York, if I feel like it. Maybe for the rest of your life!"

To punctuate her tantrum, Mary Beth swung her heavy bag at Grant with such force that it threw her off balance and one of the heels snapped, sending her into a reel that left her in a heap on the asphalt.

"Baby!" Lisa yelled, running to her rescue.

"He shoved me!" wailed Mary Beth, although only she could understand the accusation, since everyone else had witnessed her clumsiness. "Did you see that? He shoved me!"

As the women huddled several yards away, Jamie sidled up to Grant and quietly said, "Now *you're* a man who knows how to throw a party."

Grant turned from Mary Beth to Jamie, but nodded in her direction. "Shut up or you're going down next."

It was because he was talking to Jamie that he didn't hear the gravel scrunch, which is how her handbag managed to connect with the side of his head the next time she swung it. He went down in a heap, much like she had a half minute earlier.

"There!" she said triumphantly, adding an ineffectual kick at his ass, after which she thought it best to slowly back away. "Now you know how it feels!"

He stretched his foot out behind the shoe with the broken

heel and she stumbled over it, sending her back to the pave-
ment.

"Mary Beth!" Lisa was again to the rescue.

Chase shook his head sadly as his partner struggled to his
feet. "You're going to pay for that one, Grant."

"It's good for her. It'll toughen her up."

"Much as I like a good fight, you think this is smart?" His
eyes darted around the parking lot. "You know, someone
might call the cops."

Grant brushed dust off his pants. "You've got a point."

From somewhere distant down the tracks, probably still a
mile or so away, they heard the blast from an oncoming train
horn.

"That's the train," said Mary Beth, back on two feet.
"And I am *so* getting out of here and back to the city."

"Bye-bye," said Grant, wiggling his fingers at her. Just because a physical fight was ill advised didn't mean he had to
put up with her. Lisa gave him a reproachful glare.

"Yup," Jamie said, as he began slowly following the
women to the platform. "One hell of a party."

In his wake, Grant snarled, "Maybe if a *certain someone*
hadn't lost the original tape, we wouldn't have end up
stranded in the middle of nowhere."

Jamie wheeled around. "What's that supposed to mean?"

"It means that we could have avoided all of this if you
hadn't lost the damn tape. *That's* what it's supposed to
mean."

"Oh yeah? Well—well—well, if I hadn't lost the tape, I
could have taken care of this myself, and you never would
have had the opportunity to blackmail a major gay celebrity!
Did you think about that? I *gave* you this opportunity!"

Grant looked around at the parking lot and Mary Beth's
forgotten broken heel amid the swirling dust and the miles of
suburban housing tracts and farmland stretching out in every
direction.

"Thanks for the opportunity," he said, reaching down to pick up the heel. When he bent over, he felt a searing pain blaze through his back. He was getting too damn old to be sleeping on cold, hard floors and driving minivans into ditches. That was for sure.

"Here, let me help you." It was Farraday, sensing Grant's distress. He put his arm around Grant's spasming lower back and gently eased him up.

"Thanks," he said, although he didn't feel much better than he did while doubled over.

"Think nothing of it." Farraday pointed toward the platform, where the hobbling Mary Beth was ascending the stairs, followed closely by Lisa and Jamie. The still-unseen train's horn sounded again, louder this time. It was almost to the station. "You know what the problem is here, Lambert?"

"I have a feeling you're gonna tell me."

"Exactly. The problem is the two people who *don't* want to go back to Romero's are the ones who are angry about everything. The rest of us aren't fighting. That tells me that, deep down, neither of you are okay about aborting the job."

"Reverse psychology . . . analysis . . . I think you're watching too much Dr. Phil."

"Hey, I was a New York City cabbie. You don't think I know how to figure out what's going through people's heads?" He looked back to where Lisa, Mary Beth, and Jamie were almost on the platform, then to Chase, in a holding pattern midway between Grant and the others. "And there's another thing."

"What now?"

"If they get on that particular train, they're gonna end up back in the Hamptons."

"Back in the Hamptons? Are you sure?"

Farraday's face conveyed only half the disappointment he felt, but it was more than enough. "Lambert, I'm a transportation guy. Not just cabs. I can get from anywhere to anywhere faster than anyone in the Northeast . . . maybe the world. You can trust me on this."

Grant moved his eyes back to the platform, read the directional sign, and realized that Farraday was, indeed, correct. In their haste to get out of there, they had ended up on the wrong side of the tracks. For once as a fact, not a metaphor.

And Grant suddenly understood that it was like some sort of sign. Not that he believed in signs, but—if he did—this would be one. Fate wanted him to go back and get the damn evidence they needed to prove that Romeo Romero was a fraud.

Fate wanted them to get their damn half million dollars.

"We probably should tell them," said Farraday.

"Screw that," said Grant, and he began moving as quickly as his aching back would allow when he saw the nose of the train approach from around a bend down the tracks. "We're going with them."

"But—"

"Come on. You were right. We've worked too hard to walk away with nothing."

When Grant finally broke the news to them, they were enraged. But then he explained that fate wanted them to do this, and they merely thought he was insane.

Which was better, in a way, because at least they didn't talk back. And anyway, they'd be back in the vicinity of Water Mill in just minutes, ready to see this job through to the end.

While they rode, Grant huddled with Chase and they hashed out some details. When they were off the train, and after he had the chance to fill them in on his latest brainstorm, Mary Beth looked at Grant and said, "I hate you."

"You're gonna like me a lot more with almost a hundred seventy thousand dollars in your hands."

"No, I'm not. I'll probably use the money to hire someone to kill you."

Lisa tried to be the diplomat. Somewhat.

"Uh . . . I know you don't mean that, baby. But seriously, Grant, this is the stupidest fucking idea in a string of stupid fucking ideas."

"Not the way I see it. The way I see it, we've tried every other way. We tried to find Jamie's tape . . . We tried to make our own . . . We tried to do this the *nice* way. But something always goes wrong. Now we've got no choice but to march in there and get what's ours."

Farraday nodded his agreement. "I ain't been sober for twenty-four hours for nothing. We've got to do this."

"Actually," said Chase, with a glance at his watch, "you've been sober for closer to thirty-six hours now."

Farraday's hand began shaking. "Oh, Christ, I wish you hadn't said that."

"Call me skeptical," Lisa said, "but I don't see Romero going out of his way to accommodate a bunch of people who show up at his doorstep and demand a half million dollars. All I see is a call to the county sheriff, followed by a quick, brutal trial. Are you sure you won't rethink this, Lambert?"

Grant and Chase exchanged a glance and a smile. Lisa eyed them suspiciously.

"What? What is it?

Chase said, "The county sheriff is exactly the man we're counting on."

"Ugh," moaned Mary Beth, and she rubbed her sore ass in a very unladylike manner. "You think the cops are going to make this work in our favor? I don't know what you've been smoking, but I wish you'd share."

"The cops are our insurance," said Chase.

"Yeah, you're insane."

Lisa looked at Grant. "Mary Beth is right. We're out of here."

"If you girls don't want to go, you don't have to go," said Grant. "You'll still get money out of this."

To which Lisa said: "I should hope so—"

To which Grant said: "I'll repay you the five grand I owe you for those tickets."

"Wait a minute! I'm into this for a lot more than five—"

"And I'll buy Mary Beth a new pair of shoes, since the ones she's wearing kind of broke out there in the parking lot."

Mary Beth interrupted. "Those shoes cost twelve hundred dollars, Grant Lambert, and the price has probably gone up since I bought them."

"Fine," said Grant, still smiling. "Tell you what: I'll give you an even seven thou."

Lisa closed her eyes and shook her head. "You're a bastard, Lambert. You know that?"

"Hey, isn't it you who keeps telling me that people should only get a fair cut if they deliver? Well, you have a point. You're free to cut and run, but if you do, you aren't delivering."

"Bastard."

"It's fine, though. We could use your help, but the boys and I can take care of this by ourselves if we have to."

There was silence for a few minutes while Lisa lit a cigarette. Finally she said, "I really hate you right now, Lambert."

"Yeah, well, I'm getting used to people hating me. So you're in?"

She exhaled a mouthful of smoke into his face. "Guess so."

Farraday eyed the parking lot. "In that case, we're gonna need a new vehicle."

"Can you drive?" asked Grant. "Because I'm not having a great day behind the wheel."

Farraday turned his neck slightly to the right, then slightly to the left. "Still a little stiff, but better. I can handle it."

Grant nodded. "In which case I'll help you find a car."

Something had caught Farraday's eye, so they walked in that direction through the lot.

As they checked out the vehicles, Farraday asked, "What was the deal back there, when you told the girls we could do this without them? I thought we needed them."

"That, my friend," said Grant, with a genuine smile, "is how you do *psychology*."

"You're good, Lambert. You're good." He stopped and whistled. "I am in love."

Grant followed his gaze to a black Escalade parked near the road. "You think you can do it?"

"Not think, *know*. These babies were made for me."

Grant looked at it skeptically. "What about the antitheft?"

"Just saw the guy park it and head for the platform. Most likely, it'll be hours before he even knows it's gone."

"Then let's grab it."

"You know," said Farraday, as they approached the Escalade. "If they used these for cabs, I might even consider getting off the bottle."

"Seriously?"

Farraday's eyes twinkled. "Naaah."

Chapter Twenty-Seven

The plan—the new plan—was refreshingly simple and un-complicated, a welcome change from the criminal gymnastics they'd been going through for the past two weeks.

They weren't exactly going to march up to the front door, of course. That would have been a bit *too* simple and un-complicated. But that description of the plan was close enough.

Mary Beth was going to march up to the front door, convince Romero to empty the house of all remaining gay revelers and workmen, and—when only she and the actor remained—seduce him. Most of the setup had already been taken care of; she'd only have to deliver the follow-through.

In the meantime, the others would fan out across the estate, so that no matter where Mary Beth and Romero ended up, someone would be nearby to take the picture.

Deputy Henry Lemmon of the Suffolk County Sheriff's Department would be their backup. If something went wrong—Romero calling the police, for example—he would be the cop they'd use to keep the other cops at bay. And if Romero was resistant, well . . . they were sure that Lemmon wouldn't be happy to learn that the actor had been the man who had seduced Amber Arbogast away from him.

It was Grant who first thought there might be a problem,

as they rode toward Water Mill. "We don't have Lemmon's phone number."

Chase said, "What do you mean we don't have his number?"

"I know exactly where it's written down. On the pad next to the computer. Which means it's in Jackson Heights, not with us."

"That's cute," said Chase.

"What's cute?" Grant was already irritated by setback after setback, and didn't need his boyfriend to be knocking him.

Chase bounced one finger off his temple a few times. "This is my phone book, Grant. Fifteen years and you didn't know that?"

"Wait . . . your *head*? You memorize phone numbers?"

Jamie piped up from the back seat. "Jeez, Grant. You make it sound like it's magic or something."

"Jamie, what year were you born?"

"Nineteen sixty . . . uh . . . seven?"

"I rest my case." Grant returned to Chase. "So you remember Henry Lemmon's cell number?" Chase rattled it off. "Okay, Rain Man, let's get to work."

". . . eight?"

Chase dialed the number from his untraceable, off-the-street cell phone, and was relieved when the call went to voice mail. They didn't need him yet—hopefully wouldn't need him at all—so it was enough for now to reopen communication.

After a generic female voice instructed him to leave a message, he put on his "Amber" voice and said, "Hi, Henry, it's Amber. Listen, sorry I didn't meet you at the airport. Long story. But there's been some trouble, and I might need your help. Talk to you later!"

"I still don't know why we're inviting the police to join us this afternoon," said Lisa, after Chase hung up.

"You don't understand," said Chase defensively. "This guy was in *love* with me."

"With *you*?"

"Well . . . *Amber*. Still, it was love. So if we need him later, I'll just call him back and be like, the reason I didn't show up at the airport was because some guy on the plane seduced me. Promised me money and fun, and whatevs."

" 'Whatevs'?" asked Lisa.

Grant said, "He's in character as Amber. Go on, Chase."

And Chase did, embracing the traces of the "Amber Arbogast" voice he had used so convincingly up until a few weeks earlier. "So, I'm all like, I really love you, Henry, but I guess I was just a silly teenage girl, and I did a stupid thing. I hope you can forgive me. I totally want to die for what I did to you. I even wrote some poetry about it I want to share with you when we're together."

Lisa asked, "Teenage girls are like that? Why aren't more men gay?"

"After a couple drinks—" Jamie started, but Grant shut him off with a scowl.

"Anyway, it turns out this guy is bad." Chase-as-Amber's voice caught. "I mean, like really bad. He's *mean*, and he makes me do all these chores like I'm Cinderella or something. And I think he's a pedophile . . . not a man like you, who wants to take care of me. He only wants me to be his slave, and he's holding me against my will in this big house out in Water Mill."

Lisa thought for a moment. "This is the kind of thing that you guys ordinarily do for a living when I'm not around?"

"Now, Lisa," said Chase, "we're not doing anything that Chris Hansen doesn't do. Plus, he just puts the creeps in jail. *We* steal their identities."

"And their cars, if they have one that Charlie Chops would like," added Grant. He was proud of that flourish; that little value-added to their business plan.

"You should cut me in on the car action," said Farraday, who was enjoying driving the Escalade. "I could get you from Newark Airport to Chops's place in twenty-two minutes during rush hour."

"Next time," said Grant, not altogether sincerely.

"Well," said Lisa, "much as I enjoyed watching Chase pretend to be a teenage girl, we've still got a job to do."

"This time," said Grant, "I don't see how we can fail."

His was a unique sentiment inside that Escalade.

It was 2:30 when Farraday slowed as they passed Romero's estate. There was a lone catering truck in the driveway.

"Looks like the cleanup's almost over," said Grant. "Time for us to get to work."

"Where to now?" Farraday asked.

"Head into town. We have to pick up a few things."

Half an hour later, Mary Beth walked through the still-open front gate, her oversized handbag swinging from one shoulder. She had on a new outfit and new shoes, courtesy of Lisa's credit card. And clean skin, courtesy of the bathroom at Starbucks.

She rang the bell and waited. Then she rang it again and waited some more. When no one answered after several minutes, she followed the sound of high-pitched laughter around to the side yard, where a handful of those young gay men were still in the pool, going strong after almost a full twenty-four hours. She couldn't even begin to imagine the drugs that were fueling them.

"Excuse me!" she shouted over their voices. "Does anyone know where Mr. Romero is?"

"He went upstairs after brunch," said one man, whose wet brown hair flopped over his eyes. "Said he had a headache."

I can only imagine, she thought. "How about Jared? Is he still around?"

There was silence for a moment, until they all burst into giggles.

"Okay, fine," she grumbled. "I'll find them myself."

"What a biiiitch," one of them said to her back, and the others started giggling again. Somehow, she managed to ignore them, tempting as it was to spray the pool with pepper spray.

The door from the pool to the house was open, so Mary Beth let herself in. She looked around and understood even better than before why Romero had taken refuge. It was as if Hurricane Gay had made landfall in the living room. Empty and half-empty plastic cups and plates littered every horizontal surface, dry lemons and limes were scattered randomly around the floor, and the entire room had a pervasive aura of sticky staleness. Yeah, the boys had had one hell of a party.

"Romeo?" she called out. "Romeo?"

She heard something creak, then creak again, and realized they were soft footsteps on the staircase.

This time, her voice was tentative. "Romeo?"

He walked into the living room clad in a blue robe and slippers, and carrying the remnants of a Bloody Mary.

"My darling," he said. His smile was weak, but welcoming. He looked tired . . . or maybe hungover. "I had hoped that was your voice. It's the only thing that could get me out of bed." He winked. "Or *into one*."

"Uh . . . ha." She gestured around the living room. "This place is a mess. You want help cleaning up?" Not that she wanted to clean—she *really* didn't want to clean; wasn't even sure if she knew *how* to clean—but she had the sudden idea that a photo of Romero and his naked cleaning lady might meet their needs while keeping her out of a more intimate sexual simulation.

He didn't bite. "People are coming in tomorrow to clean." He looked around, frowned, and added, "And they were relatively good this year. Last year . . . well, you do not want to know."

She nodded, because it was true that she did not want to know.

"The boys are still here?" he asked. They heard a splash from the pool, and both sighed. "Never mind. I know the answer." He set his glass down on a sticky table and asked, "So, you are here to pick up Jared Cockring and take him home, I suppose?"

She took a few steps toward him and licked her lips. "Actually . . . Jared knows his way home. I was hoping to see *you*." She glanced down and noticed his robe twitch where she wished it hadn't. *Disgusting.*

He took a step toward her, and she might have recoiled had she not remembered that the gay boys playing in the pool offered a degree of protection.

"You know what would make me feel better?" he asked.

"Another Bloody Mary?"

"No. Well, *yes*, actually, but I think what would make me feel better is to relax in the hot tub."

"Uh . . . oh, really?"

"Would you care to join me?"

Mary Beth didn't answer right away. Instead, she calculated how much time it would take the rest of the gang to get in position to capture the picture, because there was no way she was going near that hot tub if they weren't ready.

"Mmmmm . . ."

"Yes?" he asked.

"Mmmm . . . maybe. But . . . uh . . . can we warm it up first?"

"It is like you are reading my mind." He smiled as he walked gingerly toward a pitcher of Bloody Mary mix on the other side of the room. "We'll set it at the right temperature—it's clouding up and cooling off a bit, so the warm water will feel good—and then in fifteen minutes or so . . ."

She recalculated. "Perfect!"

His drink refreshed, he led her back through the house toward the guestroom, and as they walked, he talked.

"I do apologize for last night, Mary Beth. I was a bit of a cad . . ."

"You don't have to . . ."

"But my image. You must understand what I mean to all the homosexuals of the world. If they were to discover that I also crave beautiful women, well . . . they would be crushed. So I hide that side of myself. I hide it for the good of my fans." He opened the door to the hot tub enclosure and said, "But with you, I can be— *Jesus Christ!*"

It took Mary Beth a beat before she realized that he was not suggesting a sick role-playing game.

"*Jesus Christ!*" he yelled again, and added, "Get out of there! *Out!*"

She looked over his shoulder through the doorway.

Lesbian Blindness!

In the hot tub were Jared and another young man, both doing something like she was supposed to be doing.

But they weren't doing it for the benefit of cameras.

And they weren't pretending.

"Well, *brother*, you sort of ruined the hot tub plan."

"Why? It's nice in there."

He was back in his bathing suit, drying his hair. They had been left alone in the guest room because Mary Beth told Romero she wanted to give Jared a strict talking-to; which, in fact, she did.

"If you think either one of us is getting into that stew of communicable diseases you were brewing out there, you're out of your mind. What were you thinking?"

"Hey, everyone left me and I sort of liked the guy. So get off my back."

"*Someone* has to." She sat heavily on the edge of the bed,

inches from where she had been sitting before Romero knocked her off the night before. "It's time for you and your friends to clear out so we can wrap this thing up. You can see your, uh, 'hot tub boy' when you're back in New York."

"I will. But maybe we can give him a lift home!"

"Do yourself a favor and do *not* mention that idea to Lambert." She looked him over. "Do you have any clothes besides your flip-flops and that bathing suit?"

"They're in the minivan."

"Hmm. Well, that's gonna be a problem for you." She thought for a moment before a very satisfied smile came to her face. "But there's a change of clothes in the *new* car for you."

"New . . . ?"

"They'll explain outside. Look for a black Escalade parked down the street. And now you'd better get going, because there's work to do."

He started to obediently leave, but stopped, much to Mary Beth's annoyance. "One thing you should know."

"What?"

"Down the basement, I found some stuff we might want."

"What were you doing . . . ?"

"Looking for a private place to be alone, until we found the hot tub. Not that *that* worked out so well for us. Anyway, there's all this stuff . . ."

Mary Beth had a moment of hope. "Please tell me Romero's one of those pervs who likes to tape himself. Anything to take the burden off me."

"No, sorry, no tapes or anything. But there are a lot of paintings and shit, and they're all wrapped."

"Wrapped?"

"In brown paper. Styrofoam on the edges, and all that. Like they're gonna be shipped somewhere. I peeled off the edge of the paper on a few of them, and they looked expensive."

She shook her head. To Jared, "expensive" probably meant *Dogs Playing Poker* or *Velvet Elvis Meets Jesus*.

"You know what he's doing?" she said. "He's protecting his valuables from people like *you*." She thought about it again. Just in case: "When you get outside, mention it to Lambert. I doubt it's anything we want, but valuables are valuables."

He looked at her hopefully. "So I did good?"

"Doubt it. Now get the hell out of here. Remember: black Escalade. *Black Escalade.*"

Jared spotted the blue Escalade and walked over to it, peering through the windows but not seeing anyone inside.

"Can I help you?" asked the sixtyish man who was suddenly walking toward him from the garage, wondering why this kid was checking out *his* car in *his* driveway. Must have been one of Romeo Romero's guests, given the way he was dressed. Or rather, *wasn't*.

Jared was unshaken. "My friend is waiting for me, and I thought . . ."

"There's a black one just like this parked down the street. Maybe that's your friend. I *know* he's not in my car."

"Oh." Jared shrugged and smiled. "Nice to meet you."

The older man watched Jared walk away and wondered again why he and the missus had thought it would be a good investment to buy a house across the street from an actor.

Now they were alone. Romeo Romero had finally rid his house of his loathsome guests and sent the last catering truck away, even though they complained about leaving a lot of their equipment in the kitchen. It could all wait until later. Or tomorrow. Or, hell, Tuesday.

Now was all that mattered, and now he was *finally* alone with the delightful Mary Beth.

"Well," he said, sadly, "I guess the hot tub is out of the question."

"Uh . . . yeah." She was certain of that for so many reasons. Jared and his new "friend" had only sealed that deal. But maximum accessibility was also on her mind. "Maybe we could lay out by the pool."

He glanced out the window, looking for an excuse, because he had no intention of exercising his true Kinsey 1 status so carelessly.

"The clouds are coming in, my dear. It will be cool, and unpleasant. Maybe even rain. But there is so much more to this house. My bedroom is upstairs . . ."

"Oh, no!" she said instinctively. "I'm afraid of heights."

He thought about that. "The *second* floor?"

"*Especially* the second floor."

"I don't . . ."

"Do you know that most accidents in the home happen on the second floor?"

"I . . . uh . . ."

"Which is why I don't do second floors, Romeo. No offense. *Third*, though . . ."

"I have an attic."

She thought fast. "Like I was about to say, third is even worse than second."

"Uh . . ." He was trying to find the sense in her argument and drawing a blank. Then again, the girl was also afraid of locked doors. So many psychoses in one woman . . . he'd have to remember not to make a habit out of her. "Okay. No second floor. No third floor." Fortunately, he had an alternative. "The guest room?"

"Will the door be unlocked?"

He was ready for that. "Yes, my darling. The door will be un—"

"Do you mind if I powder my nose?"

"Huh?" He was having a hard time following her, which

he blamed on the party, the gay boys who wouldn't go home, and just maybe those five Bloody Marys.

Mary Beth smiled. "Powder my nose. It's an American euphemism for 'go to the bathroom.' "

"Oh, well . . . of course. You know where it is, correct?"

"Correct. And have another Bloody Mary while I'm gone."

Inside the bathroom, which was as big as most living rooms in New York City, Mary Beth turned on the tap and called Lisa.

"He's ready to go," she said, in a whisper over the running water, when her girlfriend answered. "Are they in yet?"

"I don't know. I'm in the car."

"Well, find Grant and tell him it's time. I don't care if he has to *fly* over that hedge. I am not gonna let Romero touch me for one second longer than I have to." She paused, then added, "Speaking of the car, did Jared find you?"

"He's walking down the street right now. Oh, Lord, Lesbian Blindness."

"Tell me about it. Okay, Romero wants me in the guest room. Got that? The door will be unlocked. It's back by the hot tub . . . Jared knows exactly where it is." With that, she remembered what she had seen in that hot tub and felt her stomach churn.

"Guest room. Door unlocked. Got it."

"Okay," Mary Beth said in parting. "Make this fast."

"Okay—hey, who drives a white Mercedes?"

Mary Beth thought about that. "White Mercedes? I don't know. Why?"

"Because one just passed our car and it looks like it's pulling into Romero's driveway."

While Mary Beth went to powder her nose, Romeo Romero took advantage of the opportunity to walk to the kitchen and punch in the alarm code, which closed the front gate and activated the motion detectors for the first time since the previous morning. After scanning the pool area and spotting a few unclaimed bathing suits, he was afraid some of the boys would be back, and didn't want to risk being interrupted.

God knew how those men without their bathing suits were going to get home, but that was their problem. They were *not* getting back in the yard to retrieve them. His problem—*all* his problems—were about to be relieved with a hot multi-hour, multiorgasmic session with the lovely, busty, luscious Mary Beth.

Seconds after the white Mercedes pulled into the driveway, the gate began to close, missing the car's rear fender by inches.

"That was close, Ian," said J. P. Hunt from the passenger seat, still looking every inch a New York cop despite being one hundred miles away from the city. "A split second more and it would have clipped us."

"Life is all about that split second," said Ian Hadley from behind his Ray-Bans, which he wore despite the cloud cover. He spun the wheel slightly to conform to the curve of the driveway, then eased to a stop at the front door.

"So you think the party is finally over? That kid we just passed in the Speedo and flip-flops . . ."

Hadley had already erased that memory from his mind. "J. P., if the party isn't over already, it will be within three minutes." He parked next to the front door. "Wait for me here."

"Sure you don't want me to go in with you?"

"Quite."

Jared watched the white Mercedes pass, then crossed the road to the Escalade. He looked for Chase, but—no Chase in sight behind the tinted glass—identified the front seat passengers through their half-open windows as Farraday, behind the wheel, and Lisa.

He was sort of afraid of Farraday, so he went to Lisa's window.

"Hi." He waved.

"Christ," she rasped, blowing a plume of smoke sort of past him, but not quite. Jared coughed. "Put some clothes on."

The lock switch flipped, and Jared let himself into the back of the car. "Where are my bags? I need to change into my traveling clothes."

Lisa said, "Oh, uh . . . well . . ."

"We had a little problem," growled Farraday. "So figure out something else to wear."

Jared was almost in a panic. "Like what?"

Turns out, like an orange T-shirt and denim cut-offs.

Chapter Twenty-Eight

Mary Beth asked, "Are you ready, Romeo?"

"I have been ready for a woman like you all my life."

"Then let's—"

DING ding . . .

"What's that?" she asked unhappily, thinking about Lisa's tip about a possible mystery visitor in a white Mercedes who would have to be gotten rid of quickly.

He faltered for a moment. "It's the doorbell."

"Those kids are gone, right?"

"Hmm." He thought about the abandoned bathing suits, and wondered if one of them had managed to get back onto the grounds before the gate closed. "I thought so, my dear. Let me see who it is."

He walked to the peephole in the door and frowned.

"What's the matter, Romeo?"

"It's not the kids. Apparently, I have a business call."

DING ding . . .

"*Well, tell them to go away!*" And even Mary Beth was shocked by her loud tone.

Romero sighed. "It's not that easy. You see, I have some, uh, business to discuss with this gentleman."

"So . . . you want me to hide?"

Despite his desire to have Mary Beth, and despite his disappointment at this interruption, that was the last thing he wanted.

"No, my darling. Our guest is someone who is aware of my Kinsey Five-ness. Please, I must insist you stay."

Mary Beth didn't like that. It put another hitch in their plan. Still, she said, "Okay." And hoped to play it out.

When the newcomer started knocking, Romero finally opened the door.

"Ian," he said, pumping his arm. "So glad you could stop by."

Hadley was colder. "You knew I was coming this afternoon, Romero, so why the formal . . . ?" That was when he spotted Mary Beth. And flashed his sharp white teeth in an approximation of a smile. "Hello, miss. I didn't see you there."

Romero made the introductions, after which Hadley asked Mary Beth to leave them alone for a moment. When she was gone, Hadley drew close to the actor.

"You're getting a bit bold in your old age, eh, Romeo?" he asked in a hushed tone.

"What you already know, I cannot take back. But this is staying between us."

Hadley shook his head with disappointment. Somehow, when it was just their secret, it seemed a bit more special.

"Just be careful. Some people might use this sort of thing against you."

The irony was not lost on Romero. "Indeed, some people *might*." He caught a flash of gray hair through the window at the side of the door. "Did you bring someone with you?"

"My Number Two. Don't worry, though. He's a retired police officer from New York. Doesn't know a thing, but even if he did, he's absolutely discreet." Hadley leaned uncomfortably close to Romero's ear. "I wanted him along because I'll be taking a sizable amount of cash with me when I leave."

"But he doesn't know?"

"He knows nothing. He won't even be coming into the house. So just relax, Romeo." He looked around. "Is anyone here other than the girl?"

"No, I sent everyone home."

"Good." Hadley smiled. "So let's take care of our business."

The house next door to Romero's was vacant for the weekend. The very proper owners—who, like the owner of the blue Escalade, had once thought buying a house near Romeo Romero would be a good investment—had opted to spend the weekend in Manhattan, as they did every year when it was time for the Pool Party. The clamor of Midtown was vastly preferable to the clamor from the house next door.

Not that Grant would have known or cared; he only cared that there had been no sign of life in the place for the past two days, and the yard was covered in overgrown foliage near Romero's hedgerow, which, if they stayed mostly on their hands and knees, would conceal them pretty well.

When Lisa and Jared approached, stooped over to minimize their visibility, Grant was carefully hacking through the hedge with the electric trimmer they had bought in town while Lisa was buying Mary Beth a new wardrobe.

"How's it going?" she asked.

He turned them off. "Slow. These bushes are thick at the bottom."

Chase took the clippers from Grant's hand. "I'll spell you for a while."

"Make it fast," said Lisa. "Mary Beth says that it's time." Her cell twittered. "And there she is now." Lisa answered, not saying much as her girlfriend gave her an update, then hung up and said, "New problem."

Grant sighed. "Because we haven't had enough of them?"

"Ian Hadley is there."

"At Romero's house?"

"At Romero's house."

Grant thought about that. "Okay, so he must be there to pick up his blackmail. Maybe that's good. He won't be staying long, and in the meantime it gives us more time to cut through these bushes."

"Yeah." She shrugged, without commitment. "Maybe."

Mary Beth had retreated to the kitchen to call Lisa while the men consulted, no doubt over Hadley's *successful* blackmail effort . . . unlike the one she seemed to be engaged in. After ending the call, she figured she'd given them enough time alone, and was on her way out of the kitchen when the blink of a red light caught her attention.

It was coming from the alarm control panel on the wall behind the door.

And last night, when she had first seen it and the house was overrun by guests and caterers, the light had been green.

It *was* green, and now it was red. Meaning . . .

"Shit," she muttered, fishing her phone from her handbag. She flipped it open and looked for the text message she had sent herself, the one with the alarm code.

4363.

She plugged the numbers into the keypad and held her breath for what felt like minutes, but was only a few seconds. She didn't breathe again until a green light flashed.

That was close. Too close . . .

In the living room, Hadley assessed the damage. "It looks like you had one hell of a party last night, Romeo. I do hope our press coverage helped."

Romero forced a smile and took a swig from his Bloody Mary. "I'm sure it did, Ian."

Noting the drink, Hadley had a sudden craving. And what

better reason for a drink than to celebrate a successful black-mail effort? "Perhaps we should toast our new partnership."

"Eh?" There was nothing Romero wanted less. Ian Hadley was supposed to pick up the first part of his payoff and just *go away.* Fortunately, Mary Beth had returned, which meant that Hadley wouldn't want to stick around.

He was wrong.

"Why not?" Hadley extended his arms, as if he was the host, welcoming Romero and Mary Beth to his own private party. "J. P. can drive me back to the city. We should have a toast—the *three of us* should have a toast—to celebrate."

"What do we have to celebrate?" asked Romero, without the slightest effort to be cordial.

"Your successful party . . . our partnership . . ." Hadley gave a little bow to Mary Beth. "Your *very* attractive lady friend."

Mary Beth, hoping to buy a little more time, added, "A toast would be great! Romeo, didn't you say the refrigerator was stocked with champagne?"

"Uh . . ."

"I'll just go check. I'm sure there must be some—"

"No," he said, resigned to his fate. "I'll get it."

As Romero began his slow walk from the living room, Hadley smiled wolfishly and said, "Wonderful. That will give me time to get to know your friend better."

Yeah, thought Romero. *Just fucking wonderful.*

He walked to the kitchen, passing through until he reached the basement door. He wanted Hadley out of there—he wanted Mary Beth in his bed, and Hadley *out*—and there was one sure way to make that happen.

Cash.

A bag of cash big enough to quiet Hadley until . . . well, not much longer.

As he descended the staircase, he thought that Ian Hadley was worse than the taxman. Neither would leave him alone until they had more than their pound of flesh, but at least the taxman didn't fake geniality to rub it in. The sooner he had both of them out of his life . . .

Ah, but soon enough.

He stopped his determined walk through the basement when he noticed the brown paper peeled from one of the paintings stacked vertically on a pallet, leaning against a cabinet.

"How the hell . . . ?"

And then he saw it wasn't just *that* painting. Several of them had been disturbed.

The caterers? Those damn homosexuals? *Someone* had been rummaging through the basement, where they did not belong, and he wasn't happy about that. If he didn't already know this would be his final party, it would have been the last straw.

And then he was gripped with a sudden panic. If people had been prowling around down here . . .

In a corner of the basement, back behind the furnace, he found a plain brown shopping bag. Looking inside, he was relieved to see it still contained bundles of neatly stacked bills. At least the vandals hadn't penetrated this far into the basement.

Romero fanned a handful of the bills, part of Ian Hadley's first installment. It was more than he wanted to part with, but it least it would quiet him for a while. Which would buy him enough time . . .

Back in the kitchen, the shopping bag dangling from one hand, he grabbed a bottle of champagne from the refrigerator. He thought about also taking three Waterford flutes, but then thought better of it. No need to make Hadley too comfortable; he could drink out of a plastic cup. Whatever it took to get him to leave.

He would have felt the same way even if Mary Beth wasn't there. The fact that she was, though . . . waiting for him . . . yes, Hadley would have to leave.

He was out of the kitchen and back in the hallway—shopping bag in one hand, champagne bottle in the other—when something belatedly registered in his brain.

Did the alarm panel flash a green *light?*

He backed into the kitchen and saw that, indeed, it had. *Strange.* He punched 4363 on the panel and waited for the red light to flash before returning to the living room.

They could only see Jamie's cargo shorts, legs, and topsiders. The rest of him was buried deep in the hedge.

"Are you almost through?" Grant asked.

"Almost," said his muffled voice from somewhere in the bushes over the quiet hum of the hedge clippers.

Grant said to Chase, "I had no idea this was gonna be such a nightmare."

"I know," said Chase with a sympathetic shrug. "Who'd think that a couple of bushes would be so hard to cut through?"

And then Jamie was wiggling backward, and they all took a step back to give him room. Finally out of the hedge, he stood, brushing some of the dirt and twigs and leaves off his clothes, then giving his hair a fresh tousling. A twig remained stuck in his forelock.

He handed the clippers to Grant and said, "Okay, we're through. But it's tight."

Grant looked over his crew. "We're all pretty slim. Except Farraday, but he's back with the car. We can make it." They all looked at the hole in the hedge, which already seemed to be filling itself with sagging branches. "Now we just have to wait for Hadley to leave and Mary Beth to give us the go-ahead, and we're golden."

Lisa said, "I'll text her and get an update."

"You do that."

Jared—now shirtless, for once not because he wanted to be, but because Grant decided it'd be better if he wasn't hiding in the greenery in a blaze orange shirt—said, "I'm the thinnest one!"

Grant snorted. "And your point is?"

"That I should go first."

Chase nudged Grant. "That does make sense."

"All right. But we'll have to get you a shirt. You don't wanna go through the bushes without one." He looked around. If they were all going, they were all going to need the shirts on their backs. Which left . . .

"No way," said Farraday, when Chase returned to the car with the proposal. "I ain't wearing a T-shirt."

Chase offered him the orange tee. "You can wear this."

"Wear Jared's shirt? Maybe I could get into *two* of them, but not one."

"So it'll be little snug. This won't last long."

Farraday leaned toward him and, in the gruffest voice he could manage, said, "Listen, Chase, it's Sunday and I haven't had a drink since Friday night. And now you want me to squeeze into this tiny little orange shirt? Are you *begging* me to go postal?"

When he returned to the hole in the hedge, Grant asked, "Did he give you a hard time?"

"A little bit." Chase handed Farraday's shirt to Jared, who looked at it suspiciously. It was totally not his style. "So I had to make him an offer."

"Yeah?"

"Soon as the job is done, we're buying him a bottle of Dewar's for the ride home."

"Fair enough. So let's get back to this hole . . ." Jared giggled, but a glare from Grant stopped it. "Boy Wonder goes through first, then me, and then Jamie. I want Chase and Lisa to bring up the rear. Maybe not even go in until Hadley's out of there, 'cause he's seen 'em. Does that work for everyone?" They all agreed except Lisa, who was staring at her cell phone. "Lisa?"

Lisa looked up. "That was Mary Beth." She looked again at the message. "Hmm. Must be nice to be in the house;

they're drinking champagne. Anyway, Hadley doesn't seem to be in a rush, but she's turned the alarm off, so . . ."

"So it's time," said Grant.

Lisa closed her phone. "It's time." She reached into the plastic bag at her feet and handed them each a disposable camera. The last one went into her own pocket.

Jared put his camera in the back pocket of the denim cutoffs, slipped into Farraday's shirt, squared his shoulders, and said, "I'm ready."

"Is there something more interesting than me on your phone?" asked Ian Hadley with a chuckle, and Mary Beth looked up from Lisa's text telling her the gang was about to invade the estate.

She gave him her girlish giggle. "Oh, nothing. My brother was texting me"—Romero groaned involuntarily, thinking of the violated hot tub—"to tell me he made it home."

"Oh, good," said Romero. "We wouldn't want anything to happen to him."

Another giggle. "The important thing, Romeo, is that *he's* gone. And *I'm* here. And when Ian leaves, we'll be alone."

"Ahhh, yes. Yes, that *is* the important thing." She saw his robe twitch again in that inappropriate place and looked away. *Men!*

Hadley smiled. "You want me to leave, Romeo? But we're having such a pleasant afternoon."

Romeo reached for the paper bag at his feet and winked in Mary Beth's direction. "Ian, I should probably give you that, uh, *thing* you came for, so you can get on your way."

She hadn't paid much attention to the bag when he carried it in along with the champagne—figured it was plastic cups or something equally worthless—but now that she realized it was going to be passed to Hadley . . .

For the briefest moment her calm wavered, and she was afraid that dollar signs might have actually flashed in her eyes.

*How much is Hadley getting from Romero? A quarter million?
Is that bag big enough to hold a quarter million dollars?*

And Mary Beth Reuss decided that Ian Hadley was going nowhere until she liberated that bag from him. A sure quarter million was better than Grant's hoped-for half million, especially because that would be *her* quarter million, and she could share—or not—on her own terms.

"More champagne, Ian?" she asked brightly.

"Uh . . ." Romero was confused. "But I thought . . . ?"

Hadley smiled broadly with self-satisfaction and patted the bag. Now that he had what he wanted, he thought it was an excellent time for more champagne. "Don't mind if I do." He turned his smile to Mary Beth. "Madam, you are a true gentleman."

Even though the bottle Romero had brought was still one-third full, she said, "I'll grab another." She picked up her handbag and was gone before Romero had the chance to object.

In the kitchen, Mary Beth started pawing through drawers, looking for another brown shopping bag.

She was so intent on her search that she didn't notice the red light blinking on the alarm panel.

Jared squirmed through the hedgerow, the sharp twigs and branches scraping his arms, back, and legs, until he reached the other side. He poked his head out, and, seeing no one, wiggled through the narrow opening. Seconds later, Grant was at his side; then Jamie. The three men crouched close to the shrubbery, not that it would really hide them.

"All clear?" asked Chase, whose head was six inches or so away, back inside the hedge.

"You and Lisa hold back for a minute."

" 'Cause these branches kind of hurt."

"I know, baby. But just stay where you are until we're sure no one's gonna be shooting at us."

"*Shooting?*" Jared and Jamie had perfect timing.

"Keep your voices down. It's just, we don't know what might happen. Like, if Romero has a gun."

Jamie shook his head. "Now is not a great time to tell us that, Grant."

Grant looked at the motion detector, high up on the tree a few yards away, and hoped that Mary Beth had done what she was supposed to do.

"Chase?"

"Yeah?" said the hedge.

"Me, Jamie, and Jared are gonna make a break for the house. Wait a bit . . . if you don't hear anything going wrong, you and Lisa come through."

"Okay."

Grant looked at Jamie and Jared and said, "Okay, guys, let's do it. Just the way we discussed."

Mary Beth finally found her paper bag folded up with some other bags under the sink. That bag went into her handbag, then she grabbed a bottle from the refrigerator and was leaving when . . .

A red light?

Oh, no! This is bad.

She rushed to the alarm panel—one hand in her bag, not finding her phone—and began punching in the code from memory.

4-3-6—.

Six?

No, three?

She struggled. *Think, Mary Beth, think. Four-three-six . . .*

Three? Her hand groped inside the bag, but the phone was eluding her grasp.

She stared at the panel and tried to remember the last digit to disable the alarm.

* * *

Grant took two steps forward and stopped.

"What's wrong?" asked Jamie.

Without a word, he pointed toward the front of the house, where they could see a gray-haired man standing with his back to them.

"Who's that?" whispered Jared.

"No clue. But he's not with us, so let's make this fast." And he began a mad dash across the open yard toward the rear of the house, running faster than any of them—Grant included—thought he had in him.

Mary Beth pushed the 3 and hoped for the best.

Unseen by anyone except the lone dispatcher sitting in a sterile office at Wilbourne Security LLC, the alarm was disabled a split second after Grant's foot landed a few inches into the beam. A single *ting* rang out and a light flashed on and then abruptly off, and the dispatcher looked up from his peanut butter and jelly sandwich. It had only been a fraction of a second, which probably meant a chipmunk or something had broken the beam.

Damn millionaires kept building out in nature, then were surprised when nature walked onto their lawns. It was the bane of his existence.

But he had a job to do.

The home address and phone number of Romeo Romero were already on his monitor, even after only a split second of interruption, so the dispatcher put his sandwich aside, picked up the phone, and dialed the Romero residence. The hand that wasn't holding a telephone was poised above a switch that would immediately send a patrol car to the house to personally check on the security breach if no one picked up or, if someone did, they couldn't give the safe word.

Fucking chipmunks.

Chapter Twenty-Nine

The phone was ringing when Mary Beth passed it, walking back into the living room carrying champagne in one hand and her handbag over the opposite shoulder.

"Want me to get it, Romeo?" she asked.

"Good heavens, no!" He laughed as he stood and smoothed his robe. "How would that sound? A *woman* in my home?"

She glanced down at the phone, and didn't like what she saw. The display read *WILBOURNE SEC.*

He approached, but she stood her ground between him and the phone. "I could say I'm your assistant."

"Everybody knows my assistant. They also know she doesn't work weekends when I'm not filming." He tried to move around her to the right; she shifted her body to block him.

"Then your cleaning lady."

He moved to the left, and again she mimicked him. "Cleaning ladies do *not* answer telephones. Now if you'll let me get that . . ."

The ringing stopped.

"Well," said Mary Beth, with a desperately wide, desperately cheery smile, "if it's important, they'll call back!"

"That's *my* philosophy," said Hadley.

Romero hiked an eyebrow. "I suppose."

Mary Beth sat, and over Romero's shoulder saw Grant,

Jamie and Jared race across the lawn past the window. She hoped they'd have the good sense to get out of sight when the security patrol inevitably showed up.

"So, *Ian*," she handed Hadley the bottle, and her voice became a purr, "would you be so kind as to . . . pop my cork?"

Behind her, she heard Romero mutter something, but she didn't care. Ian Hadley was not leaving *this* house with *that* paper bag.

A few minutes later, Chase was still in the hedge, branches digging into his skin.

"Think it's safe to go?" asked Lisa, from somewhere behind him.

Chase poked his head out slightly and looked across the yard. The others had vanished. He listened carefully for the sound of shouts, or dogs, or—God forbid—gunshots, but heard nothing but blissful silence.

"I think we're—" He stopped as a metallic groan—*the front gate?*—filled the air.

"What?"

"*Shhh.*"

Seconds later a blue car with some sort of red lettering on the door—Chase couldn't read it from this distance—pulled up the driveway.

"What is it?" hissed Lisa, but he ignored her.

The car doors opened, and two uniformed security officers stepped out. And then a gray-haired man seemed to appear out of nowhere and was talking to the officers.

Chase slid back to obscure his face, then felt Lisa tug at his foot and whisper, "Come here." So he did, painfully worming his way back through the hole in the hedgerow, the branches pulling at his shirt and scratching his skin.

When he got to the other side, Farraday was there, looking perfectly ridiculous in the orange T-shirt that threatened to burst against his thick frame.

"Say one word about the shirt and I'll break your neck."

"I wouldn't dream of it," said Chase, fighting a snicker.

"The blue car is Wilbourne Security. I saw them drive up and let themselves in. Someone must've set off the alarm."

"So where does that leave us?" asked Lisa.

"On this side of the hedge," said Farraday, and Chase nodded his agreement.

Where others would see plans destroyed and lives potentially ruined, Mary Beth saw nothing but opportunity.

True, it wasn't great for the blackmail scheme to get a visit from the Wilbourne Security team. But it *could* make it easier to separate Ian Hadley from his paper bag, so she was going to make the best of it.

The front door opened and a gray-haired man in a polo shirt said, "I've got some security guards here. Someone set off the alarm by mistake, maybe?"

"Probably a squirrel," said Romero. "Just send them away."

Mary Beth looked at the gray-haired man as he closed the door, then back at Romero. "Who's he?"

Hadley said, "He's with me."

Damn, thought Mary Beth, *how many people are running around this place?*

The door opened again. "They say they've got to talk to Mr. Romero."

Romero shook his head. "No."

"Or else they say they have to call the county sheriff."

Romero sighed unhappily. "Very well. Let them in."

The gray-haired man stepped aside and the two guards entered, looking like they had come from the same parents. Both were tall, dark-haired, not particularly attractive, and unsmiling.

"Mr. Romero?" one asked the room, until Romero waved

slightly to acknowledge that he was the one they wanted. "We got a report of an alarm."

"I think there's something wrong with the control panel. I've set it a few times, and it keeps turning itself off. Probably just a wiring problem."

"You didn't answer our dispatcher's call," said the other. For Romero's benefit, his eyes shifted slowly toward Hadley, then back again. "Is anything wrong?"

Romero caught the guard's implied accusation, and was tempted for a split second to throw the blackmailer to their mercy. But no . . . that would just complicate things, and things were already complicated enough.

"I was unable to reach the phone in time."

"Well, sir," said the first. Or was it the second? Mary Beth had already lost track of their individual identities. "According to your contract with Wilbourne Security, we have to make a search of the premises when the alarm is tripped."

Romero frowned. "Very well. Do what you have to do."

One of the guards asked, "Can you show us where the control panel is?"

He stood and led them back to the kitchen. J. P., reacting to police instinct, followed.

When they were alone, Mary Beth said, "Ian? Could you do me a favor?"

"Possibly."

"I'm very thirsty. Would you be a dear and get me a glass of water?"

He smiled. "Maybe you should have more champagne."

"No." She faked a dry cough. "Water."

"But I don't know where the kitchen—"

"Just follow the rest of them."

From his hiding place in the pantry, which happened to be a bit too close to the alarm panel for his comfort, Grant heard the sounds of a group of people tromping into the kitchen. Then Romeo Romero said, "See? That's what I'm trying to tell you. I set the alarm, and when I come back it is off again."

A new voice Grant didn't recognize said, "Well, it was on when it was tripped."

And then another voice he didn't recognize—one that sounded exactly like a New York City cop—said, "Maybe you should check the perimeter. See if an animal set it off."

There was a pause, then another set of footsteps into the kitchen, followed by Romero saying, "I didn't realize I was giving a tour of my home."

To which someone with a British accent, which could only be Ian Hadley, said, "Mary Beth wants a glass of water."

"Over there." Seconds later Grant heard the tap start and Romero said, "I don't know what to tell you. Search all you want. The problem is with *your* equipment."

The tap turned off and the guy who sounded like a city cop asked, "Want me to search the place with them, Ian?"

"No, J. P. All this activity is giving me a headache, and I already got what I came for. Let me give this to Mary Beth, and we'll head back to the city." There was a pause, and he added, "I'll be in touch, Romeo."

"I'm sure you will, Ian."

And, with that, there was another series of footsteps walking away, the sound of the door swinging closed, and . . .

Silence.

Grant decided it was best to hide in the pantry for a while longer. He had ducked out of sight when he heard the doorbell and figured they must have somehow tripped the alarm, which meant security guards would be prowling around. Hopefully, not for long, but who knew? He hoped the others were hiding, too, or else they were going to have a bad afternoon.

Correction: a *worse* afternoon.

And it was good he stayed in the pantry, because no more than thirty seconds later the kitchen door banged open again and Romero's voice said, "I don't know about this, Ian."

"It's perfect. Not to pat myself on the back, but my idea is *brilliant*. Trust me on this, Romeo; I'm a professional. Burglar breaks into actor's home! Actor bravely defends his property."

"No . . . no. Bad publicity."

"Not if we spin it the right way, Romeo. What if we highlight all the good you did for the homosexual community last night with that Eastern Seaboard Pride party, and then make this sound like retaliation."

There was a pause. "Tell me more."

"You did a good thing for your fellow homosexuals last night—we'll have to call it a 'swishy soiree,' of course, and I apologize in advance, but that's just what we do at *The Eye*—and today you're doing what you do best: sitting home, alone, working intently on your next prestigious project . . ."

"The action movie with Jamie Foxx."

"Uh . . . okay. Anyway, you hear a disturbance by the back door. You're home alone, remember, and concerned about your personal safety when confronting the ruffians, especially because this could be—wait for it—*anti-gay retaliation*! Payback from the local yokels for hosting that swishy soiree!"

"But it's *Water Mill*! We don't *have* yokels."

"Nonsense. There are yokels everywhere. Trust me on this; I make a damn decent living thanks to them."

"Hmm. I'm starting to like it."

"I thought you would. So . . . you then call your security company. They arrive quickly, but not before the brutes *crash* through the back door and attack you."

"Attack me? And then what do I do?"

"Why, you fight back, of course."

"With my fists?"

"No, not your fists. With something *my* readers and *your* fan base will eat up. Let's see." There was a pause, followed by what sounded like various kitchen implements banging. "Frying pan . . . no. Rolling pin . . . no. They're both clichés."

"Well, then *what?*"

There was a long pause before Hadley continued.

"A whisk."

Again there was silence in the kitchen, until Romero finally said, "A *whisk?*"

"It's perfect," argued Hadley. "A whisk just screams 'gay'!"

"I don't know if I want people to think I'm *that* gay."

"It doesn't matter what you think," said Hadley. "I am *The Eye*, so the story will be written the way I've created it."

"What about the security guards? How do you keep them from talking?"

"We'll include them in the article," said Hadley. "I've found that it's easy to get people making fourteen dollars an hour to share my vision of a story if their names will be in print." He clapped his hands together. "I've got to get back to the city to write this up. Have the security guards call me at *The Eye* tomorrow."

Grant, ear pressed to the pantry door, heard the sound of Ian Hadley leaving the kitchen. When he was gone, Romero muttered, "A goddamn whisk. Why not just give me a *loofah.*" Then he, too, left, and the only sound was the swinging kitchen door.

In the cramped pantry, Grant's back hurt. But probably not as much as Romeo Romero's pride.

Ian Hadley, accompanied by J. P. Hunt, returned to the living room, took Mary Beth's hand, noted without comment she hadn't touched her glass of water, and said, "It was a pleasure to meet you."

"The pleasure," she said, smiling sweetly, "was mine."

"Read 'Between the Streets' tomorrow," he said, and he

picked up the brown paper bag. "We're going to make your Romeo a hero."

"I'll buy ten copies!"

Fifteen minutes later, the security officers also left, with a promise to call Hadley, having completed their thorough search of the premises without finding the three crooks hiding in the house or the hole in the hedgerow. Which was probably why they would always be security officers—and never *good* security officers, at that.

When the house was empty of uninvited guests, at least as far as *he* knew, Romero turned to Mary Beth and said, "I do apologize. I was not expecting the day to become so . . . *frantic*. But now, there are just the two of us . . ."

She flashed him a broad grin. "Yes, Romeo. We're finally alone . . ."

Farraday watched the white Mercedes drive out through the gate and away, followed a short time later by the blue car with the red Wilbourne Security sign on the doors. He waited a few minutes, then got out of the Escalade and crept back to where Chase and Lisa were still hiding behind the bushes. They saw the orange T-shirt before they saw the rest of him.

"They're gone."

"All of them?" Chase asked, and Farraday nodded. "Okay, Lisa, ready to go?"

"Ready."

After he hadn't heard any noise for quite a while, Grant screwed up his courage and opened the pantry door a few inches. Then a few inches more.

It took him a few tentative minutes, but he finally crept the handful of steps to the kitchen door and pushed it ajar. From down the hall, he could hear the voices of Romero and Mary Beth in unintelligible conversation.

"*There* you are!" said Jamie, suddenly behind him, and

Grant let go of the door. It swung to a gentle close, not the slam he had feared.

"Would you keep your voice down?" Grant snarled.

Jamie dropped his voice. "Sorry, but I've been looking all over for you."

"How about you concentrate on getting the picture instead of looking for me."

"Yeah, we'll get that. First, though, I need to show you something."

"What?"

Jamie tugged on his elbow. "In the basement. Come on."

As they crept down the basement steps off the kitchen, Jamie explained. "Jared found this during the party—don't ask why he was down here; you won't like the reason—and figured maybe we can make a few bucks. So he showed me, and you know what? I think he might be right."

Grant wasn't convinced the intellectual wattage between the two of them was enough to swipe a pencil from a blind peddler, but, well . . . he was already in the basement, so he might as well take a look.

"So what am I looking at?" he asked, when they were standing in front of a sheet of ripped brown paper.

Jared pulled the flap aside with a flourish. "Ta-da!"

"Keep it down." Grant looked behind the flap at an apple. "What the hell is that?"

"It's art," said Jared. "It's a painting. And there are a few more."

"Okay." He took another look. An apple . . . a pear . . . big deal. "So why am I supposed to care?"

Jamie said, "If Romero's hiding it down here, that must mean it's valuable."

"And *why* must it mean that?"

Jamie shrugged. "Why else would he be hiding it?"

Grant looked at the apple and the pear, and also at the part of a banana he thought he could now make out in the shadow of the brown paper. "I don't know art. Don't know what it's worth . . . don't know how to sell it . . ."

"But *I* can get rid of it," said Jamie. "I know a lot of collectors."

"You know collectors who *trust* you?"

"Well . . . Okay, maybe I'll have to re-earn some trust, but the point is I know these people."

Grant shook his head. "Maybe some other day. We have a job to do, and an art heist isn't that job."

"But—" Jamie began, but the groan of floorboards above their heads silenced him.

"They're making their move," said Grant, taking the camera from his pocket. "Let's get that blackmail photo and get out of here."

Jamie looked back at the paintings. "Can we talk about this later?"

"Doubt it."

They were in the guest room, the door open wide to the empty house, the curtains open to the yard. Mary Beth looked around the room as she slowly unbuttoned her top and thought, *If those jackasses can't get the picture under these conditions, they're never gonna get the picture.*

Romero smiled at her from the edge of the bed, where he sat with the top of his robe open and hanging off the shoulder, exposing a broad patch of graying chest hair. She tried not to look, but . . . *Honestly! How do men live with those bodies?*

"My dear," he said, reaching for her. "Perhaps I can help you."

She took a step back. "No, no . . . I've got it."

She glanced at the window and saw a flash of Chase LaMarca out there before he ducked behind the hot tub. Good. Maybe they wouldn't screw this up after all.

"Mary Beth, this will be heaven for both of us." His accent was almost at full force. "I cannot wait . . ."

"I can't either, Romeo." She turned, feigning modesty as she slipped her top off, leaving her wearing nothing but her slacks and bra. She looked up and saw a fragment of Jamie's face peeking around the corner; he disappeared behind the door when their eyes met.

"Come to me, darling," Romero said, and when she turned to face him she saw that he had now hiked the robe up almost to the top of his thigh, which she supposed he thought was seductive. She tried to act appropriately instead of doing what she really wanted to do, which was to cover his face in pepper spray.

"Are you ready, Romeo?" She closed her eyes and licked her lips.

"Oh, yes, darling! Yessssssss . . ." He trailed off, drawing out that *s* as the sound of a loud crash boomed from the front of the house . . .

The sound of the front door being flung open.

"*What the . . . ?*"

"*Romero?*" roared a voice they both recognized as Ian Hadley's, and they both thought, *What's* he *back for?* "Where the bloody hell are you?"

While Romeo again recovered from coitus interruptus, Mary Beth glanced around and saw the heads of several of her cohorts duck out of sight.

"*Romero?!!*" The voice was getting closer. "I know you're here!"

The actor pushed his robe back into position and stood, just as Hadley—trailed closely by J. P.—stormed through the open door.

Recovery finally complete, Romero snapped, "Ian! What the hell do you think you're doing?"

"I've come for my money!"

"But . . ." Romero was confused. "I *gave* you your money."

"You gave me," he shouted, "a bag containing one thousand dollars placed on top of last Sunday's *New York Times*!" His voice shook with anger. "If you wanted to be clever, Romeo, you could have at least used the Sunday *Eye*."

"I don't know what you're talking about."

"Give! Me! My! *Money*!"

They had heard it all, and there was still more for them to hear, so Grant wasn't surprised when Chase texted him.

LEMMON?

And Grant replied: NOW

Chapter Thirty

Henry Lemmon took the bait, to their great relief. That meant that after two weeks, he still didn't know that his credit had been bled dry. He also didn't blame Amber for his stolen car, which was the great thing about a lot of suburbanites—including, apparently, lawmen. They blamed the Evil City of New York, even if the crime took place at Kennedy Airport, which was practically in the suburbs.

In fact, Henry was only troubled by one thing when he talked to the very frantic Amber Arbogast for the first time since the day she didn't get off that plane—meaning, of course, when he was talking to Chase, who was at that moment huddling behind the hot tub, faking the voice of a teenage girl. To Henry, there was no difference.

Why hadn't she called him earlier? He could have rescued her! Unspoken was the "again," since Henry was all about rescuing Amber; first from her parents, and now from this guy who Amber said was called Ian something.

Chase explained that he wasn't allowed to use the phone— *"Ian is harsher than my dad"*—and that was that. Like the best bait, it went down hook, line, and sinker.

But there was one more piece of business that had to be taken care of.

"I need you to come alone," implored Chase, in his best "Amber" voice.

"Alone?" Henry thought that over. "But if this Ian is as sick as you say . . ." He didn't want to think about that any further. Who knew what this creepy pedophile Ian was up to? Who knew what he was capable of?

As always, Amber had thought that through. She was such a smart girl.

"This could be very embarrassing. For both of us. You know what I mean? If you call the cops—the *other* cops, not you—my parents are bound to find out, and I'll have to go back to Albany."

"Oh yeah." He certainly didn't want *that* to happen.

"And," Chase continued, "the other cops are gonna wonder how come you're getting calls from an underage girl."

"Oh yeah." He absolutely didn't want *that* to happen. No, that would be a very bad thing. It was one thing to put one over on the neighbors; quite another to convince his brothers in blue that a niece—a niece they had never heard of before—had suddenly come into his life, and now had to be rescued from a pedophile. You could probably get away with that shit on *The Young and the Restless*; not so much with the Suffolk County Sheriff's Department.

So they were in agreement. Henry Lemmon would come alone. It was better that way . . . for both of them.

Chase gave him the address in Water Mill and begged him again to hurry. Then he hung up. And he smiled.

"I give him ten minutes," he said to Grant, hiding with him behind the hot tub.

Grant didn't smile. He frowned. "Well, it's good we're doing something, but I'm wondering if we should have asked him to come later."

"What was I supposed to do? Get him to come rescue me, but tell him to come at eight o'clock tonight, because that was more convenient for me? Jeez, Grant, it was *your* idea to use him to get rid of Hadley."

"Yeah, yeah . . ." Grant thought for a moment. "We've got

to get rid of Hadley, and Lemmon will be good for that. But we've got no Amber, and he's going to be looking for her."

Chase began to object—he *was* Amber, after all—but then understood what Grant was saying. Not that he'd be all that convincing in the harsh light of day—airport security lines manned by bored screeners were one thing; an obsessed, lovelorn cop quite another—but he didn't even have his drag with him. That was back at the apartment in Jackson Heights.

So Deputy Henry Lemmon was going to show up at the house, confront Ian Hadley, and then discover there was no Amber Arbogast to be found. Which probably wouldn't work to their advantage in the way they needed.

"So we need a plan," said Chase finally.

"We need a plan," Grant agreed. "And we need it to come together in about seven minutes."

From the ground floor, they heard the doorbell chime.

And Chase sighed, "Or maybe now."

Grant looked at him. "We've got to talk to Mary Beth."

"Gotcha."

The argument had slowly worked its way from the guest room, down the hall, and back into the living room, with Ian Hadley demanding his money and Romeo Romero insisting he had already given it to him and wouldn't be giving him another dime. Even though Mary Beth and J. P. were supposedly in the dark about their blackmail agreement—and, in J. P.'s case, really *was*—the two men, lost in their rage, didn't care. Accusations and counteraccusations flew in the loudest voices they could manage, each trying to scream over the other.

Which worked to the advantage of the criminals in the house—those that weren't huddled by the hot tub, that was—since they could move around without worrying too much about an errant footfall giving them away.

"I am telling you one more time!" shouted Romero, the

blue robe flowing with every gesture. "You *have* your first payment!"

Which is when the doorbell chimed with its *DING* . . . *ding*.

Mary Beth looked out the window to the driveway, where she saw a Suffolk County Sheriff's Department patrol car. Hopefully it was the same guy Chase had on the line, although it would have been nice if someone let her in on the plan, because she had no idea what she was supposed to do or say.

"It's the sheriff, Ian," said J. P., who was also looking out the window. He jabbed a thumb in Romero's direction. "Want me to let him in so he can take care of this joker?"

"What?" Hadley sputtered. "Of *course* I don't want you to let him in!"

"But if he ripped you off . . ."

"I will deal with Mr. Romero on that matter *privately!*"

Mary Beth felt her cell phone vibrate and stole a quick glance at the screen. The message was from Chase, and simply said, KITCHEN.

The doorbell rang again, immediately followed by a banging fist. Romero stepped toward the door.

"Everyone *please* calm down." The room quieted. "It's the sheriff's department. We have to let them in." Hadley began to object, but Romero added, "Let me handle this, Ian. I give a lot of money to the PBA. I'm sure we can take care of this quickly and discreetly."

He approached the door and Mary Beth said, "I have to powder my nose."

"Again?"

She smiled shyly. "When you've gotta go . . ."

J. P. eyed her as she walked away and, out of the corner of his mouth, said to Hadley, "I wonder what *she's* hiding from the cops."

"Oh, J. P.," muttered Hadley. "Stop being such a *cop* all the time."

In the kitchen, Mary Beth found Lisa, Grant, and Chase.

"It's the county sheriff!" Her voice was as muted as possible, which was still louder than advisable.

"We know," said Grant, keeping his own voice barely audible. "Is it our guy?"

She shrugged. "How am I supposed to know?"

"Kind of dumpy?"

"Aren't they all?"

"Well, it's probably our guy. In which case, just pretend to be Amber."

Chase shook his head and pointed unhappily at Mary Beth. "She can't be Amber. She's at least ten years older than Amber."

Mary Beth tried not to take the pointing and "older" comment personally. "And if it's not our guy? What if the security guards got suspicious and called the cops? Then what do we do?"

Grant shrugged. "Probably five to seven for breaking and entering, if we're lucky. More if they think this is a home invasion."

She shook her head. "That's not what I meant. Anyway, I am not going down for this. As far as *they* know, I'm a guest of Romeo Romero."

The others looked at her with a combination of respect for her self-preservation instincts and, well, *contempt* for her self-preservation instincts. But it was Grant who finally said, "We all hang together or *you* hang separately."

Her hands went to her hips. "What's that supposed to mean?"

"It means if we get busted and you try to worm off the hook, I am telling the cops that this was all your idea."

She looked over at her girlfriend. "Lisa, are you going to let him do that?"

"That depends," she said. "Are you going to sit on your tush and play innocent while they haul me away?"

Mary Beth rolled her eyes and blew a stray wisp of hair out of her eyes. "Okay, okay. I'm in." She glared at Grant. "We all hang together. Satisfied?"

"Satisfied enough. So what's the argument about?"

She played innocent. "Hadley thinks Romero shorted him on the blackmail."

"And did he?"

Again with the innocence. "How should I know? Anyway, back to my original question: what do I do out there?"

Grant thought for a moment, then said, "It's probably our guy, so let's work on that angle. Here's what you're gonna do . . ."

While the discussion was taking place in the kitchen, Deputy Henry Lemmon was finally let into the house by one Romeo Romero. Henry knew who he was, but out here in Suffolk County the locals didn't gawk at the celebrities. In any event, Romeo Romero's celebrity was of the lesser variety, mostly limited to the snobs who liked boring movies set in pastoral nineteenth-century European estates or homosexuals, two groups that definitely did not include Henry Lemmon.

The fact that this Romero character had kept him waiting at the front door for two minutes aggravated him and made him more certain than ever that the quick call from Amber had been legitimate. Delay him . . . ask questions . . . ask for ID beyond the badge he wore pinned to his uniform . . . keep insisting that the alarm company had already come and gone, whatever that was supposed to mean . . .

Those weren't the actions of a law-abiding citizen. Those were the actions of someone with something—or *someone*—to hide. If he was a betting man—which, come to think of it, he was every now and then—he'd lay odds that Ian the Pedophile was somewhere in the house, secreting Amber away.

"Mr. Romero," he finally said, when he had had enough. "I need to inspect the premises."

"But, again, why? I already told you the alarm company—"

Another stall tactic. "I don't care about the alarm company, Mr. Romero." He looked around the room and pointed at the expensively dressed man lounging in an end chair, as if he had never had a care in the world. "Who's this?"

Romero played indignant. "*That* is none of your business, Officer."

Officer? Had this Italian homosexual just demeaned a Suffolk County Deputy Sheriff by calling him "officer"? Henry tried not to focus on the slight, but it was difficult.

"Mr. Romero, please identify the gentleman for me."

"He is a guest."

Henry's voice grew stern. "Mr. Romero."

The expensively dressed man took the initiative to try to defuse the situation, and leaned forward in his chair.

"Busy day at Casa Romero," he said with a chuckle, then looked at the actor and said, "Romeo, it's quite all right." Henry grimaced; he was English. A Brit and an Italian . . . it was like the United Nations moved to Water Mill. "I certainly have nothing to hide. My name is Ian Hadley."

Ian! Which meant that Amber hadn't been playing him, as he knew she wouldn't . . . even though a little twinge in his gut told him it could be a possibility.

The Brit started to reach into the breast pocket of his blue blazer, and Henry instinctively lowered his right hand to the firearm holstered in his belt. Seeing that, the man pulled back his hand and put it back in his lap. Then, in the most infuriating gesture yet, he smiled. Henry thought his teeth were too white.

"I was just reaching for my identification, Deputy." Well, at least the Brit knew proper protocol. "But if you'd prefer for me to give it verbally, I am the editor of the 'Between the Streets' column at the *New York Eye* and I live on East Fifty-seventh Street in Manhattan."

Henry's face was stone. "And what is the nature of your business in Water Mill, Mr. Hadley?"

Hadley and Romero looked at each other quizzically. Henry couldn't quite tell if they were genuinely confused by his visit or were communicating something much more evil and devious and sleazy. Probably the latter.

In any event, the Brit gave him an answer.

"Mr. Romero and I had some private business dealings to transact, and we are also personal acquaintances." He paused, then tried to look concerned. "Have I—well, has either of us—done something wrong?"

"That's for me to determine."

Romero's temper was beginning to get the better of him. "This is my home. You cannot come into my home and start interrogating me and my guests. I must insist you leave right now, and I *will* be reporting this to the sheriff. I happen to be a major contributor to the PBA."

Go right ahead, you sick, loathsome excuse for a man, thought Henry, but the words came out as, "I'm just doing my job, Mr. Romero."

The Brit chimed in again, a slight smile on his lips. "Perhaps we could be of more assistance if we knew the nature of your, uh, *visit*. I can assure you that Mr. Romero and I will be quite cooperative."

Henry decided that it was time to tell them—to see if they'd cooperate and make this easy, or stonewall and make it ugly—and he was just about to start the interrogation when a young woman burst through a door at the far end of the room.

Amber?

Chapter Thirty-One

She was not what he expected.

She looked much older than sixteen. That was one thing. If he had seen her on the street, it would have never occurred to him that she was underage. She could pass for her late twenties.

Then again, an older-looking Amber wasn't necessarily a bad thing. There would be less talk in the neighborhood, and maybe he could even take her out in public.

But she also looked different than he thought she'd look from those pictures she'd sent him over the Internet, which granted weren't the best quality. It was all so confusing.

Maybe, he thought, he shouldn't jump to conclusions.

Maybe this wasn't really Amber.

There was one sure way to find out.

"Miss," he said, with great authority in his voice. "Can I speak to you in private?"

"I was just going to ask you the same thing," she said, from the other end of the living room. Then she winked—taking care that the British editor and the Italian actor didn't notice—and added, "We can talk in the kitchen . . . *Henry*."

Romero and Hadley reacted to her use of his first name. *Ah, let 'em wonder about that for a few minutes*, Henry thought. *They'll find out soon enough.*

When the kitchen door closed behind him, he asked, "Amber?"

Mary Beth threw her arms around him. "Henry, thank you for coming!"

"Amber?" He tried to return the embrace, but she had his arms pinned, so instead he made an awkward nuzzling motion.

She let go so quickly he almost lost his balance. "We don't have much time, so listen."

"Amber?"

"No. That's what I have to tell you. I'm Amber's older sister—"

"Aha! I *thought* you looked old."

"—and . . ." Mary Beth stopped. "Old? I do *not* look old."

Henry tried to take the words back. "I don't mean 'old' old. Just old*er*."

She swallowed her pride and waved the comment away. "No time for that right now. Like I was saying, I'm Amber's sister. I got here just before you did."

He tried not to betray his disappointment. "But I thought she wanted *me* to rescue her."

"She did. I mean, she wanted *someone* to rescue here. I just happened to get here first. But we can work that out later."

"When?"

"*Later*. When you see her *later*." Mary Beth tried to remember where she was in the narrative. "Oh yes . . . Anyway, I got her out the back door, and I was trying to distract those men in the living room until she's far from here. But now that you're here, maybe you can just arrest the English guy. Then Amber can be together with you, and life can return to normal."

Henry thought about that. "But without a victim, I can't arrest him."

"It's easy. Just walk in there, pull your gun . . ."

"We only pull our guns if we're prepared to shoot."

She shrugged. "So *shoot* him. That's not my problem. I am just looking out for my baby sister . . . uh, and trying to make sure the two of you live happily ever after."

"But I need some sort of evidence. Or a witness."

Mary Beth sighed. This was dragging on too long and getting far too complicated for her liking. "Fine. You want a witness? I'm your witness." And with that, she opened the kitchen door, marched down the hall to the living room, pointed at Ian Hadley, and said, "Deputy Lemmon, that man is the pedophile who molested my sister Amber."

"What?" said Hadley, rising from his chair. "Pedophile? *That* is ridiculous."

Henry Lemmon puffed out his chest. "Sir, I'm going to have to ask you to come with me."

"The *hell* you are! Romeo, are you going to let him do this?"

Romero was wondering the same thing, and decided that the answer was yes. He had no idea what was going on with Mary Beth—this was probably her way of getting Hadley out of there so they could *finally* be alone—but anything that would remove that angry, blackmailing liar from his home was fine with him.

"Deputy," the actor said, oozing every bit of charm he could muster. He even thickened the accent again. "I had no idea that Mr. Hadley was up to anything untoward. If I had known . . ."

"Why *you . . . you . . .* You're a *dead* man, Romeo Romero!"

"And now he's threatening my life."

"Not your life! Your *career*! You will never work again! *Never!*"

Henry asked, "Mr. Romero, do you know the whereabouts of a young woman by the name of Amber Arbogast?"

"Oh, no," said Mary Beth, rushing to his defense, because the last thing they needed was for the actor to be taken away in the patrol car. "Romeo never even saw her."

Henry asked, "You're sure?"

"Amber told me that Mr. Romero knew nothing about it."

Romero shrugged. "Uh . . . well, there's your answer."

J. P. took a step forward and looked to Hadley for direction. "You want me to . . . ?"

"I want you to shut up," Hadley spat, then he turned and stared down Romero. "You're really going to let this moron arrest me?"

"Please don't disrespect the badge, sir," said Henry.

"*Screw* your badge," said Hadley. His attention back to Romero, he said, "I still have the tape, Romeo. This isn't over."

That caught Romero's attention. "The tape? You told me the tape would be destroyed."

"Which tapes are these?" asked Henry, but he was ignored again.

"You think I didn't make a copy?" Romero blanched. "You played your little games, and now you're going to end up getting burned. You made your own fate this afternoon, Romeo."

Henry asked again, "What tapes are you talking about, Mr. Hadley?"

The anguish etched on Mary Beth's face almost looked sincere. "Pornographic tapes. Including *child* porn! Maybe including *Amber*!" And then, for good measure, she covered that anguished face with her hands.

"And who the hell is this Amber?" asked Hadley, but Deputy Henry Lemmon was already bearing down on him. When he made his first pass at snapping on the cuffs, Hadley wormed away.

"Sir," said Henry, dancing a little jig as he tried to stay in front of Hadley. "We can do this the easy way, or the hard way."

"Let me help, Henry," said Mary Beth, reaching into her handbag. "The rest of you should probably cover your eyes and mouths."

First they heard Ian Hadley scream, followed by a brief scuffle. And then doors were slamming.

Grant, Chase, and Lisa, still standing in the kitchen, just looked at each other and shrugged.

And then, a few mostly silent minutes later, Chase's cell phone rang. He looked at the Caller ID.

"Your buddy Henry?" asked Grant.

"No." Chase shook his head, confused. "It's Hadley's cell." He flipped the phone open and said, "Chas—uh, *Charlie* here."

"It's J. P."

"On Ian's cell?"

"Yeah, well, he had a little problem. He sort of got pepper-sprayed and arrested. I'll fill you in later. Right now I'm out in Long Island, bringing Ian's car back to the city. But he wants you to go to the office to pick something up. I can meet you in a couple hours."

"Is everything all right?"

"It will be. But you and me, we're gonna have to remove some of his personal effects, 'cause there's a chance the cops will be looking for them, and we don't want them to find them."

"What kind of personal effects?"

"Videos . . . DVDs . . . that kind." And then J. P. Hunt told him where he'd find a hidden key that could get him into Hadley's office, and where he'd find the tapes. "Just get 'em together and I'll meet you at Galan's when I hit town, after I pick up some things from his place on Fifty-seventh. When we have everything together we'll figure out what to do with them." He hung up.

"So?" asked Grant.

"I have no idea what's going on, but they're moving the tapes." He recounted his conversation with J. P.

"Then you'd better get moving." Grant gave him a quick kiss. "Good luck."

Chase darted across the lawn, crawled through the hole in the hedgerow, and was back at the Escalade in minutes, just as the clouds began to open up with a light sprinkle.

"How fast can we get to Midtown Manhattan?" he asked Farraday as he leaped into the passenger seat.

"Water Mill to Midtown on a late Sunday afternoon on a three-day weekend? Most people, it'd take about two hours. Me, eighty-five minutes."

"I'm timing you."

"And now, my dear . . ." Romero began, gently stroking Mary Beth's hair. "I think everyone in the county has interrupted us this afternoon—Ian Hadley, the sheriff, the security guards, the gay boys—but, *at last*, we are alone."

Which is when Grant and Lisa walked into the living room.

"Not so fast, Romero."

"And get your hands off my girlfriend."

"Girlfriend?" He pulled his hand away from Mary Beth's hair and stared at her. *Girlfriend*? He sighed. "This isn't my day."

Grant took out his camera. "Let's see if we can brighten it up for you."

Chapter Thirty-Two

"Here's the deal," said Grant, sizing up the waning light in the living room. "I'm usually a very patient man, but not anymore. I'm tired of things going wrong. Now we're doing things *my* way, so nothing else goes wrong."

Romero, clad only in red-striped boxer shorts, nodded. "*Your* way."

"Exactly." Grant moved a stack of books from an end table; he was afraid they might block the camera. "See, we know your secret. True, we tried to play around for a while and do this the old-fashioned way. Get you in a compromising position . . . capture it on film . . . But every time we almost got our shot, something screwed it up." He adjusted a picture on the wall. "This time, there won't be any screwups, because this time we're not waiting for the seduction."

Lisa added, "Anyway, it amounts to the same thing, Romero. Just in this case, it's not voluntary on *your* part, which it would have been if our luck had been better. But it works out the same in the end."

"Okay," said Romero. "So you take a picture of me with Mary Beth. Then what?"

"I thought that would be obvious," said Grant. "Then you pay us a half-million dollars to get the picture back."

"A half-million . . . *Five hundred thousand dollars?* You can't be serious!"

"Dead serious." He looked around. "Okay, I guess we're ready."

Mary Beth started to strip down, then stopped and turned to Grant. "By the way, Hadley said something about having a duplicate of the original tape. You know, before I sprayed him with pepper spray and they dragged him out of here."

Grant cocked an eyebrow. "You mean, if we kept searching his office, we could've saved ourselves all this aggravation."

"Exactly." She looked unhappily across the room at Romero in his boxer shorts. "But here we are, so . . . ."

Grant thought for a moment. "Actually, Chase is on his way back to the city to get Hadley's video stash out of his office. But I don't think it occurred to him that the Romero tape was still around."

"Oh, right," she said with a dismissive wave. "They're all in a panic 'cause they think it's kiddie porn." She laughed. "My bad."

"We can always make use of the original. Do me a favor and call him about this. Tell him to see if he can get his hands on Hadley's tapes. And then we'll do your photo shoot. Between the video and *our* photos . . ."

She narrowed her eyes. "He's your boyfriend. *You* call him."

Grant rubbed his lower back. "I don't like phones."

Mary Beth shook her head, opened her cell phone, and walked to the foyer, where it was at least a bit quieter.

While they waited for Mary Beth to complete the call, Jared and Jamie walked into the living room. Each man was carrying one of the paintings from the basement. Romero looked from one to the other, then at their loot. He wasn't sure if he was more enraged that they were stealing his artwork, or that it was being stolen by Jared Cockring and that vacuous Jamie fellow that had been pestering him a few weekends earlier. He decided to be enraged by everything.

But Grant beat him to the verbalization of irritation. "Where have you two been, and what the hell are you doing?"

"Miss us?" asked Jared.

Grant eyed the paintings. "Not really. Barely noticed you were gone, now that you mention it, even though everyone *else* has been working."

"We've been working," said Jared, oblivious to Grant's sarcasm.

"Right. We've been in the basement," said Jamie, also oblivious. "I'm telling you, Grant, I think these are really valuable."

"They are *not* valuable!" Romero raged from the couch. "They are family heirlooms. *Worthless* family heirlooms."

Grant turned back to Jamie and Jared. "Okay, so apparently they're valuable. But we've got no way to get them back to the city. And even if we did, I don't know a fence who handles paintings."

"But . . ."

"Plus, you violated the first rule of burglary, which is to not let your victim see what you're carrying out. We leave with those, and Romero is on the phone before we hit the town line. Meaning we'd never be able to sell them."

Jamie sighed. "Okay, we'll put 'em back."

Jared added, "Some people have no imagination."

"Oh, I've got imagination," muttered Grant. He pointed at Jared. "And in a few minutes, you are gonna know exactly what I mean by that."

Mary Beth walked back from the foyer. "Okay, I took care of Chase." She unhooked her bra strap. "It's time for some photography." With that, she turned to Grant. "Be very, very careful, because if my face shows up in one single picture I will hurt you."

"Don't worry about it."

She walked toward Romero. "*Heeey*, Romeo. How much do you want me now?"

From the couch he said, "You realize that there is no possible way I can get an erection, don't you?"

"You'd better *not*," said Mary Beth. "You do and I'll Bobbitt you."

Grant picked his camera angle. "Mary Beth's a hot young girl. Romero. Just go with the flow."

"Oh, for God's sake!" The actor squirmed, and Grant shook a finger at him. "The longer it takes us to get these shots, Romero, the longer you're gonna be posing for us. Now, off with the boxers."

"You people are going to hell."

"Okay," said Grant, "if that's your attitude, we've gotta do what we've gotta do. Mary Beth, you still got your pepper spray?"

"Some. I used a lot of it on Hadley."

Grant smiled faintly. "In the immortal words of Amber Arbogast: 'whatevs.' "

As Grant clicked away, filling the disposables with blackmail photos, each of them began to think that there was something almost *noble* about what they were doing. Sure, they were criminals, engaged in an illegal activity, but their victim was far from sympathetic. He was a heterosexual lecher who had spent decades deceiving the public—especially their own gay community—by pretending to be one of them. And now they had the power to expose him.

Although given the choice between nobility and cash, they would take the cash without thinking twice.

Romero squirmed, and Grant cautioned him. "Keep that up and your next naked photo will be with *me*."

That settled him down.

The photo shoot with Mary Beth was over, and Romero had pretty much calmed down. Grant was certain that was about to change.

"Okay, Mary Beth, you're done." Grant gave her a wink

as she passed, one hand covering her upper region, the other covering the lower. Then he said, "Jared, you're on."

Romero looked up from the couch. "Wait a minute . . ."

"For our own amusement," said Grant. "And as a guarantee that you won't talk."

He shook his head. "You're blackmailing me for . . ." He swallowed hard. "For five hundred thousand dollars. *Of course* I won't talk."

"Wish I could trust you. But I can't."

"But—"

Jamie, who had been mostly quiet to that point, said, "What's the matter, Romeo? You're a big-shot gay movie star! You should be thrilled to be seduced by a man like Jamie."

"Jamie?" rasped Lisa.

He looked confused for a half second, then recovered. "I mean Jared."

Lisa whispered to Grant, "What the hell was that all about?"

"I dunno. The expert on psychology is Farraday, but he should be halfway to Manhattan by now. But I think part of it's called transference, along with some wounded pride on the part of Jamie Brock."

She shrugged. "Okay. Just asking."

Grant said to Romero, "These are for what I like to call the 'consensual sex' collection. You go to the cops and claim we forced you to take the photos with Mary Beth, and we trot these babies out."

"What would that prove?"

"That, along with the picture in this morning's *Eye*, would be evidence you were having a normal, homosexual relationship with Jared. So why would he—and his friends—try to blackmail you? You tell your story to the cops, we show the photos with Jared and tell him you're just trying to get back at him for dumping you. That sort of makes everything neutral, right?"

Jared pulled off his denim cut-offs without bothering to turn away from Lisa and Mary Beth.

"Again?" moaned Mary Beth.

"Lesbian Blindness," said Lisa.

"Exactly."

Mary Beth, still only half dressed, said, "We don't really have to watch this, do we?"

"No," said Lisa sternly. "It's nose-powdering time."

"Okay, but no sex in there," said Grant. "We're out of this place in a few minutes."

He found an angle he liked and Jared, now naked, positioned himself against Romero, pouting his lower lip. It looked to Grant like Jared's "masculine" look.

Whatevs.

"You're a trouper, Romero," said Grant as a flash went off. "No wonder you win all those awards."

He was about to take another picture when the front door swung open and someone yelled, "*Aha! I finally caught you!*"

They turned and saw a round, sweaty man in a stained windbreaker standing defiantly in the doorway, a battered camera dangling around his neck.

"Who the hell are you?" asked Grant.

The man didn't answer. He simply took in what he was seeing—Romero Romero, naked, with a naked young man in his lap and two other guys watching—and then he moaned.

"Dammit," he muttered, shaking a fist in frustration. His shoulders slumped and, without another word, he turned and walked back out the door, closing it quietly behind him.

"What was that all about?" asked Jamie.

"Wasn't that the crazy guy from the party last night?" Jared asked Romero. "The one who knocked down Tori Spelling?"

The actor sighed. "I can no longer tell one crazy person from another."

When the photo session was over and everyone was dressed, Lisa asked, "So how are we getting back to the city?" Grant shrugged. "We'll take Romero's car. He won't mind." The actor was pulling on his red-striped boxers when Grant approached. "I don't think you're gonna especially miss us, but we should figure out when we're gonna meet again."

"It will take me quite some time to get half a million dollars in cash."

"How long?"

"Three weeks. Maybe four. I may be able to get a smaller amount together by the end of the week, if you'll settle for that."

"I won't, but I'll take that smaller amount as your first installment. Fair enough?" Romero looked at him with wounded eyes. "Okay, 'fair enough' wasn't the best way to word it. Just think of this as a way for you to pay back the gay and lesbian community for all their support over the years."

"Mmmph . . ."

"Good." Grant smiled. "I'll be in touch."

They began to walk away, but Mary Beth doubled back. For a moment, Romero hoped she had come to her senses, and was about to turn on her confederates. But, no, she only retrieved something from beneath the couch. Brown paper bag in hand, she left to rejoin the others.

And he thought, *A brown paper bag?*

Wait!

Mary Beth had to duck when Deputy Sheriff Henry Lemmon's patrol car, en route back to Romero's house, passed them a few blocks down the road, but the rest of the trip back to New York was uneventful.

For them, if not for Chase.

"You got everything, Charlie?" J. P. Hunt asked when they met at Galan's just after 9:30 that night.

Chase patted the plastic bagel bag, once again put to good use. "Every last DVD."

J. P. opened the Duane Read bag he was carrying. "And here's the stuff from his apartment. Now we've just got to stash it for a while."

Chase took a sip from his Guinness.

"I've been thinking, J. P. . . ."

"Yeah?" He eyed him up and down. "What?"

"You're Ian's number two man, right?" J. P. nodded. "If he's in trouble, won't the cops search *your* place if they can't find what they're looking for in Ian's house or his office?"

He thought about that, and didn't like the way he could see it possibly playing out. Especially if Ian really *did* have some child porn. It seemed unlikely—his boss really liked the *adult* ladies—but when he was a cop he'd seen enough dark secrets of otherwise respectable citizens to know that, well, you never really knew what was going in someone's head. Murderers, pedophiles, serial killers . . . sometimes they lurked under the crispest starched collars.

"So what do you propose?"

"No one knows *me*, right? I've only been there for a week. I'm hardly the kind of person who'd be entrusted with Ian's personal effects."

J. P. saw where Charlie was going. "So you'd be willing to hold this stuff until everything blows over?" Chase nodded. "I don't know . . ."

Chase could be very persuasive when he put his mind to it. And when he was done persuading, J. P. toasted him.

"I wasn't sure about you at first, Charlie. But you know what? You're a real stand-up guy."

Chase lifted his Guinness. "I try, J. P., I try."

* * *

Despite all the setbacks, when they were all sitting around Grant and Chase's kitchen table just before midnight that night, they had to agree that it had turned out all right.

They got their blackmail photos, and they got their half million dollar agreement with Romeo Romero. As a bonus, they even retrieved the original video from Hadley's collection, plus the $30,000 partial blackmail payment Mary Beth liberated from Hadley's brown paper bag. They were disappointed it wasn't the full quarter million, but it made for some nice icing on the cake.

Not to mention they brought home the Escalade and Romero's car, which they could sell to Charlie Chops.

They had been through a lot, but they finally hit the big one. It was a moment worth celebrating.

Grant Lambert wasn't one for sentimentality, but when the gang—*his* gang—broke up their gathering around 2:00 in the morning, he hugged them as they left.

"We did it!" said Jamie. "I knew we could do it!"

"Great weekend," said Jared. "And I got a few numbers! Oh, and can I get copies of the pictures?"

"Ummm . . . thanks, I guess," said Farraday. "And this hug is, uh . . ."

"Always a pleasure, Lambert," said Lisa. "Maybe next time we'll do a job that's less intense."

"Get your hands off me, Lambert," said Mary Beth. "I swear to God I will kill you."

"Really?" Grant asked Mary Beth. "Because . . . okay, I know we don't like each other all that much, but you did pretty good."

She held her grimace as long as she could, but finally smiled. "Okay, maybe we can work together again. But no more nude scenes."

He hugged her again. It was a bit awkward, but it was a hug. "I promise."

* * *

Much later, when Chase was climbing into bed next to Grant, he said, "It was sort of crazy, but it all worked out. Good job, baby."

Grant's voice was tired. "And now I can retire."

"On a few hundred thou? You must be dreaming. Even if we don't work for a while, that's only going to get us through a few years." He rolled over and let one hand ruffle through Grant's silvery hair. "Plus, you'll never retire. None of us will. Even Lisa. We'd be bored. This isn't like some factory job or something, where you do the same thing every day until you make it to sixty-two. This is . . . well, it's *exciting*."

"Sometimes a little too exciting."

"You're just tired. Look at what you did. You cobbled together your bunch of misfits and put together a half million dollar job. That's, like, the major leagues."

Grant allowed himself a faint smile. "It did come together in the end, didn't it? I was starting to wonder, what with everything going wrong for us. But in the end, it fell together." He turned slightly toward Chase. "And you know what? My back doesn't hurt so much anymore."

"It was tension. The job's done, so you're starting to relax."

"Maybe that's it."

And Chase said, as he drifted off to sleep, "It's over. Nothing else can go wrong."

Chapter Thirty-Three

When his home phone rang early in the morning two days later, Grant—freshly minted man of leisure, or at least almost one—didn't answer. After six rings it stopped, and the call went to voice mail. When the ringing began again, thirty seconds later, he also ignored it.

But three calls in rapid succession in just over a minute meant that someone wanted to reach him urgently, and since he didn't owe anyone money, he figured it probably *was* important.

"What?" he asked, finally answering.

"It's Lisa. Are you sitting down?"

"Sitting down is for bad news."

"Yeah, well, I don't know how to tell you this, Grant, but we have a problem."

He sat down. He *knew* everything was working out too well. "What?"

"Romero has left the country."

"Huh? So what does this mean, he 'left the country'?"

"He ran. Fled. Vamoosed. Whatever you professional criminals are calling it these days. He packed up and took off for Italy."

"Italy?" He thought about that. "But ... he was just here."

"And now," she said, "he's not."

"Ah, shit."

"I'm with you on that." She paused, and he heard her light a cigarette. Her office building—every office building in New York State, for that matter—was nonsmoking, but that wasn't going to stop her. Not this day.

"So how do you know this?"

"You'll like this one," she said. "Well, actually, you *won't*. But I have some irony for you, if you like irony."

"I don't."

"Okay. Well, about an hour ago, a new listing came in to the office: six bedrooms, six full baths and two half-baths, media room, pool, move-in condition . . ." She expected him to get it right away, and when he didn't she added, "In Water Mill."

The figurative light bulb went off over Grant Lambert's head. "Don't tell me," he said. "It was formerly owned by a celebrity."

"Uh-huh. According to the information I got, the owner has relocated to Italy and is desperate to sell. Anyway, I checked around a few places and get this one: the town clerk tells me there's a tax lien. That bastard hasn't been paying his taxes. If the house doesn't sell fast, the town takes possession." She took a drag on her cigarette. "It sounds like Romeo Romero left some unpaid bills behind, because my experience is if they stiff one creditor, they stiff them all."

"Yeah, like us."

"Funny how the world works sometimes, isn't it? But hey, if you want to invest in some Hamptons real estate, the price tag on this baby is really low. Rumor—*unconfirmed* rumor, but rumor—has that his pied a terre in Manhattan will also be on the market within a week. A city real estate tax lien. So if you're looking for something smaller . . ."

Grant frowned. "Maybe next time." Despite his better instincts he had to ask. "So what's the asking price for the Water Mill place?"

"Twelve million. I can probably get a buyer for ten and change, given the circumstances. That means Romero, *theoretically*, will be able to pay the town and whoever else he owes. Probably the IRS, if I had to guess . . ."

"And us?" Grant asked, vaguely hopeful.

"Uh . . . yeah. Sure. You keep thinking that. I'm about as confident of that as I am he's gonna pay his tax bill."

"Listen, you must have a way to contact him. There's information on the owner, right?"

"Uh . . ."

"Just tell him that you're going to sell the place, and when you do, he has to pony up the money he owes us."

"Yes, well . . . uh . . ."

"What?" he asked. "It sounds like a plan to me." As he finished that sentence, the door opened and Chase walked in. Grant offered him a weak wave and a shake of the head that connoted a throbbing migraine.

"Yes, it's a plan," she agreed. "Just not a good one, Lambert. You see, Romeo Romero doesn't know I was part of your little scheme. He's seen me, yes, but has no idea that I have a legitimate job. So if I—as a Realtor—approach him, let alone try to shake him down . . ."

"Yeah?"

"Well, first, it exposes me. And second, he could easily get my license yanked. And third, well . . ."

"Go on."

"Are you sure?"

"Go on."

"Okay. Third, if I sell it for a decent price, I could make a great commission; maybe as much as I would have made from the blackmail scheme. And legitimate money, at that. Do you understand *that*?"

He thought about that. "Can't you cut the gang in for a share of your commission?"

"*Lambert*!" she squealed, and, for a rare moment in Lisa

Cochrane's life, she sounded almost girlish, albeit in a husky-voiced kind of way. "That's real estate money! That's my *professional* money, not income from our, uh, sideline."

When Grant hung up the phone, Chase gave his partner a quizzical look.

To which Grant Lambert sullenly said, "There *is* no honor among thieves. I think I finally understand that now."

For the first few days after Romeo Romero hightailed it back to Italy, the press was mute. Then again, Ian Hadley had a hard time getting out of jail and back to the office before Tuesday afternoon thanks to the interference of Henry Lemmon's uncle, the Honorable Judge Howard Lemmon, which helped delay the news. Eventually, though, his good name was cleared of child abduction and child pornography accusations, and he was allowed to finally leave Suffolk County, looking much the worse for wear. Although the Calvin Klein blazer held up quite well, all things considered.

But even upon Hadley's return, it took a while before the story warmed up. There was a lot of reporting to do, which caught many of the reporters off guard because it involved actual reporting. It was a full week after the actor fled before "Between the Streets" broke the tawdry story wide open on the cover of *The Eye*, launching the gossip column feeding frenzy that quickly followed.

Hadley felt good about that. Romeo Romero had swindled him out of a quarter million dollars of perfectly good blackmail money, and that son of a bitch would pay.

No matter how long it took Hadley, he would *pay*.

ROMEO IS BURNING U.S. GUV

Tax Cheat Fled U.S. for Europe; Fake Gay Connection Eyed—An *Eye* Exclusive by "Between the Streets" Senior Editor Ian Hadley

Internationally acclaimed actor Romeo Romero, mired in debt to Uncle Sam, has fled the country for his native Italy, and "Between the Streets" has learned that the swishy sexagenarian left American taxpayers footing a tax bill that could approach $50 million, a sum substantially higher than had been initially reported.

Romero, who is admittedly gay, owes the IRS more than $20 million, and also skipped out on millions in New York state taxes and years of unpaid property taxes on his sprawling estate in exclusive Water Mill, Suffolk County.

The actor's career has been in decline in recent years, contributing to his severe financial problems. In addition, *The Eye* has learned that his popularity was further endangered by a spreading rumor in the gay community that Romero, who proclaimed his homosexuality in 1982, was not actually gay. According to a well-placed source in the gay community who insisted on anonymity, Romero merely used the gay community's well-known affinity for their fellow gay entertainment figures to further his career.

"This was about to blow wide open," said the source. "His reputation in the gay community was about to implode."

Attempts by the staff of *The Eye* to disprove this charge were inconclusive.

Ian Hadley set the newspaper down on his desk and sighed. As he wiped smudgy newsprint from his fingers, he thought that "inconclusive" was just about the saddest word in the English language. For a journalist, at least.

There was a knock at his door, and Hadley looked up to see J. P. Hunt waiting expectantly.

"You wanted to see me?"

"Oh, yes." He reached into the jacket pocket of his Ralph Lauren suit and pulled out an envelope. "Charlie came through for us, and I want to reward him."

J. P. looked at the envelope. "But you fired him."

He handed the ex-cop the envelope. "The fact is that Charlie delivered when I needed him. Yes, I had to fire him, but . . . really, can I blame *him* because his hot water heater burst and destroyed my tapes?" He chuckled, then flattened his hands on the desk. "I guess by firing him, I did just that. But all things considered, I want to make sure he thinks of his time at *The Eye* positively. The last thing I want is for him to be disgruntled."

"He was a stand-up guy," said J. P. "I'll miss him." J. P.'s eyes misted just a little bit; the Irish in him. "I'll take care of it."

When J. P. was gone, Hadley picked the tabloid up again, skimmed down toward the bottom of the article, and continued to read.

Most recently, Romero was in negotiations to star in an action-adventure buddy flick with actors Jamie Foxx and Scarlett Johansson. On Friday, publicists for the actors had no comment.

Sources tell *The Eye* that, in recent months, Romero had smuggled funds, furnishings, antiques, and artwork worth millions—enough to satisfy at least part of his liability, according to one well-placed associate—to Italy, where they will be out of the reach of American tax collectors. The associate went on to detail the elaborate lifestyle indulged in by the actor in recent years: everything from black-tie galas to private jets to weeklong Bacchanals at the Water Mill home where the weekend liquor tab for the guest list could reach $100,000.

Hadley liked the information that acquaintance gave him; all the more so because Hadley *was* the acquaintance, right down to the probably exaggerated and *certainly* made-up liquor expense.

IRS officials were not optimistic they would be able to recoup the amount owed by Romero.

"The guy knew what he was doing," said one senior department official, speaking on the condition of anonymity. "He emptied his home of everything of value before he fled. All that's left is the house itself. This guy is going to prison if he ever sets foot on American soil again, but as long as he stays on his side of the Atlantic, there's not much we can do about it."

Police sources speculate that the actor used delivery trucks—provided by Eastern Seaboard LGBTQI Pride, a gay advocacy group—to move the valuables from his home without detection. Romero hosted the group's annual "pool party" fund-raiser at his home in late May.

Among paintings Romero apparently smuggled out of the county were several still lifes by Henri Mortengenser, each valued at a minimum of $750,000. Mortengenser, known for his apple, pear, and banana combinations . . .

Blah, blah blah, thought Hadley, and he skipped down a few paragraphs.

As for the international tax cheat's future, his stardom affords him another degree of protection. "Someone like Romero doesn't need the American film industry," said a well-placed Hollywood insider. "He's untouchable, like (Roman) Polanski. He's got

a European fan base, and a gay fan base, and he
can keep making movies for another thirty years if
he lives long enough. He doesn't need to be in the
U.S. to have a successful acting career."

Attempts to reach Romeo Romero through his
agent were unsuccessful.

Ian Hadley read the article one more time, then dropped
the newspaper in the trash.

At the same time, just a few miles away, Grant Lambert
was doing the exact same thing. He even sighed regretfully at
the very same moment Hadley did, and never in a million
years would either man think that someone like Romeo
Romero could bond them like that.

In Grant's case, though, he retrieved the paper and reread
the paragraph about those still lifes. Could those paintings
with the apples have been . . . ?

Nah. Impossible.

Had to be impossible.

Chapter Thirty-Four

At 8:42 AM the following Wednesday, Grant, in a brown delivery uniform, sat in the driver's seat of a car he had picked up in a nearby parking garage ten minutes earlier. Once again, the brown uniform was guaranteed admission, even though he could not imagine why the garage attendant thought it was normal for a deliveryman to be wandering unaccompanied to the lower level of a parking garage.

Whatever; not his problem. If they wanted him to have the unsupervised run of the garage, that was fine with him. He'd have to remember that scam for future reference.

He chose a nice, older car with a garage ticket tossed on the passenger seat, not just for the reasons he preferred nicer and older but also because the ticket meant he could pay cash for his transaction and drive away.

He got the car running and drove up the ramp. After paying the attendant—*"Twenty-two dollars! But I was only here for . . ."* he said as he paid, because he had to make it look real, and also it was significant money out of his pocket—he drove a few blocks and double-parked.

And then Grant Lambert, the Man in Brown, was staring through the windshield a half block away at a somewhat familiar York Avenue storefront.

Roughly three minutes later, he saw a black woman in her

forties walk up to the front entrance of Kievers Realty and twist her key in the lock. It wasn't the first receptionist and, thank God, it wasn't evil, elderly Stanley Kievers. It was someone new, whom he could hopefully work with.

He gave her a minute to get settled, but not so much time that one of those familiar faces would arrive and ruin things. He had no doubt that he would not escape from Stanley Kievers's grasp if their lives ever again crossed.

And then, almost before he knew it was happening, he was pressing that buzzer at the side of the door frame.

"UPS."

Once inside, Grant forced a smile that was passably convincing and avoided eye contact. "Some boxes were delivered to the wrong address a few weeks ago, and I need to pick them up."

"You're sure they're here?"

"Yes, ma'am." He looked at his clipboard. "A Mr. Stanley Kievers wants us to pick them up." He began to follow that well-worn path in the formerly green industrial carpet to the door he now knew led to the goods. Which he hoped were more or less still there, because otherwise he had just been engaged in the most massive time-waster in criminal history.

For a moment, he thought he was going to get away with it. Out of the corner of his eye-contact-avoiding right eye, he saw her looking at him. But not with alarm; more like uncomfortably strange curiosity.

Until she said, "Grant Lambert?" Which was much, much more uncomfortable and much, much stranger.

It was hard to play the UPS card when someone knew his name, so he looked up, finally made eye contact, and hoped prison wasn't as bad as he had imagin—

"Constance?"

"Grant? That's really you?" She ran at him before he had an opportunity to form a reaction, and when she reached him she hugged, throwing him dangerously off balance. "What are you doing in this shithole? Don't tell me you've gone straight and you're really working for UPS!"

He shrugged. "Nah. I'm just here to pick up a few things."

She stared at him. "Those boxes stacked up in the storage room?" He shrugged again, and she frowned. "Damn. Well, there goes *that* scam."

Which reminded Grant: "So what are *you* doing here?"

She smiled and pulled him close, even though they were the only two people in the office.

"For the keys."

"The keys?"

"Every day my girlfriend comes by to bring me lunch. In exchange, I give her a few keys that won't be used for a couple of hours." She leaned closer to his ear. "You'd be surprised what you can find in an empty apartment when no one's around."

Grant suddenly got it. Or at least thought he did.

"You mean like a bunch of delivery boxes?"

"No, like the microwaves and—" She stopped, and offered Grant a hurt look. "Those boxes in the back? Oh, *hell* no. Old Man Kievers found them himself, but I'll make sure you leave with them. Me and my girlfriend are just stripping out their microwaves, fixtures, and every now and then a refrigerator, if her brothers are free to help move it. Lot of money in that stuff, Lambert." She put her hands on her hips. "And I don't steal boxes of people's shit, Grant Lambert. That's Old Man Kievers's deal, not mine."

He apologized, then, with a worried glance at the wall clock, knew that it was time to end the reunion, pick up his boxes, and get the hell out of there. Constance offered to help.

"We should get together soon," she said, as they carried the last load to the stolen car.

"I'll mention it to Chase," he said, without commitment. "Maybe we could all go to dinner."

Grant didn't want to fiddle with jimmying open the trunk, so they had been cramming boxes into the backseat until there was no room left, and then went to work on the front passenger side. As they worked to make things fit, Constance said:

"Oh yeah, well . . . dinner could be all right. But I was thinking maybe we could do a job together again someday."

"A job?" Again, his voice was without commitment.

"Yeah." She handed him a small box to pack. He was pleased to see it was the electric toothbrush he wanted. "Like that time we swiped that yacht from the guy in Jersey. Remember that? Those were some good times."

Turned out the electric toothbrush was the last item, so Grant closed the door, putting his weight on it until a *click* told him it had latched. Then he turned to Constance and said, "Let's stay in touch."

She smiled. "I know how to find you."

After they got rid of the motor vehicles and split up the cash Mary Beth had lifted from Hadley, they figured they were marginally ahead of the game. No one cleared anywhere near what they'd hoped for, but they all got something. At least they could keep the landlord at bay and the utilities on for a while. In this business, they knew, only getting something wasn't the worst thing that could happen.

But as hard as he tried to make the numbers work in his favor, Grant couldn't find a way to squeeze them enough to pay the necessities *and* buy a plane ticket to Italy, where he had some unfinished business in the amount of one million dollars.

Patience, he told himself, refreshing a discount airfare Web site over and over again and trying to figure out what would come next.

A few minutes later, Chase interrupted him at the computer. "Hey, did you see the mail?"

"I saw you had an envelope from *The Eye*. Pay stub or something?"

Chase smiled. "Better than that. A personal check from Ian Hadley for a grand. I guess that's his way of buying my silence."

"It's not a million . . ."

"But we'll take it."

"Exactly." Then Grant asked, "You ready?" and Chase nodded.

They switched places—Chase taking the chair, Grant watching over his shoulder—and in a few clicks Chase was in a chat room.

"Who's Todd Mulcahy?" asked Grant, reading as Chase typed.

"A curious sixteen-year-old gay kid in New Rochelle with a homophobic family. Looking for a mature gay adult to rescue him."

Grant smiled. "With body by Jared Parsells?"

Chase uploaded the photo with the head cropped off and said, "With body by Jared Parsells."

"Okay, then. Hook us a big fish. One with a nice line of credit."

"And," Chase added, as a *ping* announced an incoming instant message, "an older model luxury car . . ."